W9-CBW-507

JIM MUNDY

JIM MUNDY

A Novel of the American Civil War

Robert H. Fowler

HARPER & ROW, PUBLISHERS
New York, Hagerstown, San Francisco, London

 For information address Harper & Row, Publishers, Inc., 10 East 53rd Street, New York, N.Y. 10022. Published simultaneously in Canada by Fitzhenry & Whiteside Limited, Toronto.

FIRST EDITION

Designed by C. Linda Dingler

Library of Congress Cataloging in Publication Data

Fowler, Robert H
Jim Mundy : a novel of the American Civil War.
1. United States—History—Civil War, 1861-1865—Fiction. I. Title.
PZ4.F7867Ji (PS3556.0847) 813'.5'4 77-3789
ISBN 0-06-011303-0

---

77 78 79 80 81 10 9 8 7 6 5 4 3 2 1

To Bell Irwin Wiley

Acknowledgments, Denials and Apologies

There is no county in North Carolina called "Oldham" and no town by the name of "Meadsboro." Neither was there a "10th North Carolina Volunteers" regiment, nor a "Ferro's Brigade." Otherwise, the regiments, brigades, divisions and corps mentioned in the text are based on real units.

Historical personages such as Robert E. Lee, Richard S. Ewell, Braxton Bragg, Jacob Thompson and Zeb Vance do appear in the book, but deliberately have been given little to say. Other characters are wholly fictitious and are not based on anyone, living or dead.

I do have friends and business colleagues named John Bradway, Jack Davis, Ed Engerer, Frank Kugle, Dave Lewis, Bob Miner, Rich Noel, Bob Perry, Fred Ray and John Sutton. For their amusement and with their permission, I have used their names for the members of Jim Mundy's squad. In the book, these characters are described as "good old boys from Oldham County, but not one of which could write his name." My friends thus named all are literate and bear no resemblance whatsoever to the characters in the book.

Separate portions of the manuscript were read for historical accuracy by William C. Davis, President of The National Historical Society; John H. Foard at the Blockade Runner Museum, Carolina Beach, North Carolina; and Joseph P. Cullen of Fredericksburg, Virginia, and James V. Murfin of Harpers Ferry,

West Virginia, both National Park Service officials. I am grateful for their help.

Finally, I wish to express the debt I owe to Dr. Bell I. Wiley of Atlanta, Professor Emeritus at Emory University and author of *The Life of Johnny Reb* and *The Life of Billy Yank,* two books that inspired a new generation of scholars to study and write about the common people of the Civil War. Bell Wiley's work and his personal example did much to inspire this fictional treatment of the war from the viewpoint of Jim Mundy. I am most grateful to him.

ROBERT H. FOWLER

JIM MUNDY

Baltimore, Md.
January 20, 1917

Dear Jimmy,

It was good to get your letter of January 15. You are a good boy to write to your old grandfather.

I am lonely as hell now that your grandmother is gone. Your Uncle Vance and that lot of pissants he employs at the printing company have to be polite when I go down to the office but I know they regard me as a nuisance.

Your own mother, the lady Estelle, condescends to write me a duty letter once a month but I haven't laid eyes on her since last summer. She is too busy with her Philadelphia Mainline friends to waste time with an old Confederate veteran down in Baltimore, especially one that always embarrassed her anyway. (Guess you heard that she asked me not to chew tobacco anymore when I visit your splendid home there in Rosemont.)

Who gives a damn? Thank God I've got plenty of money and still own the printing company. Otherwise I would be out on my ass in the cold.

Anyway, you wrote that your history professor there at Harvard told your class that he could not say for certain just what "the War Between the States" was all about and that you wanted my opinion on the subject.

First off, I wonder where he gets that "War Between the States" shit from. Has the influence of the almighty United Daughters of the Confederacy spread all the way up to Boston? I was in that war for three and a half years. I lost an eye at Gettysburg. I was captured and left to rot in a Yankee prison camp but escaped. I was the only man remaining in my regiment to be paroled at Appomattox. And I say, by God, it wasn't any war between the states; it was a real Civil War between real men. You tell your Harvard professor that for me.

The fellow is right, though, when he says no one knows for sure what caused the war. I don't know anybody in Baltimore that has a better library than me on the war. Generals' memoirs, regimental histories, Miller's Photographic History, Battles & Leaders. I've read them all except for the 128 volumes of the Official Records. I was up to my neck in the war and, Jimmy, I wouldn't know what to say to a college class about the causes of the war.

The nigger question had a lot to do with it, of course. Yet you would have had a fist fight with most Confederates if you accused them of fighting for slavery. Maybe they were, but they didn't realize it. No, it was more like the people were itching for a fight, at least in parts of the South. And by God we got our fight.

Your grandmother, God rest her sweet soul, did not like me to talk about the war. Felt that it made me more profane and overexcited. Calm, lovely woman. She is not here to curb my tongue or review what I write, so I can reply frankly to your question. Sherman said war was hell and it was, partly because of him, the son of a bitch. The war was full of pain and suffering, more than your spoiled generation could understand, much less bear. But it was glorious fun, too. I wouldn't have missed it for the world.

Why does any war get started? Things like slavery and states' rights and King Cotton and all that malarkey don't explain very much. At the bottom of it all, men like to fight. Then, when they find it isn't all glory and fun, it is too late.

That is happening in France right now. The Germans, with their Schlieffen plan, thought they could whip the French and be home for breakfast. Three years later, they are still dying in the trenches, them and the French and the English, as well.

Now it looks like Wilson is going to let us get drawn into it as well. Man never learns.

Stay out of it yourself, Jimmy. That is my advice to you. Time for my afternoon toddy. Not used to writing such a long letter.

Love,
Grandpa

Baltimore, Md.
February 4, 1917

Dear Jimmy,

Glad you enjoyed my letter so much and glad your professor did, too, although I must question your judgment in letting him see what I wrote. If you are going to be showing my letters around, I'll have to mind what I write.

Don't know why you should be surprised at your old Grandpa's being able to express himself with the pen. Didn't you know that I edited and wrote most of the Cigar Makers and Tobacco Traders News? They could not pay their bills with Mundy & Son so I took over and ran the publication for nearly twenty years. Tripled their circulation and you can guess who got the printing business. Finally sold it for a grand sum when I turned the reins over to your Uncle Vance. Your grandmother and I took a tour of Europe on part of that money.

Anyway, you say your professor thinks I write clearly and colorfully and that you both hope I will tell you more about my views on how the Civil War got started and describe some of what I did in it.

Well, why not? I have nothing better to do. I just go to the office three days a week to make sure Vance has not given the business away and to my Masonic Lodge meeting one night a week. And the Presbyterian Church most Sundays. I do that because your grandmother liked me to go to church. Mostly damned foolishness I hear from the pulpit.

All right. You and your professor friend want to hear more. I'll go you one better. Give me a few months and I'll send you the entire story. I will scrawl it out at home and get one of the girls at the office to typewrite it so you don't strain your eyes. I have nothing better to do in my old age and I have never cultivated the vice of modesty.

So brace yourself for what I am going to tell you.

Love,
Grandpa

BOOK ONE

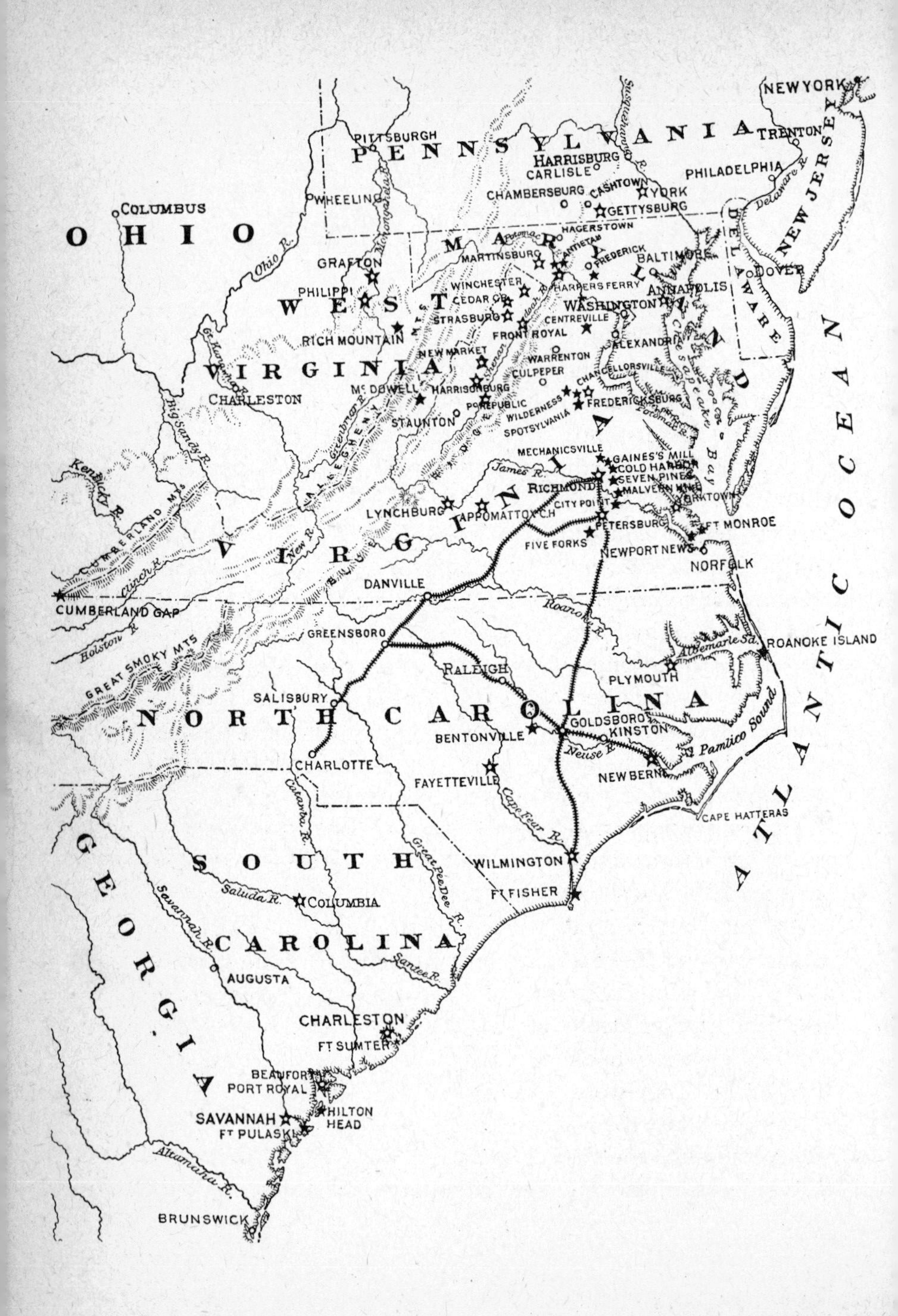

NEW YORK
PENNSYLVANIA
TRENTON
PITTSBURGH
HARRISBURG
CARLISLE
PHILADELPHIA
CHAMBERSBURG
CASHTOWN
YORK
GETTYSBURG
COLUMBUS
WHEELING
OHIO
Ohio R.
HAGERSTOWN
MARYLAND
DELAWARE
NEW JERSEY
MARTINSBURG
ANTIETAM
FREDERICK
BALTIMORE
GRAFTON
DOVER
PHILIPPI
HARPERS FERRY
ANNAPOLIS
WINCHESTER
WEST
CEDAR CR.
WASHINGTON
STRASBURG
CENTREVILLE
FRONT ROYAL
RICH MOUNTAIN
ALEXANDRIA
NEW MARKET
WARRENTON
VIRGINIA
CULPEPER
CHANCELLORSVILLE
McDOWELL
HARRISONBURG
CHARLESTON
PORT REPUBLIC
FREDERICKSBURG
WILDERNESS
STAUNTON
SPOTSYLVANIA
Potomac R.
Chesapeake Bay
ATLANTIC OCEAN
Kentucky R.
Big Sandy R.
MECHANICSVILLE
GAINES'S MILL
COLD HARBOR
James R.
SEVEN PINES
RICHMOND
MALVERN HILL
CUMBERLAND MTS
YORKTOWN
LYNCHBURG
APPOMATTOX C.H.
CITY POINT
FT MONROE
PETERSBURG
VIRGINIA
FIVE FORKS
NEWPORT NEWS
NORFOLK
Clinch R.
DANVILLE
CUMBERLAND GAP
Roanoke R.
Holston R.
GREENSBORO
Albemarle Sd.
ROANOKE ISLAND
GREAT SMOKY MTS
RALEIGH
PLYMOUTH
SALISBURY
NORTH CAROLINA
GOLDSBORO
KINSTON
BENTONVILLE
Neuse R.
Pamlico Sound
CHARLOTTE
NEW BERNE
FAYETTEVILLE
Cape Fear R.
CAPE HATTERAS
GEORGIA
Catawba R.
Great Pee Dee R.
SOUTH
WILMINGTON
FT FISHER
Saluda R.
COLUMBIA
Savannah R.
CAROLINA
Santee R.
AUGUSTA
CHARLESTON
FT SUMTER
BEAUFORT
PORT ROYAL
SAVANNAH
HILTON HEAD
FT PULASKI
Altamaha R.
BRUNSWICK

1

I was born in Oldham County, North Carolina, on March 3, 1843. The Mundys, who then spelled it Monday, came to that section from Virginia just before the Revolution. Our people had been Quakers until then; came from England to Virginia around 1650. In North Carolina, after the Revolution, they deteriorated into Methodism. Hosea Mundy, or Monday, who was my great-grandfather, went off to fight against Cornwallis in the last two years of the Revolution. Oldest son in his family he was. He returned to become a Methodist preacher when that pious bunch of hypocrites swept over the country. There has been at least one Methodist preacher in each generation since. My own father preached and farmed. My younger brother, Wesley, became a Methodist minister full time and remained so until he died ten years ago. Your grandmother was a Presbyterian and she turned me into one.

Like most people in Oldham County, the Mundys owned no slaves. My father wasn't an abolitionist exactly, but he was uneasy about the so-called right of one human to own another. Up in the hill country around the Big Rock Camp Meeting area where we lived there weren't more than half a dozen families that owned as much as one nigger. Down in the lower part of the county, below Meadsboro on the old Manawee Indian lands, several families owned fifty or more slaves, like the Ferros and the Liddles. They were the aristocrats, so called.

Anyway, when the war came, humble folks like the Mundys, rich people like the Ferros, and in-between like some of our distant cousins, the Sheltons and the Winchesters, they all signed up to get in on the fun. They wanted a fight and by God that is what they got.

North Carolina was the last state to secede from the Union. She was slow to make up her official mind on the point. South Carolinians as a class have always been too full of piss and pepper in my opinion but us Tar Heels tried to stay out of it. You want to know what finally brought us in, and the high-and-mighty Virginians, too? It was Lincoln's calling for 75,000 volunteers to put down "the Rebellion." That tore his ass with the Southerners who had been hanging back but I must confess that I can't see what else he could have done. Hindsight tells me he should have called out half a million men right off and had it over with.

I went into Meadsboro, the county seat, with my daddy and little brother Wesley on a pretty day in May of 1861 to hear two speakers from Raleigh whip up support for secession. One of them, a feisty little lawyer wearing a swallow-tail coat, told the crowd the Yankees were "bloodthirsty oppressors" preparing to invade Oldham County at that moment to despoil our women and destroy our homes. The other fellow, a great fat ex-Baptist preacher named Elmer Fincastle, assured the crowd that the Yankees were cowards, and we could go off early in the morning and whip them before breakfast in time to get in a day's plowing. That set up a roar of laughing from the crowd. When the noise died down a bit, Old Man Hiram Winchester, one of our second cousins, a miller by trade, called out, "By God, if they're as bloodthirsty as the other fellow says, it may be a long time before we get our breakfast."

Some of the roughnecks in the crowd grabbed old Hiram and rode him around on a rail and then dumped the poor old man into Mead's Creek down the hill from the courthouse. He was the only man in that crowd of five hundred to speak against secession. There were others, like my daddy, who saw no point in secession or war, but they were afraid to speak up.

Hardly one of them bully boys that rode old Hiram on a rail came back from the war in one piece. I had the brains and blood of Big Bill Utley splattered all over my coat at Sharpsburg when a cannon ball took off his head. And I nursed Clarence Crump in camp when he was dying of measles. He cried for his mother with his last breath, but that May day in 1861 there in front of the new brick Oldham County Courthouse Clarence Crump was running around bellowing like a bull: "Down with Abe Lincoln" and "Let's go whip the Yankees and get it over with."

Oldham County was thirty miles long and twenty wide, and it had a white population in 1860 of about ten thousand people and a black count of about three thousand. In addition, there were two pockets of mixed bloods. One was Indian and white mixed and the other Indian and nigger. The Manawee tribe used to live in that area, strong people, but white traders came in and corrupted them, and then runaway slaves from South Carolina interbred with them. Then the smallpox hit them about 1750 and almost wiped them out. That's how the area opened up for white settlement. Our folks came down from Virginia. Huguenots came up from South Carolina with slaves. Germans and Scotch-Irish came down from Pennsylvania, only they called themselves Irishmen then. Some Welsh and English settlers came over direct via Wilmington to take up the land as well. We raised cotton and corn and hay. Most of the white people in the county worked in the fields, even those that had slaves. There wasn't much romance there.

And that was the way it was in most of the Old North State. Now there was a state with a total white population of only 600,000 and they sent off 125,000 men to the Confederate service, the most of any state. And even with that kind of showing, there were whole counties in the mountains along the Tennessee border where the few men that did go to war went off to the Union side; yes and some poor counties in the middle of the state showed little enthusiasm for the Confederacy. Their men hid out and bushwhacked for a living. But Oldham County was ready to fight and so was I. So on October 4, 1861, I found myself lined up in front of the new brick courthouse to enlist in the North Carolina Volunteers. My mama had cried and begged me not to go. My daddy wore out the knees of his britches praying I'd change my mind. I was their oldest and they depended on me, but I was determined to go. I was afraid the war would be over before I had a chance to get into it. Besides, I was tired of sweating behind a plow while Pa was out conducting revivals and working on his sermons. Let precious little Wesley have his turn at the work; he was fourteen and big enough to handle a plow: that was my attitude.

So there we were, about 400 men or I should say farm boys, mule drivers, store clerks and carpenters getting ourselves formed into three companies of about 125 each to be signed up for twelve months. Three officials of the state government, now technically transferred in all its glorious sovereignty as one of the eleven components of the Confederate States of America, were on hand to sign us up properly. Some of the local politicians and aristocrats were present as well to harangue us about doing our duty for the beloved Southland.

I saw Jane Ferro that day for the first time in my life. Her daddy, Ernest Ferro, was one of the speakers. He went on for half an hour about the constitutionality of secession and how it was the North that had ruptured the Union and not the South. Never a word about the hundred thousand dollars' worth of black flesh he owned. He was a stocky, dark-haired man, very proud-looking. That day he was dressed in a white linen suit and one of those shoestring ties that professional Southerners around Baltimore like to wear today.

Mrs. Ferro was one of your blond Scotch-Irish types. Pretty woman in her way. She was sitting in a carriage, not a buggy mind you, but an open carriage drawn by two fine horses and driven by a dignified-looking black servant. A big brown woman with high cheekbones was in the carriage holding their youngest child, a little boy. As for Jane, she was only eighteen, just like me at that time. She had dark-red hair and a milky-white complexion with just a few light freckles across her forehead. I had never seen anybody as pretty and fine. I kept cutting my eyes at her, but she took no notice of me, a ragged-assed string-bean of a preacher-farmer's son.

Half of the boys and men in our company of 125 had to sign their names with an X. That's the kind of thing the ladies in the U.D.C. don't tell you. With them it was all gallantry and honor. I doubt if they knew what a miserable job of education the South did. Well, that day one of the fellows from Raleigh, when my turn came, said, "Here, son, scratch an X on this and tell me your name." I took the pen and wrote big as life, "James Asbury Mundy," in a good, clear script and the man was surprised. Said, "Why, you must be educated."

I said, "I attended Professor Mead's Latin Academy for five years." And so I did. The academy was just two miles from our farm and I rode a mule there. Even though I worked off most of the tuition cutting wood for the boarding students, mostly planters' sons from the old Manawee Indian lands and some from down in South Carolina. But my daddy let me off from the farm work, I give him credit for that. He scrimped and saved to give Wesley and me a good education. Professor Mead considered me one of his finest scholars. Wanted me to go on to the University at Chapel Hill, but there just wasn't enough money. And, besides, the war came along.

So there I was, eighteen, standing six feet and a half-inch in my stocking feet and weighing 148 pounds, hard as a rock, holding up my hand and swearing to serve the Confederate States of America for the next year of my life. Hot damn.

I cut my eyes over at the carriage where the Ferros were waiting. Tom Shelton, who had the honor of being my second cousin, was standing beside the carriage with his hat in his hand, talking to Mrs. Ferro and her daughter. I didn't even know her name but I felt jealous at the sight. I never cared for Tom Shelton. He was three years older than me. Strapping fellow about six feet tall and 180 pounds. Wide shoulders and curly brown hair. He had gone to Professor Mead's school as a boarding student and he was a great bully.

Now he and I had the same great-grandfather, Hosea Monday, but he never bothered to acknowledge any relationship at school or later in the army. The Sheltons ran a store in Meadsboro and a cotton gin. His own daddy, who was a first cousin, mind you, to my own pa, owned three nigger families and he had three hundred acres and so they considered themselves aristocrats with nothing in common with us poor Methodists up in the hills. They even joined the Episcopal Church and sucked up to the really big families like the Ferros.

I went home that night tired and excited. Next morning I put my clothes in a sack. My pa gave me a New Testament and three dollars. I kissed him and Ma goodbye, shook hands with little Wesley and started walking the four miles into town. Caught up with a neighbor hauling cotton to the gin on a wagon drawn by a team of oxen. He gave me a ride for a while, but I got impatient and hopped off and ran the last mile to the little camp of tents the recruiters had set up on the courthouse grounds.

They took the rest of the day for the election of officers. Our company elected William Ferro, son of Ernest, as captain, Charles Cadieu as first lieutenant, and Tom Shelton as second lieutenant. The recruiting man from Raleigh recommended that I be named a sergeant. Ferro called me over and talked to me about it. He was twenty-three, very refined, posh type. Elegant. I told him I could do the job and so he took me on. Hot damn.

They hadn't finished the railroad to Charlotte, so the next day they marched us over to that town and next morning put us on the cars to be hauled off to Raleigh. There were crowds in Charlotte to cheer us and give us cider. And we got into open boxcars and chugged off toward Raleigh. The war had started for me.

2

Took us all the next day just to get to Greensboro. The rails were of wood covered with iron strips and they wouldn't take much speed. All along the way there was people out in buggies and wagons waving to us and shouting encouragement.

We stopped in Salisbury for an hour to take on water and wood for the engine and they let us off to stretch our legs. There were girls to talk to and plenty of free cider and cake brought out by the patriotic ladies of the community. Believe me, I took advantage of my opportunities.

There was a couple of black legs in the crowd selling gourd dippers full of corn liquor for fifty cents, and you could pay in U.S. or Confederate money as you wished. Noah Rhine and Harry McGee—two boys I had been to the academy with—persuaded me to join them for a dipperful of that rotgut. Me, who had never before tasted anything stronger than a cup of sweet grape wine at a dance and that taken on the sly so my folks wouldn't know. I hung back for a minute and then Harry says, "Ho, Jim boy, you're away from your mammy's apron strings now," and I says, "Hot damn, you're right." Could always resist anything but temptation. I took that dipper and tried to drink her down like spring water. Well, you know what happened. It scalded my throat and made me sputter and cough, but I drained her down to the last drop and then wiped my face on my sleeve to hide my expression and conceal the tears in my eyes. "Mighty fine," I said. "Best liquor I ever tasted."

Harry was one of those peppery little Scotch-Irish fellows,

dark-haired and wiry but tough and mean when you crossed him. Professor Mead could never teach him much. Anyway, he says, "Let's have another," and I says, "Boys, my daddy only gave me three dollars and if I spend it on liquor I won't have any money for camp." Harry says, "Noah Rhine is rich. Why, his pa has piles." We fell over each other laughing at that. Noah did come from a big family of German Lutherans, hard-working, careful people and his pa, like mine, was unenthusiastic about the war. The Rhines had no slaves and they wouldn't raise cotton. Noah's daddy, old Jacob Rhine, grew hay on his land and ran a grinding mill on the side. Always had money while Harry McGee's family was practically poor white trash.

I hate that expression "poor white trash," but I guess it says a lot in a few words. God help anybody that ever called me that, then or now.

Anyway, to get back to my friend Noah Rhine, he was a quiet, muscular fellow with sandy hair and a sideways grin. His pa had given him a pocketful of U.S. coins. Noah reached in his pocket and says, "One more wouldn't hurt us, I reckon."

The man with the gourd dipper passed her around again and before we had time to feel the first slug's effects, we had put down a second one. Then Tom Shelton, Lieutenant Shelton that is, sees us and yells, "All right, you peckerwoods. Back on the train." Loud and bossy. We ran back and sat down in the straw again. The sun and the clouds began to wheel over my head and pretty soon that backwoods white lightning had laid me low. Yes sir, Noah Rhine, Harry McGee and Jim Mundy was three of the drunkest country boys you ever saw. First we were happy, laughing and insulting each other in fun and yelling out the car at every pretty girl we saw. Then Harry got sick and threw up over the side of the car. That made Noah puke too. But I held mine down; always had a strong stomach. I don't remember getting to Greensboro at all. Harry and Noah recovered enough to haul me off and help me into an open-air market where our company spent the night.

Next morning I woke up and could hardly get the coffee down. But in a little while I felt better and managed the corn mush with brown sugar but passed up the fried fatback that particular morning. Tom Shelton comes swaggering over and says, "Mundy, word has reached me that you got drunk in Salisbury yesterday. If you want to remain a sergeant in this company, don't let that happen again."

By God, I wanted to hit him across the mouth but (one) he was strong as a mule and (two) I was in no condition to hit anybody. Plus, the son of a bitch was an officer. So, quiet as a mouse and meek as a lamb, I got on the North Carolina Railroad car that took us on to Raleigh. Every mile or so, Harry or Noah would say, "Mundy, word has reached me that you got drunk . . . " and they would bust out laughing and the other would say, "If you want to remain a sergeant . . ." I wouldn't have taken that ribbing from anybody else.

We got to Raleigh that afternoon, Raleigh the capital city of the great state of North Carolina. What a madhouse. Trains like ours had been pouring in for days, hauling in thousands of men from all over the state. North Carolina did a job for the Confederacy, let me tell you. If the other Southern states had done as well, the war might have ended differently.

The authorities had established a training ground called Camp Mangum near town. Harry McGee, Noah Rhine and me got ourselves a piece of canvas, set it up and called it our tent. There was all sizes and shapes of shelters there.

Now at that point in the war, it looked like the South had just about won. The papers were still bragging about the great Confederate victory at Manassas Junction back in July. Fort Sumter was securely in Confederate hands. I remember lying under our new blankets in that tent, Harry, Noah and me, talking about it one night.

"I just hope we get there before the fun is over," says Harry.

"My pa says it's going to last a long time," Noah replies. "He says the North has got it all over the South when it comes to factories and money and population and they ain't about to step aside and have a new nation to the south without putting up a real fight."

And then yours truly speaks up: "We don't need the factories or the population. One of us can whip three of them." And with that we went to sleep.

It took a while to get ourselves organized. As previously noted, we had formed ourselves roughly into companies back in Meadsboro. Now, the idea was to take companies of a hundred to 125 men and combine them with nine companies from other counties into regiments. So as a result, those three companies that were recruited in Oldham County each got put in a different regiment there in Raleigh.

As for our company, we were designated Company H and we went in with nine other companies to form the 10th North Carolina Volunteers. That was step one. Then came the politicking. We got to elect our regimental officers, unlike some regiments where only officers could vote. There was a heap of campaigning going on that first weekend. Men were out talking up their friends as candidates. One candidate I kept hearing about was Elmer Fincastle.

Kind of a skinny fellow with a big nose comes around our company and I asked him who he was drumming for and he replied, "The Reverend Elmer Fincastle."

I says, "A big fat fart with a bald head and a red face and a set of leather lungs; a Baptist preacher from Raleigh?"

Fellow got flushed in the face and says, "Reverend Fincastle is a fleshy, well-set-up gentleman but I would hardly designate him as you just did so impudently."

And I says, "You designate him anyway you like, but I heard him come to Meadsboro last May and sling so much shit it took us a week to clean up the yard around the courthouse."

It was a mistake to cause the fellow to look such a fool in front of my companions. One word led to another and he finally says, "You're a mighty smart-mouthed young man. Where did you learn to insult your betters like that?"

I replies, "I have seen and heard the Reverend Elmer Fincastle and if you say he is my better you have insulted me, you big-nosed bastard."

I don't know how anybody stood me in those days. Or now, for that matter. Next thing I knew that fellow was coming at me swinging. I ducked one blow and another and then he caught me one over the eyes as I moved toward him to get under his guard. Made me see stars but he hurt his fist and he started dancing about and yelping, which gave me a chance to get him around the waist and throw him down. I then proceeded to pound him good until Harry and Noah pulled me off him. They had seen Tom Shelton running toward the commotion. Up comes Lieutenant Shelton and starts to give me another lecture. But Harry and Noah swore on their sacred honor that the other fellow had struck the first blow and that ended that for the time being.

The fact that our uniforms arrived the next day helped us forget this altercation—or so I thought at the time. Wagonloads of jackets, shirts, trousers, drawers, shoes and so on were hauled into camp and the outfitting got started.

North Carolinians generally were better dressed and equipped than other Confederates because (one) we fought closer to home than, say, Alabamians or Floridians and (two) our state government looked after its boys better than other states did. Anyway, by the end of that day I found myself possessing two pairs of cotton drawers, two pairs of socks, a pair of uncomfortable "brogans," gray trousers with a blue stripe to denote infantry, a woolen hip-length jacket, a heavy gray overcoat and, to top it off so to speak, a precious little short-billed kepi or cap.

Later in the war we changed to more sensible clothing, but that is how they started us out there at Camp Mangum in the fall of 1861.

The next day after that was Sunday. There I was, all dressed up and nowhere to go and show off my new uniform. I had a slight black eye and a lump on my forehead from contact with the bony fist of my camp-politician friend, but that didn't stop me. I was hell bent to show myself off.

It had occurred to me that my pa wouldn't be very happy if he knew that I had got drunk and engaged in a fist fight all in the same week. So out of a mixture of remorse, respect for him and vanity about my new garb, I took myself into town to a little Methodist Church.

It was the Methodist Episcopal Church South, of course. The slavery issue had split the Methodists into Northern and Southern branches some years before. But there was a third branch that called itself the Methodist Protestant Church. Something to do with some theological question which doesn't matter. Anyway, I heard a good Bible-thumping sermon and as I was leaving church a nice fellow and his wife struck up a conversation and invited me home for Sunday dinner, which I accepted, as the fellow says, "with alacrity." Enjoyed the food immensely. They had several children the oldest of which was a big rawboned girl of about twenty, ugly enough to stop a clock, and she keeps grinning at me and acting coy. Her pa worked for the railroad and he was full of opinions about how the war should be fought. They invited me to come back the next Sunday, but I lied and said I had drawn guard duty and that a sergeant could not run off and leave his men even to dine with good Christian folks like them.

Got back to camp to see a great revival meeting going on. In fact, I heard it before I saw it. I heard the familiar voice of the Reverend Elmer Fincastle bellowing from the platform. He was giving it to the boys straight from the Old Testament. David and Goliath he was telling them about, quoting scriptures to his own purpose, which was, of course, the election of Elmer Fincastle to the position of colonel of the 10th North Carolina. It made me sick to see the way the crowd ate up his windy oratory. Made me wish Cousin Hiram Winchester had been on hand to heckle him again. In fact, the South could have done with a lot more Hiram Winchesters and a lot fewer Elmer Fincastles. Would have saved itself a lot of grief. Maybe it had too many Jim Mundys as well, thoughtless, bored boys spoiling for a fight.

To make a long story short, the regimental election was held the next day and the Reverend Elmer Fincastle won by a landslide. Excuse me, Colonel Elmer Fincastle.

Guess who he chose as his adjutant? The fellow I beat up. His name, it turned out, was Zachariah Swan. He was a half-assed schoolteacher.

Harry and Noah got a big kick out of guying me about my friends in high places. They didn't laugh long though. Day after the election Tom Shelton comes around and says they needed a sergeant to supervise the construction of the latrines for the entire regiment. Said Major Swan had particularly asked for me to have that duty. Me, given the job of building shit-houses for a thousand men.

My two buddies could hardly wait for Shelton to get away so they could laugh, but then he turns and says, "By the way, Captain Ferro has appointed you, McGee, and you, Rhine, as corporals, to serve with Mundy. Here is a list of your squad members. All of you will report to Major Swan for your tools and instructions." With that he hands me a piece of paper on which were written the names of Jack Davis, Robert Miner, Fred Ray, John Bradway, Frank Kugle, Ed Engerer, John Sutton, Dave Lewis, Bob Perry and Richard Noel, all good old boys from Oldham County, but not one of which could write his name.

It was my turn to laugh after that. Harry and Noah threw me down and sat on me until I apologized for making trouble for them.

3

We did a good job on those latrines and privies. Had to, for Major Swan came by twice a day just hoping I would make a mistake or be found loafing on the job. But I was military courtesy itself, "yes sirring" him right up to the edge of sarcasm.

Swan and Colonel Fincastle had got themselves copies of *Hardee's Tactics* and also the 1860 U.S. Army handbook and they had us out twice a day drilling and instructing. Our colonel gave us a patriotic lecture for about an hour every day as well. He and Swan ran that regiment like a little political kingdom. Fincastle seemed to have the idea that once our rifles came through the blockade we would all march north and fight another big battle like Manassas and parade right into Washington to receive the surrender of Abe Lincoln and the abolitionists.

So there we were, left-facing, right-facing, forward-marching and halting on the parade ground. We were reviewed twice by Governor Clark.

We carried broomsticks as we drilled. The Confederate Army generally was very well equipped in the weapon line. We sometimes needed shoes and our new uniforms wore out; we didn't get our rations on time, but we generally had good weapons, brought through the blockade, or captured from the Yankees, or, more than you might think, made in our own factories. But those first few weeks there at Camp Mangum we had only broomsticks with which to present arms, right shoulder arms and so on. Up close we cut a ridiculous sight, but I remember one chilly day around the first of November our entire regiment was out with three others on the parade ground executing a grand maneuver and I caught a vista of four thousand or more men moving as one body. It was a thrilling sight.

During those early days of camp life, I formed a great respect for Captain William Ferro, head of our company. I had to report to him as one of his sergeants and I found him to be a natural-born leader of men. Slender, blond gentleman with good manners and a calm way about him. Always made me feel a little rough cut but anxious to please him. Never knew him to do anything that was unfair.

It came as a surprise to me years later to learn that William Ferro had written letters back to his family in Oldham County telling details of camp life and describing some of the men who served under him. Here is what he said about me, as it was repeated to me:

> One of my best sergeants is a spirited young fellow from north of Meadsboro up around the Big Rock Camp Grounds. He is James Mundy, son of the Rev. Robert Mundy, a Methodist preacher of the community. He went to school to Professor Mead and I must say that despite his humble family background he is as lively and intelligent a chap as we have in our company.
>
> Tom Shelton regards him as a trouble maker but Charles Cadieu, my first lieutenant, agrees with me that the Confederate Army could use a lot more of Jim Mundy's kind.

Now I tell you this, not to blow my own horn, but to show what a generous-hearted, perceptive person William Ferro was. My grandson Jimmy makes me think of him.

Well, cold weather came in earnest and some of the people who had voted so eagerly for Elmer Fincastle began to have second thoughts. We still didn't have our rifles and most of us were still in tents with frost on the ground. But not him, no. He lived in his own home in Raleigh and rode out to camp in a buggy every day to supervise things. We'd have been a lot better off if we had elected William Ferro colonel, let me tell you. He took pains to look after his men. Used his own money to buy a side of beef; hired wagons and sent work crews out several miles to cut firewood. And where some slaveowners' sons had body servants along with them, he refused his father's offer of a slave at that time. Said he would live as his men did. Just as well. A lot of those servants disappeared when they got the chance, mostly the young ones. Some of the older ones did stick it out, but they were rare. All this talk about loyal slaves is so much poppycock. Black, green, yellow or white, nobody wants to be a slave. Niggers just never had a choice to be anything but slaves before the war; when it came to a chance at freedom, you see how many took it.

Our regiment never had as many men as it did in those days of drilling with broomsticks because it was about that time that the measles and mumps moved in. Now today here in Baltimore we got the finest hospital facilities in the whole world at Johns Hopkins. The difference between that kind of medicine and what went on fifty years ago in both armies is beyond belief. Our regiment had a surgeon, a young fellow who had been to the university and had been apprenticed to old Doctor Bailey for only six months. Well, he was one of the first to die of the measles. I had caught the stuff when I was just ten and had had the mumps as well, so I was immune. But those two diseases, especially the measles, ran through our camp like wildfire. We lost a dozen men in our company alone. It got so bad our hospital tents were filled and we had to take over some public buildings in Raleigh. It was pitiful, let me tell you.

They turned the little Methodist Church I visited that Sunday into a hospital. Captain Ferro learned I had had the measles, so he detailed me to go and help run the show. The people of the church pitched in and helped as well, including the railroad man's wife and raw-boned daughter. That girl would do anything I asked her, so I took advantage by keeping her hard at work. My patients were the best cared for anywhere. I organized the boys into foraging parties and I didn't ask any questions about how they came by the chickens they brought in.

William Ferro came every day to visit the men from our company and a couple of times he sat up all night with a dying boy. As for Colonel Fincastle, he was so afraid of catching the measles the best he could do was stop his buggy at the church door to "make enquiries."

While this measles epidemic was decimating our ranks, we got word that the North wasn't just sitting on its ass waiting for the South to do as it pleased. The Yankees had the freedom of the seas and they had the navy to boot and they used them both to good advantage. They sent an expedition to the coast of North Carolina. If you have read your history books, you know that General Burnside commanded that expedition of fifteen thousand men and they descended on the coast of North Carolina before we were prepared. First took Hatteras Island and then Roanoke Island, closing off Albermarle Sound. They never took Wilmington until almost the end of the war, of course, but they gobbled up the Outer Banks. That force was to remain a thorn in the side of the Old North State for the rest of the war, threatening the rich farm land of the eastern counties and, worse, the railroads that fed Richmond from the south.

The Confederate authorities started shifting troops down to protect the port of New Bern against this threat, while our regiment was still back in Raleigh getting over the measles and waiting for our rifles to show up, that and enduring the everlasting sermons of Reverend Elmer Fincastle, excuse me, Colonel Fincastle.

4

Smart young officers like William Ferro and Charles Cadieu got fed up with having their men shiver in tents with winter coming on and they practically forced Colonel Fincastle and Major

Swan to let them put up wooden barracks for our regiment. They pointed out that the barracks could be used by other men when we moved out.

So it was that Captain Ferro came up to me one day and says, "Sergeant Mundy, you and your squad did a superior job of running that hospital and I want to congratulate you."

I says, "Thank you, Captain. My boys deserve the credit. But I do thank you for them."

Then he says, "We need to get ourselves a barracks thrown up in a hurry. We have finally got permission to go ahead and I have requisitions for tools and nails and several wagonloads of lumber, green lumber, I'm afraid, but it'll have to do."

"It'll be good to get out of our tents and under a roof like Colonel Fincastle," I says, smirking.

He ignores the jibe. "Yes, well I wish you and your squad would take charge of the construction of our company barracks."

With that he pulls out a piece of paper with some rough plans drawn on it. I looks at the paper and says, "We can have her up in a week."

And that's what we did. There was some grumbling at first. Jack Davis said by God he had signed up to fight and not to dig shit holes and hammer nails. So I told him, "Good, you can saw wood and carry lumber instead." Dave Lewis said it would be impossible for thirteen men to build a complete barracks by Saturday. So I says, "In that case we'll just work right on through Sunday."

First thing Monday morning we turned to and by noon Friday we had a little low building long and wide enough to accommodate 110 men, which was what we were down to after the measles epidemic and after two men had got homesick and deserted.

Colonel Fincastle came around to admire our handiwork, saying over and over again, "Mighty fine. Mighty fine." But Major Swan pointed out the cracks in walls and places in the floor where the boards hadn't been sawed exactly true.

Anyway, we were settled in that barracks by Christmas. And it was on the morning of Wednesday, December 25, 1861, that I got a Christmas gift I'll never forget. A Confederate States of America wagon comes out from the depot in Raleigh and stops right in front of our barracks. Lieutenant Charles Cadieu was setting beside the driver and on that wagon they had crate after crate of brand-new Enfield rifled muskets, caliber .577, made in England and brought through the blockade to Wilmington. The finest weapons used in the Civil War, in my opinion. Confederate purchasing agents let the Yankees go over with their ready money and buy up useless guns that Belgium and Austria didn't want. The Southerners went for the best and that's what we got.

The Enfield was a beautifully balanced gun that felt good in your hands. It loaded just as fast as a smoothbore, but it was as accurate as some of the old-fashioned flintlock rifles the Germans and Scotch-Irish brought down to the Manawee country from Pennsylvania.

We got rags and lined up while Captain Ferro handed each man in his company—except for clerks and cooks and officers—his own personal Enfield. Then we all sat around wiping the grease off the guns and listening to an ordnance officer lecture us on how to care for this fine weapon. We got so excited that the captain took us all out on the parade ground and let us drill with our new guns, this on Christmas afternoon. I even slept with my gun in my arms that night, and next morning we got up early to draw our ammunition: Minié balls, black powder, rag patches and percussion caps. Then off we marched to the firing range to try out the muskets.

Later we learned to make cartridges so we could load fast in battle, but at that stage we had to measure out each load and pour the powder loose down the barrel. Then you wrapped the ball in a cloth patch and rammed the load down hard so the rifling would bite into the lead. Then you either put your ramrod back in its holder under the barrel or stuck it in the ground and you put a little brass percussion cap on the nipple, after cocking back the hammer, of course. You then held in your hands a weapon that could be aimed accurately up to three hundred yards and which could kill a man a thousand yards away.

One of the dumbest things both sides did in the war was to keep their men in massed ranks just as the British did against Great-Grandpa Hosea Monday while fighting with and against a rifled musket firing a conical bullet. The war was half over before both sides learned to stop advancing like they were on parade.

So that was the Enfield. I'd rather have it than one of them 1903 Springfields our army has today. Would shoot just as far and just as accurate. A good soldier with practice could get off three shots in one minute. I carried my Enfield for over eighteen months. Never felt as much of a man as I did with that musket on my shoulder and a box full of cartridges and another containing caps on my waist.

So that was our Christmas present for 1861. Unfortunately we had only one week to drill ourselves with our new weapons and to learn how to fire them or generally to care for them. We had lived only three weeks in our barracks my squad and I worked so hard to build when the order came.

The 10th North Carolina was to be moved east to Kinston to give battle to General Burnside if he tried to press inland from Albemarle Sound. Hot damn!

5

Once again we loaded ourselves on the boxcars and set out for the town of Kinston, ninety miles east of Raleigh. A little over halfway there we stopped for dinner at Goldsboro, which was an important rail junction on the line leading from Wilmington to Petersburg, Virginia, one day to become the lifeline between the Confederate capital at Richmond and the blockade-runners' docks on the Cape Fear. From Goldsboro we moved on to Kinston and there went into camp.

There were several regiments already down in New Bern on the Neuse River just where it enters the Albemarle Sound. But they held us back at Kinston as a kind of reserve until we could see which way old Burnside would jump.

Now Kinston was an unprepossessing village normally, but with all those newly armed Confederates it was a bustling place in January of 1862.

The Reverend Colonel Fincastle couldn't bring his buggy down from Raleigh, but his wife, a pretty little woman about ten years younger than him, did come along and they took a small house in Kinston while the rest of us shivered in our tents. Naturally the colonel could not be expected to walk so he bought himself a big old dapple-gray gelding from a planter near Kinston. It must have been ten or twelve years old and seemed the gentlest, most phlegmatic beast you could imagine. Colonel Fincastle was not one of your natural-born riders. He weighed close to 250 pounds. To mount his horse, he had to climb up on a box, and when he settled himself into the oversized saddle, you'd see that old gray brace his legs out to the side and hear him give a huge sigh. It was a three-gaited horse, but I never saw but two gaits—a slow walk and a reluctant trot—there at Kinston.

Thus mounted, Colonel Fincastle would draw up his regiment on the field and deliver his now familiar lectures on patriotism and duty. How he loved to bawl commands and see his regiment wheel this way and that. We wasted an awful lot of time on parade drills, time that should have been spent in learning to fast-load our Enfields, fire from a prone position, advance by rushes and so on.

Captain Ferro gave me another special job at Kinston. He

came up to me one morning and says, "Mundy, how would you like another assignment?"

I thinks to myself, "Hut-oh, another barracks for somebody else to live in."

But he says, "I'd like you and your squad to forage for our company while we're in Kinston. You can rent a wagon and we'll provide you with the funds and you go out and buy meat and such vegetables as you can find this time of year. I want you boys to have something more than fatback and corn mush."

Well, that suited me just fine. And the boys, too. For once I heard no grumbling, not even from Jack Davis or Dave Lewis. I found a free mulatto in town who was willing to drive us around in his little wagon, drawn by a blind mule, for a fee, of course. That way I got acquainted with a new way of life. There is a lot of difference between eastern North Carolina and the Piedmont section where I came from. In the east the land is flat and sandy with long-leaf pines and even cypress trees along the black water streams. And there were more black slaves about than white folks. Big plantations with huge white columns, surrounded by carriage houses and, farther out, slave cabins. Here lived the men who called the shots in the Old South.

I learned a lot about human nature and business, buying supplies for our company in those days. First time out I had our yellow friend drive Noah Rhine and me down a tree-lined lane and stop his wagon at the front of one of those palatial "big houses." I goes up to the front door and knocks. A white-haired Negro in a black suit comes to the door and asks what do I want.

I says, "Howdy, Uncle. I want to see your master."

He says, "What is your business?"

I says, "I do not discuss my business with servants. Just tell your master that Sergeant James Mundy of Company H, 10th North Carolina Regiment, wants to see him."

He draws himself up and replies, "Colonel Rankin is on duty with the army in Virginia. You'll have to state your business to me so I can decide just whom you should see."

About that time a dignified middle-aged woman comes out in

the hall and says, "Justin, who is at the door?" Then she sees me and I speak up, repeating my spiel about wanting to see the master of the house.

She says, "Young man, my husband is away with the army just now and I am mistress of the plantation. But if you have business to conduct, let me suggest that you go around to the plantation office in the rear. I will send someone to fetch the overseer."

I started to protest that I was there to see the top person, but she cuts me off in a patrician way with "We just do not conduct business at our front door here. Please wait at the back yard for the overseer."

Noah Rhine and that mulatto heard all this and they had sly grins on their faces as I walked off the porch and said, "Follow me around back."

We had to wait half an hour for the overseer. As I waited, burned up by the highhanded way I had been sent away from the front door, I remembered something else Hiram Winchester had shouted that day the previous May when he interrupted the secessionist meeting. "You are going to find it'll be a rich man's war but a poor man's fight."

The overseer, a lean, dried-out sort of fellow of about forty, finally came and he did sell me a hundred pounds of potatoes, just to get rid of me, I expect.

After that I did my trading with ordinary folks, occasional small farmers and free Negroes. I didn't go to the front doors of any more plantation houses. And I was able to keep our company well stocked with potatoes and chickens and even an occasional ham while we were there at Kinston.

Along about the second week of March they lined us up on the parade ground early one morning and Colonel Fincastle, sitting on his sagging gray horse, tells us, "Men, we have our new marching orders. We have one hour to break camp and begin our march to New Bern to defend that city against the depredations of the Yankee invaders."

He took up half an hour haranguing us, so it was two hours

before we could gather our belongings, fold our tents and load them on wagons, empty our bowels and bladders and set out on the thirty-five miles of sandy, rutted road that led from Kinston to New Bern. The Atlantic and N.C. ran on to New Bern and beyond to Morehead City, but they didn't have cars available for us.

We had a small band in those days, not more than six pieces, and it struck up "Dixie" as we marched through Kinston. That song was worth more than an entire army to the South. I still love it. Play it slowly, in a minor key, and it would serve as a funeral dirge. But played with a snappy spirit as it was that day, it made you want to turn handsprings. Years after the war, when my wife dragged me to a concert here in Baltimore, the orchestra struck up "Dixie" and the next thing I knew I was on my feet giving the Rebel yell. By God, a dozen other old Confederates in the crowd joined in. My wife was humiliated by this, but she forgave me as she so often did, saying, "I guess you just can't help yourself, James, can you?"

"No, ma'am, lady," I replies. "I am just unregenerate."

So, with "Dixie" ringing in our ears, our bellies filled with nourishing food, and our new Enfields on our shoulders, off we marched, following Colonel Fincastle and his gray horse, headed for battle with the "Yankee invaders." Look out, Burnside, we're coming to get you.

Incidentally, as we marched through Kinston I noticed Mrs. Fincastle watching the procession from the porch of the little house they had occupied there. I felt embarrassed to think of some of the rude remarks my friends and I had made about her husband and her. Some parallels drawn about whether he had to use a box to mount her as he did his horse, I believe. She was a plump little partridge with jet-black hair and a milky-white skin. Struck me as we marched past her that she had a mighty faraway look in her eye. Wondered what she really thought of that vast buffoon of a husband so much older and less attractive than she.

6

It took us three full days to cover those thirty-five miles to New Bern. We were soft from too much food and encumbered by too much equipment, extra blankets and items from home. Even so, we should have marched that distance in two days but we were held back by Colonel Fincastle and his broken-down gray horse. He insisted on leading the regiment, and his horse just would not or could not carry his bulk any faster. This was all right with us. The boys passed the time larking and singing ditties such as:

> I'd rather be a private, and carry a private's pass,
> Than to be a lieutenant, and kiss the captain's ass.

Tom Shelton's ears would turn red when he heard that, but he couldn't do anything about it without appearing ridiculous.

The countryside changes as you move from Kinston toward the coast, or I should say, sound. Swamps on either side of the road, great oaks and cypresses with long trails of Spanish moss. Long-legged birds with curved beaks and damned few people of any color. Everything was so different from the red lands of Oldham County.

We got to New Bern late in the afternoon and found the town in a turmoil. New Bern was quite a port at the outbreak of the war. Had a boat-building industry and docks with tobacco and cotton warehouses around. Even had a rope factory. With nearly six thousand people, it was the largest town in the state.

There were five regiments already there. Plus an odd collection of militiamen from the general area, family men and mama's boys who found it inconvenient to sign up for a full year's service as I had done but who had to make a show of defending their own homes. They were armed with odds and ends such as old single-barrel shotguns and flintlocks. I even saw a pompous little militia captain who carried nothing but one of those silly little pepperbox pistols in his belt. That was the militia. Fit only for guarding prisoners. They wouldn't have made a pimple on the ass of a real Confederate soldier.

Give them credit, though. Those militiamen did make a pretense of protecting their area, more than could be said of the big slaveowners. It took a lot of hard work to construct the various fortifications along the Neuse River below New Bern. The Confederate authorities advertised in local papers for slaveowners to hire out their black property to dig earthworks and they got exactly one nigger sent down. A few free men of color came in to work for wages. That's all. Slaveowners would send their sons off to die, but risk their valuable slaves? Never.

So that left Confederate soldiers to do the dirty work, and they had only enough shovels, picks, wheelbarrows and such to employ just a few hundred at one time.

Some weeks before, the soldiers then on the scene had built various entrenchments and earthworks seven to ten miles below New Bern plus Fort Thompson, a truly formidable fort on the Neuse River just four miles from the town. By "formidable" I mean heavy cannon protected behind high mounds of sandy earth with piles driven in the water nearby to keep the Yankee gunboats from steaming in under the guns.

The Confederate Government, getting nervous about New Bern, had recently sent down General L. O'Bryan Branch to take command, and he had decided the earlier fortifications were located too far from the town. He had decreed that a new line of defense be manned from Fort Thompson, inland for two miles. With our arrival, General Branch had 7,000 men plus 19 pieces of field artillery and 41 heavy guns, enough force and material to have held New Bern forever, if properly deployed.

It turned cloudy and cold as we approached New Bern, tired

and footsore near dusk on our third day of marching. Our morale wasn't helped by the sight of boxcars that could have hauled us down from Kinston in three hours, standing about waiting to be unloaded so their contents could be added to the piles of tents and uniforms and various gear. The Confederates had just sent men and equipment down without much planning.

We awoke the next morning in a cold drizzle. Colonel Fincastle rode his gray horse out to camp from the snug hotel where he and Major Swan had spent the night. We were getting our usual after-breakfast lecture when we heard a booming from the Neuse River below town. Yankee gunboats were shelling Fort Thompson. We could hear the guns boom, and the sharper, nearer explosion of the shells. Soon the heavy guns of the fort were replying. Our first sounds of war.

The noise died down after a bit. Captain Ferro came over and says, "Men, we are going to move through the town about four miles and take up a position near the railroad. We are to occupy a brickyard which we must turn into a fort covering the railroad. This is important work and I know I can count on you to do it well."

With that, our band gives us "Dixie" as we march through the streets of New Bern, following Colonel Fincastle's gray horse, which managed a halfhearted trot for the occasion.

I could have strode those four miles out to the brickyard in an hour, but it took us nearly three to maneuver a thousand men over that same distance. Colonel Fincastle, instead of following the railroad's straight line, led us along the Old Beaufort Road, a half-mile from the brickyard, and into the rear of the 37th North Carolina, whose men were busy digging their new entrenchments. After disentangling ourselves, we moved through the ranks of the neighboring 7th North Carolina to the brickyard, whose premises were graced with the militia huddling about doing nothing.

General Branch rides up and directs the militia to vacate and take up a new position across the railroad, to our right. The brickyard was an assortment of kilns and piles of brick plus a stable and a low, sturdy little office building which, of course, became Colonel Fincastle's headquarters.

Two years later, in a similar situation, well-seasoned Confederates or Yankees could have dug themselves a deep, secure trench, throwing the dirt up on the side facing the enemy, and been prepared in two hours to repulse three times their numbers. Instead, we farted around that brickyard, recovering from our "strenuous" march, grumbling about the poor quality of the shovels and hoes available. We were far more concerned with our comfort in the cold drizzle now falling than the possible approach of an enemy.

Fort Thompson with its mighty guns lay about one and a quarter miles to our left, on the Neuse River. Three Confederate regiments occupied shallow breastworks between our brickyard and Fort Thompson. The railroad, guarded by the militia, lay on our right. Several hundred yards behind and beyond the militia, two regiments covered a three-quarter-mile front with their flank resting on low swampy ground only a water moccasin could cross.

It was a strong position, covering both land and water approaches to New Bern. The only drawback was that you could not see beyond a narrow field of fire that had been cleared along a drainage ditch in front of us.

That night the rain fell in earnest. After a cold supper, soaked to our skins, Harry McGee, Noah Rhine and I huddled under our stretch of canvas and complained.

"I signed up thinking we would march up to Virginia and have another glorious battle like Manassas and it would all be over," says Harry. "And here we are in the asshole of the entire state to protect a port that is no damned good to the South anyway. The Yankees have the place bottled up."

"Yes," replies Noah Rhine, "but just think what a grand place it would be for them to unload their supplies for an advance against Kinston or Goldsboro."

"You are nothing but corporals," I tells them. "Leave the planning to officers."

"Like Tom Shelton, who is a bully, and the Reverend Fincastle, who is a horse's ass?" Harry comes back at me.

"How would you like to have permanent guard duty? Keep sassing your sergeant and that is what you will get."

I will not repeat what he said to me.

A thick fog had rolled in during the night, so that we could barely see the woods beyond the clearing in front of us when we were awakened early to the sound of musket fire in the distance.

"Skirmishers from the 7th Regiment, sent out to scout the area and reoccupy some old works downriver," Captain Ferro said. "Sounds as if they found something."

A bit later, all hell broke loose on our left as the gunboats came up and began bombarding Fort Thompson. For two hours they poured shells into the works, and the guns in the fort gave it right back, hot and heavy. An occasional shot from the boats exploded above the trees and soon we could even smell the gunpowder. It was exciting.

Then a courier comes galloping up out of the fog and consults with Colonel Fincastle who was still on his gray horse. The color drained out of that great red face as he bawled for his captains to gather round him.

It seemed that while we horsed around in the rain the day before, the Yankees had moved up their transports and had landed a large force about ten miles below us. The earlier fortifications that had been constructed were either unmanned or only lightly held. Anyway, they were all in Yankee hands now.

"Up in line of battle," Captain Ferro orders as he comes running back to us. "Load your pieces and keep them dry." We flung ourselves down in a line before our pitifully inadequate piles of sand and waited.

The noise of the muskets came closer, finally terminating in a continuous rattle. Across the cleared space beyond the drainage ditch, the strange coastal birds left their treetop perches in alarm; soon thereafter rabbits came dashing out of the woods across our front, followed later by several deer. Then came our skirmishers at a dead run, skedaddling back to their lines. One of them angled off from the railroad toward the brickyard. He was sweating and out of breath. "Thousands of them and they got cannons, too," he panted.

"Now, boys," Captain Ferro called out. "We've got a good position here. Don't fire until I tell you to. When I give the order, aim at their legs. We've got a clear field of fire in front of us. Relax."

Relax, hell. I heard no chaffing among my squad then. Nobody was bragging about how one of us could whip three of that mysterious horde out there in the woods. There was a steady traffic of men going back behind the brickyard to void their bowels in the bushes. I went twice myself.

A bit later and we could hear the sounds of hundreds of men moving in the fog beyond the cleared area. Some of my boys were actually shaking with fright, their teeth chattering and their hands trembling.

Colonel Fincastle was still on his horse. He stayed there until a shell shrieked over his head and exploded in the latrine area behind us. I never saw a fat man move so fast. He slid off that horse in a flash and moved his hindquarters back into his snug little solid brick headquarters.

Three more cannon shot followed. The shells sailed through the air, trailing spumes from the fuses, and burst well behind us. The Yankees had four small howitzers back along the railroad and although they weren't the most practiced artillerymen in the world, you couldn't have proved it by us. It was terrifying for green country boys to lie there with bombshells bursting about them. The Yankees gave our brickyard their particular attention until a battery of our own guns next door began replying and then the two sets of artillerymen dueled with each other, which was fine with me.

As the smoke cleared, I says to my squad, "Now if anybody

else has to shit, he'll have to do it in his britches. Stay on the firing line."

Two men had been wounded by shell fragments during the bombardment, and had to be carried back to the stable where our new regimental surgeon had set up shop. I never saw men with so many solicitous friends clamoring to help carry them back out of danger. There were enough volunteers to have hauled away a pair of elephants. Tom Shelton yelled, "Just four of you, damn it. And get back here as soon as you can."

The noise beyond the cleared space intensified, bushes cracking, bayonets clanking. Looking back in the *Official Records,* I know that Burnside had only about ten thousand men, but on that foggy morning of March 14, 1862, I would have sworn he commanded one hundred thousand, all headed in my particular direction. I desperately wished my pa's prayers had been answered and that I was home helping my beloved parents and my dear little brother, Wesley, with the chores around the farm. I had to do something, being a sergeant, so I calls out, "Here it comes, boys. Get ready for the fun."

7

Every eye strained to see through that damned fog as we caught the ringing sounds of ramrods and bayonets. Colonel Fincastle remained secure in his hidey hole in the little office; Major Swan stood outside on a pile of brick, gazing through his field glasses at the fog-obscured woods and shouting back at the colonel. Off to our right, our glorious militia knelt along the railroad with their shotguns and flintlocks at the ready.

Suddenly the air over our heads became alive with Minié

balls, followed by a crash of sound from the woods. The bullets sang around us, slamming into the brick kilns and stripping leaves and bark from nearby trees, a storm of lead hornets. Two men in the squad to my right pitched backward as if someone had kicked them in the face. To our left another man was screaming that he was hit.

"Cock your pieces and keep your heads down," Captain Ferro shouts.

All along our shallow entrenchment came the "click" of hammers being drawn back. Forms began to take shape across the cleared space, hundreds of them, and suddenly all of them began roaring "Hurrah" and coming toward us at a dead run. On the forms came, until we could make out their faces, then:

"Fire!"

Our one thousand Enfields, firing all at once, sounded like a gigantic door slamming. All across our front, the Yanks simply stopped in their tracks.

The smoke cleared. A line of blue forms lay around the feet of the stunned enemy. Dozens of them lying on their backs, some still and others writhing about. Their comrades reloaded, and standing in the open, began peppering away at us at will, which was a great mistake, for that kind of firing is ineffective.

"Reload," came the order. *"Fire!"* Another crash of sound and the Yankee line fell back into the trees.

Then a massed column of Yankees charged along the railroad, headed for our militia, firing as they came. Within seconds they were almost on top of the poor home guards, who took off to guard their homes, I reckon. I mean they simply broke and ran, every man for himself, dropping shotguns and flintlocks that had been in their families for generations.

Next thing we knew, three Yankee regiments were occupying the railroad and were dressing up their ranks for a go at our flank. A good colonel would have wheeled half his strength around to face this threat while sending for reinforcements to hold a natural strongpoint like the brickyard. But there was no one to direct us. Colonel Fincastle was in his lair wringing his hands as Major Swan kept shouting the bad news to him. And we were still taking fire from the Yankees across from us in the woods. In fact, the flash of muskets could be seen far off to our left toward the river, as well.

The fire from these three flanking regiments, plus the one on our front, produced a terrifying crisscross effect. Captain Ferro saw the danger and pulled our company from behind the breastworks to form a rank to the right. As we ran over to try to stem the tide, Colonel Fincastle comes out and sees the mass of Yankees about to burst upon us. His faithful horse was tied behind the brickyard office. There was no box to use for mounting and he didn't need one. Up he hauled his 250 pounds of blubber into the saddle, shouting back to Swan, "Tell the men to fall back, for we are flanked. Tell them to take up a new position to the rear."

With that he flails away at his horse's sides with his hat, and for the first time that gray beast broke into an honest-to-goodness gallop, toward New Bern.

Three volleys the Yanks gave us, and then came that mighty roar as they deliberately moved toward us. We fired two volleys into them, but it was like farting into a hurricane. Within seconds the other companies of the 10th began fleeing their breastwork back across the brickyard toward New Bern, following the example of our glorious colonel. In a moment a stream of men were high-tailing it to the rear.

Captain Ferro saw that we'd be overrun if we tried to stand our ground any longer. "Don't panic," he shouts. "Join the 7th Regiment to our left." That was a smart move and if the other companies had done the same, the battle of New Bern would have turned out differently. Instead, they had scurried to the rear, many of them leaving their new Enfields behind.

The Yankees had broken our line, and now were intent on rolling it up. After scampering over to the 7th, we threw ourselves on our bellies and resumed our fire. We were soon joined by other companies of the 7th.

All along our front, between the brickyard and Fort Thompson, came a steady rain of bullets. The Yanks sent volley after volley into us. Poor John Bradway was hit in the throat and died without a sound. Fred Ray suddenly spun around and fell, hit in the leg, squalling like a stuck pig. We tried to be good Christians and give better than we received, but they were too many for us. They came crashing toward us with bayonets fixed, a fearsome sight. We fell back across the camp of the 7th Regiment toward the Old Beaufort Road, where the 37th N.C. held firm. There we halted, reformed, we remnants of the 10th and 7th Regiments, reloaded our muskets, fixed our bayonets, and stood ready.

"Charge!"

I have said how the song "Dixie" was worth an army to the South. The "Rebel yell" was worth another army. Nobody ever taught it to us. That bloodcurdling scream is in the blood of every Southerner. It sprang from our bellies and throats spontaneously that March afternoon as we charged into the momentarily bewildered enemy.

The edge of the Yankee mass gave way before our charge, but a handful of the braver ones stood and were soon cut down or battered to their knees. We rolled halfway over the old camp of the 7th Regiment before the Yanks recovered from their surprise enough to counterattack. We were standing in among the dead and wounded. It was a shocking sight to see at your feet a blond young fellow with a great bloody hole where his forehead had been not ten minutes before. And over there was an officer with a gray mustache, sitting up and holding his belly, trying to stop the blood from gushing from a bayonet wound.

Here the Yanks came again, and it was fall back or be captured. So we raced to the Old Beaufort Road and held them there for a while with our musket fire, until a fresh Yankee regiment cut toward us from the railroad, joined by the men who had been firing across the clearing originally. And now the 27th Regiment, which held the line next to Fort Thompson, was catching it from the Federal gunboats. Once the militia broke and ran, it was just a matter of time, since we had not properly fortified the brickyard. Now, all the Confederates began abandoning their breastworks and falling back to the rear toward New Bern.

Our company followed the Old Beaufort Road, turning to fire at the Yanks when they pressed too close. During one of those brief stands Captain Ferro fell to the ground with a mangled arm. Noah Rhine, Harry McGee and I made a stretcher out of two muskets and a blanket, and that way lugged him halfway back to the Trent River bridge. There we encountered Major Swan, waiting on his bony nag, left behind by Fincastle to observe.

"Get off your horse," I says to him.

"Who do you think you are talking to?" he replies.

"I am talking to a dead major if you aren't out of that saddle by the time I cock my musket," says I. "We got Captain Ferro here and he needs your horse. He's wounded."

"Why didn't you say so?" With that he slides down and watches while we put the captain in the saddle.

Our company and the men of the 27th Regiment were the last to cross the bridge. We set fire to it, which gave us a chance to catch our breath at New Bern. I found a surgeon and he agreed to haul the captain beyond the city and see to his wound. Hauled him in an ambulance, too. Most of our wounded were back at the battlefield, so he wasn't busy.

General Branch was storming about, ordering the destruction of the military stores amassed in New Bern. Up in flames went wagons, turpentine and barracks. For a while it appeared as if the entire town would be destroyed, houses along with all that horde of supplies so painfully extracted from the rest of the state.

We retreated well beyond the town, where I caught up with the surgeon who had set up shop in a little church. Fortunately he had a good supply of chloroform and he removed the captain's right arm about midway between the elbow and shoulder.

They wouldn't let me watch, and frankly I was glad. Soon the captain was on his way back toward Kinston in an ambulance drawn by two strong mules.

It was a sad-assed collection of beaten, bitter men that finally reassembled beyond New Bern that night. We had left behind well over five hundred killed, wounded or captured. Before dawn the next day, we were on the road back toward Kinston. The Yankees had taken too much punishment to try to close up on us for another battle. Besides, they had what they had come for, possession of New Bern.

The official report on the battle said that our regiment "left the field in the utmost disorder."

We simply got the shit kicked out of us in our very first battle, thanks to the North Carolina militia and Colonel Elmer Fincastle. That was what happened.

8

Back in Kinston, we went into camp to count our losses and lick our wounds, but I personally got little chance to rest. First morning there Captain Ferro sends for me to come and see him in the hospital, which was nothing more than a converted warehouse. He was propped up on a cot, looking drawn and sickly enough to break your heart.

"Sergeant Mundy," he says, "I observed you in the battle at New Bern and I thought you handled your squad very well."

"Why, thank you, sir," I answers. "They are a smart bunch of boys, brave and true, every one of them."

"What's more, I owe you a word of personal thanks. If you hadn't taken the initiative, I would have been left behind in

Federal hands. I want to thank you for that."

"I simply did my duty, nothing more," says I, fairly bursting with pride at his praise.

"Well, Sergeant, the general himself has been around to see me and he and the surgeon have ordered me back to Raleigh for an examination by the doctors at the hospital there, and if they give their approval I am to return to Oldham County for a few weeks to recover at my home."

"That's good, sir."

"The general directs that I must be accompanied by some man who acquitted himself especially well in the battle. He wants to reward valor and hopes that I can choose a man with enough initiative to help recruit some replacements back home. Would you like to go with me?"

I would have done almost anything to get away from Messrs. Fincastle and Swan. And, besides, I wanted to help the captain. So I replies, "It would be an honor to accompany you, sir."

The camp was seething with angry talk as I packed up to leave. Seems Colonel Fincastle had come out and tried to make one of his speeches but the boys had whistled and made so much rude noise that he had given up and stormed home to his ripe little wife. I told my squad to stop that sort of thing. He was still their colonel and it was bad for an army to show disrespect in public for an officer of his rank. That's what responsibility can do: make you into a prig.

Harry McGee reminded me of what I had said and done to poor Major Swan and I tells him to "Do as I say do and not as I do. Besides, those were unusual circumstances."

Word spread of my assignment and soon I was surrounded by men giving me letters and packets of money for their families, generally making nuisances of themselves and paying no attention to my protests that the doctors in Raleigh might not find Captain Ferro well enough to travel back home. These homesick fellows were the same who had been so anxious to leave their families just a few months ago. Human nature!

At the hospital, a couple of stout fellows put Captain Ferro on a stretcher, despite his protests that he could walk, and loaded him on an ambulance. The surgeon took me aside and said, "Now, Sergeant, he is healing satisfactorily. The sutures are holding up well, but he must not be jostled about. Keep him quiet. Here is a letter to give the doctor in charge at Raleigh about his case. We will telegraph ahead so there will be an ambulance to meet your train. Under no circumstances is he to walk about."

So off to the depot we go in our ambulance. They set the stretcher gently into the baggage end of a combination car. I made sure the captain was comfortable, but he says, "Now, Mundy, you go and sit down in the other end. I'm going to sleep and you might as well take your ease in a seat."

Beyond the partition, in the passenger compartment, who do I see getting aboard but Colonel Elmer Fincastle and his pretty little wife? He was looking somewhat subdued but still booming about, making sure that the conductor knew he had the wife of a colonel on board.

"Goodbye, dear Elvira," I hear him say to her. "I'll come back to Raleigh when this mess gets sorted out and I am vindicated."

"Goodbye, Mister Fincastle," she replies in a low voice. "I do hope everything will turn out all right."

"Well, don't worry about it in any case. I have many influential friends in Raleigh and Richmond, too, and they will look out for my interests."

I sat there and acted as if I was not listening. But as Fincastle starts to leave he calls to me, "Soldier, come here."

I gets up and walks up to him and gives him an exaggerated salute, which he returns and then asks, "Aren't you in the 10th North Carolina?"

"I am indeed, sir. I am Sergeant James Mundy, of Company H."

"Yes," he replies. "Captain Ferro's company from Oldham County. Fought a brilliant rear-guard action, I hear. Unfortunate about Captain Ferro's loss of a leg."

"An arm, sir," I corrects him. "His right arm."

"His arm, of course. Well, where are you headed for?"

Now a good colonel would have known my name and my business. He would have come to see his captain loaded on the train. But not this windbag. So I tell him and he asks, "You mean Captain Ferro is on this car?"

"Right through that door in the baggage compartment, but he is sleeping just now."

"In that case I won't disturb him." And he kisses his little wife goodbye and gets off the train.

It was an uneventful trip to Raleigh. Several others rode in our compartment as far as Goldsboro, where I got off to buy a bit of lunch for the captain and me. He said he wasn't hungry. When I got back to the passenger compartment, Mrs. Fincastle was alone so I tipped my hat to her and, seeing she had no food, offered her the captain's portion. To my surprise, she accepted.

"Won't you sit down and eat with me?" she asks.

"Yes, ma'am," says I, thinking to myself what the boys would say if they could see me.

It was a most pleasant ride to Raleigh. I was glad the train had to go on a side track for half an hour to let a special car carrying the governor and some high Confederate brass pass us, headed east. According to the conductor, an overbearing, chatty fellow, they were going down to Kinston to investigate the army there.

"Understand we had a rough time down at New Bern," he says, interrupting my conversation with Mrs. Fincastle.

"It was rough, for a fact."

"You were there?"

"In the thick of it."

"Is it true that some of our boys ran in the face of the enemy?"

"Not in their faces," I replies, getting a little annoyed with this officious ticket puncher. "In the opposite direction. And only militia from down here in your section of the state. The rest of us withdrew."

"Well, I think it is cowardly to run or withdraw in the face of the enemy. It is a shameful way to act. And I heard in Kinston last night that one of the colonels actually rode off the field and abandoned his men. If we are going to win this war, we Southerners must show more courage than that."

Even though I despised her husband, I did not want to let Mrs. Fincastle hear any more of that kind of chat, so I cut the conductor off with "Perhaps you will have the opportunity to enlist in the army yourself and can teach courage to the boys."

With that he gives me a dirty look and mumbles something about five children and a hernia. But at least he got on with his business.

Up close, Mrs. Fincastle was not quite as pretty or young as she appeared at a distance. She was developing a few wrinkles around her nice light brown eyes and I could see the beginnings of a double chin. Still, she was a pert little woman with a full bosom and a pleasant smell about her. What's more, she paid me the compliment of making me feel like I was somebody. Wanted to know all about me and my family.

"A Methodist preacher's son. Well."

"Yes, ma'am."

"And very young for a sergeant, aren't you?"

"Just turned nineteen."

"Sergeant, now that we are alone, you were at the Battle of New Bern. Is it true that we were so badly beaten there?"

"It was not a victory, that's sure, but we did handle the Yankees pretty rough. They knew they were in a fight."

"Well, I shouldn't talk out of school but my husband is just worried sick that his action in that battle may have been misunderstood by some. He says he risked his life to ride back and get reinforcements but before he could return the line had given way."

It was all I could do to keep from letting out a snort of laughter at that, thinking what a sly, fat hypocrite he was. Instead, I says, "Well, I was too busy in the fight to know what was going on behind the lines. But I'm sure the colonel has nothing to fear from a full exposure of the truth in this matter, Mrs. Fincastle."

"Oh, thank you for saying that. And you will not repeat what I told you, I trust."

"I will keep your confidence," I promised.

By this time we were drawing into Raleigh. Unlike her husband Mrs. Fincastle took a personal interest in Captain Ferro, going back to the baggage compartment to chat with him and inquire after his health.

As she started to go, she says, "I have been conversing with this fine young soldier, Captain. When you are feeling better, I would be pleased to have both of you call for coffee or tea."

The captain gave one of those polite responses you learn early in the South which gets you off the hook and makes the other person feel good. At least his class learns it. I never was very good at it.

9

We remained in Raleigh for a week. The hospital let me sleep in the barracks with the orderlies. Most of the patients in the hospital were suffering from diseases and injuries from accidents. We brought damned few of our wounded away from New Bern, of course. The captain got excellent attention, which left me free to stroll about the city, seeing the sights.

Lo and behold, as I was walking along Fayetteville Street our second day there, someone calls to me, "Sergeant Mundy." I turned and there was Mrs. Fincastle carrying a market basket and accompanied by a dried-up old black woman.

"How is Captain Ferro?"

"He is mending nicely."

"Do you think he is able yet to come and have coffee with me?"

Thinking very fast, I reply, "I think not. The doctor allows him to walk about very little, I'm afraid."

"Oh, too bad. Perhaps I may visit him tomorrow." Then she looks at me and says, "How about you? There is no reason you cannot take refreshment with me, is there?"

At that point, I wasn't interested in sitting about drinking coffee with a woman twelve or fifteen years older than me, but I couldn't think of any excuse. "I guess . . . why, no, ma'am. No reason at all."

"Then you can carry our purchases and come right along with Mandy and me."

Mandy, it turned out, was an old free woman who had been working for the Fincastles for some time. Mrs. Fincastle led the way to a neat little clapboard cottage surrounded by thick shrubbery. She and I sat in the living room talking while Mandy rustled up our coffee. Later in the war I would have crawled through the streets of Raleigh for a cup of genuine coffee, but at that stage the blockade hadn't taken hold and the coffee beans could get through. At first I sat wishing I was out strolling about but she had the knack of putting you at your ease and soon I was entertaining her with cleaned-up versions of some choice Oldham County stories.

Mandy hovered about with coffee and tea cakes. After about an hour, though, she puts her head in the door and says, "Miss Elvira, is it all right if I goes on home now?"

"Why, certainly, Mandy. But do come first thing in the morning so we can get the wash started early."

With that I rises to go, saying, "Mrs. Fincastle, it has been a great pleasure visiting with you. I reckon I should be going now."

She says, "Please call me Elvira and I don't think it is necessary for you to go at all."

"Why, Mrs. Fincastle, that's mighty—"

"Elvira," she corrects me.

"Well, Elvira, I just didn't want to impose myself on you."

"You are not imposing yourself, believe me, James. Here, let me refill your cup."

I reckon I was naïve. Hell, I know I was naïve and, for all my vulgar talk, innocent as well. I had never been intimate with a woman. Had stolen a few kisses and hugs at backwoods parties and dances but I didn't understand life until that afternoon in Raleigh, North Carolina.

Mrs. Fincastle, excuse me, Elvira, told me how lonely it was being the wife of a busy officer and how she missed having someone to talk to. Then she wanted to know how many sweethearts I had back home. When I said none, she replies, "A tall straight handsome young man like you doesn't have a girl. Now, James, you aren't telling me the truth."

My daddy would have said the devil made me make my next remark. Whoever it was, out comes the words "Well, Elvira, I guess we just don't have girls as pretty as you back in Oldham County or I wouldn't be able to say I never had a sweetheart."

"You dear boy, how sweet of you to say that."

Then, with tears glistening in her eyes, she walks over to me and puts those soft white arms around my neck and plants a wet kiss right on my mouth. I didn't quite know what to do, but she soon showed me. Led me right through an adjoining door into her bedroom and there I learned the delights of the flesh. Learned them at the age of nineteen in the arms of a woman in her thirties, and the wife of my colonel at that.

Let me tell you I was like a young bear that just discovered honey. Couldn't get enough of it. I was back again that night and again the next.

Captain Ferro was getting much stronger now, able to walk about the hospital grounds. He looked at me closely, saying, "You appear peaked, Mundy. Are you getting enough sleep?"

"Yes, sir. I am."

"You must find Raleigh very boring."

"Not at all, sir."

"Well, we will know tomorrow if my stump is well enough to stand that trip to Oldham County. If it is not, I expect you ought to rejoin the regiment. If the doctor says yes, we'll take the cars for home."

The last thing I wanted was to leave Raleigh, whether for Kinston or home. That night I was lying in Elvira's big feather bed and she said, "Even if you do have to go back home, you'll be returning through Raleigh and I'll be waiting for you. In fact, James, I have been thinking that perhaps Mr. Fincastle could be persuaded to make you a member of his staff. You could help him out with his paper work and that way you and I could be close to each other. What do you think about that?"

"That would be nice." And I buried my face between her two great sweet breasts and she wrapped those lovely soft arms about my head.

It was a fine place to rest your head but a damned poor place from which to hear anything. Such as the sound of a buggy drawing up in the yard and a large man alighting from it and saying good night to the driver. In fact, the first indication I had of something being amiss was the vibration of a heavy foot on the porch.

I raised my head from its resting place to ask, "What's that?"

Then the voice of Elmer Fincastle roars through the front door, "Elvira. It's me! I'm home!"

"Oh, my God," she whispers. "Hide over there," pointing to a curtained cubicle in which she hung her dresses. I leaped out of bed stark-naked, scooped up my shoes and uniform and dove behind that curtain, all covered with goose bumps.

"Dear Mister Fincastle," says Elvira as she dons her nightgown. "What a pleasant surprise. Have you had supper? Do let me take you in the kitchen and feed you."

"I ate on the train. I'm exhausted and ready for bed. I have been through the valley of desperation these past two days, Elvira."

"Oh, my dear, what is the matter?"

I soon heard what was the matter as I huddled behind that curtain, cold with fear, trying to keep my breathing low and easy. Fincastle undressed and slid a ridiculous nightshirt over his great pink paunch, then blew out the light he had brought in from the living room. Soon he was in the same spot I had been so happily occupying a few moments earlier.

"Oh, Elvira. I am a defeated man. Surrounded by enemies and sorely misunderstood."

It seemed that the governor and the Confederate brass had been in Kinston conducting a full inquiry into the Battle of New Bern and that certain criticisms had been made of Colonel Fincastle's conduct. Seemed they were most critical of his failure to fortify the brickyard and of his leaving the field of battle before his men.

"And the worst part is the disrespect my own men have shown me. Oh, Elvira, I am so misunderstood."

"Poor dear," she murmured.

"It was all I could do to avoid a demotion."

"What did they do?"

"Why, they relieved me of my regimental command and are transferring me back to Raleigh as a special colonel. I will assist in recruiting around the state and will act as a liaison between North Carolina and Richmond. It will be a post of honor and that way you and I will not be separated so much."

"How nice."

"But the humiliation I have suffered. Oh, Elvira, I need you so. . . ."

I had to remain cowering behind that curtain and listen to the bed creaking as old Fincastle caught up on his homework. It may sound funny now, but you wouldn't have thought it humorous at all if it had been you behind that curtain, freezing to death and afraid to breathe. I had no idea how I would ever get out of that room.

In a minute, Fincastle moaned and the bed stopped its infernal racket. Then Elvira said, "Mr. Fincastle, would you do me a favor?"

"What's that, my dear?"

"I left my slop jar out on the back porch and I really must have it."

"Of course, my sweet. I will fetch it."

As soon as he was out of the room, Elvira raised the window

and whispered, "James. Out the window quickly."

Like a flash I emerged from the cubicle, gave her a final kiss, and tumbled out into a frightful bush covered with tiny thorns. They tore into my skin from every angle. It was all I could do to keep from crying out.

"James," she whispered into the darkness. "Don't forget when you come back to Raleigh."

The window closed softly and I was left to disengage myself from that fiendish bush, get dressed and limp back to the hospital barracks. Hot diggety damn!

10

The next day Captain Ferro was found to be sufficiently healed to allow a trip back to Oldham County. So I goes to bed early and get my first full night's sleep in some time. Rested from the labors of love, you might say.

And early the following morning we boarded our train for Greensboro. I bullied the conductor into setting aside a seat just for the captain. With hospital pillows to lean back on, it was a smooth ride to Greensboro, where we were lucky enough to transfer to another train ready to head south to Charlotte.

I enjoyed that trip. The captain asked me questions about my family and discreetly got my ideas about how soldiers should be trained and disciplined. Seemed to find my outspoken ways amusing. Wanted to know, too, why I had not gone on to the University, which rather flattered me.

Between our chats, he dozed. I tried to, but my brain was aflame with restless thoughts, first of lying in bed with Elvira and then of standing with musket leveled at charging Yankees and then of digging my face into the sand while shells burst all around me and then of running while Minié balls gave chase and once again back to the ripe body of my colonel's wife. I had been through a great deal in a short time; it was more than a nineteen-year-old could easily absorb.

Elvira was in my blood. The experience behind the curtain and in the thorn bush had cooled me down a bit, but as I rode on that train all those hours I could not keep my mind from running back to that delicious woman. Mind you, I was not in love. It was an obsession. She had taken possession of me.

The train was crowded, almost every seat was taken on the ride from Greensboro to Charlotte. Even though the windows were closed, the dirt and ash still sifted in. There were lots of soldiers on the train, but no longer did I see crowds lining the way.

We reached Charlotte late in the afternoon. Captain wanted to hire a buggy and set right out for home, but I prevailed upon him to take a room in a local hotel and get a good night's sleep. He looked awful pale and, although he wouldn't admit it, I could tell his stump was paining him.

So after supper in the hotel dining room, I squared him away for the evening and strolled out to a livery stable on Tryon Street, where the proprietor was overseeing the night feeding of the animals. Told him I had a wounded hero of the Battle of New Bern in my care and we required the very best transportation down to Oldham County. He agreed to provide it after I had haggled him down five dollars.

That night I slept in the same room as the captain, he on the bed and I on a pallet on the floor. Undressed in the dark so he wouldn't see all the scratches across my backside, from the thorn bush. Up early next morning for the kind of breakfast I have always loved and which you can get only in the South, to wit: good strong coffee with yellow cream and two spoons of sugar, salt-cured ham with red-eye gravy over grits, two eggs fried in the ham grease, big flaky biscuits coated with rich butter topped off with honey in the comb and sticky peach preserves. Talk about eating, that is it.

"You have a good appetite, James," Captain Ferro said as he watched me have my second round of biscuits.

"Well, I am tired of the army's fatback and corn mush," I replies.

"So am I." But still he hardly touched his food.

To my surprise when the buggy showed up at the hotel, the livery stable owner himself was driving. Said he had lain awake thinking about what I had told him of Captain Ferro and he wanted to hear more about the Battle of New Bern. It was a comfortable buggy, big enough to allow the captain to stretch out. Even had pillows and a lap robe. And two strong matched sorrels pulling the rig.

I sat up on the driver's seat with the fellow and answered the questions he kept pumping at me. What was it like being in battle? Were the Yankees the cowards everyone said they were? Could you see a cannon ball in the air? How many dead men had I seen? I gave him such a good story that he cut another five dollars off his price when we finally got to the Ferro plantation.

Let me say a word about that place, which I had never seen even though it was in our county. The first Ferro (then Ferreaux) had left the low country of South Carolina before the Revolution. His name was Jacques and he still spoke French. Brought along a dozen slaves, most of them skilled workmen, and took up lands formerly inhabited by the Manawee Indians. He was a Huguenot, and the religion that came closest to his was the Presbyterian, so he marries into the Scotch-Irish that were coming down from western Pennsylvania. Every generation had improved itself. For instance, the captain had gone north to college, to Princeton. The Ferros brought in more slaves as time went on until by the time the war began they owned sixty.

To get to the plantation, which they called Beaulieu, we turned off before we got to Meadsboro and headed southwest, away from my own home, which was northeast of the town. I had never been down in that part of the county before. I pictured a house like those I had seen near Kinston, big white mansion with pillars across the front. To my surprise I saw that it was a hulking three-and-a-half-story brick structure with a porch completely around. The first story was a kind of half-basement containing the kitchen, dining room and common room for lounging. You walked up a set of steps to the first floor, which contained the parlor, library and so on. The bedrooms were on the next floor plus some low-ceilinged rooms in the attic, under the eaves. An imposing, but very practical sort of house. Old Jacques Ferreaux and his slaves had made the brick themselves, I later learned.

The slaves lived well away from the big house in a collection of brick huts, two dozen of them at least, set in among some low shade trees, chinaberry and such. There were blacksmith shops, barns, corncribs, a plantation office, all well maintained and orderly-looking. Some layout they had there.

That plantation was a world unto itself. They raised sheep and made their own cloth; kept bees, ran a small winery for everyday drinking and a still for the hard stuff. Cotton was the big cash crop, of course.

I had thought I might hook a ride with our livery stable chap back up near my neck of the woods, but as the captain paid him off it appeared that he expected me to hang around. So I did.

The family came pouring out on the porch. Mr. and Mrs. Ferro, their youngest son, little Pierre, a middle boy, Ernest, Jr., and last but not least, Jane, the girl with the dark-red hair I had seen the day I enlisted. They all clustered about the captain, embracing and kissing him and all except little Pierre avoiding any glance at or mention of his empty right sleeve. Then came the four house servants, greeting him warmly and a bit shyly, all except that big brown woman with the high cheekbones. She put her arms around him just as the members of the family had. And the dignified black man I had seen holding the horses at the courthouse embraced him, too.

I was beginning to wish I had gone back with the livery stable man, feeling somewhat left out, when the captain said, "And here is the sergeant I wrote you about. He is still looking after me. Father, Mother, this is James Mundy."

Mr. Ferro took my hand and says, "Sergeant, I understand you saved William's life. We are most grateful to you."

Mrs. Ferro, looking very handsome, takes my hand as well. "Yes, Mister Mundy. That was such a brave thing for you to do. I am so glad you came home with William. And we do hope you will stay the night with us."

Mr. Ferro frowns at that. "Now, Eunice, this young man has a family of his own and he may be anxious to see them."

But the captain says, "It is so late that you would be traveling into the night. Stay the night, James, and I'll see you go home in style in the morning. I do have some army business to talk over with you."

So, stay I did. They showed me a splendid feather bed up in the attic. Later, we assembled in the dining room for supper, only they called it dinner.

I may have given the wrong impression earlier about my own family. They were gentle, well-mannered people, considerate in their dealings and calm-spoken. Don't know where I got some of my rough ways. A natural-born rebel, I guess. Anyway, we did not reach across the table for food or quarrel with each other as I saw the McGees do. But the kind of elegance I experienced at Beaulieu was from another world. They ate around a huge polished table of mahogany set with a confusion of heavy, English sterling tableware. The plates were of imported china, so thin and delicate I feared they would break. Exquisite crystal and linen napkins. What's more, three servants stood about to fetch things.

They seated me between little Pierre and daughter Jane. For

once, in the midst of all that splendor, I was speechless, very conscious of being in a Confederate uniform that was showing its hard wear and wondering which fork and which spoon to use. Finally decided it was monkey see, monkey do. Just followed the captain's suit and that way averted a disaster.

Mr. Ferro directed Cassius, the butler, in the opening and pouring of the wine, saying to me as he did so, "Sergeant Mundy, normally I would ascertain your age before offering you wine, but I suppose that anyone who has done what you have is old enough for anything."

The cat still had my tongue so I mumbled something like "I reckon so."

The conversation around that table amazed me as much as the good wine and superb food. These people talked so easily, in polite tones, asking for each other's opinions and acting interested in what you said. Never felt like such a backwoodsman in my life.

But I never was repressed for long. The wine began to loosen my tongue and they drew me out more and more. Decided the best way was to act natural. They seemed to like my jokes or at least pretended to.

After supper, I mean dinner, we repaired to the great common room where a small fire was burning and lo and behold I soon found myself with a snifter of brandy in my hand, swapping opinions with Mr. Ferro about how the war should be fought. Later, while there was still enough light to see a bit, I strolled about the grounds with young Ernest as my guide, visiting the slave quarters, the barns and various outbuildings.

At that point, the flow of life at Beaulieu was little disturbed by the war. Their oldest son had gone off and lost an arm. Coffee was getting expensive and no more French wines could come in through Charleston. Mr. Ferro complained about the Confederate Government's policy against raising cotton and was alarmed at the way prices were beginning to rise. Still, generally the war had not affected his life much. He still had his land, his slaves and the wealth accumulated over three generations. And he was investing current profits in good sound Confederate bonds.

Back in the house that night, Captain Ferro takes me upstairs into the library, where they had more books than I had ever seen, to tell me that the next morning they were going to lend me a good saddle horse to ride home and to use while I was on furlough.

"Why, that would be fine," says I. "I appreciate it."

"Jane has a nice gentle bay mare and she has volunteered her for your use."

Now Jane and I—the same age and all that—had sat beside each other all through the evening without once saying a word to each other. And here she was offering me the use of her mare. I was flabbergasted and tried to thank him again.

"Wait a minute. There is a method in all this. The general thought it would be well if we took some recruits back when we return. I'm not in condition to run all over the country, so I thought you might be willing to visit families in your area and see if you can't persuade some of the young fellows to go back to camp with us. Between the measles epidemic and the fiasco at New Bern, we are about twenty-five men under strength. How about it?"

That suited me just fine. Went to bed that night and dreamed of shells bursting about me again, only this time my face was not buried in the sand as it had been at New Bern; instead, it was pressed into the bosom of Elvira. I woke up half-smothered, my face in the goose-down pillow, and lay there letting my mind drift back to the elegant meal, sitting beside that quiet girl with the dark-red hair. Up early the next morning. Breakfast around the same table with the same well-mannered conversation. This time I got up my courage enough to say to Miss Jane, "I do thank you for the loan of your horse."

She replies, "I'm glad you can use her."

"I'll take good care of her if you will tell me how."

"Well, perhaps I can come out after breakfast when they are getting her ready for the trip."

She strolled out to the barn with me and we talked some more as the groom saddled up the little mare. Turned out that Miss Jane had spent three years at a girls' boarding school in Charleston and had been there when Fort Sumter had been fired upon the year before. She told me how exciting it was to hear and see the bombardment. Now, at eighteen, her education had ended, as it had for me. Formal education, that is. I have never stopped learning.

We were talking a mile a minute when her father appears, saying rather gruffly, "Now, Jane, we have kept Sergeant Mundy from his own family long enough." That man never liked me, I'm sorry to say.

One last talk with the captain. He asked me to come back in one week to report to him on my recruiting activities. Meanwhile, he had a duty of his own to perform. Had taken it on himself to bring a list of every one of his men who had died, whether of disease or wounds, and as soon as he felt strong enough he planned to visit every one of their families. That's the kind of man that was William Ferro. One of the finest.

I must have cut a ridiculous figure riding away from that mansion in a Confederate infantry uniform, a blanket roll over the front of a flat English saddle and an Enfield rifle on my shoulder. I rode like any farm boy, but the mare did not take advantage of my lack of horsemanship. She settled into an easy saddle gait that ate up the miles.

I never felt as much like a king as that day riding that fine mare, my head reeling with all my recent experiences, and looking forward to seeing my family again.

11

My exuberant mood lasted all the way into Meadsboro. It lasted until I started to ride past the Oldham County Courthouse. There, on a low brick wall outside, sat old Hiram Winchester.

"Howdy, Cousin Hiram," I calls out.

"Hey, pull up there." He walks out in the street and takes the mare's bridle, making me his prisoner. "You're Robert Mundy's boy, aren't you?"

"Yes, sir. I'm James."

"And what are you doing in that silly uniform? Playing soldier?"

"I'm not *playing* soldier, Cousin Hiram. I've been off and fought my first battle. I'm home on furlough to do a little recruiting."

The old man snorted. "Seen the elephant, huh? Let me tell you, you ain't been in your last battle by a long sight."

"I expect not, Cousin Hiram."

"No, sir. If you come back alive from this war, you can count that your blessing."

"Well, I'm pretty tough. It's good to see you looking so well. I'll tell Pa I saw you. Now, if you'll excuse me, I haven't seen my family since last October. . . ."

Hiram kept his iron clutch on the bridle.

"We have made our bed with this secession business and now we must lie down in it. Mark my word, boy. There is going to be weeping and wailing and gnashing of teeth. Tribulation. Suffering like nobody has known since Bible days. This war ain't even warmed up good. Nobody would listen to me but you'll see

I am right someday. This war is going to ruin us all. Nothing will ever be the same again. You married, young man?"

"No, Cousin Hiram. I'm just nineteen."

"At least you won't leave a widow. Tell you, Oldham County will be filled with widows before this is over."

Well, I had had a bellyful of that talk. If there had been anyone to help me, I'd have liked to give the old man another ride on a rail. I jerked the reins so the mare would pull her head free of his grasp, tipped my cap and wished him goodbye. "Tiresome old fart," I muttered under my breath. Tried to recover my mood, but it wouldn't return until I came in sight of our two-story, unpainted house. Had only written a couple of letters home and them before the battle. Nobody was expecting me.

Little Wesley saw me first and came loping across the barn lot shouting for Ma and Pa. Pretty soon they were all around me asking questions and generally making a fuss. I was home.

I loved my daddy and mama and hope I have not given a wrong impression of them. My father was a tall, gangling man who never exchanged an angry word with anyone. He preached the gospel of love and I must say that he lived up to it. Great one for praying and talking about the sweet mercy and grace of God. Despised the Presbyterian notion of predestination and hated sin and strife.

My mother had more pepper. Sometimes got short-tempered. Got my whippings from her, not Pa. Snappy little woman with a ready tongue. Come to think of it, my rough ways must have come from her side. One of her first ancestors in America was a Welsh boy who ran away to sea and ended up in Virginia, where he eloped with a fifteen-year-old daughter of a prominent landowner. Without benefit of clergy, they fled to Indian country to escape the wrath of her father. They lived there among the savages until the old man forgave them. So the story ran.

As I say, I loved my parents but I had not been home for one day before I got restless again. So I set out on my mare and went about the countryside talking up the army among the boys and delivering all the letters and such that had been pressed upon me. Rode up to Professor Mead's academy and the old man invited me in to talk to the boys, who ranged from ten to seventeen. On Saturday, I rode into Meadsboro and chatted with some of the men around the two general stores the town then boasted. And on Sunday I went to church to hear Pa preach on the parable of the Good Samaritan and stayed for the Sunday school that followed. Lo and behold, the Sunday school superintendent asked me to give them a talk about the war and I made it sound like it was a great adventure, concluding with "Now you young men, Captain Ferro will be at the courthouse next Friday to take your oath. You are going to miss out on some fun if you stay home from this war."

After services, the girls hung about, making eyes at me. One tall beauty in particular who had never given me a second look before. I acted as if I didn't have the time of day for her and in fact I did not. My mind was on others of her sex. Common country girls had no appeal for me anymore.

That night as we sat around the living room after the evening Bible reading and prayers, my father tried to have a serious talk with me, beginning, "James, army life seems to be agreeing with you."

"Yes, sir. Out of doors and lots of exercise."

"You are reading the Testament I gave you, I trust."

"Well, you must understand that they keep us pretty busy during the day and we have no candles for evening reading. But I did go to church in Raleigh."

"Expect you hear some pretty rough language from some of the men."

"Yes, sir. There are some tough characters in the army and their language is shocking sometimes."

"And drinking, I expect."

"Now, Pa, the army does frown on drinking."

"I just pray that you steer clear of men who swear and drink. God will not give his blessing to blasphemers and drunkards.

This is going to be a long and bitter struggle and the South will need the help of the Almighty."

"Yes, sir. We are going to need the help of everybody. The Yankees are tougher than we thought."

My mother, who was shrewder than my daddy, listened to my evasive responses with narrowed eyes. "You haven't fallen in with any loose women hanging about the army, have you, son?"

"Oh, Mama, the only woman hanging around our camp has been the colonel's own wife. And he is, or once was, a Baptist minister and she a middle-aged woman."

"Well, I don't want you bringing home a wife from down east or up in Virginia. Lots of nice girls right here at home."

"Yes, ma'am."

I was glad when Wesley asked me to tell him about New Bern. I told him the entire story for the third time to head off further questioning.

The middle of the next week I rode over to Beaulieu on the little mare and found Captain Ferro much improved. Color back in his cheeks. Beginning to pick up some weight. He listened to my report and then insisted that I ride in the buggy with him to call on a couple of families of men who had died. I had already visited the Bradway and Ray families of course.

The first visit went all right. It was a big family. They had already done their grieving. Mainly they were flattered that one of the local aristocrats was paying them a visit, I think.

But the next stop was one of the worst experiences I ever had. The house was little more than a cabin way back off the main road, on a wagon trail the buggy could barely go on. The widow was a faded young woman with two little children hanging on her skirts and a widowed mother who sat in a rocker chewing tobacco. I remembered the husband. He was in the next squad at New Bern. I had seen him fall. He was a kind of sour, quiet fellow.

Well, word of his death had not reached this cabin in the woods, only we did not know that. Captain Ferro tipped his hat, identified us and said, "We have just come to pay our respects.

I know your husband's death was a great shock to you."

The two women stared at us blankly. "His death?" the young woman asked.

The captain didn't quite know what to say so I broke in with "Yes, didn't you hear that Oscar died in battle three weeks ago?"

Well, you never heard such screaming and crying in your life. Then the mother and two children took it up. And there we were, two men not knowing what to do or say, just sitting in the buggy until that storm of grief abated. That poor woman had nothing much to live for anyway and in a wink she had lost that little.

The captain and I tried to offer words of comfort, but the old woman wouldn't listen. "He had no business running off to fight in a rich man's war. Gave his life to help high and mighty people like you to keep your niggers, that's what he done."

Only time I ever saw the captain lose his air of self-possession. Just turned scarlet.

She was a bent old woman with mean little eyes, full of a lifetime of bottled-up bitterness. Once she got wound up, there was no stopping her. Men were no good anyway. Her own husband had been a shiftless drunk who died and left her on the mercy of her daughter and son-in-law. Her daughter's husband had volunteered against her advice. I began to appreciate the poor fellow's motive for signing up. Expect it was to escape life with his wife's mother.

Finally the wife gets control of herself and tells her mother to hush. "These gentlemen didn't kill Oscar. It was the cruel Yankees. Oscar died protecting our home. You mustn't insult his captain."

"No," says I piously. "Captain Ferro lost an arm in the same battle, as you can see."

The widow invited us to come in and eat with them, but we excused ourselves. Meanwhile the old woman sat there wiping her eyes and staring at us with pure hatred.

As we drove away, the widow started wailing again at the top of her voice with the old woman and the children chiming in. Their lament followed us all the way out to the main road. The captain and I didn't say a word to each other on the way back to Beaulieu.

12

At Beaulieu, I offered to return Miss Jane's mare, thinking I had kept her long enough. The captain said no, I was doing such a great service for the Confederacy I might as well wait until we met at the courthouse the following Friday before giving back the mare. I was becoming awful fond of that little animal and was glad to accept.

Miss Jane herself came out on the lawn as this conversation was taking place. For a bit my tongue was tied up on me as I admired how the sun gleamed on her long red hair, but I could see she expected me to say something so I blurted out, "I do apologize for appropriating your horse for so long."

"Oh, Mister Mundy, I'm just glad she is useful to you."

The captain excused himself to go in the house, so I stood holding the mare, wondering what to say next. She made it easy for me by asking, "Is Nellie behaving herself?"

"She is going just fine. It's a pleasure to ride her. I rub her down every night and even clean her hooves. Nellie and I are getting to be good friends."

"She's the best horse I ever had. Father bought her mother in Virginia ten years ago when he was up there to buy a family of slaves. Her sire belongs to a neighbor. Do you ride much, ordinarily?"

"All my life," I replied, forgetting to mention that it was mostly mules.

"William thought about forming a cavalry company, but there don't seem to be enough horsemen in these parts. Wouldn't you rather be in the cavalry?"

Truth was I would have, but cavalrymen for the most part had to furnish their own horses, which is one reason why they tended to come from better-off families in South Carolina or Virginia. But I answered, "Not really. The infantry is a lot more important than the cavalry. Our cavalry was no use to us at New Bern." That was the truth, too. Cavalry should have covered our retreat, but they were scouting off somewhere else when we skedaddled.

"I suppose it gets lonesome being away from home."

"I haven't been homesick much."

"Do you get many letters?"

"Just from my daddy and mama."

"The way to get letters is to write letters, Mother always says."

She looked right into my face as she said that, and I into hers. Seemed to me I had never seen eyes of such clear blue. My natural boldness broke through.

"If you wouldn't mind, maybe I could write to you. Wouldn't you like to hear all about the war?"

"Why, yes, I surely would. But I'm afraid life is pretty dull around here. I don't know what there would be to write back to you."

"It would be good just to get some letters from Oldham County."

As this was going on, the big brown woman came out of the kitchen and stood near us with her arms folded, watching us with a frown on her face.

"Your slave woman acts like she wants something," I says.

"Oh, that's Reba. She's not a slave."

"Doesn't she belong to your daddy?"

Miss Jane laughed. "Reba doesn't belong to anybody. We belong to her."

"I don't understand."

"Reba's grandfather was a Manawee chief. She isn't really a darky. Her mother was mostly Indian and free. Her father was a mulatto slave, a cabinetmaker, who belonged to my grandfather. Reba just came to live with us soon after my parents were married. She is the wife of Cassius, our butler." She stopped to speak to the brown woman. "What is it, Reba?"

"You supposed to be helping your mother with the embroidery. She is getting tired of waiting for you."

"All right," Miss Jane says, "you go tell her I'll be right along." Then to me, "Reba and Cassius run this family, I think sometimes. So you will write to me, Mister Mundy?"

"Mister Mundy won't write to you but James Mundy will, Miss Jane," I says grinning.

She gave me the merriest smile in return. "Miss Jane will not reply to your letter but just plain Jane will."

"I wouldn't call you plain, Jane."

We stood there for a moment just smiling at each other, two healthy and (excuse my lack of modesty) good-looking youngsters. Then she went in the house as her brother came out again.

After a bit of business talk about recruiting, I mounted the mare and rode back up to the Big Rock Camp Meeting Grounds area of Oldham County, a different part of the world inhabited by different people.

13

Come next Friday, I met the captain at the courthouse and we set up our recruiting desk in the corridor outside the Register of Deeds' office. The first three recruits were waiting for us when we got there, the Wiley twins and one of the Alexander boys, a towhead who stuttered. Later in the morning there comes in a half-white, half-Indian from the settlement of half-breeds who lived in the piney woods east of Meadsboro. (There was a community of part free-nigger, part Indians who lived on the other side of the town. Although they all sprang from the old Manawee tribe and were all hard-shelled Baptists, never the twain did meet. Despised each other.) The half-breed's name was Jimmy Golightly. I drew Captain Ferro into the Register of Deeds' office to confer with him about whether to accept this fellow's enlistment.

"Why not?" he asks.

"Well, he is not white."

"Neither is he black. We aren't allowed to sign up free blacks because of the notions that it might give the slave population, but I know of no regulation against accepting Indians. Besides, this man is at least half-white."

So we took Jimmy Golightly into the Confederate service. In time he became one of the best soldiers we had.

Another of our recruits was "Preacher Sam" Elkins, so called because he spent every free moment reading his Bible, praying and lecturing his comrades on their morals. Of which more later.

By afternoon, Captain Ferro had sworn in fourteen men and boys and made them promise to show up early Monday for transportation to Raleigh and Kinston for induction into the ranks of the 10th North Carolina.

"You did a good job of recruiting, James," he said to me.

"I think maybe some of them got the idea that the Confederacy furnishes every man with a fine saddle and horse like this one."

The captain laughed. He liked my sense of humor.

"Good for Nellie. Incidentally, Jane says to keep Nellie until Monday and she will ride into town with me in the carriage and pick her up here."

That pleased me, not so much being able to keep Nellie a little longer as the prospect of seeing Jane again. In fact, that girl was much on my mind over the weekend as I sat in church once more, at my mother's last few meals and endured her pampering. It had occurred to me that Elvira Fincastle no longer seemed so real to me. In fact, I hardly thought of her anymore.

It was a sad scene at our house Monday morning. My mother wept and my father blew his nose. They both hugged and kissed me and made me promise to be good and to be careful and to "drop them a line." Wesley shook my hand and asked for the tenth time if the army wouldn't take him when he turned sixteen.

I mounted Nellie and rode out of the yard. Stopped at the road for one last look at our rough, unpainted house with my tall, gangling old daddy and little short mama standing on the porch watching me. That scene stayed on my mind for the next three years.

In Meadsboro, I found that we had fifteen recruits, not fourteen. The Alexander boy came up to me and stammered, "J-J-Jim, this here's my C-C-Cousin Brady and he wants to c-c-come with us."

Brady was about six foot four and must have weighed 220

pounds, with shoulders like an ox. Turned out he had the brain of an ox, too, but we were glad to have him. Captain swore him in.

With fifteen recruits, the captain and I, that made seventeen men to get to camp. Captain Ferro had brought along two extra buggies. Turned out he didn't feel strong enough either to ride a horse or walk to Charlotte. Rather than ride while we walked, he had brought along buggies so we could all ride in equal comfort. His house servant Cassius had it all organized.

Jane was there in a long, pleated riding dress, a kind of derby covering her red hair and a crop in her hand, looking even prettier than I remembered her. I led Nellie over to her and says, "Well, Jane, here's your mare back at long last. Thanks again."

"You are welcome, James. Now you won't forget your promise to write?"

"That's one promise I will keep."

We were standing with the mare between us and her brother, who was busy loading the recruits into the buggies. I didn't know what to say to her next.

"James, thank you again for what you did for William. We are all so grateful to you for saving his life. You are a brave boy."

In that day, decent young people did not kiss in public and anyway it was unthinkable for a poor son of a Methodist preacher-farmer to take liberties with the daughter of an aristocrat. But I didn't get where I am in this world by being shy. Quick as a flash and without thinking about it, I bent down and kissed her on the lips, the sweetest kiss I ever gave or received, and to my surprise, she kissed me back. The only person to see us was old Cassius. He frowned.

"Take care of yourself, James," she said. "Now, hold Nellie and give me a hand up."

Off she rode, mounted side saddle, a graceful, natural horsewoman. I crawled into a buggy and turned my head to watch her riding down Meadsboro's muddy main street, watched her until we turned the corner.

Oh, to be nineteen again and falling in love like that.

14

It took us two days to get our recruits as far as Raleigh. The strain of so much military traffic was beginning to tell on North Carolina's meager nine hundred miles of poorly laid railroad tracks. In Charlotte we had to wait to find space for seventeen men. Near Concord, a rail had split. At Salisbury we had to wait for a wagonload of firewood to arrive. And there we let the boys get off to stretch their legs.

Lo and behold, who do I see hanging around the station but the very same black leg that had sold me the liquor the previous October. "How would you boys like a dipperful of good Iredell County corn liquor while you're waiting?" he asks. "It's only two dollars."

"Two dollars?" I reply. "I was through here last October and you were charging only fifty cents."

He gives me a mean look and says, "You can still have a drink for fifty cents U.S. The price is two dollars Confederate."

As I mentioned earlier, responsibility makes you priggish. So I sends him away with "These young men are in my charge and I won't have you selling them your bad liquor at your exorbitant prices. These men are not to buy or drink any liquor while they are in my control."

I was glad that Harry McGee or Noah Rhine was not around to hear that piece of hypocrisy.

So it went. An overnight stay at an army depot in Greensboro, a derailment near Durham Station, and it was the middle of the afternoon of the second day of travel before we reached Raleigh, a trip that could be covered today in three or four hours if you hit your connections right.

Captain Ferro marched us to the office of the adjutant general of the state. An officious little bald-headed man kept us waiting while he filled in papers. The captain was annoyed but was too much of a gentleman to speak up. At last I could not bear it any longer.

"We have fifteen men here, new recruits from Oldham County, and if we can ever get them registered, we intend to take them down to Kinston to help replace the losses in the Battle of New Bern."

The little man looks up, irritated, and says, "You'll have to wait your turn. As you can see, I am very busy just now."

"I can see you are busy shuffling those papers about your desk. But you are keeping seventeen men waiting. Is what you are doing more important than gaining fifteen new Confederate soldiers?"

"Young man," the fellow says, "I see you are a sergeant. I am preparing these papers by order of Elmer J. Fincastle, who happens to be a colonel. He is taking the night train to Richmond and he requires these documents for his official business there with the Confederate Government."

"You don't need to identify Colonel Fincastle to me. Captain Ferro and I were in his regiment before and during the Battle of New Bern."

"If I were to stop what I am doing every time someone comes in that door, I would never get any work done. Besides, if you have fifteen men, it would take me past our normal closing hours to list them all. You had better just come back in the morning and then I can give you my full attention."

Captain Ferro took charge. "Enough, James. Very well, sir, at what time in the morning?"

"Nine o'clock."

"And at nine o'clock we will have your full attention?"

"You shall indeed."

"Then I will find us bunks tonight and return in the morning." Then to me, "I must go by the hospital while it is still light and let the doctor examine my stump to see if I am fit to return to duty. Please arrange for accommodations."

I found room in a barracks and they fed us a foul supper of dried beans, the everlasting fatback and corn bread, topped off with molasses. After supper, I took the boys out to see the wonders of the state capital. Meadsboro at that time did not have a single paved street. Here they saw cobblestone streets and sidewalks covered with planks or gravel. They couldn't believe their eyes.

Nor could I mine when I observed Elmer J. Fincastle himself dashing past us in a buggy, apparently headed for the train station. It was getting on toward nine o'clock and time for the boys to be turning in. All I had to do was direct them back to the barracks and then duck down a back way to that little cottage and I'd soon be back in the arms of Elvira. She would be delighted to see me, I was sure.

It was a struggle. I broke into a sweat thinking about it. But then there came to mind an image of Jane Ferro with her long hair bobbing as she rode her little bay and of the quiet, amused way she had of listening to me talk. I thought of her merry laugh, too. And I went back to the barracks with the boys.

At long last we got back to Kinston. There was nobody around the camp except for the company clerk and cook, both of them busy cooking grub.

"Where are the boys?" I ask.

"On the drill field where they have been since seven o'clock this morning."

"Drilling for nine hours straight?"

"Oh, they had half an hour for dinner at noon."

"That's a hell of a long time. How come?"

"Because Colonel Rankin is a son of a bitch." This was from the company clerk, whom I had never known to do any useful labor previously.

"Colonel Rankin?"

The clerk and the cook gave me the news. The 10th had got herself a new commander, not one elected by the men at all but one assigned by the Confederate Government. He was Colonel Mark Rankin, a forty-five-year-old West Pointer and veteran of the Mexican War. In fact, the very man whose house I had called at on my first foraging expedition. He had been second-in-command of a regiment at Manassas and was a professional soldier. He had taken the 10th in hand, a very strong sure hand, it seemed.

"He drills the boys till they are ready to drop and then he takes them out for musket practice until they are ready to drop from that and then he runs them through classes in military discipline."

"What kind of man is he?"

"You'll find out for yourself soon enough. You'll have to watch your step from now on, Mundy."

About an hour later, the boys come in all dusty and dog-tired. Harry sees me and says, "Well, looky there. If it ain't our beloved sergeant back from his leave. Who you got with you?"

"Captain Ferro and I brought back fifteen recruits."

"Hey, boys," Harry shouts. "Fresh meat on the hoof from Oldham County."

The other fellows came up and, recognizing certain of the recruits, started shaking their hands and telling them awful lies about what was expected of them.

Later that night, after a supper that included real meat, Noah Rhine filled me in. I already knew that Fincastle was gone. Major Swan had been transferred to another regiment. Captain Ferro had been named adjutant to take Swan's place.

"I'm sorry to hear that," I says. "They just don't make better officers than him."

"Well, don't feel sorry for him. It's a step up. I hear that he will become a major now."

"Yes, but who is our captain?"

"They moved up Charles Cadieu from first lieutenant to captain and they made Tom Shelton first lieutenant. For a while there it looked like you would become second lieutenant."

"Me?" I exclaimed. "Me a lieutenant. An officer?"

"That's what I said, but Foster Liddle got the job instead."

I remembered Foster Liddle only too well. He had been part of Tom Shelton's crowd at Professor Mead's academy, a pleasant kind of ass-kisser, hardly officer material.

"Foster Liddle and Tom Shelton, now there is a pair of lieutenants for you."

"Yes, don't tell anybody but some of your friends went to Captain Cadieu and told him Jim Mundy was just the man to become second lieutenant of Company H. He didn't say anything but we heard through the grapevine that Captain Ferro had recommended you for the job already."

"I'll be damn. Then why did they give it to Foster Liddle?"

"Tom Shelton put his oars in. Told Cadieu that you were too young and too hotheaded and outspoken. Now I got this from the company clerk, who overheard them talking. Shelton told about you getting drunk in Salisbury. Said you encouraged your men to mock their officers and finally said you had threatened the life of Major Swan during the retreat at New Bern."

"That low-lifed bastard."

"Don't worry. You are lucky. This new colonel is hard on us men but he is twice as hard on the officers. Tom Shelton is having to turn to. You should see him jump when Colonel Rankin speaks."

"Hell. I didn't want to be an officer anyway. Who needs the responsibility? I would rather be a sergeant and carry a sergeant's pass."

That was a lie, however. I thought how grand it would have been to be able to tell Jane Ferro in my very first letter that I had been made an officer, one of the youngest lieutenants in the entire Confederate Army. She would have been impressed and so would her father.

But Tom Shelton had spoiled it for me. The overbearing son of a bitch.

15

There was no doubt about it. The 10th North Carolina was a changed regiment. And it was to change even more during that May and June of 1862. We became real soldiers, commanded by a real colonel.

Oh, yes, everyone professed to hate Colonel Rankin and to wish him in hell with his insistence on good order and promptness and preparation. But we spoke of his harshness with a kind of pride. I have observed this trait in children as well as men all my life. We admire a certain amount of sternness in teachers and parents, anyone in authority. Same goes for employers, I believe. I always ran my printing business with a stern hand.

But getting back to Colonel Rankin, there was a man with fire in his belly and a ramrod down his spine. He was not a tall man, but he carried his slender frame so erectly he gave an impression of height. Had a way of looking you square in the eye when he spoke to you. Had clear gray eyes that penetrated your very brain. Couldn't imagine anyone telling Colonel Mark Rankin a lie; those piercing gray eyes demanded the truth.

That man made soldiers out of the rabble that had fled at New Bern. We learned to move quickly and in concert. No more slouching about like backwoodsmen on a possum hunt. God help you if he caught you with an uncleaned musket or if you misplaced your weapon. We kept our uniforms neater and our equipment better polished. Our camp layout was reorganized so that our tents no longer looked like a gypsy settlement. And the food improved one hundred percent.

Colonel Rankin was a wealthy man, as I had surmised from my visit to his plantation that previous year. I realized in time that there lay a good heart under that immaculate gray officer's uniform. He cared about his men. Mutton and good potatoes began to appear on our menu. I asked the cook about it.

"Why, Colonel Rankin personally oversees our food supply. He buys a lot of it with his own money. And that mutton came off his own plantation."

Something else about that colonel. He could rip you apart when you were slothful, but when you gained his approval, you felt as if God himself smiled down on you. He was not gushy, but a word of praise from his lips was to be cherished like a precious jewel.

He took pains to call me to his tent to say, "Sergeant Mundy. Major Ferro has told me of your fine recruiting efforts back in your home county. That's the spirit."

Damned few such words of praise came from his lips during that May and June of 1862. I don't intend to write a history of the great Civil War, but I should point out that things generally were in a crisis for the Confederacy. First Manassas had made it seem we might be invincible. Only now the coast of North Carolina was in enemy hands from the Virginia border to Morehead City. Out west, Forts Donelson and Henry had fallen and most of Tennessee lay open to invasion from the north, while from the south a Federal fleet had opened up the lower Mississippi, taking the great city of New Orleans. Of course up in the Shenandoah Stonewall Jackson (and there was a general for you) was making idiots out of three Yankee armies, but meanwhile George B. McClellan, with an enormous army of well-trained, well-supplied men, was working his way up the Peninsula toward Richmond as a second great force under General Pope prepared to descend on the capital from the north. The war could well have ended in the summer of 1862, ended with a bang, and in the long run it would have been better for the South to have lost the fight then and had done with it. Surely my life would have been different if McClellan and Pope had captured Richmond and with it the Confederate Army of Joe Johnston. But professional soldiers such as Colonel Rankin would stave off the disaster.

We got our news in those days mostly from newspapers printed in Raleigh. I used to read aloud to those of my boys that were illiterate. Sometimes I would make up tall tales just to josh them, you know, pretend to be reading aloud while making up some farfetched story such as, "Looky here, lads, the Raleigh *Standard* says the Confederate Government has sent out to India to buy a herd of elephants. They are going to bring them back and give us all elephants to ride, just as Hannibal used them against the Romans."

They soon caught on to my funning. When I tried to read to them out of an old issue about the fight that had taken place in Hampton Roads between the ironclad ships *Monitor* and *Merrimac,* the Alexander boy stammered, "N-N-Now, Jim M-M-Mundy, you just pulling our legs again."

"Yeah, Jim," says another. "Ain't no such thing as an iron ship. Iron can't float."

That was nearly two months after the battle, but they hadn't got the news down in Oldham County and they wouldn't believe me until Noah Rhine read the same story to them, word for word. I guess I wouldn't have made a good officer after all, at least not when I was nineteen.

I was back with the regiment for a week before I wrote my first letter to Jane Ferro. I must have composed that letter in my head a hundred times. What would I say to her? I wanted to set the right tone. Wanted to make a good impression. Finally got time off from Colonel Rankin's incessant drills and classes on a Sunday afternoon. Using a pencil stub and ruled paper borrowed from the company clerk, I started scrawling:

Dear Jane,

I take my pen in hand to keep the promise I made to you, namely that I would drop you a line from time to time and tell you about army life. I only hope that you will not find my descriptions tiresome.

Then I went on to tell her about almost becoming a lieutenant, but leaving out the reason why I didn't get the job. Laid it to my age. Told her about the ride back on the train. As I got wound up, I stuck in some humorous accounts of camp life, ending with

You made me promise to stop "Miss Jane-ing" you but I must confess that I have not kept that promise. For I do miss Jane very much and only wish that I could see her again.

Respectfully,
James Mundy

P.S. Tell Nellie hello for me.

Took me all of a Sunday afternoon in April to write that first letter. How I enjoyed it. Later learned that she had enjoyed it, too. Only I had to go through weeks of torment wondering if she really would write back.

So the time passed until, in the middle of one night, the bugles sounded and we got our orders to gather our gear and be prepared for marching within half an hour. We thought it was one of Colonel Rankin's drills until we found ourselves hiking toward the dawn. Old Burnside was acting up down at New Bern and we must teach him some sense.

What had happened was that Burnside had sent out his men to tear up the Atlantic and North Carolina tracks as far as he dared toward Kinston and then proceeded to construct forts north of New Bern to protect his foothold on our coast. There were rumors he intended to advance out of his bastion, and the higher-ups thought to slap him back and maybe retake the city in the bargain.

We marched all day and into the dark, covering twenty-five

miles and arriving at a crossroads, exhausted and footsore. Colonel Rankin ordered us to throw up a breastworks to guard against surprise. After that and a cold supper of hardtack and dried beef we slept "on our arms" in the open. Next morning our skirmishers went forward until they encountered Yankee pickets. We heard the "pop pop pop" of their muskets. The skirmishers came back in, soon followed by a heavy skirmish line of the Yanks. They stopped short when they saw our breastworks and we tossed shells back and forth without much effect on either side.

They were gone the next morning and in probing ahead we found that they had retired into their new fortifications. We stayed in the neighborhood for several days, and a poor neighborhood it was. With the railroad to Kinston torn up, we had to live on the grub we had brought in our knapsacks and wagons. For a while we had the notion we would be reinforced and resupplied so as to press an attack on New Bern or at least bring the town under siege. But, no, in the end they turned us around and marched us back to Kinston. Things were getting hot and heavy up around Richmond. We were to stand ready to join the big war in Virginia.

A letter was waiting for me back in Kinston. I got it in the morning mail call and carried it in my breast pocket all day, waiting for a chance to read it. My fingers trembled when I at last got the chance to steal off to myself.

Dear James,

Your letter of April 20 arrived and I was so glad to receive it. Don't feel badly about failing to be promoted to lieutenant. You are young and father says he is beginning to think the war may drag on at least for another year. Personally I would rather you came back, now, alive and well, than as a lieutenant in the condition of poor William, later.

She told me about life on the plantation, about riding Nellie around the countryside and how her mother was asking about that tall young man from the other end of the county and so on, in a light vein, ending with

I do pray that you will take good care of yourself and that you will write again.

Affectionately,
Just Plain Jane

I wouldn't have taken a hundred dollars for that one word, "affectionately."

16

By today's standards, the railroads of the Civil War were puny and inadequate. Tiny boxcars, ramshackle, uncomfortable passenger cars and weak little locomotives. Some very sorry, poorly built roadbeds and differing track widths so that goods and passengers might have to be moved to continue a journey on another company's line. Still I say, "Thank God for the railroads." I hate to think of the marching we would have done if it hadn't been for them.

The 10th Regiment learned to know and appreciate the railroads for it was to be shifted about constantly between eastern North Carolina and Virginia. The first time came in late May of 1862. Throughout that month we read in the newspapers of how McClellan was working his way up the Peninsula from Fort Monroe toward Richmond. He had a vast, well-equipped army, supported by the Union Navy. Looking back, I can see how, if he had acted with any gumption, he could have taken Richmond. But no, he moved so slowly the South had time to gather its forces to hold that city. And the railroads played a big part in the reinforcement of Richmond.

Stuck down in eastern North Carolina, playing cat and mouse

with Burnside, it seemed that we would remain in a backwater of the war forever. Then with one day's warning, they loaded us onto a special train to Goldsboro, where we shifted to the Wilmington and Weldon up to where she connected with the Petersburg Railroad. That was the lifeline of the Confederacy, the direct rail link between the blockade-runners' port of Wilmington and Richmond. We passed through Petersburg and soon were in sight of the church spires of the great capital city. Then we crossed the James River into a new and different world.

Except for a few of our officers, I doubt that one of us had ever seen a city like Richmond. Church steeples halfway to the sky, paved and cobbled streets galore, lit with gas lamps, great, fine hotels and theaters. A state capitol that made the one in Raleigh seem like a county courthouse. Not to mention factories such as the great Tredegar Iron Works.

I saw more people in Richmond than I knew existed. By that time there were more than 100,000 human beings packed into the city. Politicians, well-off families from Yankee-occupied sections of Virginia, men and women come to work in Confederate bureaus or in various arms and uniform factories, flashy-looking young women with painted faces come to work in different kinds of establishments, and soldiers, thousands and thousands of them. The city teemed with men in gray. Never before or after, in my opinion, was the South as strong as she was in May and June of 1862. The war spirit still ran strong; the ranks were full of eager young men; we were well equipped; we still felt invincible, despite the loss of New Orleans and the occupation of mid-Tennessee.

By that time, McClellan's vast horde was in sight of Richmond's church spires. We could hear the faint sound of cannon fire to the east. Yet there was no panic in the overcrowded city. For one thing, Richmond was ringed with fortifications, outer works and inner works. Not only were there tens of thousands of Confederate soldiers to man those works; the clerks and industrial workers were organized as last-ditch militia if required. And the rail connections to the south and west were secure.

We went into camp on the outskirts of the city. The first night we went out on the town, strolling about marveling at the sights. We went to the Spottswood Hotel and gawked about in the lobby for a bit, staring at the beautiful appointments and the important people; then over to gape at the White House of the Confederacy where Jefferson Davis himself lived, and so on up and down the streets until we came to a dark area of one- and two-story row houses. An evil-looking fellow sidles up to us and asks, "You boys looking for a good time?"

I said, "We're having a good time."

"I mean with the girls. You fellows want a girl?"

Harry McGee says, "I don't know. How much?"

"Five dollars Confederate."

"I got that much. I think I'll have a go at it. How about you, Jim, and you, Noah?"

Noah grinned and said he reckoned not. Harry looked at me. I shook my head. "I'm not interested just now," I said. The Wiley boys were with us and they said they wouldn't mind a bit of fun with the girls. So Harry McGee said to hell with Noah and me and he and the Wiley boys followed that man into an alleyway.

Next morning, they told us what a grand time they had. "They had five girls in there and you could take your pick." I couldn't explain that Jane Ferro was too much on my mind to allow me to consort with whores. I let them think it was because I was a preacher's son that I was so squeamish.

That same day, we learned that our regiment was to be temporarily attached to the division of General Huger. We came to be glad it was temporary. The general was a nice old gentleman, easygoing and pleasant, but he moved slowly and appeared almost feeble.

After we became part of Huger's division, Jefferson Davis himself came out in a carriage to inspect us. Now there was an impressive-looking man, tall and well set up. I'm sorry to say that he didn't inspire much warmth, however. Had a prissy quality about him. At that time we regarded him as worth ten Abraham Lincolns, but I can now see that the reverse was true. Lincoln had the heart of the people in the North, or at least gained it by his easy, down-to-earth ways. Jefferson Davis had the respect of Southerners at first, but he lost it by his aloofness. The South would have done better to have elected Zebulon Vance as president. There was a man of the people. The best governor North Carolina ever had. He was colonel of the 26th North Carolina, one of our sister regiments, until his election to the governorship in the fall of '62. Earthy, outgoing, man with lots of gumption, just the opposite of cool, inward-looking, cautious Jefferson Davis.

Anyway, Davis came out to look us over and with him there rode a gray-bearded man in the uniform of a brigadier. Struck me that he was one of the handsomest men I had ever seen. Around fifty with a self-assured manner.

"Who is that with the President?" I asked Captain Cadieu.

"That is R. E. Lee, the President's military adviser and head of the forces of the Commonwealth of Virginia. Now keep quiet, Mundy. A sergeant should know better than to talk in the ranks on parade."

So Davis and this Lee fellow looked us over and seemed to think that we Tar Heels were good enough to help defend Richmond. At any rate the next day we were made ready to join the fray.

The Battle of Seven Pines or Fair Oaks was fought on May 31 and June 1 of 1862. That's where the Confederate Army under Joe Johnston tackled part of McClellan's south of the Chickahominy. I wish I could report that our regiment played much of a part in that battle. It seemed we were going to for they marched us through Richmond and out the Charles City road. There we stopped and fell out to await our fighting orders.

Soon we could hear the battle booming away, not three miles from us. We could tell that whatever was going on would have made New Bern look like a skirmish. The cannon fire made a bass rumble, with the higher, sharper pitch of musket fire providing the tenor melody. We had time to wander off into the bushes to pick the partly ripe blackberries. It was a good way to pass the time and, for me, to get away from Harry McGee's constant retelling of his exploits at the whorehouse. You'd think nobody ever had a piece of tail before.

The sound of fighting trailed off that night and we slept under the stars alongside the road. The battle started up again the next morning and, after breakfast, General Huger comes up in his leisurely way and orders his colonels to prepare to move toward the sound of the guns.

"Here we go again," I says to my boys. "Here is our chance to pay the Yanks back for New Bern."

But it was not to be. After moving forward for half a mile, we stopped again. That is when the wounded started flowing back. Surely that is one of the most pitiful sights in the world. First the men with arm and shoulder wounds, or maybe a superficial head wound, say from a spent shell fragment, all able to walk. A bit later the ambulances started coming along our road, laden with stacks of men, all of them groaning and crying with pain, the ambulances trailing a dribble of blood.

The Battle of Seven Pines took place along a three-mile front between the Chickahominy River and Richmond, so it was the handiest thing to haul the seriously wounded back to the city for hospitalization and further surgery. Our regiment, which had left its wounded behind at New Bern, had never seen anything like this. Too bad that Kaiser Wilhelm and his Prussians weren't present at Seven Pines and many of the later battles of our Civil War. They might have thought twice about bringing on the present slaughter in France.

One of the men wounded at Seven Pines was General Joseph E. Johnston, who commanded the Confederate Army. Johnston had a checkered career in the war. That was the nearest I ever came to serving under him for they had to take him off the field of battle and replace him with R. E. Lee.

General Huger formed our regiment up into a hollow square

and after a bit here came a long line of Yankee prisoners to be marched into our midst. Our other regiments picked up and moved again toward the battle, but the 10th had to stay there and guard prisoners, something the militia would have been given to do if there had been a militia. We took our feelings out on the miserable-looking Federals put in our loving and tender care.

"Hey, hey, bluebellies. Hey, look at the Yankees," says Harry McGee.

"Hey, damn Yankees, what do you think of Lincoln now? Still glad you voted for that nigger lover?"

"Come to free the slaves, or find yourself a black wife?"

That particular group didn't see any humor at all in the catcalls. They had been through hell and were a dejected bunch of men, their faces black from gunpowder smoke and drawn with fatigue. Some had light wounds as well. I think they expected we were going to execute them, the way we had them penned up, with muskets and bayonets held in a threatening manner.

Before long, we found ourselves headed back toward Richmond, herding our prisoners along like cattle. Some of our crew still jeered at our poor charges as we entered the city.

"You Yankee bastards came to take Richmond. There she is."

17

We remained on guard duty for most of the month of June on Belle Isle in the James River. At that time during the war, it was pleasant enough, for us guards, that is. Don't think there is such a thing as a pleasant prison camp, not for the prisoners.

We kept the Yankees penned up like chickens in a barnyard. We stood guard duty with loaded muskets, two guards to the tower, and we had strict orders to shoot at anyone who tried to escape. Funny thing. I felt like I was back on the farm, looking down on a barnyard full of dirty blue chickens, nothing to distinguish one Yank from the other. They slept in crowded tents. They lined up twice a day for food that was shockingly bad. I know because us guards were eating the same thing. And they took care of their necessaries out in the open in a latrine that stretched for fifty yards. Latrine, hell. It was an open ditch with a log rail for squatting.

After a few days, the prisoners became more human, more individuals that is. I learned to know the bald-headed fellow with the beard, the tall man with the frizzly red hair, the Irishman with the red cheeks and the young German with round shoulders. I discovered that just as we looked on the Yankees with scorn and hatred, they regarded us with contempt. After a couple of days, they recovered their spirits enough to respond to our insults in kind.

"Hey, Yankee, how does it feel to be in the Confederate States of America?"

"I ain't in the Confederate States of America, you ignorant Rebel. This is still part of the United States."

Or, in response to some gibe about freeing the slaves: "We've come to free you, Reb, for the slaveowners have you in their power."

"Yeah, yeah. The abolitionists have you in theirs. They're the ones that started this war."

"Abolitionists didn't fire on Fort Sumter. You Rebs started this war."

"Yes, and we're going to finish it, too."

"Aw, go home and learn to read and write."

The exchanges between the guards and the guarded were not always so hostile.

"Hey, Reb, I'm dying for some tobacco. Got any on you?"

"Maybe I have and maybe I haven't"

"I'd give a dollar for a pouch of pipe tobacco. How about it?"

"Let's see your dollar."

Or, "Hey, Johnny, this food ain't fit to eat. I can't stand corn mush."

"Same thing us guards are eating."

"Yes, but you get to go into the city. Can't you buy some fruit, or cake, or anything for me?"

"If I had some money, maybe."

"How about a watch? I'll trade you my watch."

A pretty brisk trade developed in that way between the guards and the prisoners. Tobacco, food and whisky flowed into the prison pen, while U.S. money, pocket knives and watches flowed out. Our officers forbade us to trade with the prisoners, but they couldn't enforce the rule.

Harry McGee traded a pint of corn liquor to a Dutchman for five dollars and went off to his whorehouse again, taking several other boys with him. I had just got another letter from Jane Ferro and couldn't wait for him to go so I could read it undistrubed and write a reply. In her letter Jane told me that Reba, the big part-Indian woman, had warned her about writing to a soldier without first getting her father's permission. "But I told her that one did not need permission to write to a Confederate hero." Too, she had read reports that a big battle was brewing below Richmond and wondered if I had been in any more fighting.

I wrote back about the thrill of seeing Richmond, leaving out descriptions of the saloons and houses of ill repute that had sprung up. Also told her about being on the fringes of the Battle of Fair Oaks. Made it sound as if the 10th had been given a very special assignment in escorting prisoners to Belle Isle. Women like to be impressed by men, especially men in whom they have a special interest. Gives them a sense of shared pride.

Talk about sharing, Harry McGee discovered that his Richmond whore had shared something with him. We were standing side by side at our latrine one morning, I taking a leak and he just standing there.

"What's the matter, Harry?" I ask. "You don't look very happy."

He made a face. "It burns so when I try to piss."

"Why don't you see the surgeon?"

He did and found that he had a raging case of clap. What's more, both the Wiley boys had it as well. Finally the surgeon had the entire regiment line up company by company. Don't know about the others, but he discovered a dozen doses of clap right in our company. These men were marched off to a hospital for treatment, something to do with reaming out their dicks and dosing them with a mercury compound. And they had to sleep in separate tents while they underwent the treatment. I will not repeat the taunts we inflicted on our erring brothers.

I was never so glad of anything as of my decision not to follow Harry McGee down that alley with that pimp. Whatever would I have told Jane Ferro? What would her brother have told her, for he surely would have known? Truly, virtue is its own reward. Ah, to be nineteen again and in love. And not to have the clap.

18

I have read postwar accounts of how worried some Confederate officials were during that period in which McClellan stood in his tracks outside Richmond, hauling up supplies and siege cannon along the railroad from Yorktown. My impression was, however, that morale ran high in the city. The papers were full of the exploits of Stonewall Jackson out in the Shenandoah Valley. He was the hero of the moment. There wasn't so much admiration for Robert E. Lee, the newly appointed general of the forces around Richmond. There was much grumbling about all the spadework Lee had the men doing, strengthening and extending the earthworks around the city. We didn't realize it then, but there was a man! Lee could be seen riding that big gray, Traveler, in and out of Richmond, on his way to and from conferences with Jefferson Davis. He had a commanding presence. Had that extra strength that comes from perfect self-control. Of course, he had courage and intelligence as well.

Had Lee been in McClellan's place, he would have pounced on Richmond while he had the initiative. Instead, "Little Mac" edged up toward the city, extending his right north of the Chickahominy, reaching out to connect up with a Federal corps under McDowell due to advance south from Fredericksburg, taking his own sweet time.

His own sweet time enabled Jackson to finish his work in the Shenandoah and arrive in Richmond. Lee began his countermoves. The rest is history. After the war, U. S. Grant was called a "butcher" because of the way he spent the lives of his men in the great battles of 1864. Actually, you could just as well call Lee by the same name for he was bold in battle, sending his men forward without hesitation to die when he saw some military advantage to be gained.

The story of how he slammed away at McClellan during the Seven Days' Battles is too well known for me to bother relating it here in detail. With Jackson on the scene, he commanded the largest single army we Confederates ever fielded. He sought first to destroy that part of McClellan's army that was isolated north of the Chickahominy. Oak Grove on June 25, Mechanicsville on the twenty sixth, Gaines's Mills and Garnett's Farm on the twenty-seventh and twenty-eighth. The cannon roared and the men fell. Because of Jackson's slowness and other factors, Lee failed to destroy McClellan, but he did cause him to abandon his base on the York River and switch it to Harrison's Landing, seventeen miles downstream on the James River.

Make no mistake about it: the Federals fought back stubbornly, inflicting more casualties than they suffered, although they did leave behind many prisoners and most of the supplies and heavy artillery they had so laboriously hauled up the Peninsula. Lee was like Jim Jeffries trying to knock out a heavier opponent but never quite landing his biggest punches. He drove his man across the ring, however, and into a corner. The corner was Malvern Hill, fourteen miles below Richmond on the James.

While the guns rumbled away at Oak Grove and Mechanicsville, we continued to guard our prisoners at Belle Isle. Then, on June 27, two things happened: a new batch of prisoners came into the compound and a regiment of untrained Georgia conscripts arrived by rail. Lee needed us to help finish off McClellan. The new prisoners were being relieved of their money and valuables by the old ones as we turned over the guard towers to the Georgians. We marched through the crowded streets of Richmond, around the noisy wagons and their shouting Negro drivers, past the refugee-packed hotels and the busy saloons.

I'll never forget those next few days. I didn't know what war was. Prisoners trudged past us in droves, so many that it was no longer fun to insult them. They went past in an endless line, crying out to us for water or tobacco. At times both our regiment and the prisoners had to give way to ambulances, scores of them bearing delirious men along the rutted road toward the hospitals and churches of Richmond. Many of the wounded had undergone amputation of legs and arms at field hospitals. Now the chloroform had worn off and there was no one to offer them morphine or even brandy. The lucky ones were unconscious.

We came to Savage's Station, where just the day before a terrible battle had been fought. I had seen a few freshly killed men at New Bern, of course, but nothing like this. Confederates and Yankees lay in windrows, already swollen and stinking. The smell simply overcame you. There was no way to escape it. The odor penetrated a handkerchief or hat held over your face. If you tried holding your breath, that dreadful stench of rotting flesh was waiting, twice as bad, when finally you had to breathe again.

And wouldn't you know who got halted there for burial detail. They handed out shovels and showed us where to dig a wide, shallow ditch. While one squad labored in the sandy loam, another followed wagons out to pick up the bodies. Every man in my squad threw up at least once. I stood it as long as I could, until we came across the horrible remains of a South Carolinian who had been cut almost in two by a cannon ball. Nearly fainted I vomited so hard at the sight.

That was what we were doing on June 30, burying the dead while the Battle of Glendale or Frayser's Farm raged just six miles away, south of the intervening White Oak Swamp. We worked away in a heavy rain, gathering in the bodies, identifying them as best we could, laying them in that shallow ditch, covering them up, and then penciling names on pieces of plank set up as headstones.

We were glad when that day came to a close and we learned that we were to leave the Yankees to bury their dead and rejoin Huger's division. I am ashamed to say that some of our boys did not entirely neglect the Yankee dead. They sneaked about, stripping the dead of both armies of money and valuables. Yes sir, there are men still living in Oldham County who played the ghoul then and later, too, which just goes to show how war debases human beings.

All along our march across the Peninsula we passed abandoned U.S. Army knapsacks, muskets, blue overcoats, piles of tents, ambulances and stacks of canned food. Most of the paraphernalia McClellan had hauled up the Peninsula for four weeks his men abandoned in four days. Talk about the waste of war! I hate to think about my tax money going for equipment to be left to rust and rot over in France today. But it is happening now as it did then.

All this valuable loot was too much for many of us to resist. At last Captain Cadieu halted us and read the riot act. "I personally will shoot the next man in this company who leaves the line of march to steal gear left by the road. Everything you see properly belongs to the Confederate Government. You can't possibly carry anything more and you are delaying our progress."

Cadieu generally was a patient, mild-mannered fellow, but we could tell he meant business. So we marched past temptation thereafter. Besides, we had all we could carry in the way of extra blankets, overcoats and rain shelters, not to mention canned meat.

The sound of battle had stopped by nightfall of the thirtieth. We ate a good supper of canned meat and dried vegetables, courtesy of the U.S. Government. We enjoyed a good night's sleep atop our captured Yankee blankets.

We made quite a picture the next day when we finally caught up with old Huger's division south of Glendale around noon. By that time most of us had discarded the silly little kepis, those ridiculous caps with tiny stiff visors. We had replaced them with soft gray slouch hats whose brims were broad enough to shade a man's face in the sun and keep the water off the back of his neck in the rain.

At that time I had never heard of Malvern Hill, the stretch of high ground lying along the James River opposite Turkey Bend. That was the corner into which R. E. Lee had driven George B. McClellan.

19

We moved with part of Huger's division at what seemed to me a snail's pace southeast along the Quaker Road, getting ourselves entangled with jams of other units. We marched with a feeling of expectation. There was a smell of some great event about to take place. We were moving in for the kill. Lee had shoved McClellan away from the gates of Richmond and forced him to sullen retreat back toward the protection of his naval guns at Harrison's Landing on the James. The Confederate Army had picked up enough tents and small arms and overcoats and blankets to re-equip itself entirely. More important, it had saved Richmond and now sought to destroy McClellan.

To read some accounts of Malvern Hill you would think it was a small mountain. Viewed from a distance, as we saw it that July 1 of 1862, it was merely a stretch of high ground sloping northward from the James River, gradually losing itself in the flat terrain of the Peninsula. Cultivated fields and a few houses along the crest, patches of woods and some overgrown ravines on the lower slopes, and along the west, a small creek called Turkey Run, emptying into the James. That was Malvern Hill.

Noah Rhine had the eyesight of a hawk. I think he could read a book a half-mile away.

"Jim," he said as we halted on the Quaker Road to let a battery of our artillery rattle past, "I never seen so many cannon in my life."

"Hell, Noah, it's just our usual artillery."

"I mean way out over there along that slope. The Yankees have that hill covered with cannon. Can't you see?"

I could in fact make out clumps of guns lined up in tiers, with limbers and caissons neatly arranged behind them. Waiting. Colonel Rankin rides up to see what was the delay and he noticed us all craning our necks to stare at the hill in the distance. By this time we were all buzzing at the sight. Captain Cadieu and Tom Shelton were trading a set of field glasses back and forth.

"The Federals have scores of guns on that hill, Colonel," Cadieu says. "More artillery than I knew existed."

The colonel takes out his field glasses and studies that hill for several minutes. "Yes. They're not in retreat any longer. And I see considerable infantry on the slopes around the guns. Looks as if they mean to fight again."

With that he orders us to fall out and feed ourselves.

Harry McGee and Dave Lewis were as excited as terrier pups as we ate our captured rations.

"At last we are going to have a real battle," says Dave. "This will be better than Manassas."

"I just want to pay them back for New Bern," Harry said.

At this point, Huger had allowed his division to be separated into two sections. Our regiment and others were all mixed up with a horde of Jackson's men for a while and then our artillery.

The result was that we sat beside the road for hours, well out of the action, giving the right of way to our artillery.

At that point I wouldn't have paid two cents for the artillery of either army. At New Bern, for all the noise they made, the damage done by the cannon was trifling. It was the infantry with their rifled muskets that gave and took the punishment. That was my opinion at noon on July 1 as our cannon came hustling past amidst a great rattle of wheels and harness with the artillerymen in a fine sweat, hurling curses at their straining horses and each other and generally acting as if the war depended on them.

After 1 P.M. the Federal gunners began to show their hands. I know now from having read various accounts that they had about 250 field pieces on Malvern Hill, backed up by naval guns aboard boats in the James behind the hill. But as the artillery duel progressed I would have sworn the Yankees had a thousand cannon. They concentrated their fire on our poor artillery. One of our batteries would come racing up, get in position, haul their limbers back a ways, tether the horses and open up at the hill. About the time they got off their third shot, the Federals would start their counterfire and you could see the shells arc up and sail right down in among our guns. It was hell on our poor artillerymen. They couldn't get started. First off, the Yanks were all ready, sitting on high ground with a grand view. They had far more guns than we to begin with and ours were being hastened into the action piecemeal. Finally, I might as well say it, generally throughout the war the Federal artillery outshone the Confederate. Man for man, give me Southern infantry or cavalry. But those Yankee gunners were something else. Malvern Hill was their show.

Of course all this bombarding back and forth made a grand fireworks display for us North Carolina hicks lying alongside the road watching the fun. It was a most exciting sight, the flashes from the guns on the slope amid the growing cloud of smoke and the "whoosh-whoom" of hundreds of shells raining upon our batteries. What did any of this have to do with us infantry? It was a private dispute between artillerymen.

By later afternoon, our gunners had simply quit trying to respond. It was hopeless. Infantry would have to do the job.

"Off your asses and on your feet," someone shouted. We scrambled up and got in marching ranks.

Now the front stretched for a mile along the approach up the northern face of Malvern Hill, that part of the hill lying between two creeks. From the Yankee skirmish line near the base of the hill to the crest measured nearly a mile and a half, and that elevated terrain seemed designed by the Almighty as an artillery platform.

While we maneuvered our way across a creek and over fields, D. H. Hill sent forward one of his brigades. Up the lower slopes it went, its regimental colors flapping. We could hear the crackle of their muskets and see a line of smoke as they ran into where the Yankee skirmish line waited, a line manned, we later learned, by Berdan's sharpshooters carrying repeating rifles. Hill's men had to fall back.

By now it was well past 5 P.M., but the attacks were just beginning. To Hill's right, one of Huger's brigades, commanded by Armistead, went into action, soon followed by another of our sister brigades, Wright's. Soon a storm of noise could be heard, followed by fresh clouds of smoke. The Federal artillery had fallen silent while the Yankees swabbed out their guns and changed their loads from exploding shell and round shot to infantry-killing canister.

Now Berdan and his deadly sharpshooters were finally flushed out of a wheatfield. The Yankee artillery began thundering again. As Wright and Armistead faltered, Magruder began to feed brigades into the fray, all this in piecemeal fashion. We could see our boys follow their regimental flags up in grand style, rank upon rank, halting to fire off a volley and then move forward again with that piercing Rebel yell. Up they pressed until the Yankee artillery spoke. They would stop, fire and move forward again toward the lines of flashing guns.

All told, the Confederates fed fourteen brigades into the slaughter. If they had all gone forward in a grand rush, maybe, just maybe, they might have succeeded. But sending forward one or two brigades at a time, that was playing right into the Federal hands.

As our lines pressed forward, we could see the gray forms they left behind lying on the hill. Yet again the guns lashed out and Magruder's men began drifting back down the slope, turning now and then for a parting shot at the relentless cannon.

William Ferro, now that he was a major and the regimental adjutant, rated a horse. He came riding by to speak to me, as he always did when we met. "We're catching it from those confounded guns, James," he says.

"Yes. I thought sure we were going to drive them off."

"It'll take more than one or two divisions to do that. They're using canister and the closer you get, the deadlier it is."

The major spoke the truth. You could dig in and ignore shells unless one landed on top of you. Canister was different. Basically this was a cylinder filled with lead balls, fired from a cannon at attacking infantry. The can disintegrated on leaving the muzzle, spraying those balls across the landscape. The effect was like firing an enormous load of buckshot. The closer you got to the cannon, the worse the effect.

So Lee sent his brigades up the slope, and although they cleared the lower reaches of Malvern Hill and occasionally got in among the forward artillery crews, they could not stand up to that massed artillery fire. In the end they straggled back, driven into a frustrated rage.

Our turn came near dusk. They maneuvered us into long ranks, regiment by regiment, close packed, almost shoulder to shoulder, told us to load our muskets, fix our bayonets and advance. We went forward at a walk, over bushes already tramped down by our artillery and by the feet of the men who had gone before. No joking now. Just the voices of our officers shouting to keep our ranks dressed.

We'd show them how to silence those damned guns, I remember thinking. Let us Oldham County boys do the job. Another brigade moved to our right, another to our left, and still another a hundred yards in front of us, all advancing to strike the Federals from their left. The fading sun fell on our backs, illuminating the crest of the hill where the dreadful artillery flashed, boomed and spewed out smoke.

For a brief while as we crossed a thicket, some very heavy shells began falling in the area, making a noise like an approaching freight train and then bursting with greater force than we could believe.

"Gunboats are throwing shells over the hill blind," Captain Cadieu yells. "Move faster and we'll get past their target area."

Soon those enormous shells were bursting well behind us as we advanced up the lower reaches of the hill. At that point a heavy line of blue skirmishers opened on us. The brigade ahead halted and dispersed them with a single volley. As we passed up the slope, we stepped over the bodies of men who had fallen to the fire of the Yankee skirmishers. Ahead of us, the leading brigade fired again and were answered by a blast of musket fire that sent Minié balls whirring about our heads.

"Close up on the troops ahead. Come on, get moving," Cadieu shouted.

We broke into a trot and just as we caught up with the other brigade a line of Federal guns lashed out, spraying our area with those dreadful canister balls. The leading brigade halted, gaps appearing in their ranks. We raced up to fill those gaps, most of us in time to level our muskets and fire off a volley at the offending artillery a bare 250 yards ahead.

I looked right into the muzzles when they spoke again. The sound rocked us as the air became alive with lead canister balls. They sang around our heads, they kicked up earth in front of us, some bouncing up to strike about our legs. And they ripped into the flesh of our men.

"Charge!" the cry rang out. We burst into the Rebel yell and raced forward. The guns flashed again, this time tearing holes up and down our line. It was maddening. I remember being infuriated, lusting to get among those artillerymen and smash their skulls.

Those damned Yanks kept serving their guns until we were on top of them. I angled off to one side to dodge away from their last blast, but even so the force almost knocked me down. With Harry McGee at my side, I flung myself on a middle-aged artilleryman who still had his back turned having just pulled the lanyard of his Napoleon. I rammed the butt of my musket into his back, knocking him against the cannon wheel and then fell to beating him over the head and shoulders. Another gunner came running up with his rammer over his head to bash me. Harry McGee stabbed him in the chest with his bayonet.

Now our infantry was all over that first line of guns, jabbing and clubbing. We should have pressed right ahead, but instead we stopped to herd our prisoners down the hill and to try to turn that battery around to face their late owners. Thus we wasted precious minutes and our advance lost its momentum. Next thing we knew the guns farther up the slope opened up on us, their canister balls ricocheting off their captured guns. Then a line of blue infantry, with bayonets fixed, gave us a volley and moved toward us. It was hopeless. We had spent our force.

We turned around and trotted back down the hill. I started to follow but saw the artilleryman I had beaten sit up and put his hand to his head which was streaming blood. I dashed over and put my musket muzzle against his forehead.

"On your feet or I'll blow out your brains."

He staggered up and with my gun at his back we walked back down that hill, over and around the bodies of our comrades who had fallen for the sake of a brief and futile triumph. There lay the Alexander boy who stuttered, on his back, his eyes wide open. And there lay brave Dave Lewis and Richard Noel. Three men out of my squad alone.

"Hey, look at Jim Mundy," Noah Rhine said. "He brought his own personal prisoner back."

They rallied us at the bottom of the hill, gave us time to rinse out our mouths and reload and then ordered us forward again. I looked at my prisoner, who sat on the ground, holding his head between his hands. "Over there, Yank," I says, pointing to where a dozen or more prisoners were collected. "Over there quick or I'll make you go up that hill with me."

The terror was gone. I was not afraid anymore. I simply yearned to get among those gunners again and kill them.

Up we moved, once more, grim and desperate men. I pulled my slouch hat down over my forehead so I could not see the guns, just followed the shouted orders of our officers.

"Charge!"

I screamed the Rebel yell and broke into a dog trot. The cannon roared. Suddenly I didn't have a hat. A ball had carried it away and I found myself staring at the line of guns, the same ones we had taken, now manned by fresh crews.

"Fire!"

I leveled my musket and squeezed the trigger. At the very instant I fired, that infernal line of guns flashed again and men fell all around me.

"Fall back, fall back! It's no use."

So back down the slope we straggled, past fresh corpses and newly torn bodies, back through the woods and among our own crestfallen artillerymen.

It was a blessing that Lee waited so late in the day to try to knock out McClellan. The Yankee artillerymen had that much less time to slaughter us. Our brigade of five regiments left over six hundred men lying on Malvern Hill that afternoon. Those dreadful Union guns made a widow out of many an Oldham County woman and many an orphan as well. Throughout the long night we could hear the pitiful cries of our wounded begging for water and sobbing for their mothers.

In our camp, we got a lecture from "Preacher Sam" Elkins, a skinny fellow with a big Adam's apple, the one who was the religious fanatic. "Tell you why we lost," he says to Harry McGee. "It's God's judgment on us because you and the Wiley boys and others have forsaken your Christian upbringing. You went into a house of prostitution and God is punishing us all for your sins."

He went on like that until Harry McGee was ready to strangle him. So like a good sergeant, intent on keeping peace and goodwill among his men, I says to Elkins, "Oh, shut your mouth. God has punished Harry enough with the clap. No more of your preaching or I'll volunteer you for picket duty tonight. You can preach to the Yankee pickets. I expect you will find some sinners among them as well."

"Fine talk for the son of a minister of the gospel," he mutters.

"One more word from you and I'll run a red-hot bayonet up your self-righteous ass. We've suffered enough today without listening to you."

Blessed are the peacemakers. We fell into a restless sleep, expecting to resume the battle in the morning. But as the dawn of the new day fell upon Malvern Hill, we looked in vain for the glint of light from cannon barrels and bayonets. The Yankees were gone. They had slipped away during the night, down to Harrison's Landing to the protection of their gunboats. We were left to treat our wounded and bury our dead.

20

I have made myself sound awful tough and hardhearted in those days, but the truth is that I had my dreams and soft spots just like any other youth. Perhaps more than the ordinary nineteen-year-old for I was most ambitious. If my parents had been better off and there had been no war, I could have gone to the University like Tom Shelton. Might have come out to practice law or go into cotton factoring or maybe got into railroad building, or God knows what. Anything but farming or preaching. Or I might have won a place at West Point and gone off to the cold North to become an army officer. Southerners were successful in the old army. But, no, the war was on. I was in it. And I couldn't even become a junior officer, thanks to Tom Shelton and his clique. So I lived in my dreams.

While on guard duty or on the march, I used to let my mind drift to what might be. In my fantasy, our regiment under this new General Lee, having chased McClellan away from Richmond—albeit at a high price—would march upon Washington, crush the intervening army of Pope, seize the Federal capital and dictate peace terms to the Yankees.

There would be a final grand battle in which I would play the hero. General Lee himself would witness my deed of valor and make me a brevet captain on the spot. The U.S. Government would recognize the Southern states as a separate nation. I would return to Oldham County as a war hero and Jane Ferro would be waiting. Her father would overlook the gap between our family stations and would welcome me as a son-in-law of great promise.

Ma and Pa and Wesley would not embarrass me at the huge wedding on the lawn at Beaulieu. In fact, Pa would assist the Presbyterian minister with the ceremony.

We would buy five hundred acres and Mr. Ferro would give us a half-dozen slaves as a wedding gift. We would be kind but firm with our blacks. I would not be cruel, but neither would I put up with laziness. We would have a small house at first, Jane and I, but would plan it so it could be added to as our prosperity increased.

Our plantation would flourish under the hand of a good overseer and I would go into some other field, perhaps politics. After all, I did have the gift of gab. Had lots of push and brass. Maybe I'd be governor of North Carolina someday, or anyway a U.S. Senator, excuse me, a C.S. Senator.

Jane and I would have five children—two boys and two girls plus a late child who could be of either sex. It would be a happy life for James and Jane Mundy, free of strife or strain and full of honor and respect and all good things.

I was, indeed, ambitious.

As I said, I had my dreams and my soft spots, too. The day after Malvern Hill, I wandered over to the prison pen to inquire after the health of the Yankee artilleryman whose head I had cracked the day before. Found him lying on his back, his eyes closed and blood caked all over his head. I stirred him with my foot. He groaned and opened his eyes.

"What do you want?"

"I'm the one that captured you yesterday."

"Go to hell."

"You're in a poor position to tell anybody to go to hell. You look like you've already been there."

"Leave me alone. Mind your own business."

"Come on, Yank," I says. "Don't be rude. Just wanted to see how you are."

"You should be able to see that I am in a bad way, thanks to you. You tried to kill me."

"You and those Goddamned cannon killed enough of my friends."

"Wish I had killed you, too. Now they are going to haul me off to prison and I will never see my family again."

"Cheer up. Here, I'll give you some fresh water. Maybe you'd like a nip of liquor as well."

With that, my Yank sat up so I could get a better look at him. He was one of your heavy-set fellows with sandy hair going a bit bald on the top. In his thirties. He drank most of my water and then poured the rest on his head.

"Where's the liquor?"

I passed him a small flask and he drained it like liquor was going out of style.

"Where you from?" I ask.

"Pennsylvania, a town called Carlisle. Where are you from?"

"North Carolina. A town called Meadsboro."

"I'm sorry about yesterday. But you Rebels were stupid to come up against our guns. It was like shooting fish in a barrel."

"Except one of the fish cracked your head and took you prisoner."

He made a face. "Don't rub it in. What's your name, Reb?"

"Jim Mundy. Sergeant Jim Mundy of the 10th North Carolina."

He held out his hand. "I'm Jake Detweiler, 1st Pennsylvania Artillery. Got any tobacco?"

"Don't use it, but I'll get you some."

To make a long story short, we had a very pleasant conversation. He scribbled off his parents' name and address and asked me to drop them a line to tell them he was alive, although not very well and they were not to worry.

Even though I knew there was no way to get a letter into Pennsylvania, I promised I would write to them.

"You sure you can write?" he asks.

"Of course I can write. Don't insult me. You want your head cracked again?" I said this with a grin and he laughed in return.

"Sorry, Reb. No offense meant."

"All right, Mundy, you aren't supposed to be fraternizing with the enemy!" It was Tom Shelton, using that scornful tone of voice I had learned to hate. "Get back to your squad."

"Your officers are bastards, too, I see," says Detweiler.

"Especially that one," I reply, holding out my hand for a final shake.

I went back to my squad and a bit later I saw my prisoner limping off toward Richmond, with his comrades, under guard. Found myself wishing I had left him lying beside his cannon, for I knew that he was being marched off to hell.

Our company became a special brotherhood after Malvern Hill. We had been through the fire together and that had bonded us as one. I still felt a grudge against Tom Shelton. Captain Cadieu would never be as fine an officer as William Ferro. "Preacher Sam" Elkins was an irritating prig and big Brady Alexander remained a stupid oaf, but we all had proven our manhood on the bloody slopes of Malvern Hill.

Our company strength had fallen to only eighty-five men. It and the other nine companies of the 10th Regiment worked as parts of a machine under the fine handling of Colonel Rankin. I can't explain the process by which we had been turned into veteran soldiers, but there it was. Maybe it was largely mental. We had lost our fear and had gained respect for ourselves. Praise was heaped upon our regiment for its part in overrunning that line of guns.

No praise was heaped upon General Huger, poor old man. He was already under a cloud for his failure to hold Roanoke Island against Burnside back in February. All during the Seven Days' Battles, he had mishandled his division, either arriving too late at the battle front or getting in the way of other divisions. They turned him out to pasture after Malvern Hill, giving him some sort of inspectorship.

Despite our bloody repulse at Malvern Hill, the Confederate Army felt good about itself after the Seven Days. McClellan had been outgeneraled. Richmond was secure. No longer did anyone call Robert E. Lee "Old Spades." Neither did anybody add up the cost in killed and wounded, not just then, at least not for publication. It came to over twenty thousand. But once the dead were under their two feet of dirt and the wounded hauled off and out of sight, we—the unscathed—put them out of mind. We could not hear the sounds of mourning back in Oldham or hundreds of other counties across the South as the casualty notices were sent home. We were eager to fight again.

21

The next six weeks dragged by. The 10th Regiment drew a variety of duties. We buried more dead. We went about gathering up equipment strewn over the countryside below Richmond by the Yankees. We scouted down the Peninsula as near as we dared to Harrison's Landing, which remained a Federal strongpoint, impossible to take without a huge navy. And we did a lot of plain old nigger work with spade and pick to improve Richmond's fortifications.

To help pass the time, I began keeping a diary during that period. Still have it, but in rereading it I am embarrassed at the entries. Not by what I wrote but by what I failed to record. For instance:

JULY 10 '62—Guard duty all morning. Afternoon my squad loaded captured tents on wagons for transport to Richmond. Evening, wrote letter to J.F. How I dream of her.

JULY 11 '62—Awoke with loose bowels. Too much rich food left by Yankees. Mosquitoes bad. Letter from Pa saying how he is visiting families of men killed in battle.

JULY 14 '62—Rumor that regiment to be moved to Richmond again. Weather hot. Why does Tom Shelton always put me down for sergeant of the guard?

Even though the entries don't tell very much, I do find them useful in jogging my memory as I write these memoirs. Seemed to be writing most about the weather, guard duty, letters to and from home, and the state of my bowels.

We got to see a lot of Richmond in those days and what a city it was. Full of self-confidence again now that McClellan's tide had ebbed. The hospitals were overflowing with Lee's wounded. The big prison in Libby's warehouse was jammed and so was the compound on Belle Isle. The streets had become a madhouse as both private and C.S. wagons and carts dashed back and forth with their Negro teamsters bawling at each other and their mules. Every street corner now seemed to have either a saloon or café and at night drunken Confederate soldiers would congregate in and around these dens. The Tredegar Iron Works now employed hundreds of men for casting cannon barrels and forging iron plate. Several factories employing both men and women had sprung up to turn out paper cartridges, shoes and uniforms or blankets. The gayer blades in our company discovered that they didn't have to buy a piece of pussy unless they were in a hurry; some of the females who drifted in from the country to work in factories or C.S. bureaus were girls of a generous nature; like the shoemaker's daughter, willing to give their "awl" for the boys in gray.

I took a lot of funning because I wouldn't go along with the boys on their tomcatting expeditions. They knew it had something to do with the letters I got every week or so. I was grateful that few of them could read and therefore did not know that I was corresponding with the daughter of one of the richest men in Oldham County. Noah Rhine knew, but he was too much of a gentleman to guy me about it. Good old Noah.

I'd be a rich man if I were to be paid in gold for all the hard work I did in those days digging pits and packing the earth up into ramparts. Our regiment seemed to get all the dirty jobs. But the exercise was good for us and it did give us the opportunity to see Richmond and send and receive letters.

Noah and I spent a good deal of time in that period writing letters back home for men who were illiterate. How many times have I sat with pencil in hand while some earnest yokel furrowed up his brow and dictated:

Dear Ma and Pa,

I am here at Richmond with the Army. We was in a big battle at Malvern Hill two weeks ago. Many of our boys got killed there. We are having a good time at Richmond. It is a big city. Don't worry about me. I am fine. Jim Mundy is helping me with this letter. Say hello to Grandma and Aunt Ode and Cousin Bartlett. Your son,

Brady

That's what they would say. Only I would work in a few descriptions of the terrain and generally flower up their message. And God, forgive me for the love letters I wrote. Red-faced and tongue-tied, the fellows would take me aside and try to tell me what to say to Helen Mae or Samantha Ann back home.

"Let me see, now, Jim. 'Dear Helen Mae. Uh . . . uh . . . how are you? Hope you are fine. I am fine. Uh . . . uh.' "

"Why don't you say you miss her?" I would prompt him.

"Yeah, 'I am missing you. Uh . . . uh.' "

"How about saying you can't wait to be with her again?"

"Aw, now, Jim, ain't that going a little too far?"

"Not at all."

"Okay. Say I can't wait to see her. Uh . . . uh . . . what shall I say next?"

"Well, look, Homer, why don't you let me write the letter and read it back to you and you can send it off?"

"Yeah, Jim, that's the way to do it."

My own letters to Jane Ferro, while growing more friendly in tone, remained discreet. I didn't dare speak of love at that stage. Was waiting for cues from her for I did fear she might rebuff me. However, I had no such restraint in writing letters for others. Thus I would write, over Homer's name:

Dear Helen Mae,

Well here we are at Richmond having come here after helping clean up the battlefields to the southeast. It has been hard work. This is the first chance I have had to write to you. Our regiment conducted itself with valor at Malvern Hill but, as you must know by now, our losses were rather heavy.

Richmond is an exciting city. Wish you could be here so I could escort you around and show you the sights. Wouldn't that be nice?

I think of you often and long to be at your side again. I see lots of pretty girls here but few to compare with you.

That's all for now. Keep me in your thoughts and heart as I keep you in mine.

Love, Homer

Homer would listen with awe at what he was half-persuaded had come from his own lips.

"Hey, that is pretty good, Jim, only I don't know about that 'love.' "

"Well, do you love her?"

"Sure."

"Then leave it there as your closing. It can't make her mad."

"All right, but what does 'valor' mean?"

"It means bravery."

"I see. And you think it is all right to sign it off with 'love'?"

"Indeed I do."

"Then, by God, let her go."

God knows how many marriages resulted from my pen as I stuck in an extra word here and there or added a bit of pretty sentiment. Noah Rhine generally wrote very matter-of-fact letters. It got to where I cornered the love letter trade and he was stuck with those to Ma and Pa and Aunt Nellie.

So July came and passed. In August, Lee, full of confidence in himself and his newly forged Army of Northern Virginia, began moving north before McClellan's old army could be brought back from the lower Peninsula to reinforce Pope up above the Rappahannock. Off went half of his army under Stonewall Jackson, followed by the other half under Longstreet, and the cavalry under Jeb Stuart. We remained behind at first to guard Richmond against a possible surprise dash from the southeast. Then in late August we learned that our regiment was being detached from Huger's division to become a part of a two-brigade division under General J. G. Walker. Next came an urgent call for Walker to join Lee in northern Virginia. Off we marched again, this time toward Washington.

22

I'm sorry I said we marched. Actually they loaded us onto flatcars and hauled us out of Richmond up to Gordonsville, where we transferred over to the Orange Railroad line to Culpeper Courthouse. We traveled along at ten miles an hour or less through picked-over countryside that got more barebones the farther north we progressed. Fence rails gone, long since burned for campfires despite the rules against such depredations, poorly dressed people, generally riding on or behind second-rate horses and mules, the best long since snapped up by the army, fields poorly tended with the Negroes taking time to stare at us as long as they liked. Central and northern Virginia bore the brunt of the war, let me tell you. The people in that beautiful stretch between Richmond and Washington paid a high price.

As for the men of the 10th, we were in high spirits. We all had shoes, either captured from the Yankees or produced by one of the C.S.'s new factories. There was plenty of grub. Our morale was good enough to allow a bit of larking as we rattled along over ill-repaired rails to Culpeper. The boys funned me about the new slouch hat I had bought to replace the one carried away by the canister ball in our second charge up Malvern Hill. Said I was lying about that, the truth was I had run so fast my hat blew off.

We got off at Culpeper and slept in rows alongside the tracks. As Major Ferro explained to me, Lee had brought Pope to battle and they wanted us up quickly for reinforcements. The railroad had been torn up beyond Culpeper, so it was shanks' mare for us. With barely time to take a leak and gobble our cold corn bread, we set off for Manassas Junction, a good thirty miles away. And it was route step all the way. Yes sir, Colonel Rankin kept us moving smartly.

There is some pretty country up above Culpeper. Beautiful rounded hills and fine, sweeping fields, but we had damned little time to admire the view.

"Close up on the rear. No straggling. Keep up," Colonel Rankin would encourage the weary.

They let us fall out for water and rations for thirty minutes at noon. By that time we had covered about twelve miles at what then seemed a furious pace.

"By God, I believe he's trying to kill us," says Harry McGee.

I had to agree. Before I had choked down my hardtack and drunk my water, the call came to fall in. On we marched toward the north. We marched right into the night, not stopping until we had covered over twenty-five miles for the entire day. There was no insomnia in our camp that night. Just wrapped ourselves in our blankets and with our knapsacks as pillows slept right through until dawn. The bugle blew, we had corn meal mush for breakfast and were on our way by the time the sun cleared the horizon.

We came upon the familiar backwash of a big battle shortly. Wagon trains parked about. Prisoner corrals filled with men in blue. And the inevitable surgeons' tents. Apparently the butchers had been at it all night for outside one tent I saw a heap of white legs and arms ready to be hauled away.

They halted us near an unfinished railroad cut. Nearby a group of lightly wounded Confederates lay about.

"Who are you greenhorns?" one called out to me.

"We ain't greenhorns. We're the 10th North Carolina."

"Oh, Tar Heels, huh? Now I know why they call you that. It's because you stay stuck in one place so long you miss out on the fighting."

"What do you mean? We covered twenty-five miles yesterday."

"You still too late. The battle's over. We chased the Yanks right off the field."

He was right. The great Battle of Second Manassas had ended that day before, ended in a grand victory for the Confederacy, with Longstreet's entire corps arriving a bit late but in a position to sweep in on Pope's flank and drive the Federals off in headlong panic.

It is my contention that this was Lee's greatest victory and was also the best chance the South ever had to win the war at a single stroke. Lee had saved Richmond and now he was in a position to advance on Washington or at least bring it under siege.

I never got used to the sight of a battlefield after the shooting ended. Second Manassas was a big battle, with 9,500 casualties on the Confederate side and 15,000 on the Federal. From the railroad cut where Jackson's corps had fought off superior numbers with rocks and musket butts across fields where Longstreet's mighty juggernaut rolled to the Henry House past which the Yanks fled, the terrain was littered with discarded canteens, blankets, knapsacks, muskets, cartridge boxes and the bodies of men and horses.

Mind you, this was the same area where Beauregard and Johnston had beaten McDowell little more than a year before. The Yanks retreated right over the same ground as they had then, yes sir, retreated just as precipitously as we had at New Bern. Lee simply put them to flight.

We lingered in that area for a week waiting to see if Lee would send us to take Washington. Many of us thought we could do it. We didn't know about the enormous system of fortifications that ringed the Federal capital. Pope's army had been scattered, but it was not destroyed. And many of the same Federals who had fought so stubbornly on the Peninsula were now in Washington as well, although McClellan had been removed from command. It would have been suicidal for us to have attacked head on a city so strongly held. Lee knew that, but he saw a way to advance into the North, avoiding Washington. He had the initiative and he knew how to use it.

23

September 1862—that was a month in which all things seemed possible for the Confederate States of America. Never did the South have as many battle-tested men both in the east and the west. The new conscription law was producing a new batch of volunteers to avoid the draft. The great Northern advances had been halted. The initiative had passed to the Confederacy.

Out in Tennessee, or I should say northern Mississippi, Braxton Bragg began gathering his forces to march across Tennessee and deep into Kentucky. Fort Hudson and Vicksburg remained securely in Confederate hands on the Mississippi. The Shenandoah Valley with its rich harvest was free of Yankees. And up along the plains and pleasant hills of northern Virginia, Robert E. Lee began his move toward Maryland. For once the 10th North Carolina would not be left out of the fun. As part of Walker's little makeshift division we would be attached to Stonewall Jackson's corps and that corps was already leading a Confederate advance into Maryland.

"Roll out, boys," Captain Cadieu called to us on the morning of September 5. "Get ready to march."

We thought we knew all there was to know about marching. The papers had been talking for months about Jackson's "foot cavalry" and how his men had covered twenty-five and thirty miles a day, time and again in the Shenandoah the previous spring. And, of course, it was Jackson who had moved like lightning to march in upon Pope's rear at Centreville the month before to bring on the Battle of Second Manassas. Reading about these swift strokes was one thing; being part of them was quite another.

Stonewall Jackson. I saw him on many an occasion. He was a big man, well over six feet tall, with a dark beard and a high forehead. I never saw him smile even when his troops cheered him. He rode a sorrel horse that was too small for him. Rode it as clumsily as a farm boy.

We moved along at a terrible pace trying to catch up with Jackson's corps. We went almost at a trot for fifty minutes and then rested for ten and then on again for fifty minutes. Old Stonewall had it worked out and God help any colonel who did not enforce the rule.

I was a strong, long-legged lad and even though we traveled light, with just our muskets, a pouch full of ready rolled cartridges, and a blanket roll over our shoulders, that was a killing pace even for me. It was murder on some of the older men or those who had a touch of dysentery or those who didn't have their hearts in the war anyway, such as the conscripts that had just come into our ranks.

By the time we reached the Potomac River, we had left a trail of stragglers stretching for miles behind. Men fell down with heat strokes. A few ducked into the bushes and never showed up again, none from our company, I am proud to say. A few even died from exhaustion.

"I can't go on no more, Jim," one of the Wiley boys said to me as we took one of our half-hour noon meal breaks, lying beside a farmer's well that had been literally drunk dry. "My left leg keeps getting a cramp in it."

"Then you'll have to hop along on your right leg," I reply, ever the sympathetic sergeant.

"Can't I stay here in the shade and rest for an hour? I can catch up tonight."

"You know what would happen? Old Jackson would have you shot. He's got cavalry patrolling the road back behind us with orders to arrest any stragglers. You just rub that leg and keep it moving. Exercise is the best thing for leg cramps. Any fool knows that."

One of our conscripts, a fat married man, was a different story. He had been assigned to us at Richmond and hadn't got himself in shape. I noticed he didn't get up after one of our ten-minute breaks. I shook him.

"Come on, we got to get moving, Jesse."

Jesse was unconscious beside the road. We slapped his face and poured water on him, but nothing would revive him. Left him there in the care of an ambulance driver. Later learned he had suffered a stroke. Was sent home with a paralyzed left side. Man of about thirty-five, too.

Well-nigh worn out, we reached our crossing point on the Potomac River near Leesburg at Cheek's Ford. Little more than half of our company was still with us at that point; the others were limping along miles to the rear.

At the river bank they gave us a little time to blow. Then it was off with our shoes and into the water. We crossed in ranks of four at a time with our shoes strung from our necks, muskets and cartridge boxes in one hand and our knapsacks in the other. Slipping and sliding over the rocks, we cursed and laughed our way to the other shore, where a ragtag little off-tune band greeted us with "Maryland, My Maryland." Despite our fatigue, the music buoyed us up.

My shoes were in such a bad condition I didn't bother putting them on again. Tossed them beside the road and marched on to Frederick barefooted.

Maryland! We had come to liberate her from the abolitionist yoke, so we thought. Only thing was that few of the Marylanders seemed to wish for our liberation. We got damned few of the recruits we had thought would come flocking to the Confederate colors. All we got at our camp pitched outside Frederick was a few guilty-looking townsmen who sidled up to chat and to assure us that our states had a right to secede from the Union if that was what our citizens truly wanted.

"Yes, sir," a stout fellow of about thirty said to our squad as we sat about drinking coffee, real coffee drawn from stores in Frederick, and scraping a new infestation of lice from our uniforms. "My sentiments are with the South in this war. You are a brave set of lads and I wish you well."

"Glad to hear that," Harry McGee replied. "We got some Maryland regiments in the Confederate Army. In fact, we can sign you up right now and you can march with us until we come up with one of your outfits and you could transfer. Couldn't he do that, Jim?"

Taking it up, I says, "Of course. It wouldn't take five minutes. We can swear him in right now and he can go home and tell his folks goodbye. We can get him a gray cap somewhere and a spare musket. Say, Noah, run over and tell Captain Cadieu we got us a fellow wants to fight for the South." By this time our Southern sympathizer was getting red-faced and spluttering. "No, no, I didn't mean I wanted to join your army. Just thought you'd like to know that you have the sympathy of many Marylanders like me."

"That's a great comfort to us all," Harry says. "Ain't that right, boys? Don't it make your hearts just swell up to hear that this fellow came all the way out here to assure us that he is on our side, figuratively speaking of course? It takes a brave man to do that."

Now even Brady Alexander, stupid as he was, was laughing. Our entire squad, led by Harry McGee, solemnly rose and shook that poor Marylander's hand and piously thanked him for his good wishes. I am sure the fellow wished he had stayed home and smoked his pipe that night.

After he finally broke away and headed for home we rolled around on the ground laughing at the way we had treated him.

Generally there was little show of enthusiasm for us when we arrived and even less as we plundered cornfields and burned fence rails and drank the farmers' wells dry. Also, it didn't set well with storekeepers to have their goods confiscated by our quartermaster people, receiving in return C.S.A. scrip good for redemption upon the conclusion of the war.

The farms of central Maryland made a mighty impression on me. Big, solid barns set in rich limestone soil. Well-tended fields. Brick houses built close to the road. Good roads, too, some macadamized. A general appearance of prosperity. It all made quite a contrast with the country around Richmond or for that matter with the overgrown, shabby look of my own Oldham County.

I liked the looks of the town of Frederick, what little I saw of it. And that was damned little. There we were, across the Potomac with the city of Washington just two days' march to the southeast. Stonewall Jackson could have covered that ground in a hop and a skip, but it was not to be. First off, McClellan had been put back in command of the entire Federal Army, his own old force brought back from the Peninsula plus the beaten army of Pope. He had a huge army concentrated at Washington.

Meanwhile, Lee had sent Longstreet west across the mountain range beyond Frederick into the Cumberland Valley, which stretches from the Potomac River all the way to the Susquehanna in the very heart of Pennsylvania. We didn't know it then, but Lee meant to move us all into the valley and march us right up to Harrisburg, the capital of Pennsylvania. But first he had to eliminate the Federal garrison at Harpers Ferry so as to keep his communications secure down the Shenandoah Valley. That's where we in Walker's division and Jackson's regular corps came in. Lee wanted Stonewall to take Harpers Ferry.

24

We thought we had done some pretty smart marching getting from Manassas Junction, Virginia, to Frederick, Maryland. We learned what real marching was in our rush to trap the Federal garrison at Harpers Ferry.

The sick and the weak had been culled out by the time we reached the Potomac headed north. Now we, the hardy survivors, found ourselves pressing back toward the Potomac, moving at a pace that would have done justice to cavalry.

We marched like men possessed. No talking, no larking about, just left-right, left-right, like a great machine doing the fierce will of Stonewall Jackson. We were Jackson's men now and therefore more was expected of us. We ate up the miles to Point of Rocks, just upstream from our earlier crossing. Remember, I and many of our command walked without shoes. We crossed the rocky bed of the Potomac with our bare feet slipping on the stones. A heavy rainstorm began as we crossed. Old

Walker stopped to let us catch a night's sleep.

Until we got to northern Virginia I had never seen a mountain. Even then it had been the Blue Ridge at a distance, like a low-lying bank of dark clouds. Now we were in the shadow of the mountains. The next day—September 12—we took the road south to Lucketts and then turned west for a gap in those mountains.

This was all mighty exciting to a nineteen-year-old, tired as I was, to be one of Jackson's men, crossing a mountain range. We turned north again at the village of Hillsboro and headed for Harpers Ferry, where the Shenandoah flows into the young Potomac amid a scene that Thomas Jefferson described as one of the grandest in America. I and many like me arrived with sore and bleeding feet and aching legs.

We were moving to the immediate will of Jackson but to the larger will of Robert E. Lee. Lee had taken a huge gamble by dividing his army, sending part of it over the South Mountain Range of Maryland to Hagerstown, astride the invasion route into Pennsylvania, and then dispatching the remainder, under Jackson, to Harpers Ferry.

Jackson further divided the men under his command. He took his old corps across the South Mountain Range, across the Cumberland Valley and down to Williamsport, Maryland. There he would cross and herd a Federal garrison of about three thousand men out of Martinsburg back into Harpers Ferry. His corps would approach Harpers Ferry from Bolivar Heights. Meanwhile McLaws would seize Maryland Heights, overlooking Harpers Ferry from across the Potomac, and put artillery up there. As for us in Walker's division, we would occupy Loudoun Heights, across the Shenandoah River from the town. That way we would have Harpers Ferry completely hemmed in.

Having just recently seen my first mountain, naturally I had never climbed one before. Old Walker chose us and a couple more regiments to scramble our way up a narrow, stony path to the top of Loudoun Heights. From there we could look right down on the railroad bridge across the Potomac, the Chesapeake and Ohio Canal paralleling the river, and, of course, the houses and buildings of the town and the camps of the Yankee garrison. All this lay within a double-charged musket shot.

The rest of Walker's regiments arrayed themselves around the base of the heights while crews labored to bring up five Parrott cannon to join us three regiments on the heights.

William Ferro stood on a ledge of rock with Tom Shelton, the two of them peering across at the town. He beckoned me over.

"Here, James," he says. "Take a look at that little building down there."

I took his field glasses and focused on the brick structure.

"You're looking at the building where this war really started," the major said.

"How's that? I thought it started at Fort Sumter."

Tom Shelton snickered, but I ignored him.

"That's the engine house of the U.S. arsenal, the one John Brown and his renegades seized three years ago when they tried to start a slave rebellion. Robert E. Lee was home on leave from the U.S. Army at Arlington. They sent him here to take charge. Lee himself directed the Marines that broke into that building and captured John Brown. In my opinion that is what made this war inevitable, John Brown's criminal action."

"Not the split in the Democratic convention or the election of Lincoln?"

"No, either Lincoln wouldn't have been elected or it might not have mattered to the South if John Brown hadn't touched a raw nerve with his so-called rebellion. When he tried to arouse the black people to revolt, he solidified the white people of the South, regardless of whether they owned slaves. I was at Princeton University when that raid occurred and let me tell you it very nearly caused a Civil War between the Southern students and the Northern."

I could tell Tom Shelton didn't like the idea of the major standing there making small conversation with a mere sergeant. Couldn't wait to interrupt with "Shall we keep the men concealed up here?"

"Only until McLaws' guns over there across the Potomac on Maryland Heights start shelling the town. Then we are to make plenty of noise and generally impress them with our numbers. This is a show of strength. We want them to see how hopeless their situation is."

For my part I hoped it would take a long while for the Federals to give up. It felt glorious to stretch out on the mountaintop and rest from our long march.

The story of the surrender of Harpers Ferry is too well known to require me to add much. From our seat on Loudoun Heights we could watch the flash of McLaws' batteries and the explosion of his shells in the air above the town of Harpers Ferry. They were too far away to do much harm, but our five cannon were in easy range. It wasn't much of a bombardment, but I guess the garrison down there did feel like sitting ducks. We joined in the fun by sniping away with our muskets. I found that my Enfield could stand a double charge of powder that could send the ball right into the town. Only harm was a bruised shoulder from the powerful kick. Can't claim to have hit anything at that range, but I suppose each shot helped a little to produce the big white flag that finally fluttered from the parade ground flagpole on the edge of the town. We fired into the town throughout the afternoon of the fourteenth; a few Yankee guns tried to reply, but our Parrotts had the advantage of height and soon silenced them. The next morning a fog covered the town and we couldn't see much, but our guns slammed away all the same. The white flag appeared later in the day after the fog lifted. Harpers Ferry was ours.

That was the dumbest thing I ever saw a bunch of Yankees do. They had twelve thousand men. All the Yanks had to do was to dash out toward Bolivar Heights before Stonewall arrived. Or they might have sneaked out along the upper Potomac at night. They stood a good chance that way of breaking out. But no, instead, like a herd of sheep, they lined up and turned over their weapons to Jackson.

We had visions of descending to the town and re-equiping ourselves with shoes and eating some good U.S. grub, but it was not to be. Lee's bluff had been called. McClellan was not playing his role and staying holed up behind the defenses of Washington. He had advanced boldly into central Maryland and even forced his way across the South Mountain gaps to try to cut off Lee. Now old Marse Robert was backed up against the northern shore of the Potomac, one flank on the river and the other on a stream called Antietam Creek in the vicinity of a village called Sharpsburg. Lee needed Jackson in a hurry. He got part of us in a hurry, too. As our little division was not needed to handle the surrender of the Harpers Ferry garrison, they sent us off right away. It was a forced night march, across the Shenandoah and Potomac. We climbed up the bank on the northern side of the Potomac and smack into the rear of the Army of Northern Virginia, getting ready for a big battle. It was near noon on Tuesday, September 16, 1862.

25

Robert E. Lee was a great general, probably the best America ever produced. He made some mistakes, however, and one of them was standing his ground at Sharpsburg, daring a foe that outnumbered him two-to-one into a showdown fight. He invited disaster there with his back to the Potomac. He could have withdrawn his army across the river and still been far ahead of the game, having cleared the Yankees out of Virginia, tested Maryland's zeal for the Southern cause, and scooped up the garrison at Harpers Ferry. But no, the mighty Lee was a pugnacious man under that calm, aristocratic surface. He couldn't resist giving battle.

His other mistake in the Maryland campaign was in not carrying along a wagon train of spades and shovels. Lee had time there at Sharpsburg to throw up an impenetrable line of rifle pits and breastworks. If he had done that, the battle of Sharpsburg might have had a different ending.

Anyway, our little division was stationed that night, September 16, 1862, to the right of the Confederate line, on a hill overlooking Antietam Creek. It was raining, and we threw ourselves on the wet ground and slept, exhausted from our forced march. We were fortunate in that McClellan never made a rash move in his life. Everything had to be just so before he would attack. If he had pitched into Lee before we and the other of Jackson's men arrived, he could have driven the Confederate Army right into the Potomac. Could have ended the war right there. Lee gambled on his opponent to take his time and to that degree he won.

The South called the battle that followed Sharpsburg; the North, Antietam. I was there from beginning to end and I call it a day of hell. From early the next morning until that night it was one long day of killing. Never was there a silence or a respite. September 17, 1862. The blood that flowed that day!

We went to sleep the night before knowing there would be a real fight the next morning. Even big Brady Alexander, dumb as he was, realized it. "Preacher Sam" Elkins knew it, too, and urged us all to repent of our sins while we had time. Captain Cadieu reminded us to follow orders and keep our aim low; throughout the war there was a tendency to fire over the heads of your targets.

The two armies were done with strategic maneuvers. They lay nose to nose, with retreat impossible for either side. A single musket shot could touch the thing off.

It began at 5 A.M. the next morning, under a cloudy sky. At first there was heavy skirmishing to our left, but the firing grew quickly into a constant roar, punctuated by hurrahs and Rebel yells. By 8 A.M. the fighting had spread from the left flank near the Potomac across to the area in the center around the Dunkard church. It was a constant din of muskets playing treble to the artillery's bass.

Also by 8 A.M., a white fog of gunpowder smoke had drifted over the entire area. We ate our cold breakfast with the smell of gunpowder burning our nostrils. We lay there waiting, waiting until around 9 A.M., shrouded in smoke and our ears growing numb from the noise.

At last the order came. "Everybody up. Form ranks on your regimental colors. On the double!!" There was Colonel Rankin on his horse, pointing off to our left.

We formed up, regiment by regiment, and followed our flagbearers north through the streets of Sharpsburg, ducking our heads as an occasional wild cannon ball carried over our lines and landed in the village. They herded us over torn-down fences, around farm buildings and through fields of corn, toward the dreadful sound of battle. Spent Minié balls splattered around us as we drew nearer to the fighting.

I have read many an account of Civil War battles, some accurate and graphic and some so much horseshit about gallantry. Nothing I have read, however, conveys the feeling of excitement I felt at the business of war. By that I mean the total activity of a large army, not just the shooting going on up on the firing line but the rushing backward and forward of couriers, the advance of reserves toward the front, the heavy traffic of ammunition wagons and caissons, the stream of walking wounded fading back toward the makeshift hospitals set up in churches and barns, and over it all a fog bank of smoke, the whine of spent bullets and a roar of sound from scores of cannon and tens of thousands of muskets. All this can only be experienced in the rear of any army engaged in a life-or-death fight as was the Army of Northern Virginia that September morning as they shifted Walker's division from the then quiet right flank to reinforce Lee's center.

As we marched at the double through the eastern edge of Sharpsburg, I caught a glimpse of Lee himself, standing on a little rise, calmly surveying the battle raging a bare half-mile away. He might have been the chief engineer of a railroad construction job from the cool way in which he stood there, seemingly oblivious of the shells bursting about him. Cool, calm, self-controlled Lee; you'd never have known from his appearance that his outnumbered army was near disaster from the hammering it was taking. Others in our ranks saw him and we gave him a cheer, taking off our hats and waving them about our heads. He lowered his field glasses and raised his hat in acknowledgment.

Colonel Rankin stood up in his stirrups to shout, "Press on toward that little brick church over there! Keep your ranks closed up! Move quickly!"

Now we could see the backs of Hood's division, standing up, arms moving in hasty rhythm as they fired, loaded, aimed and fired again into the woods around the little church. I noted that they left their ramrods thrust into the earth while they fired, thereby saving time for the next reloading. Now and again their line would give way before the fury of the firing from those woods to reform to the rear. The ground over which they had withdrawn was littered by their fallen comrades. And a great gap had appeared in their ranks. It was obvious that Hood's men had about fought out. Their rate of firing was slackening while that of the horde of Yanks opposite them grew. Men were beginning to fall out of the line, ignoring the officers waving their swords and shouting at them. Those still on the thinned-out line looked like schoolboys who have put up a good scrap against bigger opponents but who know they are going to lose and are too proud to run. It was a matter of minutes before two divisions of Yankees, those commanded by Sedgwick and French, would burst right through Lee's army, splitting it. All that was required was for them to rush forward. It was that close.

Over my left shoulder I could see a fresh crowd of Confederates hurrying from the rear. It was McLaws' division just arriving on the scene from Maryland Heights. There was not time to wait for them.

"Forward at the double," came the command.

We stepped out smartly toward the inferno of smoke and sound, practically trampling over Hood's men who were falling out of the fight. Some of them turned and followed us forward again. One, a huge Texan, walked right through our ranks, his smoke-blackened face wearing a blank expression. "Can't stand it no more. I'm out of ammunition. They've whipped us."

But as we moved forward we came even with another feisty little Texan, who had refused to give any more ground. He stood there alone, doggedly firing a musket that had grown so hot he had wrapped a piece of blanket around the barrel. He swore like a madman each time he pulled the trigger.

The horde of Yanks gave a great hurrah. Out of the bank of smoke came a wall of blue uniforms across our front. Thousands of well-fed, robust men in a neat array, muskets at the ready, headed toward the hole in Lee's line.

"Fire!" That great door slammed around us and the Yanks fell in droves. We reloaded and then the order came, "Charge!"

I had thought New Bern and Malvern Hill terrible experiences, but they were Sunday school picnics compared to what followed for the next half an hour. The Yanks were taken by surprise, but they did not panic. They outnumbered us, but we had the advantage and did we ever press it. They took terrible casualties as we poured volley after volley into them, advancing several yards after each volley. They couldn't get swung around to face us properly. We drove them back into the woods and they made a furious stand around the little church.

Now McLaws had got his division into the fray, pouring a fresh volume of Minié balls into the blue ranks. We pressed them away from the church, through the woods and into the road beyond.

In all I suppose there were fifteen or twenty thousand men trying to kill each other around that little church. The ground seemed covered by dead, dying or wounded men in their neat blue uniforms.

As I say, the Yanks did not panic. They fought back stubbornly, trying to keep their unit formations. But once they got out in the open, in the fields across the road from the woods, they came into a vicious artillery fire from S. D. Lee's battery. This was more than they could take. Now they did panic. They fled the field, taking themselves out of range, seeking the protection afforded by a concentration of Yankee cannon on a ridge some distance to the rear. We had whipped their asses to a fare-you-well.

But the fun wasn't over. We now came under their artillery fire, trying to pay us back. The round shot came crashing through the trees, lashing us with broken branches until we found refuge behind a long, low rocky fold in the ground. There we stretched ourselves out, relatively safe from their guns. They tried to punish us with shells, but these struck the rising ground in front of us and glanced over our heads to explode behind us. Mind, it was no fun, but neither was it anything like as dangerous as receiving fire from thousands of muskets at a range of a hundred yards. We stayed in that position long past noon, lying there making jokes and bragging about the way we had chased the Yanks out of the woods, trying to release the tension.

That was where Big Bill Utley, the ardent secessionist, met his fate. Bill was a great red-faced bully who would drink when he felt like it. He had managed to find enough brandy back in Frederick to fill his canteen. Now he began to empty it; swilled it down like a hog and wouldn't share a drop. He was in the next squad, so it wasn't my place to discipline him.

"Ho-ho," he roared. "The blue-bellied sons of bitches couldn't stand up to real men." He stood up and shook his fist. His friends pulled him down. "Get your frigging hands off me. I ain't afraid of God nor man."

He stood up again and thumbed his nose. Suddenly there was a loud thump like a pumpkin bursting and the headless body of what had been Bill Utley went hurtling back. The cannon ball sent brains, blood and fragments of skull splattering over the men of his squad and mine.

There was no need to remind anyone to keep his head down after that. Our jokes ceased as we huddled there in horrified silence, trying to put the incident out of our minds and get some rest.

But the Federal artillery wouldn't let us rest. One battery of 3-inch ordnance rifles in particular pestered us. It was sited in a stone fence corner about two hundred yards away. The gunners would load up their guns while crouched low to avoid our fire. Then they would run the guns up to the fence and spray us with canister or else send solid bolts plowing up the dirt over our faces. Got to be a damned nuisance.

Early in this narrative I mentioned Jimmy Golightly, the half-Manawee that William Ferro and I recruited, and what a good soldier he became. Jimmy was small and quick, taking occasional gibes about his ancestry with good grace. But after the Battle of Sharpsburg I never heard anyone rag Jimmy about anything.

"Sergeant," Jimmy said to me. "We can take those guns."

"You think so?"

"Yeah. Notice the gunners fire and then duck down to stay safe until we stop shooting at them. It takes them a long time to reload. We could get over there before they were ready to fire again."

"What about their infantry though? Skirmishers on either side, see? We'd catch it from them."

"Well, it looks like they are having their dinner. Look over there. See? They're lying about with their muskets scattered. They aren't ready to fight fast."

I crawled over to where Captain Cadieu was sitting and told him what Jimmy Golightly said. His eyes narrowed as he examined the battery through his field glasses.

"You think it can be done?"

"I think it can."

"How many men would it take?"

"Maybe one platoon."

"Why not the entire company?"

"Too many. We'd get in each other's way."

"Let me talk to the colonel."

The captain, bending as low as his dignity would permit, ran back to the base of a bullet-pocked tree where Colonel Rankin sat. I watched them pointing and waving their arms, half-hoping the colonel would turn down the idea. But no, Cadieu turned and said to give it a go.

To make a long story short, we worked things out so that the instant after the battery fired another blast at us we were on our feet and racing toward them before the smoke cleared. As we ran toward that wall, the other boys kept their muskets leveled at the nearest enemy infantry, holding their fire as long as they dared.

You never saw men as surprised as those gunners when we —led by Jimmy Golightly—came leaping over that stone wall. They were downright unmannerly. Flung down their utensils and ran off like rabbits.

We had only seconds to spare. In a flash we had spiked all four cannon, driving nails into the firing vents or breaking off the end of a file. That done, we gave a great heave and turned the guns over on their sides. Jimmy Golightly picked up a shell, lit the fuse and threw it on the ground. "Let's get out of here."

By now the Yanks around us had come to life, but our boys across the way kept them pinned down long enough for us to race back to their welcoming arms.

"All right, Sergeant?" Jimmy Golightly said to me as we hugged the earth. His brown face glowed.

I grinned at him. "It sure is all right, Jimmy."

A little later both Longstreet and Jackson came up to our area around the Dunkard church to look things over. I heard Colonel Rankin tell Jackson about how we had disabled that troublesome battery. Old Jack nodded his head. I could have sworn he almost smiled.

The Battle of Sharpsburg was far from over. The fighting went on, picking up to the right. They pulled us out of the line for a while to back up Toombs' men along the Antietam Creek and then shifted us back around the Dunkard church when it appeared that old Yankee friends there wanted to try our lines again. The sound of battle never ceased all that day. We saved Lee's army around that little church during the late morning. That afternoon, Burnside, now in command of a corps, got across a bridge over the Antietam and was moving to roll up Lee's right flank when A. P. Hill arrived on the scene, having completed the paper work of accepting the surrender of the Harpers Ferry garrison. Just as we saved Lee earlier that day, so Hill saved him, or I should say us, in the dusk.

That night. I have already told about the pitiful cries of the wounded on Malvern Hill. It was five times more hideous at Antietam for both armies took dreadful losses concentrated in a small area. The only way I could go to sleep was to wrap a blanket around my head so I could not hear the cries for water.

The bloodiest single day of the Civil War, they call Antietam. They are right. Bloody, bloody September 17, 1862.

26

I awoke on September 18 expecting to hear the battle resume any minute. The two armies still lay nose-to-nose along a three-mile arc, we with the Potomac at our backs, they with all the room McClellan could ever have wanted for maneuver and more men than he needed to drive us into the river. Little had changed since the morning before except that more than 20,-000 men, nearer 25,000 between the two forces, had been killed, wounded or taken prisoner. But the fighting did not resume. The only activities in the tramped, fought-over and blood-soaked areas between our picket lines—no-man's land they call it in France today—were the burial parties sent out by both sides to gather in the harvest of the dead. We had no formal truce. The parties just went out with their wagons and nobody fired at them. The men in the work gangs stopped and chatted with those from the other side, occasionally trading tobacco for coffee.

As we lay about that day, our muskets at the ready, we boys of Company H, 10th North Carolina, were convinced that we had won a great victory. I took advantage of the lull to bring my diary up to date:

SEPTEMBER 18, 1862—We are near a town called Sharpsburg just north of the Potomac River in Maryland. Marched here on the double from Harpers Ferry having aided in the capture of that place two days ago. Engaged in a mighty battle all day yesterday, heaviest fighting we have experienced. Inflicted enormous casualties on enemy, repulsing every one of his assaults during a long day. We have won the day. Waiting for the fighting to begin again. Everyone confident we will drive off the enemy and press on into Pennsylvania.

Being too close to an event in time and distance can obscure your vision. Weeks were to pass before it dawned on us that Sharpsburg had not been a victory for the South. That night Lee withdrew us across the Potomac and marched us back up the Shenandoah Valley to the vicinity of Winchester, Virginia. Up to that point, the battle was a draw. But when Lee pulled back, he gave the North the chance to claim Antietam, as they called it, as a strategic victory for the North. And so it was.

We stayed in and around the pleasant town of Winchester for more than a month, licking our wounds, so to speak. Strangely, our company had not lost so many men at Sharpsburg despite the furious fighting there. Our strength had declined to about seventy-five. It was a mighty weary seventy-five, too. For a week or more we lay about, bone-tired in body and spirit from all that marching and killing. In this period our one-year enlistments expired, and to a man, we re-enlisted for the duration of the war. Then, late in October, as the nights were getting chilly, they marched us east over the mountains again and then south toward Fredericksburg on the Rappahannock. We moved at an easy pace, stopping for long bivouacs. Colonel Rankin was gentle with us. Took us nearly a month to move those ninety miles. Partly, of course, Lee was keeping himself poised to meet a possible dash by McClellan across the Potomac. But McClellan was too busy in Washington defending himself against charges of having been dilatory at Sharpsburg. I am grateful to the man that he was not more aggressive or I would not be here today. Anyway, on November 23 we reached Fredericksburg on the main route between Richmond and Washington and there we went into winter camp.

The high ground overlooking Fredericksburg and the Rappahannock would be our home for several weeks. Upon our arrival there we were set to building huts or cabins out of logs. Drawing from a supply of green timber brought in from the woods, in a few days my squad had built itself a snug hut with mud-chinked logs for walls, pine planks for bunks, and sawdust sprinkled over tamped-down earth for a floor. We even created a crude fireplace at one end, a fireplace that drew so well it poured almost as much smoke into the sky as it did into our room. Snug as twelve bugs in a rug were I and my boys.

We were a good crew. Noah Rhine and Harry McGee as corporals and Jack Davis, Jimmy Golightly, Bob Perry, Ed Engerer, Robert Miner, Sam Elkins, the Wiley twins and Brady Alexander as privates. And me as sergeant, of course. We had become tough individuals during the past few weeks. Had been through hell and back as the saying goes. We could march and fight like machines. We got on well together, looked out for each other. We were true comrades.

They had been holding our mail for us back in Richmond. It all came up to Fredericksburg a few days after we arrived, just after we had completed our hut. It was one of the high points of my life when they announced mail call and I stood in the cleared space outside our hut, feeling pleased at our handiwork, and the company clerk started calling my name each time he came to a letter for me. I had two letters from home and twelve —I repeat, twelve—from Jane Ferro. She had written to me every week while we had been in Maryland and the Shenandoah.

By now it was obvious that Jim Mundy was carrying on a mighty serious correspondence with somebody back home. Only Noah Rhine knew just who, I thought. There I stood getting more letters than anybody in the company except for some of the married men. Maybe it was my imagination but it seemed to me that Tom Shelton's scowl was directed at me as they kept calling out my name.

It was pitiful to see the fellows who had no mail, the way they turned around dejectedly after all the letters had been handed out. They had gone through the hell of battle and the torture of forced marching. Their folks back home couldn't write to them. Yet they hungered for news from home like anyone else.

I was free of duties that afternoon. It was a clear day, warm, too, for late November, so I took my packet of letters out to the edge of the camp to a clump of small trees that offered shelter against the breeze. There, sitting against a pin oak, I spent a delicious hour. Forced myself to read my father's two letters first. They reported on deaths and illnesses in the community and the rising cost of sugar, nails, cloth, almost everything, that plus prayers for the safety of my soul and body. Good old man.

That duty over, I arranged the letters from Jane in the order she had posted them and proceeded to read them slowly, aloud, one word at a time, so as to make them last as long as I could. Wish I had been able to keep those letters. They were full of news of the plantation and quotes from her father's table talk about the course of the war and even what their Presbyterian minister said in his sermons. She made coy reference to her little mare and how fond the beast had become of the long-legged soldier who had ridden her last spring. Only in her closing paragraphs did she permit herself any intimation of strong personal feeling for me. Each of these closings seemed a bit more personal, something about how she would like to see me again and urging me to take good care of myself. And, joy of joys, the fifth of her letters—written in reply to the last one I had been able to write before we marched north from Richmond—was signed "with love," rather than "affectionately." Jim Mundy, the tough nineteen-year-old sergeant who had been loved by an attractive married woman, who had saved his captain's life, who had marched into the fire of massed cannon at Malvern Hill and who had watched the bodies of Yankees pile up in front of his regiment at Sharpsburg, this same Jim Mundy broke into a sweat when he read those two words "with love."

They were beautiful letters, reflecting the innocence and intelligence of a rare, unspoiled girl. How I savored that hour, basking in the sun, reading those letters.

Two brief references by Jane disturbed me, however. One was the news—very unpleasant news to me—that she was writing to Tom Shelton as well as me. She referred to something Shelton had written about seeing Jefferson Davis in Richmond. A feeling of jealousy and resentment welled up in me. But then I reflected that after all he had known her first; apparently his family were just suitable enough so that they could be on the edge of the Ferros' social circle. And it would spoil my chances altogether if I let myself grow jealous and disagreeable over something I couldn't help anyway.

The other disturbing item was a passing reference to her father's disapproval of her corresponding with a soldier. Apparently her mother knew of our correspondence, however, and did not object. "I'm sure Father will change his mind when you come back from the war a hero." Thought little of this item at the time.

After rereading each letter twice, made my way back to our hut to ignore the sly questions from Harry McGee. Felt sorry for the fellows who had no mail, so I called them around and gave them a rundown on the news down in Oldham County. Invited others who had received mail to do the same. Forgive me for my immodesty, but for all my youth and brashness I reckon I was a good sergeant. Anyway, the boys liked me and they would work their asses off for me and the glorious cause of the Southern Confederacy when I asked them to. They trusted and looked up to me, even the older ones.

A snug hut for the winter, letters from Jane Ferro signed "with love" and, glory of glories, I was chosen as one of the guards for General Lee himself. Our squad had little work to do anyway. We generally had a brief drill in the morning and a class in tactics or military discipline in the afternoon. So Captain Cadieu put forward my name when he was asked to provide one of the guards to stand duty outside General Lee's tent.

I had seen the old man in Richmond, on the Peninsula, and at bloody Sharpsburg as our regiment marched toward the inferno around the Dunkard church, but never so close. What a man he was. Not as tall as me but broad in the shoulders and full-chested and erect. Had a fine head with a strong nose and a face like God's. His voice was easy, too. Can't imagine his ever shouting at anyone. Didn't have to, of course. Everything about him commanded respect.

But I remember his eyes best of all. They were dark and kindly yet not weak in the least. Full of quick intelligence.

Our watches lasted four hours. The first time he came to his tent when I was on guard those eyes flashed at me for an instant, past me and back again to my face.

"What is your name, Sergeant?" he asked.

My heart pounding, I told him.

"And your regiment?"

"The 10th North Carolina, sir."

"One of my brave Tar Heels. Let's see, you are commanded by Colonel Rankin, I believe."

"Yes, sir, that is right."

"And you helped save the day for us at Sharpsburg, so I am told."

"We were in right smart of a fight there around that little church for a fact, sir."

"Indeed you were. Brave, brave men. How can we fail with Tar Heels like you, men who stick to their ground?"

With that he passed into his tent, leaving me aglow with pleasure at his praise. What a man.

I stood guard at least half a dozen times at that post of honor. Had the pleasure of seeing Jackson, Longstreet, Jeb Stuart, A. P. Hill and all that lot come and go. Fine-looking men, every one of them. Jackson, brooding and close-mouthed; Longstreet, bluff and hearty; Stuart, high-spirited and youthful; A. P. Hill, feisty as they come. If the South had possessed the manpower and material of the North, with generals like ours it would have been no contest. We'd be two separate nations today, for ill or good. Ah, well.

Something happened to cloud my high spirits in that period. At our next mail call, the following week, I received no mail except for a brief scrawl from my little brother, Wesley. I was puzzled by this. That afternoon, Jane's brother, the major, came by our company huts and drew me aside. He was obviously embarrassed as he inquired after my health and listened to my enthusiastic accounts of standing guard at General Lee's own tent.

"I understand you and my sister Jane have been corresponding," he said after I finally had run down.

"Why, yes, we have exchanged a few letters. I hope you don't mind."

"No, of course I don't mind. And I do apologize for having to broach a rather painful subject."

"What subject is that, sir?"

"Well, you see, Jane is my father's only daughter and of course he feels very protective of her reputation."

"Her reputation?" I was beginning to get his drift.

"Yes, you see Jane is not a child anymore. Many girls her age are married and fathers naturally want to be sure that . . ." He paused.

I can't describe the humiliation I suddenly felt. Or the sullen anger. "You mean he objects to her writing to a common soldier, the son of a poor preacher? I'm not good enough?"

"It's not that exactly. You see, normally, since my father never met you before I brought you home with me, he would expect that his permission would be asked before you and Jane began a correspondence. That's the usual way."

There was a long pause as it hit me what a gulf lay between my social class and his back in the same country for which we were fighting. Even as my shame and resentment gathered I felt sorry for William Ferro for I could see he was enjoying this conversation no more than I.

"Do you wish me to stop writing to your sister, then?"

"Not necessarily. I am sure Father wouldn't either if he understood what a promising young man you are. Oh, look, James, why don't you seal your letters in an envelope and let me post them on with my letters to Jane? Then she can mail notes back through me in the same way. And Father need never know."

"I wonder what Jane thinks of all this?"

"She is an independent-minded young woman. I'm sure she regards it as nonsense."

"Maybe it is nonsense for a fellow from a dirt-poor family to be writing to the daughter of an aristocrat in the first place," I said bitterly.

"James, please don't take offense. I would never have mentioned this if my father hadn't laid down the law. Please think it over and see if you don't agree that my idea for exchanging occasional discreet notes between you and Jane isn't the best way. Look, this war can't last forever."

"No, but I'll be the son of a poor preacher forever."

"Yes, and you'll be an up-and-coming war veteran forever. Don't lose heart. And think over what I have proposed."

"I'll think about it."

It was a sad and hurt Jim Mundy who tried to sleep that night on his hard bunk in a crude log hut. What I would have given to have possessed the opportunities of even a bully like Tom Shelton. Don't ever think that money and family don't count in this world.

27

Everything pointed to a big battle a-brewing there along the Rappahannock. First came the news that McClellan, the Northern soldiers' beloved "Little Mac" who didn't like to spill blood, had been replaced by—guess who? None other than our old friend Ambrose P. Burnside, the very general who had inflicted that humiliating defeat on us at New Bern back in March, the same Burnside who crossed his corps over Antietam Creek at Sharpsburg and came so very close to rolling up Lee's right flank, stopped at the last moment by the fortuitous arrival of A. P. Hill's division from Harpers Ferry. And now Burnside was commanding the Yankees' "Army of the Potomac," some hundred thousand well-equipped men, and he was busy massing that huge force just across the Rappahannock, looking down with his artillery on the hapless town of Fredericksburg.

Our main lines ran along the heights overlooking Fredericksburg from the south. Our boys held the town itself right up to the bank of the river, but there was little we could do to protect Fredericksburg from the huge cannon the Federals hauled in from the north. The Yanks had their usual fine assortment of smoothbore Napoleons and 3-inch ordnance rifles. But these were popguns compared with the 32-pound Parrotts and similar long-ranged cannon they rolled into their commanding positions just across the river.

Not only did they have this heavy stuff; they also possessed an infernal observation balloon which they ran up once or twice a day to bob about in the December air, giving the chilblained fellow in the flimsy basket an unparalleled view of our lines, our camps and the countryside for miles around.

It was no good firing at this damned balloon with muskets or smoothbore artillery; she was out of range. However our 3-inch rifled cannon could make things uncomfortable for this spy in the sky. At first our gunners would fire explosive shells, adjusting their fuses by trial and error to get their bursts near the balloon. "Bang," the guns would speak, and we would all wait for the dot of light and puff of smoke to appear hundreds of feet above, below or beyond the balloon. The explosive shells fired by this particular gun had a weak bursting charge, so they would have to come mighty close to have any effect. The worst part was that those big guns of the Yanks would soon start throwing shells into our presumptuous artillery, which had a discouraging effect on our poor gunners.

Our boys had their best luck by firing several solid bolts from guns quickly and then shifting position so the Federal gunners couldn't locate them so easily. These projectiles made a fearful shriek; I suspect it was unnerving to the man in the basket to hear the noise of those chunks of iron sailing past him. He didn't stay up long when we really concentrated on him.

This sort of thing amused the infantry on both sides. As for us, we didn't need a balloon to know that Burnside was bringing in men by the thousands. They made little effort to conceal themselves, running their picket lines right down to the north bank of the river and exchanging shots with our boys on the south bank. Our sharpshooters gave them so much trouble they tried pulverizing the buildings of Fredericksburg that lay closest to the river. Their artillery banged away for hours, doing hundreds of thousands of dollars' damage to houses and businesses alike and no doubt expending an equal amount of Northern capital on gunpowder and shells. Made a grand show for everyone except the poor owners and inhabitants of the buildings. Brick walls came tumbling down; some of the wooden structures caught fire; roofs caved in. But after the noise subsided and the smoke cleared away, our sharpshooters crawled out of their holes and started potting away at the enemy once more. All the fireworks had been for naught.

I take that back. They did serve to take my mind off the humiliation reluctantly inflicted on me by William Ferro at his father's insistence. I had neither written to his sister nor received a letter from her since he had talked to me. Could not bring myself to do as he suggested and send her "an occasional discreet note." I wasn't built that way.

28

Never were two armies as well prepared for battle as those of Robert E. Lee and Ambrose P. Burnside on December 13, 1862. Burnside had a grand total of 122,000 men strung along six miles of the river, supported by superb artillery, with his main line actually closer to the now ruined town of Fredericksburg than ours. His army was separated by only four hundred feet of water; our main positions ran along the hills a mile back from the opposite shore, well away from the town but overlooking it.

Burnside could have seized the town on November 17 for that was the day the first of his corps reached the area, while Lee's army still stretched across Virginia. But no, Burnside dilly-dallied and gave Longstreet time to reach Fredericksburg from the west and block the path to Richmond. Burnside still might have got across and overwhelmed Longstreet, but his pontoon trains didn't arrive for another week. Eventually he was to throw five bridges across the river under the muzzles of our well-prepared guns.

They bombarded the town on Thursday morning, December 11. That afternoon we could hear the sounds of Jackson's corps repulsing an attack across the river downstream from Fredericksburg. It was icy cold that night up on Marye's Heights, which was where they positioned us, around and behind a large brick house, high up enough to give us a grand view of the forthcoming show, a good spot for that, only we would have preferred to have been back in our snug cabin a mile to the rear rather than shivering in the cold December air.

Below us the Yanks had crossed the river, driven out our sharpshooters, seized the town under our noses and were busy completing pontoon bridges. I suppose Lee could have advanced us down the hill to retake the town, but then we would have been exposed to a plunging fire from their artillery on the low line of hills that hugged the northern bank. No, Marse Robert was playing a waiting game. He knew what he was doing, it turned out. The morning of December 13 they roused us early. A heavy fog obscured our view. Being the sergeant, I had to spring up first and jostle my squad to life. They awoke, cursed at me through chattering teeth, and stumbled off for their morning pisses. Then it was cold rations as there was an order out against campfires. However, I did manage to wheedle a large pot of hot coffee from the army cook who had established an officer's mess in the kitchen of the Marye mansion.

We were eager to see what all the noise had been about down in the town the night before: wheels rattling, horses neighing, occasional shouts and so on. But our view was blocked by the fog that covered the town and the river. We loaded our muskets and swapped percussion caps and cartridges about so our supply was evenly distributed. Then we waited.

"I don't like this," said Noah Rhine.

"Don't like what?"

"Remember last March at New Bern we were sitting around just like this in that brickyard, waiting to receive an attack? It was foggy then, too. And the Yanks were also commanded by Burnside that time."

I lowered my voice. "Oh, come on, Noah. Things aren't the same at all."

"You don't think so? Why not?"

"First off, we are commanded by Colonel Rankin and not by Elmer J. Fincastle. Next we aren't green recruits any more. We have seen the elephant, not just our regiment but the entire Confederate Army. And, finally, we are led by R. E. Lee and not General Branch."

"I reckon you're right."

The others overheard our conversation and joined in. "Preacher Sam" Elkins as usual tried to cast a damp blanket on the proceedings.

"You are putting your faith in yourselves and in leaders who may be great but who nonetheless are only mortal men like the rest of us."

"You call yourself a man?" Harry McGee interrupted.

Sam ignored him. "We should not be sitting about here talking of vain things. We should be on our knees asking the blessings of God, seeking his divine protection."

"Oh, horseshit," says Harry. "Look at John Bradway. He went to church as regular as a preacher. Never touched a drop of liquor. Swore less than anybody I know except for you and that didn't stop him from getting killed at New Bern. Where was God's protection that day?"

"God is not compelled to grant our petitions. But if we do not ask, we will not receive. His ways are not easy for mere man to divine."

"They sure aren't. I say if a bullet has your name on it, nothing you can do will make any difference. What do you say, Jim?"

This religious, or, on Harry's part, irreligious, talk made me uncomfortable. "I say you should keep your musket clean and your cartridge box dry and full. I say you should always keep water in your canteen and some hardtack in your pocket. You should remember to keep your head down and when you fire, aim low. I think you will find God tends to favor soldiers who do these things."

"Aw, go on, Jim. Do you think it makes any difference if a bullet has your name on it?" Harry persisted.

"I know somebody whose name is on thousands of bullets and it hasn't killed him as far as I have learned."

"Who?"

"Captain Minié, the Frenchman who invented these conical bullets."

At that the boys all broke out laughing, all except for Sam Elkins.

"Now you are mocking God," he said.

"Shut up! You trot God out like he is your watchdog. Right now, down in that fog there are thousands of Yankees mumbling prayers for their safety and success and for our ruination. And I say well they might do so if we stop this silly gabbling and keep ourselves at the ready."

The entire Confederate Army was at the ready. Our regiment lay in reserve. Below us, at the base of the hill, there ran a sunken road, roughly parallel to the river. This road had a stone wall facing the river, providing a ready-made breastwork for Cobb's division. Then, farther up the hill, around and above us, there were dozens of cannons, many of them concealed behind cut cedar bushes and pine tree branches. The Yankees in the town could not have known how strongly held our positions were. Our artillery commanded the level stretch between the town and the sunken road, ideally situated to fire over the heads of our infantry. We could fire over the heads of Cobb's men as well, but that stone wall at the base of the hill would be the Yankees' undoing.

The fog persisted until nearly ten o'clock and then the sun began to break through. Very quickly the mists dissipated. It looked almost as if the curtain had been drawn back from a vast theater to reveal a military pageant.

What a spectacle! The Yanks had three pontoon bridges over the Rappahannock and their light artillery and wagons thronged across. Throughout the streets of the town, masses of men, many in bright blue overcoats, moved in our general direction. Thousands of Yanks were already grouped up in brigades on the southern edge of the town, not yet in good musket range, poised like so many juggernauts ready to roll upon us. They looked so powerful and numerous and self-confident.

To keep up my own confidence I glanced down at that sunken road jammed with our men in gray and butternut, then back at our cannon and their quietly moving gunners. We were ready for them. Sam Elkins' head was bowed in prayer; Harry McGee nestled his Enfield in one arm while running the fingertips of his other hand over the barrel. Noah Rhine fidgeted and gnawed his lips. Only Jimmy Golightly showed no emotion, his brown face like a mask.

I looked into the sky. There high above Stafford Heights across the Rappahannock rode the little observation balloon. I wondered if the man in the basket could see us. Even if his long glass could pick up the sight of our men in the sunken road, it was too late to get word to the ground and across the river to the various commands. Anyway, no one on our side was wasting any ammunition on that balloon this morning. There were more important and less elusive targets almost under our noses, tens of thousands of them ready to move against us.

29

It was nearly 11 A.M. when the Federals stepped out for their advance toward us. First three brigades, nearly ten thousand men, moved forward in neat parade-ground formation, with regimental colors flying and bayonets catching the sun. Around and behind us, a string of hoarse commands flew among our concealed batteries. Then suddenly our guns began blasting away, slowly at first but soon so furiously we put our hands over our ears.

"Wham, wham, wham," they spoke, the sound followed by their shells bursting on the slopes behind the advancing brigades. Our artillery fire slackened a bit while the gunners adjusted their pieces and then the noise crescendoed again and this time the shells began falling in front of and in the midst of the blue mass. The shells threw up billows of white smoke so thick you could hardly see the Yanks. They continued their advance, like a giant machine, until they encountered a fresh gantlet of adjusted shellfire. Now, back on the ground over which they had passed, we could see twisted human shapes strewn about. Again our guns found the new range. As the three brigades moved through the shell bursts they lost their cohesion, became an armed horde, no longer marching in step, their ranks disarrayed.

Some Yanks—those lightly wounded or the cowardly—were skulking back toward the shelter of the houses on the outskirts of the town. Some of the braver or more foolish broke into a trot, either from an anxiety to get through the cannon ordeal quickly or in a fury to put their bayonets into the bellies of our gunners.

Our guns tore at them again and again. By the time they had reached easy musket range of the sunken road with its gray division concealed behind the sheltering wall, the three brigades had merged together into a formless, maddened mass shouting futile hurrahs.

The boys in my squad let out an answering Rebel yell but I shushed them. "Son of a bitch, Jim," Noah Rhine yelled over the noise of the guns. "It's like being on the other side of Malvern Hill. At this rate we'll never get a shot at them."

Below us, Cobb's men thronged up to the stone wall, so many of them they couldn't all get places on the firing line. Still the blue infantry came, passing over a slight dip in the otherwise even ground, and then our own infantry raised their heads above the wall, leveled their muskets and, up the hill, we heard the noise of some two thousand muskets firing as one.

It was as if a hurricane suddenly swept over the space in front of the wall. The Yanks fell in droves. Some few stopped in their tracks and tried to return the fire, but a second volley struck down even more of them. The survivors began to trot back toward the town. Our artillerymen raised their sights and harassed them with fresh fire on their retreat.

"We're getting them coming and going," Harry McGee shouted. "Hot damn, look at the bastards run."

All along the hill, Rebel yells rang out, together with handclapping and shouts of laughter. The men down in the sunken road gave a mighty cheer of their own and some danced about waving their arms.

But this was only the first of the Yankees' assaults. Even as the first three brigades were falling back in disorder, another three —slightly to the east of them—began advancing. Our artillery turned its attention to them and it became the same story all over again.

By now the hillside and the stretch of frozen ground in front of the sunken road lay under a man-made fog of gunpowder smoke. Other Federal brigades came forward, together with survivors of the earlier attacks, only to be repulsed in the same fashion. On and on the killing proceeded until past noon. At times the smoke cleared enough so that we could see the growing litter of dead, dying and wounded Federals strewn along the route of their advances and retreats.

The ground in front of the stone wall was not as level as it had at first appeared. A hundred or so yards away there was just enough of a dip so that by lying flat a man could keep out of view. Many a Yank, unhurt in all except his morale, flattened himself on the frozen earth there to wait out the storm of bullets. They had a very long wait indeed.

Near to 1 P.M., during a lull, couriers came up the hill to say that some of Cobb's men were running low on ammunition.

They detailed our regiment and another to go down and spell some of the boys who had done such splendid work in the road. There were so many tired but excited Rebs we had trouble finding places for all of us up on the firing line. Officers actually had to drive some of them from their spots.

I put Jimmy Golightly, Harry McGee and myself up to the wall and arranged the rest of my squad behind us with their muskets all loaded.

"Now, boys," I said. "You keep loading the muskets and pass them up to us so we don't have to stop to load."

We didn't have to wait long. Here came a fresh lot of Yanks and they began firing well back so that we were forced to keep our heads down. Their bullets sang over our heads or splattered the face of the wall, sending up showers of stone fragments. A fellow just down the line poked his head up to see and fell back with half his skull torn off. After that I was glad to remain crouching until the order rang out, "Commence firing!"

Jimmy, Harry and I raised our heads and slid our muskets over the wall. It was like looking at a blue sea rolling upon us, topped by a line of white faces bobbing along like foam on a long wave. I aimed at their knees, pulled the trigger, shoved the musket back as I ducked my head, and reached back for a fresh weapon. Ed Engerer handed me his, I fired it, and so on. In that way we kept a steady hail of lead pouring into those poor Yanks until they had stopped coming and the order passed to cease firing.

By this time I was soaked with sweat. My right shoulder ached from the impact of the muskets' butts. It was good to sit with my back against that wall and rest.

Noah Rhine gave me a drink from his canteen. "Say, Jim. Let some of the others have a chance on the firing line. Don't keep all the fun for yourself."

"You're welcome to it, Noah. That's hard work."

In all, I believe the Yankees made six separate, major attacks on our positions plus other smaller ones. And we took a growing dribble of musket fire from unwounded Yanks who were pinned down and didn't dare rise. Some of the braver of these fellows actually pushed the bodies of their dead comrades up in front of them as breastworks and attempted to pick us off. Others, back on the edge of the town, barricaded themselves in houses and maintained a harassing fire at long range. They might as well have saved their ammunition.

By 4 P.M. it was all over but for the suffering. With no more mass attacks to repulse we began sharpshooting, going after anything that moved. Kept it up until nightfall. God knows how many already wounded Yanks were killed in that way, shot as they tried to sit up or crawl away.

Or how many died that night from the bitter cold out there on that blood-soaked plain between us and the town. The night was made hideous by the groans and the pleas for help from the wounded Yanks. Pitiful sounds of young boys crying out for their mothers and husbands moaning the names of their wives. How awful is war after the shooting stops.

Some of the South Carolinians in the sunken road couldn't bear those cries. They collected canteens from their comrades and, without asking permission from their officers, climbed the stone wall and went out into the night, tripping over bodies, to give water and comfort to the wounded enemy. I have my share of regrets as I near the end of my life, and one of them is that I and my squad did not follow the lead of those merciful Sandlappers. For that I hope God will forgive me when I come to him for judgment. For that and much, much more. No, I and my squad rolled up in our blankets and stopped up our ears, good Christian boys that we were.

All the next day we stood to our guns, waiting to receive a fresh Federal attack. But the enemy had enough. Old Burnside lost over twelve thousand men there at Fredericksburg, while Lee took only five thousand casualties. The great majority of those Yanks fell in front of Marye's Heights. The 10th North Carolina took special pleasure in this great Confederate victory. We paid Burnside back for New Bern in particular; we paid the

Federals in general back for what their artillery did to us at Malvern Hill.

I suppose that we might have been able to charge down into the town and capture Burnside's army the next day. But during the night all those unwounded Yanks stopped playing dead and slipped back to the town and there helped fortify the place. An attack would have cost us a high price. At any rate, on Monday, December 15, the Federals drew back across their pontoon bridges, leaving a ruined Fredericksburg in our hands together with the frozen bodies of thousands of their dead, from whom, incidentally, we resupplied ourselves with shoes, overcoats and blankets.

In recent years, I have visited Fredericksburg several times. I like to climb up to the cemetery on Marye's Heights and look out over the landscape, blotting out in my mind's eye the encroaching new houses and buildings, looking back to that glorious December day when I watched those smart blue legions advancing toward us and then seeing them ripped to shreds by our shells and Minié balls. I always make that trip in the daylight, however. I fear that if I went there at night I might still hear the dreadful cries of the Federal wounded and remember how I did not carry water to them. Oh, hell, what is the good of regrets?

30

Until the winter of 1862–63, I had seen very little snow. Down in our part of North Carolina it generally snowed only once or twice a year, light snowfalls at that, which soon melted. We got more of it up in Virginia and it made quite an impression on the fellows from Georgia and Mississippi, many of whom had never seen snow. They dashed about like idiots with their mouths open to catch the flakes on their tongues, they rolled about in the snow like puppies and rubbed their faces in it.

It snowed twice while we were at Fredericksburg, several inches on one occasion. And following that heavy snowfall, our company became hotly engaged in the "Second Battle of Fredericksburg," which came about in this manner:

I was lying on my bunk on a Saturday afternoon, fighting down the impulse to write one of those "discreet" notes Jane Ferro's brother had offered to forward to her, when Bob Perry comes running in to shout, "Hey, come see the fun! Ed Engerer and Harry McGee are having a snowball fight with some Georgia crackers."

I put on my short jacket and walked out into the ankle-deep snow. There were our two fellows stoutly exchanging snowballs with the Georgians from the other end of the camp and generally getting the worst of it. They were beginning to tire, it was plain to see. Bob Perry, who always liked a good scrap, squatted down, made himself three snowballs and trotted up to help Ed and Harry repulse a sortie by the Georgians. By now other fellows had come out of their huts to see what all the shouting and laughing was about.

I resisted as long as I could and then bent down to arm myself with several well-packed snowballs; the Wiley twins and Jimmy Golightly did the same, and in a moment we moved up and put the Georgians to flight behind a line of huts beyond the parade ground.

We stood about in the snow laughing and congratulating ourselves on our easy victory until the Georgians, resupplied with armloads of fresh snowballs and reinforced by a dozen of their compatriots, came charging around the other end of the line of huts. They chased us clear across the parade ground. I shouted for help to a group of Oldham County lads I recognized, from another regiment. They came charging in, pelting the Georgians at close range until they fell back for reinforcements.

Well, the thing grew, I might say "snowballed," until soon there were several hundred men on each side, pitting mostly Tar Heels and Virginians against Georgians and other boys from the Deep South.

At times the air was filled with snowballs, hurtling back and forth. We'd pelt the other side at long range, and then a group of messmates, each with a reserve of three or four snowballs, would mount a charge, running toward the other line until almost upon it and then hurling their missiles at point-blank, and withdrawing in a cloud of counterfire.

My lungs soon ached and my hands got so cold I had to rub them briskly to keep the blood circulating. As I retired behind our firing line to restore myself, my squad gathered around me, all laughing like crazy. An inspiration hit me.

"Say, we're fighting like a bunch of greenhorns, charging in head on. Let's get some more fellows, pack up a good supply of snowballs and roll up their flank."

They would have followed me anywhere. A bunch of other fellows from our company, parts of other squads coming in from guard duty, were standing about watching the fray. I ran over and outlined my plan. Within minutes, we had recruited them plus others from nearby huts. I lined up my fresh force and marched them via a roundabout route to a position on the other side of the parade ground, right on the flank of the Deep Southerners but screened from their view by the camp reviewing stand.

"Pack up four or five snowballs at least," I commanded. "And don't start throwing until you are right on top of them. Everybody ready?"

I gave them a minute and then lined them up into two columns. "Over there, you hit their flank and, you boys over here, take them in their rear. Now, charge!"

With that we burst out onto the parade ground, giving a mighty Rebel yell as we flung ourselves upon the enemy. Their flank was thrown into confusion. The snow under their feet had been tramped down, so it was hard to scrape up ammunition, whereas we had brought our own supply. Most of them gave way, backing up with hands raised to shield their faces. Those who stooped to make snowballs got hit in the back of the neck. Under assault from flank and rear, that end of the "enemy" line collapsed.

Our comrades along the front saw what was happening and they mounted their own charge. Within minutes, the boys from Georgia and Alabama were backing up. In some cases, fists replaced snowballs. Noses got bloodied and uniforms ripped. It became one glorious melee.

It went on until Colonel Rankin himself, accompanied by William Ferro and Captain Cadieu, came riding up. They saw the fun was getting out of hand and rode among us, shouting for us to "desist" and return to our cabins. Tom Shelton and Foster Liddle, our two lieutenants, ran out in front to prize Harry McGee's fingers from the throat of a beefy Georgian. Fifteen minutes later, we were all back in our hut, exhausted, some with blackened eyes and loosened teeth, but happy as a litter of bird dog pups.

"Damned, Jim, that was some idea, to make that flank attack. You should have been a general and not a sergeant," Bob Perry said.

Harry McGee agreed and said that our victory called for a celebration.

"We don't have anything to celebrate with," said Ed Engerer.

"Who don't?" With that, Harry goes scrabbling about around our crude fireplace. He pulled out a loose stone at the bottom and there, in a hole in the earth, was nestled a clay jug which we soon discovered contained some passable, if rather raw, corn liquor. At any rate it was strong.

Sam Elkins protested, but we banished him from the hut to go to the chapel and say his prayers. Unfortunately there was not enough liquor to get seven men very drunk, but we pretended to be higher than we really were. Then we got to wrestling about and Bob Perry fell in the fire. We got him out before he was burned, but in the general turmoil we jarred the chimney and loose mud and clay collapsed, clogging up the flue. Smoke soon filled the room and we had to wrap up and go outside to escape suffocation. We forced ourselves on some friends in a larger hut next door. At first they tried, without success, to make us feel unwelcome. Soon our high spirits infected them. We began laughing and telling stories about this Oldham County character and that, people known to us all. Then it turned out one of them had a banjo; one of the Wiley twins had a jew's-harp. While they were messing around trying to coordinate a tune between them, a couple of our boys went back to make sure our hut was not on fire. Apparently they had run their arms up the chimney to unclog things and then, just for a laugh, wiped their hands on their faces. That did it. "A minstrel show. Let's put on a nigger minstrel."

It took us about ten minutes to organize ourselves, to black up our faces and sort out our parts. Somebody improvised a drum and a couple of others pulled out pocket combs and writing paper for kazoos. The show began.

We sang, we told jokes, Harry McGee, Noah Rhine and I recited poetry and speeches we had learned at the academy in a mock Negro dialect. "Romeo, Romeo, wheahfo is you at?" The fun went on until midnight.

By the time we returned to our hut, the room was icy cold and stank of smoke, but we piled on the captured Yankee overcoats and blankets and got through the night fairly well, courtesy of the U.S. quartermaster, who incidentally did a grand job throughout the war of supplying both sides quite adequately. God bless him.

The next day was a Sunday. "Preacher Sam" Elkins had been talking up a big revival meeting set for that afternoon, but we hadn't paid any attention to him. It would be the next day before we could draw materials with which to repair our chimney and get the hut back into habitable condition. There wasn't much else to do, so some of the boys suggested that we accompany Sam to the revival.

Sam perked up at that. "It will do you all good," he said. "After the way you were carousing last night, drinking and blaspheming, you need to have your souls cleansed. Bill Utley died mocking God at Sharpsburg. If he could speak to you from hell right now, he would advise you to get yourselves right with the Almighty so that when the Yankee bullet finds its mark you will be in a state of grace."

Harry McGee looked as if he was ready to hit Sam. Ed Engerer intervened.

"Will it be warm at the revival?"

"Sure. We have built a large chapel with pine slab sides."

"Then I'm for the revival," says Ed. The others followed him and Sam across the camp to the chapel. Not wishing to be left alone, I tagged along.

The chapel looked more like a crude stable with the south side open. Sam and his fellow "saved" Christians had constructed a platform of rough lumber across the other end. We got there early enough to find an entire row and seated ourselves on the split-log "pews." Soon the entire church was filled.

The preacher was a squatty fat civilian who looked like a toad, but he had a voice like a bass horn and a pair of lungs to suit. Could that man preach! He warmed us up with a half-dozen or so old-time hymns such as "Amazing Grace" and "Just as I am." Then he stepped up to the pulpit, slapped his hands together and shouted "Hallelujah!" He was off and running.

He talked about the sweetness of home and how our dear families were there even now praying for each and every one of us personally. Then he went on to speak of the righteousness of the Confederate cause and how God would favor that cause if . . . if we would keep the faith of the Almighty and live up to the expectations of our families. "Amen, hallelujah!" he shouted. Sam Elkins echoed the shout and others took it up.

Then the preacher began to talk about the uncertainties of life in a great war. He told about the deaths he had witnessed in the hospitals around Richmond after the Seven Days' Battles.

That man could paint a deathbed scene with words, could take you right there and make you hear the last words of the victims.

Then he took off after sin and what a risk we all ran when we went into battle without God's grace as our shields.

"Oh, I know you have all seen terrible sights. You have seen men blown to pieces before your eyes. You have heard the screams of the dying out there on the battlefield. But that is nothing, my dear friends, compared to the horrors of lost souls in hell, the screams of agony from men subjected to eternal torment because they were not right with God when that shell exploded or that bullet struck its mark."

"Amen!" a great groan went up from the front row of the tabernacle.

"I'm telling it to you straight," the preacher went on. "The danger you face for your families and nation on the battlefield, the danger to your bodies, that is nothing. It's the danger of eternal damnation I'm here to warn you about. You get right with God and then you'll not need to fear anything the Yankees can do to you. What will it matter then if you die? God will be waiting to take you to his bosom, to bring you to eternal peace."

"Hallelujah!"

The preacher waited for a long time before finding his voice again. He stood there wiping that wide face with a red handkerchief. Sweating like a horse he was, and sizing up his audience with what seemed to me considerable satisfaction.

Now I had sat through more revivals than I could count and had heard some accomplished pulpit-thumpers in my nineteen years. But none of them could compare with this Georgia Baptist, sent to us by some Gospel Association or other.

"And just think of your old mama and daddy, yes, and grandparents, too. Think how they will feel if they learn the awful news that you have been struck down by a Yankee bullet. They will weep and they will mourn, but then what if through their tear-dimmed eyes they read on to see the words, 'You will be glad to know that your son died in a state of grace. He was saved at a great revival near Fredericksburg, Virginia, with hundreds of his brave comrades. He went to face God in a state of grace. He had accepted salvation.' "

His voice dropped and became soft. "Then those tears of sorrow will become tears of joy. For your loved ones will know that you cheated death. You will win a victory greater than any you'll ever win over the Yankees."

By now grown men all around the packed tabernacle were crying and grinding their teeth. And when the preacher made the inevitable altar call, they trooped up by the scores, plumping to their knees. Naturally Sam Elkins was one of the first up there, dragging with him poor oxlike Brady Alexander. The other boys, some of whom were moved deeply, cut their eyes over to see what I would do. They would have followed me to the altar, all except Harry McGee, I expect, but my heart was too hard to be touched by a Baptist preacher. If going to the altar would have brought me the love of Jane Ferro, I would have crawled up there. For it was not the love of God that interested me. I had been hearing about that since babyhood.

So, with the preacher still exhorting the hold-outs, the almost-persuadeds, to come forward while there was still time, I stalked out the open end of the tabernacle, followed by my squad, and went back to our hut.

31

As I said earlier, I regret that I and my boys were not among those Confederates compassionate enough to venture out the night after Burnside's attack and assist the poor mangled Federals freezing in the cold. We did, however, do a deed of mercy a week after the battle.

The people of Fredericksburg received ample notice of the Federal attack, so that by the time of the crushing bombardment of December 11, nearly all of them had packed up what they could carry in wagons and on mules and had moved south, some to the plantations of friends and others all the way to Richmond to further swell the population of that already overcrowded city.

What the Yankees did to the homes of these refugees during the brief Federal occupation of the town was shameful. They kicked in doors and smashed out windows. They stripped mattresses off beds and strewed their feathers or straw stuffings about the houses and yards. They turned fine homes upside down, looking for hidden silver. It was sickening to see the way they despoiled what had been a comfortable, pleasant river town.

My squad and I were standing guard duty in the town when the first few families came straggling back to their homes. I remember how a light wagon, drawn by a sickly old mule, rattled up to a two-story brick house. An equally sickly-looking old man with long white mustaches sat on the wagon seat, holding the reins. Beside him rode a young woman, faded before her time, holding a baby. An old woman with white hair and fierce dark eyes sat in a rocking chair in the back of the wagon, holding an older child. They obviously were people of quality, so they didn't shout or carry on, but you could read the dismay they felt from their expressions.

"Oh, my dear soul, see what they have done," the old man exclaimed.

"The ruthless, vile Northern trash," the old woman replied.

The younger woman put her hand over her face and began weeping.

Their door had been forced open and now hung on one hinge. Someone had thrown an upholstered chair half through an upstairs window. Feathers and scraps of bed linen littered the yard, together with broken bits of plates and crockery.

"No good crying," the old woman said. "Let's roll up our sleeves and start putting things back in order."

The old man seemed confused. "Rafe and Lisa will take care of that, Mother. I'll just call them."

The old woman's voice softened. "Daddy, you keep forgetting. Rafe and Lisa ran off, remember? We're going to have to do for ourselves."

"Oh, now, mother," he said as he got down from the wagon seat. "Rafe and Lisa wouldn't run off for good. They were just frightened of the Yankees. They'll come back. They're good darkies. You'll see."

He walked back to help the old woman from the wagon. "Daddy, you are deceiving yourself. They took clothes and food and my best silver spoons. They planned their departure carefully. We'll never see them again."

He started to protest, but she held up her hand. "Enough, enough. Help Mary Eleanor and the baby in the house and let's get a fire going."

At this, I stepped up smartly and introduced myself. The old woman gave me a long, hard stare before speaking.

"Young man, you can see what the enemy vandals have done to our home. Our two slaves, who have been with us for ten years, have deserted us, us who treated them as if they were our own children. We are ruined."

"Well, ma'am, if it's any comfort to you, the Yankees paid a high price for forcing their way into your fair city. They suffered a cruel defeat."

"That is very small comfort to us," she replied coldly.

I exchanged glances with my boys and they nodded. To a man, we stacked our muskets in the yard and spent the next two hours helping that family straighten up their house. We boarded up the broken windows and either patched or carried out the damaged furniture. We collected firewood and started blazes in the kitchen and front-room fireplaces. I even sent Sam

Elkins off to collect some captured U.S. blankets.

"God bless you, boys," the old man said when we were done.

The young woman shyly shook hands with each of my men. The old woman did the same, but when she came to me she put her arms around me and stood on tiptoe to kiss my cheek. Didn't say a word. I came near to crying right there in front of my men. Damned embarrassing.

Later, back at camp, Colonel Rankin arranged a charity drive for the people of Fredericksburg. He started it off with a hundred dollars. We were rarely paid in the Confederate Army. I think at that time we were getting eleven dollars a month and we had just received our first pay since spring; of course the money was worth less each time the paymaster caught up with us. Anyway, our regiment coughed up several thousand dollars for the relief of the people of Fredericksburg. Turned the money over to a local merchant and he went down to Richmond and bought flour, potatoes and beef, charging us a 10 percent commission, incidentally.

The sight of that once proud family returning to their wrecked home haunted me for days. It set me thinking about the futility of pride, all kinds of pride, including my own which prevented me from writing to Jane Ferro via her brother. I kept hoping that she would disobey her father and post a letter to me through a friend or carry it herself to Meadsboro, but no, at each mail call I was disappointed.

At last, I could bear it no longer. It was New Year's Eve and, not feeling well, I remained in our hut by the fire while the rest of the squad went carousing through the camp. It was a short, formal letter expressing my reluctance to cause any tension between her and her father, assuring her that I held her and her family in the greatest esteem and that I did hope she did not think me presumptuous in trying to resume our correspondence. I rewrote that letter three times trying to set just the right tone, with an aim to keeping the door open between us, being careful not to press myself too hard, while at the same time avoiding the impression that I was in any way offended by the necessity of sending my note through her brother.

Tired, but satisfied with my effort, I went to sleep with the sounds of shouting and muskets firing to bring in the new year.

1863

That letter never got mailed. I carried it down to our company mail call, hoping against hope there might be a message from her, in effect giving her one last chance to write directly before I turned over my ever so discreet note to her brother.

The entire company, officers and all, stood about while the mail was distributed. Our company clerk was a methodical chap and he had arranged the letters by alphabetical order. Down the line he went.

"Mundy," he shouted, handing a letter to Tom Shelton to pass back to me. My heart pounding away, I took the letter and saw it was only my father writing to me. I folded it and shoved it in my pocket as the clerk continued down the alphabet to "Roberts" and then, "Shelton."

An ugly premonition seized me. I looked over Tom Shelton's shoulder as he took his letter. There was no mistaking that graceful handwriting, learned from some fussy teacher at that girls' finishing school in Charleston.

Never had I felt so defeated and resentful. Instead of taking the letter I had so laboriously composed the night before to William Ferro, I pulled it from my pocket and tore it in two. I strode back to our hut and put it in the fire.

Seething so that my hand shook, I wrote the following or something like it:

Dear Miss Ferro:

Your brother has informed me that your father wishes us to correspond no more. I gather that he feels that I, being from a humble family, owning no slaves and very little land, am not quite good enough to write and receive letters to and from his daughter.

Your brother, for whom I have a great admiration, kindly offered me the assistance of posting my letters with his so as to escape your father's notice. I have declined to resort to this subterfuge until now, thinking it an unworthy thing to do. Your father might be surprised that "poor white trash" have principles the same as he but we do, and pride as well.

I naturally do not know what view you take of your father's attitude, having received no letter from you in some time. From your silence, I can only deduce that you respect your father's wishes and, for all I know, share his opinion of my worth. Perhaps you found it amusing to carry on a brief, teasing correspondence with a person of a lower social rank than your own.

At any rate, I am glad that you do not entirely lack for "pen friends" in the Confederate Army and only hope that Lieutenant Shelton, being of a more acceptable social class both to your father and yourself, can keep you posted as to the activities of this unit. It is good that you have someone with whom you feel free to write to openly.

I shall not further presume by writing to you again. But I do wish to thank you for troubling yourself to write to me, giving me news of your world which, though co-existing with mine side by side, yet follows a different orbit.

Do keep yourself in good health.

Your obedient servant,
James Mundy, Sgt. Co. H. 10th N.C.

With that, I sealed the letter and sought out Major Ferro, who was writing a report in the regimental office, a large tent with pine slabs nailed up outside as a wall. He smiled when I came in.

"Good day, James. I am in the midst of drafting our regimental report on the battle."

"I hope I am not troubling you," I said, not returning his smile.

"No, I am tired and welcome the break. How have you been?"

Ignoring his question, I said, "You kindly offered some time ago to post a letter to your sister."

"Yes, of course, James."

"Then please, would you send this with your next mail home?"

"Certainly," and, still smiling, "That was quite a snowball battle you and your boys had the other day."

"Yes. Here."

"What's that for?"

"For the postage."

"Oh, James, that's not necessary."

I laid the fifty-cent Confederate note on his camp table. "I don't want to impose." Without waiting for a reply, I walked out of his office and back to my own kind of people, the ill-educated, dirt-poor but proud white yeoman who suffered the brunt of the War for Southern Independence, or whatever the hell it was.

32

During the months since I had met Jane Ferro and begun corresponding with her, a change had come over me. I had stopped much of my vulgar talk and no longer treated people in such a cheeky way. In my fantasy I was anticipating the days when I would be a prominent member of the gentry with a daughter of an aristocratic family at my side. Jane Ferro was always on my mind in that period, thoughts of her crowding out rude talk and rough manners. In that way she had been an elevating influence on me; some of my friends had noticed a change for the better in me, but they laid it to the responsibility of the high office of sergeant maturing and civilizing me.

Well, all that stopped when I fired off that hurt, angry letter to Jane Ferro. I picked a quarrel with Will Parker, a corporal from another squad, over a trifling matter of guard duties. We came to blows, I striking the first one. Our friends separated us before we could do much damage but Tom Shelton put us on report so that Captain Cadieu was forced to take notice of something he might otherwise have ignored. He made poor Bill and me carry a six-foot log on our shoulders around the perimeter of the camp for one hour. It was humiliating. I was glad we didn't get worse punishment, such as being bound and gagged or made to sit on a saw horse all day on public view. I felt lucky to get off with helping Will carry that log, that plus a warning that I might lose my sergeant's stripe the next time I got involved in a fist fight.

I must admit that some ugly thoughts ran through my head during that one hour's punishment. Both armies had quite a few deserters during the war. Oh, nobody likes to talk about it to this day. In fact, back in North Carolina after the war somebody stole the ledger books containing the names of thousands of men reported absent from their commands without leave. Right here in Baltimore I have known fellows who let it slip in conversation that they were in the war but who got mighty vague when you pressed for details, especially as to how they ended their service. I have a private opinion that the West got a big boost in population from men of both the North and South who went out there rather than returning to their home communities after the war, doing so to escape the stigma of having deserted.

Anyway, my ugly thought was that I would slip off at night and cross the Rappahannock upstream and go over to the Yankees. The North was supposed to be a bustling country, full of industry and opportunity. No matter how the war turned out, I figured I couldn't amount to very much back home without money or family background or a university education. My experience with the Ferros had punctured that balloon. Up North I'd be under no handicap except for my Southern accent. I could get a good job, save my money, and—who knows?—maybe become a millionaire. Then someday I'd make certain that the Ferros learned of my great success. They would realize then the mistake they had made in regarding me as just a pushy country boy not good enough for their family circle.

This new daydream did not materialize. Two west Tennesseans tried to do just what I had thought of; a mounted provost patrol caught them trying to cross the Rappahannock. They confessed to desertion and were sentenced to death. An appeal to Robert E. Lee for mercy was turned down. They were to die as an example to the rest of us.

Our entire camp was required to witness the execution of those two hapless hillbillies. Several thousand of us were formed up into a huge U. The two deserters, pleading for mercy, were dragged out to the open end of the formation, blindfolded and tied to two posts. There, following a long roll of drums, they were shot dead.

I can't describe the shock of witnessing that execution. It was more horrible than seeing hundreds of men fall to artillery and musket fire at Malvern Hill and Sharpsburg. Nobody joked or sang in our camp that night. And nobody deserted for a while, either.

Toward the end of January my mind was somewhat relieved from its black thoughts by the news that we must load up our paraphernalia and move camp. We got the impression we simply would transfer to another camp nearby and therefore took all our precious belongings with us: extra blankets, pots and pans, dough boards, games, camp stools. We didn't like leaving our snug hut, but we assumed an equally comfortable place would soon be ours.

We were to be disillusioned. Amidst great groaning and complaining, we set off on the march with our backs breaking under the weight of our possessions. Fifteen miles later we stopped to camp overnight. There they notified us that Richmond was our destination and it was to be shank's mare all the way. Already we had littered the route south with the heavier and less desirable of our baggage items. There was a further stripping down at that camp.

Now, marching in the spring or fall can be pleasant for a healthy, eager young man, but damn hoofing it along in the summer heat or the winter cold. Sherman said war was hell, and he had a horse to ride. He would have said much worse if he had ever been a poor foot soldier in either army, covering fifteen or twenty miles a day with a piercing winter wind in his face.

33

At Richmond they put us up in some poorly constructed wooden barracks. There we made ourselves reasonably comfortable and awaited the pleasure of the Confederate Government. We heard all kinds of rumors about our detachment from Lee's army. They were going to send us out to Tennessee to reinforce Bragg, who had retreated after a terrific standoff battle at Murfreesboro. No, we were going to go to the relief or recapture of Norfolk, or was it Cumberland Gap, or maybe even New Bern? The rumors flew.

Meanwhile, there was sprawling, roistering Richmond at our disposal. Harry McGee, his case of clap but a painful memory, was surprised when I said yes to his perfunctory invitation to visit the fleshpots of the city one night.

"You mean you will come with me?"

"Why the hell not? You're only young once. Next time the opportunity comes around we could be dead. Let's go."

Go we did. Now I had very little money, not enough to finance a real night on the town, but Harry said not to worry. He had won over five hundred Confederate dollars playing poker back at Fredericksburg; the whole evening was to be on him.

It was a rainy Tuesday night, but even so there were throngs of soldiers and government clerks, teamsters and such in the streets and cafés. We stopped at a saloon for a couple of bracing shots of rye.

"Oysters. You got to have a dozen oysters to get you set up for the evening's work," says Harry.

"Oysters it will be."

We ate them on the half-shell, followed by hot corn muffins, ham and beans. Then we had another round of rye.

Some Texans were in the bar, well into their cups, and looking for a fight. They made several disparaging remarks about North Carolinians. One big raw-boned redhead was particularly obnoxious. I sat there planning the best way to sail into him for I was full of meanness and rye whisky, but Harry restrained me.

"Save that energy for something better than fighting Texans," he said.

It went against my grain, but Harry was paying the bills and therefore calling the tune. I walked right past that asshole Texan with my fists in my pockets until we got out into the cold January rain. The streetwalkers and pimps were out in force, but Harry waved them away.

"You aren't going back to the place where you got the clap, are you?" I asked.

"No, there is a high-class place I couldn't afford before. It's in back of a hotel with feather beds and all that, I hear."

And so it was. We walked into a stark kind of gaslit lobby with a registration desk. Sallow fellow on duty looked at us with a superior expression and says, "Sorry, gentlemen, but we have no rooms for the night. Full up."

"We're looking for two rooms with a nice girl in each one," said Harry, holding up a fifty-dollar Confederate note.

"Oh, you want the entertainment department? That is in the rear, through those doors, but it caters strictly to the officer trade."

"We are both noncommissioned officers, can't you see? I am a corporal and my friend here is a sergeant awaiting a commission as second lieutenant," Harry lied. "Of course, if you don't want my money, we can take our trade elsewhere."

The clerk hesitated. "Well, it would be entirely out of the question on a Friday or Saturday night, but as the weather is bad and it is only Tuesday we may be able to accommodate you just this once, until your friend's commission comes through. Let me just step back and speak to Madam Jones."

He was back in a moment. "She says if you come right in and are gone within the hour, it's all right. She is expecting a large private party later tonight."

Harry handed him his fifty and we stepped through the door and into a different world. Twelve or fifteen females sat around a huge fireplace, drinking coffee or stronger stuff. Big girls, little girls, blondes, brunettes, most of them white but a few with a touch of the tarbrush. Every eye was on us two Confederate enlisted men.

A great fat woman with dyed hair and cold eyes waddled over to us. "We don't normally take ordinary soldiers here, you know."

"My friend and I are extra-ordinary soldiers," Harry came right back at her.

"Well, just see that you behave yourselves. This is a high-class place."

I could see she liked our jaunty air. "Well, now you're here you can take your pick."

Harry already had his eye on a pretty little brunette with blue eyes. "Her." He pointed at the girl.

"How about you, string bean?" the madam said to me.

I looked into the circle of faces, stupid, bored, without personality, most of them, until I came to that of a very young mixed blood. She was mostly white with a narrow nose and a golden skin, frizzly black hair and dark liquid eyes. She looked at me in a way that was both innocent and bold.

"How about her?"

Harry sniggered. "Oh, going after some dark meat?"

The madam drew herself up, offended. "Maria is our newest girl. We are pleased to have her here. Now off you go, girls. Take rooms eleven and twelve. But only one hour. Time is money. Off you go."

Holding a candle, the girl led me back to a room that measured no more than ten by twelve feet, most of that space being taken up by a high bed topped by a thick feather mattress. Conflicting odors of perfume permeated the room.

The girl placed the candle on a narrow bureau and turned to face me.

"What's your name?" I asked her.

"Maria. Didn't you hear the madam? What's yours?"

"James."

"Where are you from, James?"

"North Carolina."

She couldn't have been more than seventeen, but she was taking the lead. "You ever had a woman before?"

"Yes. One, but I never been in a place like this."

She took my hand. "Don't be nervous. We don't get many boys like you in here. My, you are tall."

She was trying to be brassy, but there was still an elemental shyness about her. I judged her to be a quadroon. We stood for a moment like a couple of guilty children about to play house.

"You're trembling, James. It's cold in here. Let's get in bed and I will warm you up."

Now I have hesitated over relating this episode at all. Could just as well have skipped it, but my wife is dead and it warms my blood to this day as I write. Even so, I am not going to tell everything that went on in that little room at the back of a fancy whorehouse in Richmond, Virginia. Just let me say that Elvira Fincastle had taught me well. Only, she could not compare with this Maria. In bed Maria's shyness disappeared. Her body was lithe and strong where Elvira's had been soft and slow. She had rounded buttocks and neat little breasts.

I reckon she was used to clumsy boy lieutenants and furtive, guilty older married officers for when we were done she said, "James, you know how to do it. You are good."

We lay there with our arms around each other. I thought of Jane Ferro with spite in my heart. What did I want with an artificially brought-up girl like her when the world was full of eager, available women like Elvira Fincastle and this Maria?

We were just starting to have a second go at it when the madam shouted down the hall. "Time's up, Maria. Get that sergeant out of there. The general is here with a bunch of other officers. We need every girl."

"Maria, do I have to go?"

"Afraid so, James. That woman will send me back to the laundry if I make her mad."

"The laundry?"

"Yes, my mama washed clothes for a living and I helped her. She did sheets and towels for Madam Jones. Mama died last fall. I couldn't carry on the business, so Madam brought me here as a maid. Then she saw how some of the gentlemen took a shine to me and she put me on as a regular girl. Pays me the same as the white girls."

"Do you live here with them?"

"No, my mama was free. We own a little house. I live there with my three younger brothers and sisters. My daddy was white. He ran off to the West before the war."

By now we were dressing. As I fumbled with my buttons, I said, "Look, Maria, they won't let me come back here since I'm not an officer. Couldn't I come to see you at your house?"

"We're not supposed to get involved with gentlemen outside of this place."

"I'm not a gentleman."

She laughed. "Besides, I got my little brothers and sisters to think about."

"Couldn't I at least pay you a social visit?"

"You are a pistol ball, James. All right. I don't work Wednesday nights. You come after nine o'clock. I'll have the children in bed by then. You can stay awhile, I reckon."

I gave her a hug and she responded with a lingering kiss, then told me how to find her house.

"Want to know what I'm going to do to you tomorrow night, white boy?"

My flesh tingled. "No, what?"

She held her nose. "Give you a good bath and wash your clothes."

We walked down the hall, arm in arm and laughing. I hadn't felt so good in weeks. In the large room a group of middle-aged Confederate officers were standing about chaffing with the other girls. Among them was none other than Colonel Elmer J. Fincastle, himself. I slunk past him, my slouch hat pulled low.

Harry McGee was waiting in the hotel lobby. "How was it, Jim?"

"Pretty good."

"Pretty good?"

"All right, damned good."

I slept well that night but woke up the next morning feeling dirty and full of remorse. I had been in bed with a half-breed, a prostitute. What would my father or mother say? What would be the reaction of Jane Ferro? And her father, would not this confirm his opinion of my unworthiness?

By noon my juices were flowing again and I began to think of Maria's lithe, golden body. The next thing I was using all my powers of persuasion to wheedle an overnight pass from the company clerk. It wasn't easy.

"Jim, we aren't supposed to issue overnight passes. Best I could do would be until midnight and it will have to be signed by Lieutenant Shelton."

My hopes fell. "Let's compromise. Make out the pass for midnight, but don't give it to Tom Shelton to sign. Take it to Captain Cadieu."

"That's not the ordinary procedure. What's so important about tonight, anyway?"

"I want to attend a revival meeting."

I kept my face straight as he swallowed this story. "All right, I'll give it a try."

Harry McGee was hurt that I was going out without him and that I wouldn't say where I was going. That meant that I had to dip into my own little store of money to buy some sweet cakes and cider to take to Maria.

I found her little house, a one-story brick cottage, one of a row of similar buildings, largely inhabited by free Negroes and mulattoes or white renegades living with them. She had a candle in the front window and was sitting in a tiny living room waiting for me. I was surprised to see that she wore a simple, freshly ironed frock. She looked beautiful.

"I was afraid you wouldn't come after all," she said as she kissed me.

"The whole Confederate cavalry couldn't have kept me away. Here."

"Why, you brought me something. How nice."

She led me down a narrow hall past two closed bedroom doors and into a little kitchen with a brick floor. There we sat in front of a fire and ate the cakes and drank the cider.

Later I put my arms around her and kissed her. She turned her head.

"You forget what I said I was going to do to you?"

"Give me a bath?"

"Come this way."

She led me out the back door, across a courtyard and into a low brick building against the back alley. It was a warm, well-equipped laundry. She had an enormous iron tub half-filled with lukewarm water. Next thing I knew she had poured in more hot water, taken off my uniform and put it in another tub, and I was sitting up to my neck in warm water. Never experienced anything so delicious. It had been months since I had a proper all-over bath. That girl let me soak while she scrubbed out my uniform and hung it on a drying rack. Then she bent over and gave me a head-to-toe scrubbing as we laughed and teased each other.

"Why, I do believe there is a white boy under all that dirt," she said. "I took you for a nigger, like me."

"Don't call yourself a nigger, Maria."

"If you say so, James. My, you have skin like milk. Lily white."

As I dried myself I watched her smoothing out my uniform. "Maria, I shouldn't have let you do that. I've got to be back by midnight. My uniform will never dry in that time."

"Don't worry about that. Climb up in the loft there and get in the bed to keep warm. I'll punch up the fire so it will dry your clothes faster."

She soon joined me in the bed, there in that steamy, warm laundry. There was no madam now to shout that our time was up. I set aside all thoughts of any other woman and with them my ingrained color prejudice. Just gave myself up to giving and receiving pleasure from that strangely innocent-experienced quarter-blood.

When I awoke, it was nearly 11:30. I sat up and started to get out of bed, but she pulled me back beside her.

"Please don't go, James. I want you to stay."

I couldn't resist her. When I did finally leave, it was five o'clock in the morning. I made the mistake of offering her the rest of my money. She was indignant.

"You think I did that for money, white boy? Look, I make as much in a day as the Confederate Army pays you in a month. I take money from high and mighty Confederate officers and they give me gifts besides. This is a gift from me to you, James. And you come back for more next Wednesday night, you promise?"

I promised. Then, weak in the knees and feeling stupidly at peace with myself, I stumbled out into the street and into the arms of two provost guards on patrol.

"Let's see your pass, soldier."

They examined it. Saw that I was five hours overdue.

"Coming out of a nigger house at 5:30 and you were supposed

to be back at midnight. Reckon we'll have to turn you in."

I pleaded, argued and reasoned, but they were adamant, I think because they didn't approve of where I had been. So I was delivered back to my regiment, under arrest.

Captain Cadieu gave me a tongue-lashing. He canceled my pass privileges for a month and placed me on probation so that I would lose my sergeant's stripes on the next offense, no matter how trivial. He didn't know how harsh his punishment was. It meant that I could not return to Maria's house the next Wednesday.

But three days later it didn't matter. They loaded us onto railroad cars and started us off for eastern North Carolina again, to protect our native state from incursions by the Yankees from their coastal strongholds. I never saw that honey-skinned, tender girl again. By the time the week had rolled around we were back in our old camp at Kinston. I tried hard not to think of Maria sitting in her little cottage, a candle in her window, waiting for the tall sergeant from North Carolina to come. It did matter.

34

People mature at different times in their lives. My wife used to say I had a streak of devilish little boy in me when I was fifty, but in truth I grew up during the first half of 1863. My language reverted to its former coarseness and I lost my illusions about my opportunities in this world, together with my romantic notions about true love. However, I did learn to hold my temper and to cease giving deliberate offense to others. Lost something of my high spirits in the bargain.

At first it was boring to be back in our old camp at Kinston. There wasn't much to do except to shuttle back and forth along the Wilmington and Weldon Railroad to head off Yankee cavalry raids. Eastern North Carolina was good farming country, with its vast level acres, easy to plow and cultivate and occupied by a huge slave population. A lot of the hog and hominy that sustained Richmond came from that sprawling section. And, of course, the only direct rail route between Wilmington's busy wharves and the Confederate capital stretched across the sandy east. So it was important to protect this territory.

We lived well, drawing provisions from the rich countryside. I was never healthier. My twentieth birthday fell in March and to mark the occasion I had my friends measure and weigh me at a cotton gin in Kinston. Found that I had grown an inch—to six feet, one and a half inches—and had gained ten pounds. Still a growing boy.

We had several brief encounters with venturesome Yankee columns probing into the interior from their bases along the coast. Looking back over my diary, I see only one worth dwelling on. We had received a telegraphic warning that a Federal cavalry regiment was marauding inland, headed for a railroad bridge north of Kinston. They rushed us by rail and we reached the location a bare hour before the Yankees got there. We found a company of nervous boys and old men—home guards—drawn up in a field to receive the attackers. Colonel Rankin told them to stay there while we concealed ourselves in the underbrush around the bridge, that is spread out along either side of the road.

The cavalry came pounding along the road, full of confidence. They spotted the home guards, stopped, set up four little popgun howitzers, and wheeled their horses into position on either side of the road. After getting off several rounds from their little cannon, they came charging toward the home guards.

Naturally those untrained stay-at-homes flung down their weapons and ran like hell back toward the bridge. It was a lovely sight: several hundred blue-clad men on horseback, waving their sabers and shouting as they closed in to trap their prey and burn the bridge.

Their triumph lasted about two minutes, until at a command we arose, leveled our Enfields and started cutting them down, men and horses, mostly the latter. It would have been funny except for the screaming of the wounded horses. The smoke cleared and all we could see were the backsides of the horses and their riders streaming back toward the coast in terror. We cut them to pieces.

Used to be a common saying in both armies: "I never saw a dead cavalryman." There is much truth in that statement. The cavalry made a lot of noise and clogged up the roads with horseshit, but to a well-disciplined infantry unit they were just so many big targets. Cavalrymen on foot with repeating rifles were another matter, but that came late in the war. In 1863 the cavalry gave a wide berth to the infantry. Their sabers and pistols held no fears for us.

I neglected to say earlier that William Ferro did not accompany our regiment back to North Carolina. We left him behind in Richmond to serve on the staff of General Cooper as some kind of inspector. We learned later that he had been promoted to lieutenant colonel. I would have written him a letter of congratulation but still felt too bitter toward other members of his family to do so. I felt bitter toward the whole world, in fact, deep down under my devil-may-care surface.

We did have another interesting three weeks as spring came to North Carolina. They detached our regiment and marched us from the rail junction at Goldsboro down to Fayetteville at the head of navigation on the Cape Fear River. Off to the south of Fayetteville, in Robeson County, there lived a tribe of Croatan Indians, a mixed lot who owned no slaves but who were violently anti-Negro. There is a legend that these people are descendants of the Lost Colony of Roanoke, the English group that disappeared from the coast in the late 1500s. The theory is that these colonists, despairing of relief ships from England, moved into the interior and intermarried with the so-called Croatans. Whatever the truth of that story, these Robeson County Indians were then, as now, a proud and stubborn people.

The Confederate authorities did some stupid things in the war. One of them was to offend these Croatans by refusing to allow them to form a fighting unit as they wanted to; would only accept labor battalions from these Indians who, incidentally, had long ago lost all trace of their Indianhood except for their reddish complexions. One group went down to Wilmington to work on the Fort Fisher defenses. They received less pay than whites and were treated like Negroes. The result: they deserted and made their way back to their woods and swamps. They withheld their farm produce from the market. They welcomed runaway Confederate soldiers. And worst of all, they began robbing and bushwhacking wagon trains.

The largest body of these red-skinned malcontents went under the name of the Lowry gang. The state of North Carolina sent in the home guard, but the Lowry gang whipped their asses and sent them chasing home. They decided that the 10th North Carolina was just the regiment to show the Confederate flag to the Croatans. And Fayetteville was our base.

Fayetteville is a graceful town with a large pink market in the center square. I don't know how long they kept selling Negroes there, but the business was going on apace in the spring of 1863, believe me.

They didn't have slave auctions up in Oldham County, and Noah Rhine and I thought we ought to watch one. We found about thirty men, women and children herded together in a bull pen, watched over by an evil-looking man of about fifty, armed with a revolver.

The auctioneer was a portly, short man in his mid-forties. He had a white goatee and a red face. He could talk the ears off a brass monkey.

This gentleman was loudly pointing out the features of a buck about twenty-five years old, a jet-black nigger with powerful shoulders and arms and a sullen look on his face.

"Now, ladies and gentlemen, here we have a prime field hand. Sound and strong. He was born up in Halifax County on the Kendall Plantation. Name is Jethro. He's in good shape, as you can see. Good teeth, too. Show them your teeth, Jethro. Yes sir, strong as a mule. Turn around, Jethro, and show yourself off. Isn't he a fine specimen?"

At all this flattery, Jethro's expression softened.

"The owners assure me that Jethro is a willing worker and never gives any kind of trouble. He can do some carpentering and is a good mule driver. Has a way with animals, I understand. Is that right, Jethro? You like driving mules?"

Jethro grinned and nodded.

"What am I bid for this top-notch field hand?"

An old man in a white Panama hat shouted, "Nine hundred dollars, Confederate."

The auctioneer looked hurt. "Oh, now, let's be serious. He's worth far more than that in gold. This isn't some plantation cull. Let's be serious."

Another voice: "A thousand dollars, Confederate."

With that the bidding picked up and continued until the first bidder, after a long pause, said, "Four thousand, five hundred dollars."

The auctioneer tried in vain for more but finally declared, "Sold, for four thousand, five hundred, to Mr. Horace Melville."

Next they brought out a brown-skinned woman of about thirty-five with a sixteen-year-old girl and a twelve-year-old boy. The woman had a sensitive look in her eye; the children were much lighter-complexioned than she.

"Now here is an interesting family group," the auctioneer said. "Yes sir, here is a ready-made servants' staff. Cook, maid and houseboy. Mother and two children, the property of the late Major Baucom from Lenoir County. The major gave his life at Sharpsburg last September and his poor widow can't keep the plantation going. Yankee raiders have run off their field hands and all she has left is the land and a few loyal house servants. She wants to remove herself and her children to the interior and needs to raise some money for expenses. Mrs. Baucom says Miranda here is an accomplished seamstress and weaver as well. Taught her herself. She asks me to sell the family together. Doesn't want to break them up unless she absolutely has to. What am I bid for this mother and two children? Here is a rare opportunity."

Silence from the crowd. The auctioneer cajoled them. "Do I hear five thousand dollars for all three?"

Silence.

A woman in a gaudy dress and a large hat raised a gloved hand. "A thousand dollars for the girl."

The auctioneer tried in vain to get other bids. He ended up by accepting the bid "subject to review with the owner." In the same way he got two thousand dollars for the woman and another thousand for the boy.

Later Noah and I saw the white woman, wearing black, saying goodbye to the family, both she and the slave woman in tears, hugging each other. Still later we were in a saloon-café drinking and eating when the auctioneer came in with a big, flaccid-looking fellow from Mississippi. They sat at the table next to us.

"Dad-blamed this war, anyway, I say. It makes it so hard to do business," the auctioneer complained as he waited for his order.

The big man shook his head. "I admit the market is unsettled, but you can still turn a dollar. As long as we can keep the Yankees out of the Deep South there will always be money in running niggers down there. My biggest complaint is with this government. They are discouraging cotton planting. And what the army is doing to the railroads is a sin. But there is still money in niggers, you know that as well as I, Mr. Abernathy."

"Yes, yes, but up here in North Carolina and Virginia seems like everything is against the business. Now I used to have a good thing, going round from county to county between here and Richmond. Stop in the courthouses and nose around. Ask questions. Find out what plantation owner died recently and which families particularly needed money. I developed my sources, you might say. Then go out and pay a discreet call. Let the family know there is money available, cash on the barrel head. Give them time to think about it. Then call back as if in a hurry. Next thing you know you would be getting some good bargains in surplus slaves. Of course they try to sell you the odds and ends. That's only human nature. The chronic runaways or the consumptives. You have to exercise judgment like in any other business. And you have to keep up your reputation, deal only in desirable stock. My end of the business isn't as cut and dried as yours."

"You do have a good reputation, Mr. Abernathy. The best. That's why I have done business with you all these years. People in Mississippi perk up when I tell them I have a load of Abernathy niggers for sale."

"Well, that pleases me. If I go buying up bad stock just because they come cheap and then unload them on you or other dealers, why, it gives us both a bad name. I deal only in the best."

Their drinks came, two enormous juleps. The auctioneer handed one to his friend and raised the pewter goblet so that the moisture glistened.

"Here's to business."

"To business."

The auctioneer closed his eyes to savor the sweetness of the julep. When he opened them, he saw Noah and me at the next table watching him, for we were fascinated.

"Well, boys, how is the war going?" he addressed us with a wink.

"Very well, the last we saw of it."

"And where was that?"

"At Fredericksburg."

"Oh, my goodness, were you there? How I did enjoy reading of that battle in the papers." He turned to his companion. "Old Burnside tried to put a hundred thousand men across the river there and our brave boys shot them down like swatting flies in a cow barn. How glorious. All we need is another victory like that and maybe the infernal Yankees will go home and leave us in peace. How I long for peace."

"To peace," the slave trader raised his cup.

The auctioneer closed his eyes and drank deeply once more. Then, "Oh, my goodness, here we sit drinking while these fine lads have nothing but that vile rotgut before them. Such bad manners. Boys, I want to buy you each a genuine mint julep. Ever have one?"

"No, sir."

"We'll fix that. Waiter. Waiter."

In a few minutes Noah and I, practically hypnotized by the auctioneer's torrent of rhetoric, sat with huge pewter goblets filled with ice, powdered sugar, crushed mint leaves and smooth bourbon whisky.

The auctioneer asked us about our families, our schooling, what we had done in the war, and what had brought us to Fayetteville, his shrewd blue eyes playing upon us as we responded.

"Oh, yes, you are here to restore domestic tranquillity. I hope you can chase the vile Yankees right out of North Carolina after you have put down these stupid Indians. The number of fine families the Yankees have ruined with their raids. Oh, it would wring your hearts to see the plantations they have ruined, places families have labored for years to build up. And the worst thing is the way they carry off the nigras, hundreds of thousands of dollars' worth of them. This is a cruel war."

"Yes." I finally got in a word. "Noah and I watched your auction this morning. We saw you sell the family that belonged to the major's widow."

"Wasn't that a sad thing? Just one more example of the misery I have encountered. That lady's husband was an up-and-coming planter. Matter of pride to him never to sell off a slave. Must have had twenty-five or more. Went off to war and lost his life at Sharpsburg. His overseer left that nigra woman and their two children. . . ." He winked at me again. "You know how those things are. The rascal went off to make a fortune at blockade-running in Wilmington and abandoned poor Mrs. Baucom to run the place. She tried her best until a troop of Yankee cavalry came through. Stole all her winter's provisions, burnt her cotton gin, and insulted her in front of her children and servants. All the able-bodied nigras followed them back to the coast, leaving just a handful."

He took another sip from his goblet. "It breaks your heart to see the results. She is forced to sell off her remaining slaves and go to relatives up in Lincoln County for the duration. Sad, sad."

"I noticed she and the slave woman both were taking it hard."

"Yes, of course you get used to nigras' carrying on when they are sold. They are so emotional to begin with. Now that nigra woman should be grateful. A family right here in Fayetteville bought her. Old folks who need a housekeeper. She'll have a secure home for the rest of her life."

"How about the children?"

"Oh, a Confederate major bought the boy, as a body servant. He'll get a chance to see the world."

"And the girl? She was pretty."

He winked at me again. "So she was. A woman from Wilmington bought her, you may have noticed. Runs what you might call an establishment down there that caters to English sailors and other blockade-runners. The girl is a bit young but, as you say, she is pretty. She will have a secure place as well. Oh, yes, all of them have gained. Instead of huddling in a cold plantation house being harassed by the enemy, each has a new home. And the widow has enough money to keep her secure in the interior until she can return in peace to her lands."

He assumed a benign air. "I feel that I have performed yet another Christian service. Here, waiter, bring four more juleps."

The auctioneer's companion found his tongue. "Well, Mr. Abernathy, you have too tender a heart in these matters. I don't let my feelings get involved at all. The way I look at it, there is a need for strong slave labor in the Deep South where cotton grows best. There is a surplus of slaves up here in North Carolina and Virginia. I simply supply that need and don't let myself get involved in the feelings of people like the widow. Can't afford to. You are too tenderhearted."

"Oh, I reckon you are right, but it does tear my heartstrings to see a fine family have to part with its nigras. Hard for them ever to raise the money for more."

Our second, their third, round of juleps came. Mr. Abernathy raised his goblet and made a toast.

"To the end of this cruel war."

"And to business," his companion chimed in.

"Yes, sir," the auctioneer continued. "I wish you boys all the luck in the world. When you finish licking the Yankees, why don't you look me up? There is going to be a boom in these Confederate States, come full independence. We're going to have a lot of rebuilding to do. Europe will be on its knees for cotton, having been so long denied it. There will be money in slaves, let me tell you. Smart boys like you can make a fortune if you get in on the ground floor."

"Yes, sir," his companion agreed. "There is money in niggers if you know how to handle them and keep up a good reputation for fair dealing."

35

Noah and I had a hard time getting away from our slave-dealing friends. They were still drinking juleps when we thanked them and said our goodbyes.

With two mint juleps under our belts, Noah and I felt somewhat unsteady on our feet. We took the long way back to our camp so we could clear our heads. Noah had a troubled look on his face as we trudged along, and I asked him why.

"I can't stop thinking about that woman and her two children, Jim. That was not right to split up a family like that."

"No," I agreed. "Niggers have feelings, too. But that poor widow woman had no choice. She tried to sell them together and there were no takers."

"I wouldn't say this to just anyone, but my daddy thinks slavery is a curse to the South."

"I never knew your pa was an abolitionist."

"I didn't say he was an abolitionist. He just thinks that white people like us are held down by rich slaveowners. He says they care more for their human property than for the education of ordinary white people and that they control things."

Remembering my bitter experience with the Ferro family, I couldn't disagree.

"My own daddy isn't one hundred percent in favor of slavery either," I replied. "But, being a minister, he just thinks it is a sin to treat them cruelly. For instance, he would have been more upset than you if he saw an auction like the one today. I don't think he would object to slavery if everybody was kind to their niggers, never mistreated them or sold them off."

Normally Noah was not a great talker, but the juleps had loosened his tongue. "Well, what are we fighting for, Jim, if it isn't for slavery? I've been hearing remarks about how this is a rich man's war and a poor man's fight. Isn't that what it boils down to?"

It took me a while to think of an answer. "We're fighting for Southern independence just like my great-granddaddy fought for American independence from England."

"Yes, but why should we want independence? Is life going to be any better for ordinary white people like us? Aren't we just going to give the slaveowners more power?"

"Oh, come on now, Noah. You sound like an abolitionist. No,

the question is states' rights. The North has no business trying to force its way of life on us."

"You mean they want to stop slavery."

"You keep bringing up slavery."

"Of course I do. You know as well as I that there wouldn't be any issue of states' rights if it weren't for slavery. Why should you and I be risking our lives so that Abernathy man and his friend can deal in Negroes?"

Noah was beginning to get on my nerves, but he did make me think. I stopped and took him by his jacket front.

"Noah, right here in North Carolina nearly one-third of our population is black. Down in South Carolina there are more niggers than white people. If all those slaves are set free, what will become of us white people? You want your sister to marry a nigger? You want them owning land and voting? You want to see a nigger governor? Like it or not, the institution of slavery protects us against niggers taking over. That's what it boils down to."

He shook his head. "You may be right. I still don't like to see a family split up and sold off like cows and calves. Negroes are human like us, aren't they?"

"Almost, I reckon. Here, let's stop this foolish talk and get back to camp."

36

Early the next morning, Colonel Rankin lined us up and talked to us about our mission. First, we were to march through Robeson County to impress the Croatans with the military prowess of the Confederacy. Then, he intimated, there would be a further assignment "elsewhere in North Carolina."

We shined up our equipment and, accompanied by a battery of howitzers and a troop of cavalry, marched out that afternoon for Indian country, moving at a leisurely pace, as if on parade.

The weather was pleasant, and the sandy roads were easy on our feet. As we marched along, Croatan women and children would come out of their cabins to stare. There was not a man of military age in sight.

Some of the boys in the ranks made disparaging remarks about the "red savages," forgetting that one of my best soldiers, Jimmy Golightly, was at least a cousin of the Croatans with his half-Manawee blood. Although Jimmy never changed his expression, he must have heard the remarks. At our first night's bivouac, beside a crossroads, I passed the word for such remarks to cease. They did for a while.

Our expedition didn't amount to much. We spread out in skirmish formation along a front of about a mile and, with muskets loaded, capped and at the ready, we scouted through a wooded, overgrown area believed to be the lair of the bushwhackers. The cavalry had ridden around the area and waited on the other side to intercept any human "game" we flushed out. We found plenty of Indian signs, recent campfires, lean-tos and huts, but never an Indian until we came out on the other side half a day later. The cavalry had collared three men as they came running from a thicket while several others had eluded them.

Naturally we infantrymen were out of sorts, weary in leg and arm and covered with briar scratches. We circled up to see our prey, and nothing I could do would stop remarks such as "Let's scalp the bloodthirsty savages." These three Indians, two scrawny boys and one older man, knew nothing of scalping of course. They showed no fear either, their faces reddish masks, like Jimmy Golightly's.

We stayed in and around the county seat, Lumbertown, for a week, drilling and target-firing to impress the Scots who lived in the town and the Croatan women and children who trickled in from the countryside. While we did this, the cavalry, directed by the local authorities, darted back and forth into the hinterland, sometimes descending on Indian cabins late at night. By the end of the week they had gathered in about twenty redskins. I don't know what happened to them, for the next thing I knew we were headed north again.

As Colonel Rankin explained it, we were to march through the sand hills and into the Piedmont, where another pocket of rebellion against the Confederacy smoldered. This was in Randolph County and the miscreants there were poor whites, not Indians; men who refused to answer conscript calls, much less volunteer; them and deserters from states farther south.

Our first day's march carried us to the northern border of Robeson County. We felt we had done a good job of "pacifying" the Croatans and had done so without the loss of a single man. The next morning, when I called the roll, the story was different.

"Where is Jimmy Golightly?" I asked.

"I haven't seen him since late last night," Ed Engerer volunteered.

The upshot was that Jimmy Golightly had taken off with his blanket and musket. Deserted, apparently to take refuge with the Croatans. And he was the best soldier in my squad. Deserted.

37

At the end of a two-day march we found ourselves in the town of Sanford, having passed through the sand hills section of the state. The people here were staunch Confederates. They weren't used to seeing a regiment of tough, battle-hardened soldiers like us and they nearly overwhelmed us with their hospitality. Of course their means were limited, for the blockade had put the supply and cost of coffee, sugar and such out of reach of all except the most wealthy. Still, the good people of Sanford had learned to make do. They brought in cakes and pies made with honey and molasses. To our coarse palates it all tasted wonderful.

The town was short of young white men, too. The only ones we saw between the ages of eighteen and forty were cripples and half-wits. The girls of the town were starved for young male companionship, so there was a good deal of flirting and a great exchange of names and addresses and promises to correspond. Unfortunately, we weren't there long enough for these relationships to mature, but it was a pleasant interlude talking to the girls of the town. We were good for their morale and they for ours.

North of Sanford the countryside deteriorated. We entered an area of bad roads leading through scrub forests of pine and second-growth oak. The people were poor whites; hardly a black face to be seen along the way. They stared at us sullenly as we trudged along the clay-and-loam tracks.

I can't explain why Randolph County, in the very center of the Old North State, showed so little enthusiasm for the Confederate cause, except, perhaps, because there were no plantations in the county, with its hilly terrain and thin soil. They had no powerful slaveowners to lead public opinion toward secession. I understand that to this day the people there vote Republican.

They marched us into the county seat, Asheboro, where we were met by officials of the state government with a long list of men from the area who either had refused to answer their call-up for military service or who were reported absent without leave from their regiments.

Led by these civilian worthies, we marched out in company strength to this cabin and that in the scraggly countryside. Sometimes we would set up a circle of pickets and then send in a squad to the door to ask questions. As sergeant, I drew this duty on several occasions.

"Good day, madam," the government man would say to the lanky-haired woman who came to the door with towheaded, ragged brats at her skirt tails. "I am here by authority of Governor Vance and these are soldiers of the 10th North Carolina Regiment. We have a warrant for one Samuel Jennings. Is he at home?"

"Naw, he ain't here."

"Where is he?"

"I don't know. I ain't seen him for a long time."

"Is he your husband?"

"Yes, sir. He is."

"He was conscripted into the Confederate Army last year and he left his command between Raleigh and Richmond. Did he come home?"

"I ain't seen him."

"Now, madam, we have information that he has been observed in Asheboro within the last month. You surely must have seen him.

"I ain't seen him."

"In other words, you refuse to say. Well, madam, these soldiers must search your house and your barns and sheds. We would rather not do that. These men are armed and if your husband should resist or try to flee, he would be shot. It would be far better if you would summon him to come out peaceably."

"I don't know where he is."

It was depressing to enter those rude little houses with their battered cane-bottomed chairs and corn-shuck beds and see the meager rations of mush and fatback. I felt like a burglar to go poking about in their sleeping lofts with the eyes of the women and children following me. Sometimes we would find clear signs that the husband or son had recently been there, that they had even spent the previous nights in their own beds. On one occasion the fugitive was in bed, too sick with a fever to flee. We hauled him out and made him follow us back to Asheboro.

On another occasion we found a twenty-year-old lad hiding under a pile of corncobs in a shed. Our pickets grabbed two slackers who ran when we approached another house. It was a dirty business and none of us enjoyed the duty.

Through informants we learned the whereabouts of a camp of the fugitives, where the local ones hid out most of the time, sneaking out one or two nights a week to their families. It was in an inaccessible area, much like that of the Robeson County bushwhackers' camp except that the terrain was rougher, cut through with ravines and overgrown.

Here we met resistance, for the local deserters were backed up by a number of desperate characters from other states, men who had brought their weapons with them. They made the mistake of opening fire on our company as we neared their camp.

Captain Cadieu did a clever thing in response to their resistance. Instead of returning their fire, he ordered a retreat, telling us to "act scared and run like hell."

We skedaddled back to the road where the cavalry waited. The captain sent for help. Within a couple of hours, the rest of our regiment moved toward the deserters' camp again. Again they opened fire. We began shooting blindly into the woods while the rest of our regiment came up as quietly as seven hundred men walking through underbrush could.

The deserters, unaware of our new strength, continued stupidly blasting away at us. Then, suddenly, our entire regiment charged.

We were fit and well fed. They were out of shape from lying about in the woods and eating scanty rations. We burst right into their camp, but in their desperation many continued to resist. Must have been more than a hundred of them and we were able to capture a dozen or so, besides breaking up their camp. They scattered like quail at last and of course it was impossible to run down every one of them.

So, at the end of the day we collected our captives—unshaven, ragged men from the hills of Georgia and Alabama for the most part—and marched them back to the stockade at Asheboro.

After a week of this police duty, having temporarily put down the rebellion against Confederate authority, we headed north again, across Deep River and into the southern part of Guilford County.

We set up camp along the bank of a stream called Stinking Quarter, there to rest from our deserter-chasing labors. Our forage wagons went out into the countryside to buy provender for our regiment. Here we found no spirit of rebellion against the Confederacy, but in truth not very much against the United States Government either. The land was fertile but was tilled mainly by small farmers, a few of whom owned a slave or two and worked in the fields right alongside of them.

Many of the people here were Lutherans of German descent, industrious folk who worked hard and ate well. Their grandparents had come down from Pennsylvania; some of the older folk could still speak German. They were hearty, good-natured people who knew how to drive a hard bargain for their produce.

It was a refreshing contrast to see these sturdy Teutons with their tidy houses and barns after passing through the hardscrabble country to the south.

After feeding and resting us there, Colonel Rankin marched us east, our route carrying us past the Alamance battlefield, where just before the Revolution a collection of back-country rebels were defeated by down east supporters of the Royal Governor of North Carolina. Our next stop was the village of Saxapahaw on the Haw River. There we camped near a textile mill whose owners were making vast profits by turning out cloth for Confederate uniforms and blankets.

We had little to do, so some of the boys and I paid a visit to the mill. It was a bustling place with hired slaves unloading bales of cotton and wool at one end and loading lots of finished cloth at the other. Inside, scores of young women worked at the weaving machines, which were powered by a huge water wheel.

Curious thing about the effect of the war on the South. It stimulated a lot of industry. If the Confederacy had won or been allowed to go its independent way before the South got torn up, I think that all the factories started up to sustain the war effort might have made the region into a self-sufficient nation. Right in North Carolina, we had a musket factory at Fayetteville and a naval foundry at Charlotte and many textile mills. Of course, Richmond with its vast Tredegar Iron Works and similar facilities became a major industrial center. Well, who can say?

The factory girls weren't nearly as pretty or well spoken as the lasses of Sanford. A plump little blonde caught my eyes as she worked at her loom, but she also caught the eye of Harry McGee. He got her name and when the shift ended, he accompanied her to her home a couple of miles away. I spent the evening in my tent playing chuck-a-luck by candlelight with some of the boys.

From Saxapahaw we made an easy march up to Graham and there boarded boxcars for a ride into Raleigh. There, in the state capital, Colonel Rankin had us spruce ourselves up to be reviewed by Governor Vance himself.

I suppose I liked Vance because he was somewhat the same type as me or vice versa, quick of tongue and wit. Earthy. Vance came from Buncombe County, up in the mountains, near Asheville. He was a boy wonder at the University down in Chapel Hill; came out to practice law but backslid into politics, becoming first a legislator and then a U.S. Congressman.

Throughout the big debate of the 1850s over slavery, he remained a Unionist. He was never one of your mindless, fire-eating secessionists. He went right on trying to keep North Carolina in the Union up until Lincoln called for volunteers to suppress the South. Then the mighty voice and mind of Zeb Vance were turned to persuading the state to join her Southern sisters in secession.

I knew him well by sight, for he had been colonel of the 26th North Carolina at New Bern and at Malvern Hill. He left his regiment in mid '62 for the far more important post of governor of the state, and in that position he was worth an army in himself.

Vance was a big fellow, six feet tall at least, and quite stout, for he was a great eater. But how he could speak in public. Had such a reputation for pungent expression and wit that often his audience would start laughing with the first sentence delivered by that powerful voice.

He would start out with a simple, humorous story about some old mountain character, then quickly turn the climax of the story into a point of his argument. Another story would follow another until he had his listeners rolling about on the ground or slapping their legs and howling with laughter. Once he had them helpless with mirth, he would nail down his arguments. He talked our language.

There in Raleigh that spring of 1863 Zeb Vance gave us a personal inspection and then a good one-hour oration, which was short for him. He recalled our presence at New Bern, twitting us slightly about our inglorious role there, but hastened to say that he had recommended replacing our colonel with a well-trained military man. And then he told of his pride at the way we and our sister regiments had gone up against the Yankee guns at Malvern Hill. Went on to say what good things he had heard of our performance at Sharpsburg and Fredericksburg.

"That's why I asked for you when the loyal people of Robeson and Randolph counties began to complain that law and order had broken down in those communities. We found the job too big for the home guard: a case of sending old men to do boys' jobs, you might say. So I asked for the splendid boys of the noble 10th Regiment, and from all reports you did not let me down. Now it goes against my grain to send troops against my own people. I would not do it if it weren't absolutely necessary. But you have seen the kind of people who are resisting the legal authorities of your government. If we are to have a stable society, then we must have obedience to the law of that society's legally constituted government.

"I know that some people are saying that the poorer folk of the South are bearing the burden of this war. That's not going to be true in North Carolina. I want the soldiers furnished by North Carolina to be the best equipped and the best fed in the Confederacy. I want their families to be the best looked after and their homes the most secure, secure from Yankees and bushwhackers.

"The government of your state is standing up to the Lincoln government in the North and it will stand up for your interests if the Confederate Government in Richmond tries to trample on your rights as free white men. You may know that this state is operating its own factories. I am pleased to announce as well that I have sent our own purchasing agents to England. One of their missions will be to purchase one or more special ships for running vital medicines and other supplies through the blockade, with the profits going to the state and not into the pockets of some greedy opportunists."

He went on in that vein until we were completely convinced that our interests were his only concern. I had been feeling somewhat disillusioned with the war after my experience with the Ferros, witnessing that slave auction, and playing policeman in Randolph County. Zeb Vance's talk buoyed up my spirits and those of our entire regiment. Made us feel like heroes.

Incidentally, he made good on his promises. North Carolina suffered in the war, to be sure, but far less than most states and the reason was that she had a governor who was a man of the people and not of the slaveowners' interests.

Zeb Vance. I thought well of him then and I thought well of him after the war when my first son was born. That's why he is named Zebulon Vance Mundy.

38

In Raleigh those three or four days, I had quite a fight with myself over whether to chance a visit to Elvira Fincastle. On my last trip through Raleigh, the previous spring, I had just met Jane Ferro and was too full of romantic love notions to keep my promise to see Elvira again. Now Jane Ferro was a painful memory. Thoughts of Elvira's lovely, soft body and her warm arms kept rising. And as is usual in these cases, the temptation won out over natural fears of being caught tampering with a colonel's wife or of finding she had some new love interest.

So, after wangling a half-day pass from the company clerk and putting on the best shine my battered ex-U.S. Army shoes would take and shaving, I stepped out into the pleasant spring afternoon.

If there is a heaven, I suspect that it will be very much like spring in that section of North Carolina, just when the dogwood trees are in full bloom and the weather not yet too hot. Everything is ready to burst into lusty life, including me on that particular day. Never felt so raunchy or conscious of being young and strong. It was grand to be an experienced man of twenty on his way to meet an old flame, or so I thought.

I walked around her block three times to make sure there were no signs of her husband about. At last, in front of her door, I took a deep breath, squared my shoulders and advanced upon the porch.

I had to knock twice before the door was opened by the old black woman who worked for the Fincastles. She looked at me suspiciously.

"What you want?"

"I am calling on Mrs. Fincastle. That is what I want. Is she in?"

"Naw, she ain't."

"Where is she?"

"She done gone off to Richmond to be with the colonel. They going to live there for the rest of the war, I reckon. She and the baby left last week."

"The baby? Mrs. Fincastle has a baby?"

"Sho, they do. Anything wrong with that? Folks has babies every day."

"The baby can't be very old?"

"Three months old. Just now old enough to travel or Mrs. Fincastle would have joined the colonel earlier. Here, I ain't got time to be standing here talking to no soldier. Goodbye."

"Goodbye."

"Shitfire!" I said to myself as I walked away from the house. "Not only has she moved away, but she is a mother to boot. Damned rotten luck."

Later, as I consoled myself at a saloon I fell to talking with a couple of middle-aged state clerks who were praising the efficiency and patriotism of Governor Vance during his first nine months in office. They praised the way he had got rid of deadwood in Raleigh and brought in bright, energetic people. Also, they wanted to know about my regiment's experiences in Robeson and Randolph counties. It was a while before I could get back to a question of my own.

"What has happened to Colonel Elmer Fincastle?"

"Fincastle?" Both clerks laughed. "What do you know of the Reverend Mister Fincastle?"

"He was colonel of my regiment for a while."

"Of course. He was colonel of the 10th. I forgot. They sacked him after the fight down at New Bern. And his friends around Raleigh persuaded poor old Governor Clark to give him a job."

"Yes, yes. But where is he now?"

"Oh, Governor Vance knew what a windbag he was. Terminated his post, but Fincastle, for all his blubber, always manages to land on his feet. He has friends in the Confederate Congress and now he heads some sort of bureau up in Richmond. Something to do with taxes."

I was dying to ask more questions, but after eliciting the name of the bureau, I let up and the conversation drifted into a series of complaints against the Confederate Government and praise for Governor Vance for resisting what he felt were violations of North Carolina's rights as a sovereign state.

"Governor Vance has got this state solidly behind the fight for independence, but he doesn't take any guff off of Jefferson Davis," one clerk said.

"And he is right," said the other. "After all, that's what this war is all about . . . states' rights. If we are going to knuckle under and do everything the way Jefferson Davis orders it, we might as well have stayed in the Union and let old Lincoln dictate to us. States' rights are the issue, don't you agree, Sergeant?"

I mumbled a halfhearted agreement, finished my whisky and at the first civil opportunity, got away from the pair on the excuse that my pass would soon expire.

39

The next day a cold rain came in from the north and with it a wind left over from March. The dogwoods yielded their pink-and-white blossoms to the dreary weather. That same day, around noon, they loaded the long-suffering 10th onto open railway cars, flatbeds they call them now, and hauled us off through the rain to Goldsboro. We arrived there wet through and through and so out of sorts that I had to set aside my own bad temper and act as peacemaker among my own squad.

"Back in this Goddamned hell hole" was the way Harry McGee put it.

We stayed there until early May, without major incident except that we got new uniforms and shoes, all manufactured in North Carolina. The trousers weren't proper gray, being a horrible off-yellow we called butternut; the short infantry jackets that had replaced the longer early war models poorly sewn and the sleeves of uneven length; and the shoes were made of leather not entirely cured, but it lifted our morale to be reequipped.

There at Goldsboro I had the opportunity to watch the trains moving north toward Richmond or east toward Raleigh. Several passed every day, hauling up shipments that had run the blockade into Wilmington. If the Federals had been able to close off Wilmington earlier in the war, or if they had been able to break up the railroad across eastern North Carolina, the war would have ended in 1864 rather than '65, saving tens of thousands of lives.

But that is neither here nor there. In early May we were loaded on two of those trains headed north. Off we went for Richmond, or so we thought. Nearly a year and a half had passed since I rode my first train, from Charlotte to Raleigh. I was shocked at the deterioration of the rolling stock. The Wilmington and Weldon tracks were kept in better condition than most Southern lines, but they were bad enough. The boxcars and locomotives had become downright ramshackled. We puffed along at ten or twelve miles an hour, when we moved at all.

Our two trains hauled freight, most of it contained in padlocked boxcars, much like those 40-and-8 little pint-sized things they use now in France. However, there were several flatcars carrying Confederate military goods, well lashed down and covered with canvas tarps, and one passenger car at the rear, for the comfort of our officers, naturally.

As for the seven hundred men of the 10th, we, our blanket

rolls and equipment were stuck about on the tops of the boxcars and around the edges of the flatcars.

We poked around the train at its various stops for water and wood, despite the warnings of the brakeman, a good-natured chap of about forty with one of those funny Tidewater Virginia accents.

"You're a sergeant," he says to me. "Can't you control your men?"

"No, they are impossible. A bunch of peckerwoods from Oldham County. Nobody can do a thing with them."

"Well, these boxcars are locked up for a good reason. I wish they would stop trying to pull off the boards . . . and look there, they are trying to twist off the padlock there. Why don't you order them to stop?"

"Partly because I am curious myself. What have you got in those cars?"

He caught my humor and relaxed. "Oh, everything. Car up ahead there with the tight boards is carrying gunpowder. The next one has medical supplies. All that is the property of the Confederate Government. That and the stuff on the flatcars, which of course you know about since I saw you crawling under the tarp with your scroungy crew."

I caught *his* humor and flashed him my most winning grin. "How about the other boxcars?"

"They are filled with private goods. Merchants in Richmond are bringing up stuff for sale."

"Through the blockade? What kind of stuff?"

"Yard goods, mostly silks. And coffee and sugar. Noticed several cases of tea. Brandy, expensive stuff. One lot of fancy women's mirrors and combs. Must be a million dollars' worth of merchandise on this one train. Stuff is so scarce it will sell like ice water in hell up in Richmond."

In Petersburg they unloaded us, gave us rations and a good night's sleep, and next morning they marched us off to City Point on the James River. There they gave us each a pick or shovel and set us to work improving the fortifications that kept the Yankee fleet at bay . . . Chesapeake Bay, that is. I never heard so much grumbling in my life.

"Goddamned. This is nigger work. I'm a soldier, not a frigging day laborer."

"Hell, yes, why don't they get slaves down here to do this? I'd rather be chasing Indians through a swamp than to be straining my guts out with a shovel."

I employed all my charm on the boys, saying, "Shut up. You're lucky to have a job. If you weren't doing this, you'd be home looking at a mule's ass over a set of plow handles. You ain't too good for a little manual work."

Charm works every time. They told me to kiss their asses, but they kept digging, throwing up huge banks of earth to shield the enormous guns waiting to be emplaced.

We were working on those fortifications when news of Lee's great victory at Chancellorsville reached us via a Richmond newspaper. We all gathered round to hear the owner of the paper read aloud how Lee had divided his army in the face of an overwhelming force to defeat in detail the Federal commander who had succeeded poor old Burnside, Joseph Hooker.

The newspapers of that day usually had the stories of battles wrong. I have since studied the Battle of Chancellorsville and know that military historians regard it as Lee's most brilliant victory. It was a masterpiece of bold planning and lightning execution, the way Lee posted a holding force on Marye's Heights at Fredericksburg while he moved the bulk of his army west to contest the main advance of Hooker across the upper Rappahannock and then further divided his Army of Northern Virginia by sending Stonewall Jackson looping through the woods to descend like an angry God on Hooker's unsuspecting right flank. How I would have liked to have been in Jackson's command as he came bursting through the trees on the poor old XI Corps of the Federals.

It was a brilliant victory, but although the Confederates lost "only" twelve thousand men to Hooker's eighteen thousand, their losses were greater in proportion to their strength.

And worst of all, in my opinion, one of those twelve thousand Confederate casualties was Stonewall Jackson, wounded by his own troops by mistake. News of his death reached us at City Point about the middle of May. Never saw men so downcast. Stonewall Jackson. If he had lived, I wonder what difference it would have made. Does the history of a nation turn on a detail such as a musket barrel being pointed just so at just such a time? If you could go back and move that barrel a half-inch, would the entire fabric of history come unraveled? Who can say?

Another piece of disturbing news came to us on the heels of that about the death of Stonewall Jackson. It concerned the activities of Negro Federal soldiers in the vicinity of Yankee-occupied Norfolk. We had heard early in 1863 that the Yankees would start enlisting them. We didn't take this too seriously, thinking it wouldn't amount to much. For some time, Negroes running away from their masters in Tidewater Virginia or eastern North Carolina had been flocking into Norfolk. There as in the other Federal strongpoints along the coast, they were considered as "contrabands of war" and therefore not to be returned to their masters, although the Lincoln government made a pretense at that time of not disturbing slavery. Of course Lincoln's Emancipation Proclamation, put in force on January 1, 1863, designated that all slaves in rebellious areas would be considered free henceforth while those in loyal areas such as Maryland, Kentucky and Missouri would remain in bondage. What a piece of hypocrisy!

Anyway, after the proclamation went out the Federal Government started signing up niggers to wear the blue uniform, and their authorities in Norfolk started organizing the contrabands in their midst into military units, giving them arms and sending them out into the countryside to harass the good Southern people.

40

The southeastern corner of Virginia, next to North Carolina, lies amidst flat, arable land interrupted here and there by swamps. A ragtag Confederate regiment had been holding a town, both to protect the residents and to serve as an outpost in case the Federals made a serious advance inland toward the railroad feeding Petersburg and Richmond.

The Federals had decided to test their new Negro regiments against that town. It had been an easy matter for them to chase our one regiment out.

Exaggerated reports of "outrages" against the whites of the area had appeared in the Richmond papers and with them criticism of the Confederate Government for failing to protect the town. Stung by this criticism, Jefferson Davis dispatched our entire brigade—five regiments in all—to the area. We were delighted to put aside our shovels and take up our muskets for the march through Petersburg and thence southeastward. Our anticipation increased when we learned that our mission was to punish the Negro troops and save the distressed white people in that corner of Virginia. Rumor fed upon rumor until most of us believed that the black troops had burned the houses of the town, raped most of the white women, bayoneted babies in their cribs and now were defying us to do anything about it.

I can't fully explain the outrage most Confederate soldiers felt about Negroes being used as soldiers against them. At the mildest, their feelings were that it was not fair, not playing the game. This was a test of manhood between white men. Negroes might be considered an object of the game; they were not supposed to be participants. At the other end of the scale, there was a deep hatred, contempt and, I suppose, fear of the black race. Now my own attitude toward darkies has tempered since 1863, for after having spent a lifetime around them I know them to be human beings who somehow have managed to survive two centuries of buffeting. Mind you, I think they should keep in their places. Don't mistake me on that. But they must live as well as we.

Like most of the boys in my regiment, I had known very few Negroes and none of them intimately. Forget what I wrote earlier about Maria, the quadroon girl in Richmond. That was a different matter. Except for the occasional lad whose father owned one or two slave families, most of us enlisted men had not exchanged a hundred words with a member of the African race. They were simply a black presence in our midst, a shadow that threatened us even as we affected to despise it.

The closer we drew to the black garrison town, the uglier grew our mood. How many times did I hear promises that we would "teach them niggers a lesson."

Earlier in this narrative, I very nearly left out an account of my acquaintance with Maria. What I am about to relate regarding our encounter with the Negro troops is a far more shameful story, but I will tell it nonetheless.

We camped about half a day's march from the town while an accompanying cavalry regiment—a bunch of so-called mounted infantry from western Virginia—pushed ahead to mask our approach. The atmosphere in our camp that night was full of excitement and blood lust. Men who normally neglected their weapons, unless driven to it, now cleaned and recleaned their muskets and sharpened their bayonets as never before. I noticed Harry McGee busy whetting the blade of the huge hawk-billed pocket knife he carried. Others were slicing crosses into the noses of their Minié balls so they would spread on impact and thereby cause more serious wounds.

I never encountered such a primitive mood in a group of men before. It was frightening.

Our plan of battle was simple. We in the 10th did not understand it at the time, but later it became apparent. Our regiment was to be used as bait for a trap. They advanced us down the road, on the heels of the calvary with a dozen pieces of artillery rolling along behind us.

Our other four regiments marched about a mile behind the artillery, two regiments on either side of the road, spread out in skirmish lines, walking across fields and through woods.

We moved deliberately, at a slow pace, halting at every turn in the road while the cavalry scouted ahead to the next turn. Noon had come and passed but we were not allowed to stop and eat, which of course made our mood even uglier.

It was about 1 P.M. when we heard the popping of our cavalry's carbines up ahead, answered by a volley which sent spent bullets kicking up dirt in front of us. "Advance at the double," the order came. We began to trot along the road, our muskets, loaded and capped, carried before us in the manner of quail hunters, until we saw drawn up across our route three regiments of Negroes. The black of their faces contrasted with the fresh blue of their new uniforms. Here and there we saw their white officers, most of them mounted.

A roar went up from their ranks when they saw us. Our cavalry stopped their pot-shotting as they waited for us to come up.

Colonel Rankin was the very image of coolness as he sat on his horse, deploying us company by company to the left and right of the road, just out of range of the enemy muskets. He held a consultation with his ten captains, who then ran back to their companies.

"All right, men," Captain Cadieu shouted. "We're going to advance, halt and give them a volley. Don't charge them, no matter what they do. If they advance, you fall back slowly, keeping the same distance between our lines. If they come forward in a charge, you run back down the road and reform between the artillery you'll find drawn up there. We'll make a stand there."

"You want us to run from a bunch of niggers?" someone shouted.

"Do as you are ordered. You'll see the purpose."

Ahead of us, the white Yankee officers were dressing up the ranks of their black troopers, no doubt giving them a talk about bravery and such.

Colonel Rankin raised his sword, pointed it toward the enemy and shouted, "Regiment, advance!"

We went forward at a walk until we could easily see the expressions on the faces of the Negroes.

"Regiment, halt! Cock your pieces. Ready. Aim. Fire."

A line of white smoke spouted across our front. We were answered by a heavier volley from the blacks but, being recruits, their aim was poor, most of their bullets singing over our heads.

"Regiment, fall back in formation."

We started backing up. Another roar went up from the Negroes and, despite the shouts of their officers, many of them started running toward us, not stopping to reload. In a moment the others stampeded toward us, chanting as they came, "Ain't gwine take no quarter," meaning they did not intend to take prisoners.

Many of our men were cursing and grinding their teeth, but Colonel Rankin shouted the command that was repeated by our captains, "Retreat. Retreat. On the double. Fall back."

Our entire regiment turned and ran. The blacks, thinking they had put us to flight, swept around and past their frantic officers, pursuing us like an armed mob, laughing at what they regarded as our cowardice.

We ran until we reached our line of guns and then turned, loaded our pieces and waited like so many coiled snakes.

The Negroes surged along the road repeating, "Ain't gwine take no quarter."

It seemed a thousand years passed before we heard the order, "Fire at will." Our muskets began their deadly work. The Negroes began to fall, but their mass kept moving toward us until our cannon joined in the carnage, sending showers of canister into their disordered ranks.

Now they halted and began frantically trying to load their muskets. I have to hand it to those niggers. This was the first time they had been in a real battle. True, they had us outnumbered three to one, but still it took courage to stand there and return our fire. It would have been serious for us if we had been as untrained as they or if we had not been supported by artillery.

They were just getting ready to give us a charge when our two regiments on the right came out of the woods squarely on their flank. With a shrill Rebel yell these fourteen hundred men advanced to within easy range and began pouring musket fire into the black mass.

A moment later, our other column swept in from the left, bringing the Negroes under a crisscross of fire. There they were, hemmed in on three sides, being raked by twelve cannon, and completely beyond the control of their officers. Even seasoned troops could not have stood that. In fact, seasoned Confederates would have turned and raced out of range from such a hopeless situation. That is one reason we generally took lighter casualties than the Yanks; they tended to retire stubbornly, trying to fight back and thereby taking unnecessary casualties. We moved in and out of action much faster. And these Negroes were Yankee troops.

They went to pieces. Those in the rear threw down their muskets and stampeded back toward Suffolk. Others either cast themselves on the ground or raised their empty hands, giving up.

Our fire slackened. The cannon stopped firing.

"Look at them Goddamn monkeys. They have had enough."

"Black sons of bitches. Thought they didn't believe in taking quarter."

Just as their officers lost control of their men, now so did ours. What happened was a shocking thing. Various squads of Confederates ran out among the helpless and in some cases pleading Negroes and began striking them with their muskets and kicking those already on the ground, wounded as well as those merely cringing.

"Please, please, massa," I heard one cry.

"Don't massa me, nigger. I'll teach you to rape white women."

Soon hundreds of our soldiers, ignoring the orders of their officers, were pouring into the huddled clumps of the defenseless blacks.

Harry McGee is long dead and he left no children or I would not relate this. I saw him run up to a huge Negro who had been shot in the side and was kneeling, crying for mercy. Harry took out that evil hawk-billed knife and slashed him across the throat. As I reached Harry, he had a smaller soldier by the front of his jacket and was poised to slash him as well.

Harry never knew who struck him across the back of the head with the flat side of a musket butt. It was the only way I knew to stifle the blood lust that possessed him. Harry was Scotch-Irish and I expect that his Celtic ancestors had dealt the same with their vanquished foes.

Finally our officers regained control of our regiment, but only after thirty or forty of the Negroes had been put to death and many more had been battered about. We captured several of their white officers as well, our boys slapping their faces and spitting upon them or ripping their epaulets from their shoulders and cursing them as "nigger-loving abolitionists." One, an anemic-looking lieutenant with a Boston accent, was knocked down and kicked, his glasses getting broken in the process, until Captain Cadieu rescued him.

It was not our most heroic moment of the war, although I must say that the Yankee officers who mishandled their black troops were partly to blame for the massacre.

If we had gone into battle shouting that we were not going to take prisoners, our fate might have been the same. Generally, though, both sides followed the rules and took prisoners. I can't remember any other case in which a foe on either side was killed after he had surrendered.

We discovered after our rage had subsided that many of the blacks had been drinking and indeed some were drunk. They fought better than we had expected. They deserved better officers. I still say that the Confederates would have done well to have enlisted Negroes early in the war. We could have sent our Negroes to fight their Negroes just as Confederate Indians fought Union Indians out in Oklahoma. Some of my old Confederate veteran friends in Baltimore violently disagree with my opinion, which may be one reason I still hold to it and repeat it often.

Anyway, we marched into the town, greeted as saviors by the white people, not one of whom, it turned out, had been raped or had his home burned. Some had been insulted or mocked by their black oppressors; that was the worst that had happened. Nonetheless we all felt like knights of old who had just won a great victory.

Harry McGee nursed his sore head and cursed the "dirty nigger" who had hit him from behind. I was glad no one enlightened him.

41

It was June before we left the area, marching back to the railroad and then riding north again. We feared they were hauling us back to work on the James River fortifications, but at Petersburg they shifted us to another train. We soon rattled into Richmond itself.

The capital appeared more crowded and chaotic than ever. A kind of manic excitement ran through the city, now that mourning for the great Stonewall Jackson was subsiding and a full realization of the magnitude of the victory at Chancellorsville came, together with an appreciation of the opportunities available for a Confederate offensive.

Eyes turned north. Lee had won two victories in a row over the Union Army of the Potomac—at Fredericksburg in December of '62 and at Chancellorsville in May. The Union Army was far from destroyed, although we did hear many enlistments were running out and that morale ran low north of the Rappahannock. Years later I was to read that Abraham Lincoln wept when he heard the news of Chancellorsville. It would have cheered my heart to have known that at the time.

The Richmond papers told of the siege a Federal general called Grant had mounted against Vicksburg, a thousand miles to the west of Mississippi. But they made it seem that the defenses of that Confederate "Gibraltar" could never be reduced. Meanwhile, in Virginia, what would Lee do with his opportunities against a dispirited enemy army, still commanded by Hooker? There were several rumors:

1. Lee would move directly upon Washington, driving the discouraged Union Army back across the Potomac.

2. Lee would swing around the Federals, before they could fall back from their positions along the Rappahannock, and trap them between that river and the Potomac.

3. No, the seemingly invincible Confederate Army of Northern Virginia would swing even farther west and advance across Maryland and into south-central Pennsylvania, from whence he would send Stuart's cavalry westward over the Alleghenies to smash the cannon factories at Pittsburgh and his infantry divisions eastward against either Baltimore or Philadelphia, in that way destroying railroads between the Northeast and the Middle West and isolating Washington, D.C.

4. None of the above. Instead, Lee would leave a holding force along the Rappahannock while he took most of his army

west by rail to corner that upstart Grant against the fortifications at Vicksburg and, after crushing him, invade Kentucky.

While these rumors flew about the capital, Lee completed the reorganization of his army. Previously he had operated with two corps—one under sturdy old James Longstreet and the other under Stonewall Jackson. Now he would have three smaller corps, bringing the cantankerous old "Baldy" Ewell and the fiery A. P. Hill up to the level of Longstreet. Lee made many other changes in his army, getting rid of deadwood and shifting units about. We discovered upon our arrival in Richmond that Colonel Rankin would be promoted to brigadier general and be sent out to take command of a brigade in Tennessee. And he would be replaced as our colonel by none other than William Ferro.

This news sent a buzz through our regiment. We had come to respect Colonel Rankin but felt little real warmth for him as he was a stern taskmaster. But there was hardly a man in the regiment who did not feel a strong affection for William Ferro. I was the exception because I still felt resentment toward all who bore the name of Ferro for what I felt to be their humiliating treatment of me.

Our first two days in Richmond were too busy for me to brood, however. Jefferson Davis himself, looking like he had a ramrod up his precious ass, came out to review us. Unlike the warm Zeb Vance he did not deign to address us, however. I think the man had ink and water in his veins instead of rich red blood. Never mind that. At the conclusion of this review, Colonel Rankin gave us a brief talk in which he thanked us for our loyalty and praised the way we had become what he called "one of the steadiest regiments in the Confederate Army." We gave him three Rebel yells for that.

Than William Ferro stepped forward to take command. He expressed his pleasure at returning to a regiment in which he had so many friends and neighbors and promised to keep up Colonel Rankin's traditions of discipline. He looked heavier and had a more robust complexion as he stood there gesturing with his one hand while the empty sleeve of the arm lost at New Bern dangled at his side.

In his conclusion, Colonel Ferro informed us that we would leave Richmond in the morning to rejoin the Army of Northern Virginia. It seemed we were to be added to Rodes' division of Ewell's corps, most of whose men had been a part of Stonewall Jackson's "foot cavalry." The cheering and Rebel yells that greeted this news hurt my ears.

So one last night remained to us in Richmond, a night I wanted to spend "on the town." Would it be possible to find the lodgings of Elmer Fincastle, taking a chance that his bureaucratic duties would have carried him out of town and that his voluptuous little wife still would have some feeling for the raw North Carolina soldier to whom she had taught the ways of love? Or should I try to bluff my way back into that officers' bordello to have another evening of exquisite love-making with Maria? I would first get my pass and then toss a coin.

Our usually accommodating company clerk shook his head. "No, sirree, Jimmy boy. Colonel Ferro has stopped all company passes. Only way you can get out of camp tonight is to apply at regimental headquarters and I don't think they will believe that shit about going to a revival meeting."

"Kiss my ass, then," I responded.

I suppose that if company passes had been handed out freely on that last night, we would have left a good part of our strength back at whorehouses or drunk in gutters when the regiment stepped out in the morning. So I wasn't resentful as I made my way to the regimental headquarters tent.

Stepping inside, I was surprised to see William Ferro himself talking to several of his captains. Before I could approach the regimental clerk about my pass, Colonel Ferro excused himself to come over and greet me.

"James. How have you been?"

I saluted him. "Very well, sir. And you?"

"I'm fine, James, fine. My stump doesn't pain me anymore

and, as you can see, this soft city living has put some weight on me. But I am ready to get back in the field again."

I was surprised and a bit put off by the warmth of his greeting.

"James," he went on, "I have been holding a letter for you for some time now. When it first reached me here in Richmond, the regiment had moved from Kinston. Apparently you hopped and skipped all over North Carolina. I was at the point of sending the letter on to Kinston anyway but then learned you were headed back to Virginia. I am so sorry it has taken this long. Look, I'll just step into the next tent and dig the letter out of my papers."

The other officers seemed annoyed at having their conference interrupted while the colonel made small talk to a mere sergeant. My heart pounded as I waited for Colonel Ferro to return.

"There it is," he said as he opened the tent flap. "In your hands at last. Now that is over, what business brings you to headquarters?"

Looking down at the envelope I recognized the precise, feminine handwriting of Jane Ferro. He had to repeat his question.

"Oh, nothing, really," I mumbled. "I just wanted to say congratulations on your promotion."

"Why, that is very good of you, James. I do appreciate it. The 10th is a fine regiment and I think it is going to perform very well with Ewell's corps."

"I am sure it will, sir. Thank you and congratulations."

I backed out of the tent, all thoughts of Elvira Fincastle or Maria driven from my mind. Holding the letter tightly, I avoided my comrades and went off to an army stable to open it.

The letter was dated February 1, four months before.

Dear James:

Your letter arrived yesterday and I have been thinking ever since just how to reply to it. In fact, last night I slept hardly a wink, worrying over the offense my father has caused you.

It is true that my father does not approve of my writing to you, and while I love him dearly, still I think his attitude is wrong. I want you to know that I do not share it.

James, how could you accuse me of toying with your affections by carrying on "a brief, teasing correspondence with a person of lower social rank"? That was a hurtful thing to say and I only hope that you did not truly mean it.

I do not regard you as an inferior in any way. From what I know of you through our all-too-brief personal meetings and our most welcome correspondence, not to mention brother William's praise of your conduct, I feel you to be a person of superior spirit and intelligence, a young man sure to make his mark on the world.

You have been on my mind constantly ever since that happy day when you brought poor wounded William home in a buggy. I have never known a young man with your ready wit and high spirits.

You seem to be hurt because I wrote to Tom Shelton, whom I gather you don't care for. I have known Tom since we were children. Please do not think that I have been writing to him in the same way as to you.

Oh, dear James, let us not quarrel. I should not say this. It is improper of me, but I am so fond of you. I shall die if you do not take back those hard words and if you stop writing me your warm and interesting letters.

Father will come around, I know he will. Mother likes you. And even Reba, who has never thought any young man good enough for me, asked me the other day, "What do you hear from that tall young fellow, that Mundy boy? He is something."

You are something, James. Something terribly important to me. For, James, I love you with all my heart. Please write and say you love me as well.

Jane Ferro.

I was glad nobody watched me as I finished that letter for I put my face in my hands and wept for the first time since I was a little boy—wept tears of joy and regret for my stupidity and also from sheer gratitude.

Suddenly life became sweet again. That is very nearly the happiest moment of my entire life, there beside a stinking Confederate mule barn in Richmond, Virginia, on June 3, 1863, on the eve of Lee's great invasion of the North. I say "is" rather than "was" because the memory of it still brings me pleasure.

I scrounged a pencil and paper and while it was still daylight I scrawled out a reply, pouring out my heart with apologies and promising to be pure and brave so as to be worthy of her upon my return from the war—a war, that, I assured her, would soon end with a great Confederate victory on Northern soil, a victory in which Robert E. Lee would whip the Yankees worse than he had at Fredericksburg and Chancellorsville put together.

With that note in my hand, I returned to the headquarters tent to find Colonel Ferro putting away his papers.

"Please, sir," I said, "would you mind enclosing this letter to Miss Jane with your next envelope home?"

He smiled. "Certainly, James. I shall post a letter in the morning and she should have it within a week or ten days."

"I would be grateful to you."

He seemed so busy with his paper work that I did not want to detain him. As I turned to go he called me back.

"You forgot something."

"What is that, sir?"

"The postage. You don't want to impose, remember?"

We exchanged grins. He waved away my offer of a fifty-cent bill. "Just teasing, James. I'm going to add a note to Jane and tell her there is a good chance you will become a second lieutenant after this campaign. But if you breathe it to a soul, I will demote you to corporal."

I felt like skipping as I walked away from his tent. How could anyone be happier than James Mundy, Sergeant, Co. H., 10th North Carolina Regiment, C.S.A.?

42

As we set out from Richmond, we had little notion of what lay ahead for us. I was surprised to see that Colonel Ferro was mounted on Nellie, Jane's little bay mare, the same one she had lent me back in Oldham County for my recruiting work. His father had shipped Nellie up by rail from Charlotte. Seemed William needed a calm horse with an easy gait because he had only one arm. Nellie filled the bill. The sight of that little mare cheered me throughout our march north, for she reminded me of Jane.

Just as he was breaking in a new steed for the long march, so William Ferro handled our regiment gently at first, moving us along at an easy pace, often riding ahead and then stopping to watch us walk past. Or his pale blue eyes would observe us keenly as we lolled about during our rest stops or as we set up our camps at the end of the day. He kept his voice low even when correcting some fault. His way of rebuking a soldier was not to shout or criticize but to ask a question such as "Don't you think you ought to keep your cartridge box fastened? It would prevent your spilling ammunition along the road."

Each evening he walked through our camp to chat with a captain or sergeant here and there, to inquire after the condition of our feet or to taste the food prepared at individual company messes. We were convinced that he knew every one of the seven hundred men in his regiment and that he was concerned for our welfare.

For my part, I would not have minded if he had marched us twenty-five miles a day through rain and mud, for my heart sang with every step. Jane Ferro did love me. She preferred me to all the better-born young men she knew. What's more, I might soon become an officer, which would give me status back home. So my attitude was: Let's get the war over and done with so I can return as a hero to Oldham County to take my place as a young man of consequence and promise.

The members of my squad noticed how cheerful I had become. I stopped much of the vulgar talk to which I had reverted. Taking example from William Ferro, I ceased being so impatient with other people. Life was never sweeter.

We reached Culpeper, Virginia, on June 9, 1863, to the sound of small arms and light artillery fire for that was the day Stuart and Pleasonton fought the biggest cavalry battle of the war at nearby Brandy Station. It was an inconclusive fight. Pleasonton attacked Stuart across the upper Rappahannock with three cavalry divisions and gave our supposedly superior horsemen a bad time of it for several hours. Pleasonton failed to get through to see what Lee was up to so far from his accustomed camps around Fredericksburg, but he did shake Stuart's confidence. As I have said before, cavalry battles made a lot of noise but didn't amount to much and I think that is true even of Brandy Station.

We caught up with our new division north of Culpeper in the rich, low hills of the Virginia Piedmont and from then on things were different. The division was commanded by one Robert Rodes, born in Virginia and at one time a professor at the Virginia Military Institute but more recently a civil engineer for a railroad down in Alabama. Rodes was blond as a Norwegian and had long mustaches. Only thirty-odd years old but acted like a stern old man.

Hardly had we caught our breath than we found ourselves marching in a long column headed not quite due north toward the Shenandoah Valley. No more leisurely marching for us. We had become a part of Stonewall Jackson's old corps, now commanded by irascible Richard S. (Old Baldy) Ewell, just reporting back for service after losing a leg the year before at the Battle of Groveton. Ewell rode in a buggy or carriage drawn by two horses. His piercing eyes and beak nose gave him the appearance of an eagle; a bald eagle, I might add.

Old Ewell had performed well as commander of a division under Jackson. Now he commanded three divisions, a total of 23,000 men, and his corps was leading the way for Lee's army, part of which still stood guard far back down the Rappahannock at Fredericksburg. It remained to be seen whether Ewell could dominate in battle like Stonewall. But he marched us as Jackson might have. Left-right, left-right, we ate up the miles as our column pressed toward the distant blur of the Blue Ridge Mountains.

I had a sense of entering upon an exciting part of history and so I kept my diary up to date throughout that month of June 1863. Some of the entries:

JUNE 10, 1863—Clear day. Not too hot. Marched throughout afternoon north through some pretty country. Crops look good in this section. Tonight we are camped at a place called Gourd Vine Church. Our boys all excited about joining Stonewall's old corps. Ewell's other two divisions following another road west of us, I hear.

JUNE 11, 1863—This was a hard day of marching. Don't know who picked our route but he couldn't have chosen a sorrier road if he had tried. Wagons and artillery could hardly make their way along the ruts. Turned west at a place called Gaines' Crossroads and encountered General Ewell himself in his buggy. Other two divisions were held up so he gave us permission to take the pike first. From there it was easier going. We are now camped a couple of miles north of a place called Flint Hill. Encountered one brief shower.

JUNE 12, 1863—What a day! Up at 4 A.M. Marched all day right over the mountains via Chester's Gap, through village of Front Royal. Waded the Shenandoah River and stopped, exhausted, at Cedarville to wait for Johnson's division to catch up. Joined by Jenkins' Brigade of so-called mounted infantry here. (Later) Ewell is trying to kill us. Gave us a couple of hours' rest and put us on the road again in the afternoon, following along behind this Jenkins crowd of cutthroats. At last we are resting at a place called Stone Bridge, must have marched over 25 miles today.

I was too tired when I wrote that last entry to do justice to the day's activities. It took eighteen hours for Ewell's entire corps to cross over Chester's Gap, and our division led the way. During a brief rest stop in the gap, I looked back over the green foothills, through which we had passed, to see the rest of Ewell's corps crawling toward us like a gray snake, an immense column that stretched as far as the eye could reach. What a glorious scene! The tail of the column was an indistinct blur. Closer to the gap, I could make out wagons, artillery and individual regiments following their colors. Finally, toiling up the nearer slopes, I could see the faces of Johnson's division and hear the tramp of their feet, the jangle and creak of harness and the complaint of cannon wheels. The sight brought to me a thrill, a consciousness of the power of this superb army. The feeling lasted until Tom Shelton shouted, "On your feet, men. Let's move out."

The beautiful Shenandoah Valley was spread before us as we passed over the crest and down into the village of Front Royal. We marched through the town and to the banks of the Shenandoah River. We had a train of pontoons dragging along behind us, but Rodes was too impatient to wait for it to be set up. So we waded that icy stream and stopped a short distance beyond.

That is where we encountered General Albert G. Jenkins and his fifteen hundred rude Virginia hillbillies waiting to escort us north. These were a far cry from Jeb Stuart's dashing cavalry. They carried carbines and sawed-off muskets, were mounted on rough horses, and seemed to have little knowledge of military discipline.

At this point, Lee's army of some 75,000 men stretched from Fredericksburg across northern Virginia to our resting place beyond Front Royal. I don't know what he would have done if Hooker had moved smartly and started gobbling up the tail of this column. But Lee knew he could get away with it, I suppose. Anyway, he did not mind taking risks. In fact, Ewell was about to do some gobbling of his own.

Winchester was and is the chief town of that end of the Shenandoah, and it was occupied by a Federal division commanded by General Robert H. Milroy. Ewell decided to send Early's division directly north against Winchester while Johnson's division moved east of the town and seized Stephenson's Depot on the railroad that brought supplies out to Milroy from Harpers Ferry.

As for our division, we would move along the northern bank of the Shenandoah, bypassing Winchester even farther to the east than Johnson, then descend upon the railroad at Summit Point, well beyond Stephenson's Depot. Then, with the help of Jenkins, we would clear the way up to the Potomac River.

The strategy worked against Winchester. Ewell gobbled up most of Milroy's division and put the rest to flight. The survivors scattered into the mountains west of Winchester like so many chickens. My diary tells the story of our progress to the Potomac:

JUNE 13—Marched all day. Supposed to be in the village of Millwood tonight but Jenkins failed to secure the place. Jenkins had a chance to bag a large Federal detachment at Berryville but his apes failed to pin them down. Rodes marched us around the place to cut them off but they slipped away. We are camped tonight on the railroad at Summit Point, in a pouring rain.

JUNE 14—Can bearly hold my pencil, so tired. Marched against Martinsburg. Two Yankee regiments made a stand with a battery south of town. Shelled them and then attacked. They ran like rabbits. Abandoned guns in town. We camp tonight just a short march from the Potomac River.

My diary isn't much help in reconstructing the next few days. Old Rodes let us sleep late the next morning, June 15, while Jenkins crossed over the Potomac and rode north with the intent of securing the town of Chambersburg up in Pennsylvania. We resumed our march about 10 A.M. and by late afternoon we reached the Potomac River. The engineers turned to and put the pontoons in the water in short order. Most of Rodes' division, including our regiment, gingerly crossed the narrow walkway of boards, and that night we slept comfortably in a meadow just outside the village of Williamsport, Maryland. We remained in that pleasant locale for two days, waiting for the rest of Lee's army to close up with us and for Jenkins to scour the countryside ahead. He did a good job, too. It wasn't long before his men began herding back droves of cattle and farm horses. The horses generally were of little military use, but the cattle were just the ticket for a hungry army that seldom got fresh beef. We slaughtered many on the spot and sent others across the river and back toward Winchester.

The odds and ends of fleeing Federal soldiers had abandoned tons of canned meats, hardtack, flour, corn meal, sugar and coffee. How glorious coffee can be when you haven't tasted the real stuff for a long while. Most of the loot left by the Yankees was properly passed back for use by the rest of Lee's army, but we kept the coffee for ourselves.

I well remember lying stretched out on the grass after our evening mess, gazing across the Potomac River as I contentedly sipped from a large tin cup of rich coffee, laced with sugar, courtesy of Abe Lincoln and the Yankee taxpayer. All around me lounged the tough confident men of Rodes' division, men tested in battle, hardened by marching, well equipped, and now well fed to boot. Behind us lay the vast, unconquered and seemingly unconquerable South, stretching eight hundred miles across valleys, mountains, hills, forests and flat cotton lands to the Gulf of Mexico. We had defended that beloved land successfully for two years and now we were poised to carry the war into the country of the enemy.

I trembled with pleasure at the thought of the great adventure lying before me. And, to top it off, there awaited back in Oldham County the lovely, kind Jane Ferro to give me a hero's welcome after we had humbled the Yankees on their own soil and gained recognition from them of the independence of the Confederate States of America. Life seemed sweet and full of promise in that June of 1863.

43

A geography lesson is in order here. The Shenandoah curves gently northeastward from the lower left corner of Virginia to the Potomac River, a broad, fertile valley, drained in its northern reaches by the Shenandoah River. Beyond the Potomac River, it is complemented by the Cumberland Valley, which runs seventy miles across Maryland and deep into Pennsylvania, ending at the wide, shallow Susquehanna River. The South Mountain Range forms the low eastern wall of the Cumberland Valley; the steeper Blue Mountain Range, the western. Unlike the Shenandoah, the Cumberland Valley is not drained by a major river. Its even, fertile limestone earth made a natural invasion route into the North, leading to Harrisburg, the capital of Pennsylvania.

It should have been obvious to the Yankees that Lee intended to sweep the length of that valley to take Harrisburg and its rail yards and, in the process, live off the fat of the Pennsylvania Dutch country. Still commanded by the usually aggressive "Fighting Joe" Hooker, the Union Army of the Potomac hovered in northern Virginia, shifting its strength sluggishly away from Fredericksburg to act as a shield between Lee and Washington, D.C., while his cavalry ineffectively poked at Jeb Stuart's troopers guarding the tail of the Confederate column. This cautious wait-and-see strategy originated with old Abe Lincoln himself, I realize now. In effect, Lincoln gave Lee his head to proceed into the naked Pennsylvania heartland without having to fight a major battle, as long as he did not turn back toward Washington.

The only forces to stand in Lee's way were odds and ends of New York and Pennsylvania militia, invalid soldiers on leave and such. Hardly worth mentioning. So some of the richest farming country in America lay at Lee's mercy.

One other item before I relate what I did during those next two weeks. Now I was born a Southerner and I will die with the South in my heart, even though I live only on the fringe of Dixie here in Baltimore. And even though I agree with some of H. L. Mencken's vitriolic tirades against my native region. (Knowing Mencken personally for an egotistical bore, I can't take him too seriously, incidentally.) Despite all that, in the main we Southerners are good people, trapped by history and bearing up under our fate better than most of our critics ever would. Now one of the noblest things we ever did was to live up to Robert E. Lee's General Order No. 72 telling his army how it was to conduct itself during our invasion of the North. Aside from exchanging our weather-beaten hats for those of gaping civilians, some rough teasing and denuding the orchards of their fruit, we Rebels conducted ourselves better than any invading force I ever read about. Give us credit for that. I saw or heard of no incident of raping or barn-burning; no physical abuse of the civilian population. Too bad Sherman or Sheridan couldn't say the same.

Well, enough of bragging on what good boys we were. Old Rodes got us off our asses there at Williamsport and marched us smartly to the town of Hagerstown at the terminus of the Cumberland Valley Railroad. All we had to do was follow those tracks for sixty-five or seventy miles and we would find ourselves on the west bank of the Susquehanna looking across at Harrisburg, if Lincoln allowed the veteran Union Army of the Potomac to sit back nervously guarding Washington long enough, that is.

Now the population of eastern Maryland favored the Confederate cause, but up here in the Cumberland Valley the folks were pro-Union. They gathered to stare at us as we marched along, but we heard no cheering.

Jenkins, meanwhile, was busy cleaning out the countryside around Chambersburg. Down the valley pike came droves of cattle and wagonloads of medical supplies and foodstuffs, all properly paid for with Confederate scrip to be made good soon after the cessation of the war. Maybe it's a good thing for the South that she lost that war; I don't know how the Confederacy could have redeemed all those promises to pay with which our supply officers littered Pennsylvania.

From Hagerstown, we moved north to the village of Middleburg, Pennsylvania, and there our column came to a halt. The regiment ahead of us and the next after it were standing still. We could hear shouting and laughing up the road.

Colonel Ferro stood up in his stirrups to get a better view. Then he gave Nellie a dig in the ribs to make her canter forward. In a few minutes he rode back with a smile on his face.

"What's holding us up?" Captain Cadieu asked.

"You'll see for yourself in a little while."

It took us half an hour to advance through that little village. What had happened was we had come to a stone beside the road marking the Mason-Dixon line, and the boys were making a ceremony out of passing it. By squads they would parade across the line, shouting and cheering, onto the "foreign soil" of Pennsylvania.

When our turn came, I lined up my squad and said, "All right, boys. Let's carry the war into the North."

With that, I made a running jump, clicked my heels in the air and, with a Rebel yell, landed on the Pennsylvania side of the Mason-Dixon line. By pairs, my boys followed suit. By nightfall Rodes' entire division of nearly seven thousand Confederate infantrymen had joined the fifteen hundred horsemen of Jenkins' brigade in Yankeeland. Hot diggety damn!

44

It was an easy march from the Mason-Dixon line to Chambersburg, a mere twenty miles through prosperous farming country. Sturdy brick houses and enormous stone barns dotted the landscape. What a contrast with the ill-kempt country from which we had come.

I'll never forget marching through the main street of Greencastle, the first town of any size we encountered. Men, women and children stood along the sidewalk, staring at us. We must have presented quite a sight as we trudged along, out of step in an odd assortment of gray, butternut and captured U.S. garb. Lean, hard men we were with sunbrowned faces. We traveled light, carrying only a few personal belongings rolled in a blanket slung across one shoulder, with the ends tied across the opposite hip. A small knapsack hanging down to our waists along with a wooden canteen and cartridge box and percussion cap case completed our meager outfits. Plus our muskets, of course.

As I have mentioned before, we got rid of those stupid little kepis or monkey hats they issued at first, substituting gray slouch hats fairly early in the war. By the time we invaded Maryland, our slouch hats had been rained and snowed on, dried out over campfires, bleached by the sun, and rotted from our sweat. The hat game started in Greencastle. The sidewalks were lined with stocky, earnest German farmers and tradesmen staring with unbelief at the ragged Rebels streaming north through their little town. In a flash, while his officers were looking the other way, a soldier dashed to the sidewalk, lifted the new black hat from the head of an elderly burgher, replaced it with his own battered hat, and then raced back into the ranks. Soon scores of similar exchanges had taken place. The officers shouted and swore, but it did little good. The same thing happened in every town along our route. We must have done a world of good for the hat trade in Pennsylvania.

I know we looked strange to the sturdy people of Pennsylvania from the way they stared at us. They surely appeared funny to us, with their stocky figures and rosy complexions.

I like Pennsylvanians. They lack the mean spirit of many New Englanders or the overbearing rudeness of New Yorkers. But I could not compliment them on the beauty of their womenfolk. I understand they make marvelous housewives. But to our Southern eyes, they seemed just a bit too sturdy in the hindquarters and legs to be attractive. Ah, well, looks aren't everything.

Whether it was good or bad fortune, I can't say, but we did arrive in Pennsylvania just as their bountiful cherry orchards were coming in with ripe fruit. God knows how many tons of cherries we consumed in the Cumberland Valley alone. Again, our officers tried to keep us in line, but we *would* break rank and run over to a tree to grab handfuls of cherries. We paid a price for this violation of General Lee's order with many a griping gut and set of loose bowels.

I'll never forget a foraging expedition my boys and I staged between Greencastle and Chambersburg. During a noon rest, we sneaked down a country road to where several cherry trees grew behind a farmhouse. It appeared that nobody was home, so we began filling our stolen hats with stolen cherries. Happy as hogs in a mud hole we were until suddenly there came hustling out the back door of the house a buxom blond woman of about forty, shouting and shaking a mop handle at us.

"What the hell do you filthy Rebels think you are doing in my cherries?" she demanded as she descended on us.

Harry McGee tried his Southern charm with "Why, ma'am,

we were just sampling a few of your cherries to see if they are as good as they look. You surely can spare a few of—"

He barely dodged her swing of the mop handle. "No, I can't spare anything more for you lot of lousy bastards. My poor husband and son have had to drive our horses and beef cattle clear down the pike to the other side of Harrisburg to keep them out of your thieving hands and still your stinking cavalrymen came and drove off three milk cows. Milk cows, mind you."

I stepped forward. "Surely, ma'am, they paid you, gave you a voucher or receipt if not money itself."

"Oh, shit," she shouted. "What good is that worthless scrip except to wipe our asses with? It's no good and you know it."

Few of us had ever heard such rough language from a woman. Her speech bothered us more than her brandished mop handle. I held out some Confederate notes, but she wouldn't take them.

"Damn your Rebel money and damn you. Just leave my cherries alone. And get off my land."

My boys were all laughing at me now. And as she started forward with that mop handle it seemed wise to retreat.

We weren't there to witness it, of course, but we learned that there had been a regular exodus of horses, cattle and wagonloads of household goods along the Cumberland Valley Pike for the past week. Farmers and merchants alike wanted to put the Susquehanna River between their possessions and the voracious Rebels. The hordes of refugees included quite a few ex-slaves who had fled from Virginia and Maryland to refuges in the North. They feared they would be captured and returned to their owners by the invading Confederates. I witnessed one incident that supported their fears.

We marched into the town of Chambersburg on Wednesday, June 24. By this time we were all impressed by the evidence of plenty we saw both in town and countryside. These Pennsylvania Dutch worked hard, but they lived well.

The next day we rested around Chambersburg. I had the opportunity to stroll about the streets, admiring the rows of brick houses built right up against the sidewalks, unlike anything I had seen except in Richmond and Fredericksburg. Under a tree on the main street, I noticed a pair of tough-looking older men sitting in a buggy. One was a huge, heavy-set fellow with flowing mustache, and the other a spindly chap with a goiter on his neck. I took them for local citizens until I noticed their clothing wasn't as smart as that the Dutchmen wore. And then I overheard their Southern accents.

I nodded to them and they said, "Howdy."

"You all from these parts?" I asked.

"I should hope not," the spindly chap replied. "Do we look like these damn Yankees?"

"No. That's how come I asked you. I reckon you to be Virginia gentlemen."

"Right. We are from down near Staunton. And we are here on business."

"Business? It's a strange time and place for business."

I suppose I have a face that invited confidence for these two tough old birds told me exactly what had brought them up to Pennsylvania on the heels of the Confederate invasion. The heavy-set man was the sheriff of his county and the other a landowner. Seems a slave had run away back in 1861 and they had heard he settled down as a farm hand west of Chambersburg. Nobody was trying to enforce the Fugitive Slave Act by then. So they bided their time till now. They had bribed some of Jenkins' men to swoop down on the farm and try to recover the slave. They were waiting in the buggy to see what luck the horsemen would have.

I circled the center of town, and when I got back the same pair had been joined by four of Jenkins' men and two of the most frightened Negroes you ever saw.

A mean-looking cavalryman was explaining, "We found two niggers hiding in their barn. And we weren't sure which was yours, so we brought them both along."

"Well, you boys did right," the skinny fellow said. "That's my nigger right there." He pointed to a short, slight man of about fifty. "Don't know why I have gone to such trouble for such a worthless wretch. Aren't you ashamed, Cicero? You ungrateful black bastard. You ran away and left your wife in our hands. I guess you don't remember begging me to buy you so you could come and be with her."

The Negro ducked his head. The white man continued. "Yes, sir, I paid six hundred dollars five years ago when a dollar was a dollar, by God. This black ape asked me to buy him so he could live with our cook. Fed him and cared for him. He gets our cook pregnant and then runs away. I'm going to get him back down in God's Country and give his black ass a good whipping."

By now, a fair crowd of Confederate soldiers and local citizens had gathered about the buggy. The Rebs were laughing, but the citizens weren't. In fact, a stylishly dressed young woman, wearing a bonnet, became quite outspoken.

"You do not propose to return these poor men to slavery, do you?" she asked.

They tried to ignore her, but she would not remain quiet.

"You hear me? I am asking what you intend to do with these two human beings here. You, sir," she pointed to the sheriff. "By what authority are you holding these men?"

"By the authority of my county and the Fugitive Slave Act of 1850. I am the sheriff of my county."

"You are a scoundrel and so is your friend."

The slaveowner flared up. "This nigger is the scoundrel, him and the farmer who has been harboring him. They have deprived me of property that cost me six hundred dollars. For two and a half years they have used his labor and now I have been put to great expense to come up here and recover him. Allowing for interest on the six hundred dollars and the expense of myself and the sheriff here, I am out over a thousand dollars."

"How my heart bleeds for you. What about the other man?" She pointed to the younger, larger Negro. "Do you claim him as your property as well?"

The other Negro spoke up. "I ain't nobody's property. I am a free man. I was given my freedom down in Maryland when my master died. I been up here helping pick cherries. You ain't going to put me into slavery."

"What do you say to that?" Miss Pepperpot asked the sheriff.

"I say he is lying. He's probably from down in our section as well. I intend to take him back to Virginia and look for his rightful owner."

"Of all the immoral, wicked . . ." the woman spluttered. "I can't believe you are so evil."

By now the other townspeople were grumbling and shaking their fists. I don't know what would have happened if some Confederate officers hadn't come over and ordered the crowd to disperse.

Jenkins' four cavalrymen took their payment from the two men. The last I saw of the Negroes, they were walking with their hands bound behind them, following the buggy back toward Virginia.

45

Chambersburg, that pretty, prosperous little town, became the axis of Lee's invasion of Pennsylvania. It was occupied first around June 15 by Jenkins' brigade of rude mounted infantry who descended on the area so quickly there was little time to hide horses, cattle, foodstuffs or merchants' supplies. Then came Rodes' division of infantry on June 24, by which time the population was alerted to the fact that they lay squarely in the intended path of Lee's legions. During the last week of June, Lee's entire army, except for two divisions—Early's and Hill's—streamed through and around the hapless town of Chambersburg.

By that time, Hooker had bestirred himself enough to shift his army across the Potomac east of the South Mountain Range into the general area of Frederick, Maryland, still anxiously shielding Washington, D.C., against a Rebel sortie. Of course, we ordinary soldiers in the 10th North Carolina had no knowledge of these movements and, as it turned out, neither did Lee himself, for Jeb Stuart, instead of remaining back in the Shenandoah to protect the tail of the long Confederate column, took it upon himself to lead his cavalry on a long road which carried him between the Yankee army and the outskirts of Washington, thence across central Maryland and into Pennsylvania around York. That is a story in itself, how Stuart let Lee down to indulge himself in an invasion of his own.

Meanwhile, we men of Rodes' division gathered ourselves together, after two days of relaxing around Chambersburg, and resumed our northward march, moving like a string of carefree gray ants up the Cumberland Valley, deeper into the rich Pennsylvania countryside with its lush fields and huge barns.

As I have said, Ewell's corps had three divisions: Early's, Johnson's and Rodes'. Old Ewell, still acting in the tradition of Stonewall Jackson, divided his forces while deep in enemy territory. He had Early bypass Chambersburg to the east and move through the South Mountain Range at Cashtown to seize a town called Gettysburg and then press on to the city of York and finally to Wrightsville, where a bridge crossed the Susquehanna.

As for us, our division headed north for Harrisburg and the only other bridge across the Susquehanna, following the horse turds left by Jenkins' brigade. Johnson's division came along behind us. We arrived dusty and tired in Carlisle, just twenty miles from Harrisburg, on Saturday, June 27.

Carlisle, Pennsylvania, was and is one of the most attractive towns in North America, in my opinion. It looks like a town ought to look, with broad streets and graceful houses. In 1863 it had 5,600 inhabitants, not counting the students at Dickinson College.

The people had been given plenty of warning of our approach by that time. The stores were closed, which was just as well since their stocks had long since been hauled beyond the Susquehanna. Dickinson College's commencement exercises had been canceled and the students mostly sent home. Some New York militiamen, sent out from Harrisburg just long enough to make themselves unpopular with the people, had turned tail at the approach of Jenkins' men and withdrawn to the next town, Mechanicsburg. We had Carlisle to ourselves.

The fraternization began late that first afternoon as we lolled about our campfires on the edge of the Dickinson campus. First a few boys of ten or twelve sidled up to get a closer look at the fearful Rebels. Then some of the older lads. Soon their fathers came out to see the dreaded invaders. I picked out a freckle-faced, redheaded little chap and said, "Hey, boy, what's your name?"

He grinned but wouldn't answer.

"Come on. Has the cat got your tongue?"

"No."

"Then what's your name?"

"Frank."

"Hello, Frank. You want to look at my musket?"

I knew that would get him. He stepped up and I let him heft my Enfield, which was about as long as he was tall. While he was pointing the musket around, I cajoled his larger brother into coming over to examine my canteen. Pretty soon I was surrounded by several boys and then the questions began.

Where were we from? How many miles did we march a day? Had I ever seen Stonewall Jackson? What did Robert E. Lee look like? Did I own slaves? Was it true that we whipped black men and branded them? Was it true that Confederates killed prisoners?

Then their parents came closer. I began talking to them while my comrades took over the amusement of the youngsters. I found the parents mannerly, well-spoken people, not the brash, bragging types we Southerners imagined Yankees to be at all.

I discovered that their county, Cumberland, had a long record of voting Democratic. And they had good opinions of Southerners due to the number of bright young Methodists sent up from Virginia to study at Dickinson over the years, them plus army officers from Dixie stationed at the nearby U.S. barracks.

Individual conversations started going a mile a minute as we warmed up to each other. I fell in with a distinguished-looking older fellow who said he was a professor at Dickinson. He deplored the fact that politicians North and South had let the war break out in the first place.

"The killing is horrible," he said. "I think it is a scandal for Americans to be slaughtering each other as we are."

"Well," I replied, with my big mouth, "it's simple enough to stop the war. All the North has to do is leave us alone and that will be it. Let us go in peace."

"That will never happen, young man. You don't realize the depth of feeling we have for the Union. We can never stand by and see the United States of America dissolve into separate nations."

"Then that means we will have to lick you in battle."

"Yes, and you will never do it."

"We have already done it. We drove you away from Richmond in the Seven Days' Battles, we chased Pope right off the battlefield at Second Manassas, and we beat your army soundly at Fredericksburg and Chancellorsville. Now we are here to give you a taste of how it feels to be invaded."

He did not give an inch. "I admit that you Southerners are good fighters. And I wish Lee had kept his oath of loyalty to the Federal Government and was leading our army, as he should be doing. But just look around you. We still have young men who have not been called up. Immigrants are still pouring into New York. Our factories are booming. I wonder if the South realizes what you have bitten off."

I started to rebut him, but he cut me off. "Just look at your men. I see many without shoes. And I have noticed not a few with missing hands or less than entire arms still in your ranks.

You must be hard pressed for soldiers not to have sent them home to their families."

He had me there, for it was the custom to keep such men in the army as litter-bearers and cooks, or teamsters. Our own colonel, William Ferro, had one empty sleeve and our corps commander, Ewell, wore a peg leg. All I could reply was "The fact remains that we are deep in your territory and your army is not doing very much to stop us."

God, he was a stubborn man, this professor. "I don't wish to argue with you, young man, but you are not out of our territory just yet. My son is a captain in the Army of the Potomac and he has written that the Army of the Potomac learned some valuable lessons at Chancellorsville. He points out that the army, which is the largest and best equipped in the world, has never committed its full strength in battle, not at Antietam or Fredericksburg or Chancellorsville. I think you will find yourselves hard put to win a battle on Northern soil, and you can bet your boots or bare feet or whatever that you are going to have to fight such a battle in a very few days."

"I am not concerned about fighting a battle and neither is General Lee, I am sure. We will win."

"Meanwhile, you may not be aware that U. S. Grant has had Vicksburg under close siege for several weeks now. When that city falls, the western part of your Confederacy will be isolated and the Federal gunboats and commercial vessels will have full use of the entire Mississippi. Any victory you may win in the East will be only of temporary value. You haven't got the strength to subdue the North. This so-called invasion is nothing more than a raid in force and I still think it will end in a disaster for your General Lee."

This professor was too well informed about the overall military situation for me to hold my own with him. He was getting the better of me in a gentlemanly way that made it impossible for me to respond with my usual earthy remarks. I desperately wanted to change the subject. It came to me suddenly, the name of the artilleryman I had taken prisoner at Malvern Hill nearly a year ago.

"Excuse me, sir. Do you know a man in Carlisle named Jacob Detweiler?"

"There are several families by that name in Carlisle."

"Well, this would be a fellow in his mid-thirties, stocky, with sandy hair going bald. He is or was in the artillery."

"Just a minute. Let me inquire."

The professor turned to some of the other townspeople.

"Yes. His family lives three streets over and then down two to the left. A small brick house on the corner."

"Thank you, sir." With that I shook hands, agreeing with him that peace should reign again in our land and that it would if folk like us, rather than politicians, could talk out our differences face to face.

It was with a feeling of relief to get away from the professor and his relentless logic that I entrusted my musket and blanket roll to Noah Rhine and set out to find the family of Jacob Detweiler.

46

I made my way through the streets of Carlisle to a neighborhood of modest but neat one- and two-story brick houses, mostly set right against the cobbled sidewalk. The Detweiler house was shaped like an L, with a tiny garden enclosed in the L. The shades were drawn and it seemed no one was home when I first knocked. Then the door opened and a fat little woman with a round face and sky-blue eyes looked out at me.

"Mrs. Detweiler?"

"Yeah. I am Mrs. Detweiler." A slight look of alarm passed over her face as she took in my lanky form and Confederate uniform.

"Are you the mother of Jacob Detweiler, a Union artilleryman?"

"You knew our Jacob?"

"Yes, indeed, and I have come to—"

"Papa," she called into the house. "There is a Rebel here and he wants to tell us about Jacob." Then to me, "Come in once."

For the first time in my life I stepped into an ordinary Northern home. The front room was small but was furnished with good, solid walnut and oak furniture and all kept as neat as a pin.

A square-built old man with iron-gray hair and shoulders like a bull came into the room.

"How do you do?" I said. "I'm Sergeant James Mundy of the 10th North Carolina Regiment. Your son gave me your name."

"He knew Jacob, Papa."

The old man kept his eyes on me. "You are a Rebel, ain't you?"

"I am a Confederate soldier, yes."

"I'm not sure I want you in my house."

"Oh, Papa. Don't be rude. He may have news of Jacob."

"All right, let's hear what he has to say and get it over with."

"I'm not going to have this, Papa. Let's invite this young fellow back to the kitchen and let him sit down and tell his story. Please."

"All right, Rebel. Come on back."

The old man led the way to an enormous kitchen with one of those walk-in fireplaces across one wall. Two plates were set at one end of a long table. Pots of food bubbled over the fire.

"We were just about to sit down to eat supper. There is plenty. Stay and break bread with us," the old lady said.

I was tired after our march up from Chambersburg and it had been months since I had eaten a regular hot family meal. So, despite the old man's rudeness, I accepted.

Mrs. Detweiler set a place for me and then brought out hot bread and butter, stewed apples, fresh corn on the cob, peas and cold sliced ham, together with a pitcher of cool sweet milk. Made my mouth water to look at it.

We sat down and the old man muttered a blessing, then fell to eating, leaving it to his wife to talk to me.

"What do you know of our Jacob?" she asked.

A little bird in my brain whispered, telling me to leave out the way in which I had cracked that artilleryman's head at Malvern Hill and forced him back to our lines all bloody and barely conscious. I made it appear that I first noticed him in the prison pen after the battle and had acted the Good Samaritan in washing his wound and giving him whisky and water.

"God bless you for that," his mother said.

"I took his name and address but did not know any way of getting a letter to you. I expect that you have heard from him direct by now. After all, that was July 1 of last year. Nearly twelve months ago."

As I said this, there came in my mind an image of that stocky Pennsylvanian Dutch artilleryman marching off under guard toward Richmond.

"We heard from him just last week," the old man said, raising his eyes from his food at last.

"Oh, and how is he?"

"He is dead. You Rebels killed him."

"Oh, Papa. Don't be bitter. You know what Pastor Harbaugh said. We must not feel bitterness."

She turned to me with tears in her eyes. "The army wrote that they had been notified by Richmond that Jacob died of some disease in prison camp down there."

"They killed him," the old man said.

I had been enjoying the good food and was looking forward to the cherry cobbler cooling on a side table. Suddenly I could not swallow the bite in my mouth.

"Oh, my. I am so sorry. I had no idea."

"I guess you didn't. You Rebels killed our only son and now

you have come up here to steal our cattle and rape our women."

There was no point in telling the old man of the homes and barns destroyed by Yankees in Virginia. Or of how their son's artillery battery had slaughtered so many of my comrades at Malvern Hill. It would have been pointlessly cruel to describe to him the greater suffering the war had brought to the South, contrasting that with the relatively untouched Pennsylvania countryside. And, besides, there was that nagging consciousness that I had gone out of my way, even risking capture, to force their son down from the bloody slopes of Malvern Hill. Except for me he might still be alive and well with his battery mates, sitting around a campfire, prepared to blast away at us again from some other hill.

"I'm sorry. I did try to help your son."

"Indeed, you did," the old lady said. "You must forgive Papa. He doted on Jacob. I couldn't have more children after he was born and Papa loved him too much."

The old man arose and walked out of the room to the porch that ran alongside the kitchen, between it and the garden. As he got up, his face was hard and mean-looking, but as he walked along the porch I saw through the window how he let go. Tears ran down his now contorted face.

Mrs. Detweiler stayed at the table with me, asking polite questions about my own family and what I thought of Pennsylvania. I stopped all pretense of eating and tried to chat naturally, but it was an ordeal, such an ordeal that I declined her offer of cherry cobbler and another glass of milk.

At last, I pleaded duties back at our camp and said my good-bye. After she had hugged and kissed me and wished me a safe return to my own family, I walked a roundabout way through the town to the college campus, ignoring the curious stares of the occasional inhabitant as I tried to get control of myself.

"You look like you have been crying, Jim," Noah Rhine said when I rejoined my squad. "Is something the matter?"

"You're full of shit," I replied. "What have I got to cry about?"

47

Rodes' division remained at Carlisle until early morning of June 30, in place there just twenty miles from the Susquehanna River and, on its eastern bank, Harrisburg. Johnson's division lay in reserve west of Carlisle. We waited while Jenkins' brigade of horsemen scouted out the fortifications the New York and Pennsylvania militia had hastily thrown up to defend Harrisburg.

All we needed was two or three more days and the capital city of this fat state of Pennsylvania with its training camps and rail yards would be in our hands.

Meanwhile, thirty miles downstream from Harrisburg, Early's division was supposed to seize the bridge at Wrightsville and cross the river to approach the capital from the rear. I say "supposed" because on June 28 a brigade of Early's division routed a band of militia from their earthworks at Wrightsville. They scooted across the bridge, stopping just long enough to set fire to the half-mile-long wooden structure. One of my old drinking companions here in Baltimore was in Gordon's brigade and he liked to tell how prettily the bridge burned. I got damn tired of hearing his damn story.

Anyway, forty-odd miles away at Carlisle we had no knowledge of any of this as we enjoyed the good life that had suddenly come our way. A number of officers in our division had either been stationed at the U.S. Army barracks there or had been Dickinson students before the war. They renewed old friendships in Carlisle. We enlisted men were kept busy on June 28 with guard duty or cleaning our equipment or scrounging around for shoes and liquor with little success.

Early the next day, the twenty-ninth, they roused our company and moved us east of town beyond the old army barracks, there to stand picket duty. God knows what for. Jenkins had herded the militia back to within spitting distance of the Susquehanna; the Army of the Potomac was still down in Maryland.

It always made my heart leap when I saw William Ferro riding the little mare Nellie. Made me think of Jane, of course. As he rode out that morning, he was accompanied by General Rodes himself. In a bit, we saw a buggy approaching and recognized the bald-eagle profile of Richard S. Ewell, Lieutenant General, C.S.A., as well. The three men talked at length and then Colonel Ferro waved at me to join them. I trotted over and saluted.

"This is the soldier I was telling you about," he said. "Sergeant Mundy."

The two generals nodded.

"Sergeant," the colonel said. "General Ewell wishes a dispatch sent to Mechanicsburg and put in the hands of General Jenkins. We don't want to waste time sending back for a courier. I want you to carry the message."

"Yes," Ewell rasped. "And wait for his reply and rush it back to me."

"You want me to run there on foot?"

All three men laughed, making me feel like a fool.

"No, of course not. You can borrow Nellie for the mission. You and she are old friends, as I remember."

Ewell seemed in a bad humor. "Get him started. Here is the dispatch. Give him your horse and you can ride back into Carlisle in my buggy. I am meeting General Johnson there."

Colonel Ferro dismounted and took me aside while Rodes and Ewell continued to chat.

"Now look, James," he said in a low voice. "This is important. General Lee has ordered General Ewell to advance his two divisions against Harrisburg and take the city. He has to plan his advance route and he needs up-to-date information from Jenkins, who should have the situation scouted out by now. Here is the dispatch. There are supposed to be sentries posted along the road to Mechanicsburg, but this is enemy territory and we must assume there are Yankee scouts operating in civilian clothes. If anyone accosts you, we expect you to chew up the dispatch and swallow it."

"What about getting General Jenkins' reply back here?"

"That's why I chose you. Jenkins may not have time to write out a reply, so I wanted someone who can understand his response and relay it back here. Now you take Nellie and get started. Take the Trindle Road into Mechanicsburg. That's about twelve miles east of here. Ask for General Jenkins at the Ashland House Hotel."

With that he gave me the dispatch and turned the reins over to me. I mounted Nellie, pulled my slouch hat down tight over my head, and went riding past my squad members, taking no notice of their rude gestures and gibes.

Here was the way to see the beautiful Pennsylvania countryside, from the back of an easy-gaited mare. The road led over gentle hills which showed numerous outcroppings of limestone boulders, past tiny villages of broad houses hugging the right of way. There wasn't a cow or horse in sight, and hardly any grown men. These canny farmers had hustled their stock out of our reach. Off to my right I could see the northern terminus of the South Mountain Range several miles short of the Susquehanna and to my left, the steeper Blue Mountain Range running straight ahead to a notch where the river cut through.

I had enough sense not to make Nellie gallop and wear herself out. She covered the distance to Mechanicsburg easily with her comfortable, ladylike single-foot gait. Despite the harsh name, the town struck me as yet another pretty place. At the edge of Mechanicsburg, I found a toll gate in a "Y" in the road, with the Simpson's Ferry Road angling off to the right and the road into town leading straight ahead.

A surly-looking gatekeeper looked out at me as if he were getting up nerve to ask me for a toll.

"Friend," I spoke to him. "Which way to the Ashland House Hotel?"

"That way." He pointed down the main street. "Turn left at Market Street and you'll see the hotel right beside the railroad."

I did enjoy riding along Mechanicsburg's Main Street, past a nearly solid line of two- and three-story homes. A few of Jenkins' men were posted about at street corners. A Confederate flag flew from the flagpole in the town's center.

At the hotel, a Confederate sentry said General Jenkins was not there, that I would find him out at the Peace Church beyond town.

"Where is that?"

"Follow East Main Street across the railroad tracks. Then just keep right along Trindle Springs Road until you see a two-story stone church on your left on a little rise. We have a battery of artillery out there and one of our regiments. You can't miss it."

I got off and let Nellie drink from the horse trough in front of the hotel. The sentry took pity on me.

"Hey, sergeant, help yourself to some goodies. These damned Pennsylvanians are trying to feed us to death." He handed me a slab of sticky molasses pie.

"They call that shoo-fly pie," he said. "We came into town yesterday and General Jenkins told the mayor it was either furnish us with rations or he would turn the men loose to forage in their homes. You should have seen these Dutchmen bringing in baskets full of food. Most of us got bellyaches now."

With the shoo-fly pie lying heavy on my stomach, I rode Nellie on through Mechanicsburg and along the road toward Harrisburg. I was barely out of town when I heard cannonading. Soon I could see clouds of smoke drifting across a graveyard behind a pretty little stone church. The firing stopped as I drew near and it was soon followed by the crackle of musket shots in the distance.

The captain directing the artillerymen in swabbing out their guns acknowledged my salute. He had a big nose and spoke with a German accent. I told him I had been sent by General

Ewell personally to speak to General Jenkins.

"*Ja.* He is over there. The fellow with the long beard, the one looking through his field glasses."

I dismounted and led Nellie to the gentleman in question.

"General Jenkins, sir. I have an urgent dispatch for you from General Ewell."

He lowered his field glasses and took the note. After reading it, he muttered to himself. "Oh, hell. How am I supposed to know about the defenses of Harrisburg with that Goddamn New York militia screening the works? By God, I should have ridden a regiment in behind them to cut them off from their earthworks."

"Well, sir," I interrupted. "Have you an answer for General Ewell? I have been instructed to take a verbal reply back to him if you don't want to take time to write an answer."

Jenkins directed his remarks to a roly-poly lieutenant standing nearby rather than to me.

"You hear that? Old Ewell expects me to tell him how to maneuver two divisions of infantry over twenty miles to avoid jam-ups so he can attack immediately on arrival. I don't know what to tell him until I get a better look at the earthworks they have erected on this side of the river. The only way to do that is to fight a battle with the militia and yet I'm not supposed to bring on an engagement without infantry support. Old Baldy doesn't want to bring up the infantry until he knows the layout of their fortifications. Oh, shit."

Just then a soldier on horseback came pounding along the road from the direction of Harrisburg. He addressed Jenkins without dismounting.

"They had several hundred militia strung out at Oyster's Point. We waited until the artillery let up and went in on foot. Chased them back toward Bridgeport but didn't dare push farther. Colonel wants to know what to do now."

Jenkins swore and chewed on his beard. "Go back and tell him to pull back to Oyster's Point. Don't try to drive them any farther."

The chunky lieutenant spoke up. "General, this courier is waiting to take a message back to General Ewell."

"I know that, damn it. Look, get a troop with carbines and let's do our own scouting. You," he addressed me. "Ride along with us and you can see the lay of the land for yourself. We'll just cut off to the right and follow the Simpson's Ferry Road through Shiremanstown toward New Cumberland. With the road junction at Oyster's Point secure and their militia shoved back through New Market toward Bridgeport we should be able to find a position from which to take a good look at their fortifications. Hey, somebody bring my horse and let's get started."

48

Our strange entourage, consisting of one shabby-looking brigadier general, a chunky blond lieutenant, sixty evil horsemen, and one infantry sergeant, set out south from the church along a little crossroad that led over to a village called Shiremanstown on the Simpson's Ferry Road. I found Shiremanstown unlike any of the other settlements through which we had passed because of its main street, which was as wide as a boulevard in Paris. A good number of the houses were built of wood.

From Shiremanstown we trotted along at a fast clip past scattered houses, keeping a good lookout for any wandering militia, for we were far beyond our lines now. A couple of miles to our left, we could see a steep ridge running toward the river. Jenkins and his aide kept looking up at this height.

"Now, General, if we stay on this road," the lieutenant said, "it will bring us to New Cumberland. The maps show it as a town on the Susquehanna's west bank, just beside the mouth of the Yellow Breeches Creek. Seems there is a ferry across the river there to a spot a couple of miles below Harrisburg. Infantry might be able to cross there to get at Harrisburg."

"Let's not cross our rivers before we get to them," Jenkins replied. "We must see how well they have fortified the approaches to the city. Ewell particularly wants to gain the bridge across the river intact."

On our immediate right, there loomed a hill planted in wheat. Jenkins pointed to it. "That looks like our best spot from which to see Harrisburg. Let's have a go at it."

We turned off Simpson's Ferry Road into a farm lane leading up the hill. Halfway up, tucked into a hollow, there appeared the roof of a graceful stone house with the usual spacious barn nearby. A boy of about sixteen was feeding chickens in the barnyard. Jenkins called him over.

"Young fellow. What is this hill called?"

"We just call it Zimmerman's Hill."

"Can you see Harrisburg from the top?"

"Sure and you can see for miles up the river as well."

"Where does this other road lead to?"

"Down to the Yellow Breeches Creek."

"How about guiding us up to where we can get a good view? I want to ask you some more questions."

"I don't think I want to."

The boy reminded me of my little brother, Wesley. I could tell he was fascinated by us "enemy" soldiers and yet he didn't want to help us.

Jenkins caught on. "You can tell your folks and neighbors that we threatened to burn your father's barn if you didn't guide us. Come on, son. Nobody is going to harm you."

The boy grinned and set down his bucket.

"This way," he said, breaking into a trot.

We followed him along the lane to the crest of the hill. What a view! Far off to the north the ramparts of the Blue Mountain Range ran north and south of the Susquehanna as far as the eye could see. And other ranges peeked through the water gap beyond. In the nearer distance stretches of the broad Susquehanna showed through the trees, flowing right past Harrisburg.

The city presented a pretty picture with its church spires and state house rearing above a collection of two- and three-story buildings and row houses nestled between the east bank of the river and a broad hill about a mile or so inland. With thirteen thousand inhabitants, it was the largest town I had ever laid eyes on other than Richmond.

A strange-looking covered bridge stretched from the city to an island in the river and then to the foot of a bluff on the west bank. This bluff, about two miles from our vantage point, marked the terminus of the steep ridge we had observed on our ride. From Zimmerman's Hill we could see the freshly turned earth of the fortifications. The lieutenant lent me his field glasses. Gaudily dressed militiamen and civilians—black and white—teemed around the works, some still digging away and others lolling about. Several artillery pieces had been emplaced.

We rode on to the highest point on the hill, beside a young black cherry tree. Jenkins got off his horse and spent several minutes scanning the opposite ridge, then several more studying the river upstream.

"Way up there near the mountains," he said to the boy guide. "Is that the Pennsylvania Railroad Bridge?"

"Yes, sir. That's at Rockville. The main line to Pittsburgh crosses the river there."

"What is it made of?"

"Solid stone. My pa helped work on it."

Jenkins scowled. "How about the bridge across to Harrisburg?"

"We call that the Camelback Bridge. It is made of wood, of course."

"Any other bridges hereabouts?"

"Not until you get down to Wrightsville. Of course there is

Simpson's Ferry down at New Cumberland."

"I see. And over there where the fortifications have gone up. What is that hill called?"

"Hummel Heights, sir."

Jenkins led his horse away and beckoned for the lieutenant and me to follow. "That railroad bridge is one of the most important structures in the North. It carries the main-line rail traffic between the Northeast and Chicago. Tell General Ewell it will not be an easy job. We will require hundreds of men with crowbars and blasting powder. Now the earthworks are more extensive than I had thought. They cover the direct approach from Carlisle and the Camelback Bridge, to boot. Listen carefully, young man, while the lieutenant makes a sketch of the terrain. Tell General Ewell that I suggest he send one division along the main road from Carlisle to Mechanicsburg, out past Peace Church and Oyster's Point into New Market. Make a big demonstration in front of their earthworks on Hummel Heights. As a holding action. Got that?"

"Yes, sir."

"Then his other division should take the Trindle Road to the western edge of Mechanicsburg and follow Simpson's Ferry Road past Shiremanstown, following the same route we just took. That division should march right past this hill until it strikes the road from New Cumberland to Bridgeport. There it should turn north and advance rapidly against the western end of the Camelback Bridge, while the other division is making a big show in and around New Market. Got it?"

"Yes, sir. I understand."

"Repeat it back to me."

I gave him the gist of what he had just said. He smiled.

"Letter perfect. Now all I am going to give you is the sketch of what we see from this hill. You ride back to Carlisle and tell General Ewell that if he moves out early tomorrow, I think the bridge and the fortifications could be in our hands by nightfall. Harrisburg can't hold out once our artillery is posted overlooking the river and this end of the bridge is in our hands."

The lieutenant spoke up. "This boy, General. I don't like turning him loose right away. He might tell someone that we have been up here scouting around."

Jenkins nodded. "Let him ride back to Peace Church behind our young courier on his horse. Won't hurt to take him away from his mama for a few hours."

As the lieutenant explained this to the youth, I sat on Nellie, gazing over the miles of gorgeous Pennsylvania countryside that stretched north and south of the broad Susquehanna. It was long after the war that I realized our little reconnaissance party had penetrated deeper into the North than any other in the Gettysburg campaign. That young black cherry tree on Zimmerman's Hill marked the true high-water mark of the Confederacy.

Anyway, the farm boy was half-bullied, half-persuaded to crawl up behind me on Nellie's back and accompany us back to Peace Church. I resented Jenkins' doubling up the load on a mare that had already traveled thirty miles, but what could a mere sergeant say to a brigadier general?

I did enjoy chatting with the young fellow. He told me about going to a one-room schoolhouse. About how he and his father farmed, the good fishing in Yellow Breeches Creek and about his one trip to Philadelphia the year before. He asked the usual questions about the South and slavery. He was a well-spoken lad. I expect that he later bored his children and grandchildren silly with the story of how he had been kidnaped by General Jenkins himself during the great Confederate invasion of 1863.

It was midafternoon by the time we got back to the Peace Church. I let Nellie drink some water and rest a bit while I scrounged a cup of coffee and some sandwiches from the artillerymen, who enjoyed teasing the farm boy. They threatened to sign him up for the Confederate Army and take him with them.

General Jenkins saw me loitering about and growled, "I thought you were in such a damn big hurry to get your message back to General Ewell. Why don't you get moving?"

So, with these kind words ringing in my ears, I turned Nellie back toward Carlisle. It was an uneventful ride. The poor little mare was so tired I didn't dare push her hard. We reached Carlisle about dark and it took me a while to locate Colonel Ferro. He led me to General Ewell's headquarters at the barracks. I found "Old Baldy" sitting around a table with his two division commanders, Rodes and Johnson. They looked tired and worried. I saluted and after turning over the sketch told them what Jenkins had said and what I had seen.

Ewell thanked me. "There you are, gentlemen. We could be in Harrisburg by tomorrow night, I am convinced. But General Lee has changed his mind. My God, we might as well have stayed back in Chambersburg." Then, to me, "You have done well, Sergeant. You may go rest now."

Outside, Colonel Ferro explained, "It seems the Army of the Potomac has a new commander. General Meade rather than Hooker. What's more, the entire army is marching across Maryland, trying to push across the South Mountain passes to cut off our communications with Virginia. Lee has ordered Ewell's corps to draw back to Cashtown Gap west of Gettysburg. Looks like we'll make a stand there."

"What about Harrisburg?"

"It will have to wait until we have beaten Meade. Now, James, you must be worn out. I'll arrange for you to ride in an ambulance tomorrow on the march south. You wouldn't mind that, would you?"

"I'm afraid the boys will make fun of their sergeant riding while they walk."

"You aren't their sergeant any more."

"What do you mean?"

"On our ride back in his buggy this morning I told General Ewell about your fine service and he authorized me to make you a brevet second lieutenant. Your friends will have to salute you now, Lieutenant Mundy."

I went to sleep that night with a smile on my face.

49

Reveille sounded around Carlisle at 3 A.M. the next day. Captain Cadieu told the boys of my promotion to second lieutenant as they lined up for their coffee and Pennsylvania scrapple. I was to be a regimental aide, he said. Noah Rhine would take my place as sergeant, which was a good choice for Noah had a level head.

My boys gathered around me to shake my hand and pound me on the shoulder. The captain shook my hand, too, as did Foster Liddle, the insipid little fellow who had nosed me out for a second-lieutenancy back at Kinston. As for Tom Shelton, he muttered a "Congratulations, Mundy. Hope you can handle the job" and didn't offer to shake hands, which was all right with me, the son of a bitch.

Soon after sunup, our regiments started out for the South Mountain Range, leaving the good people of Carlisle to rest in peace. I tried to do as Colonel Ferro had suggested and sleep in an ambulance but found I was too excited and, besides, I wasn't all that tired from my sixty-mile journey the day before. After all, Nellie had done all the work. Anyway, as our column got to a little river, a few miles south of Carlisle, I hopped out and walked along with the boys, carrying my Enfield just like them, without thinking that a lieutenant on the regimental staff shouldn't be doing that. . . .

In a bit, we came to yet another pretty little village called Papertown, located at the entrance to a South Mountain gap. It was a picturesque place for a town, with mountains looming nearby and a brook rushing through the area. We pressed right through the town, past a paper mill and beyond to the eastern slope of the mountain range. Before us lay miles and miles of orchards and fertile farmland.

We marched at a steady, easy pace, stopping for our midday meal in a large apple orchard whose owner was nearly driven out of his mind by the depredations on his crop. Colonel Ferro called together his officers to confer while they, I mean "we," ate. Seemed strange to me to be sitting with that crew instead of my old comrades.

Colonel Ferro explained that we would continue to march southeast to a village called Heidlersburg, camp there for the night, and then turn west to rendezvous with the rest of Lee's army at Cashtown Gap, between Chambersburg and Gettysburg. Ewell had sent Johnson's division back down the valley but, to avoid overcrowding the roads around Chambersburg, he had decided to move us along a route east of the mountains.

Then he announced my promotion and introduced me to my "fellow officers" as his new aide, asking them to cooperate with me when I transmitted his orders to them.

The march that afternoon was uneventful, taking us through the village of Petersburg to a bivouac just north of Heidlersburg by late afternoon. Colonel Ferro gave me the chore of marking out the company tenting areas and seeing to it that the latrines were dug. You wouldn't believe the problems of providing facilities for a large body of men to piss and shit in. Has to be done or your camp site becomes a pigsty.

At last I found time to do what I had been looking forward to doing all day: write a letter to Jane Ferro, telling her of my promotion and of my exciting scout on Nellie's back with General Jenkins, and of my great love for her.

We are sure to meet the Yankees in battle soon for we are deep in their country and I don't see how they can tolerate the way we have been going and coming as we please. We are just as sure to defeat them once again and send them running back to their precious Washington and the security of its fortifications. Then I expect old Lincoln will realize he must let the South go in peace. I will come home and speak to your father man to man about us for I do want you to be my wife more than anything in the world.

I sealed the letter and took it to William Ferro. Found him sitting in his tent smoking a pipe and looking tired.

He took the letter and looked at me. "Forgive me for prying, but I assume you and Jane have some sort of understanding between you."

"I wouldn't call it quite that, but I must confess I feel a great affection for your sister."

"And I gather that she has for you."

"I hope so."

"Good, James. You have a bright future before you. I hope you will be happy together. Don't worry about my father. He forgets that his own grandfather was a French Protestant lad without a penny when he came to Charleston. I expect he was much like you. A family needs some fresh blood from time to time. For my part I can think of no one I would rather have for a brother-in-law than you."

He smiled to see how this embarrassed me. "And after all, I owe you something for saving my life on the retreat from New Bern."

"Thank you for saying that."

"I have done a lot of thinking about Jane's future, my own and our way of life in the South. At one time I thought the South was making a horrible mistake in separating herself from the rest of the country, but I can see now that we already were a separate nation in spirit. We Southerners are not like these people up here. Our land is different, our climate, our resources and our history. As you know, father sent me up to Princeton, and although I had many friends there from New York and Pennsylvania, still I found them so very different from Southerners. I could understand my Southern friends' thoughts by reading their expressions as much as by hearing their words. Whereas with Yankees we had to explain what we meant. And, of course, they appear so tactless to us. The Northern mind is more critical, and while they sometimes scorn us for our failure to question things, I think we are more subtle than they."

"I never spoke to a Yankee until I captured that artilleryman at Malvern Hill," I replied. "I liked him."

The colonel laughed. "Oh, yes. I told General Ewell about that exploit when I recommended you for promotion. I wonder what happened to your prisoner."

I told him of my visit with the Detweiler family in Carlisle, leaving out no detail.

"Sad. We forget how many people are affected by a single death. Perhaps one more victory will convince the Lincoln government to acknowledge what is a fact: The South is a separate country already. Then the mourning can stop, North and South."

"Do you think we'll have much trouble winning again?"

"It may not be as easy as some of us think. We can't afford to lose for two reasons: We are deep in their country with a long communications route back to Virginia. If we are beaten, Lee will have a hard time getting us back across the Potomac, I fear. And, two, the Confederacy can't afford many victories such as Chancellorsville. The Yankees lost more men than we did, of course, but, James, our proportion of killed and wounded was so much higher than theirs. They can replace their losses, but the well is beginning to run dry in the South, you must realize that."

"We haven't got many recruits recently, for a fact. And the conscripts aren't worth much, in my opinion. But General Lee himself is worth fifty thousand men."

He laughed. "That is putting it strongly, but I agree that General Lee is a great commander. I like to read about Napoleon. I think the way Lee sidestepped the Union Army and brought us up this far north without fighting a single major battle was a feat worthy of Napoleon. But the greatest strategy can be undone on the battlefield. In the matter of tactics, Lee is at his best when he lets the other side make the first move and then he makes his counterattack. I just hope that we don't get overanxious and go piling into the Yankee army. We can't afford to lose."

We talked on for nearly an hour and then I said good night.

The bugle aroused us early the next day. And speaking of Early, we discovered in the morning that Old Jubal's division, answering the same message from Lee to march back to concentrate at Cashtown, had camped on the other side of Heidlersburg the night before. Generals Early and Rodes got together with Ewell and, after consulting their maps, decided against moving directly east over an interior road to Cashtown. Instead, they would take parallel roads south to the town of Gettysburg and there follow the good, broad pike due west to meet the rest of Lee's army, the same route Early had taken a few days before on his march to York.

It seemed a routine, reasonable decision at the time. Within a few hours, we learned that its consequences made it far more than that.

50

July 1, 1863! If General Ewell or General Rodes had known at the beginning of that day what they knew at its end, the history of America would have been very different.

It began for us of the 10th North Carolina with little sense of urgency. We broke our camp there on the edge of Heidlersburg and fell into a line of march headed west, toward a place then called Middletown but now named Biglerville, I believe. We took that route while Early's division prepared to move directly down the Harrisburg-Gettysburg Road, to avoid congestion.

Our regiment marched at the tail of Rodes' division, and we were honored by the presence of our corps commander, Old Baldy Ewell himself. There he sat in his buggy with his artificial leg thrust over the edge, looking like an irritable bird of prey as he watched the progress of our column.

I should note here that his third division, Johnson's, was out of his control at that time beyond the South Mountain, retracing its steps from Carlisle back toward the Cashtown Gap. If Johnson's division had been with Ewell's other two that morning at Heidlersburg, our history books would tell quite a different story, too.

At Middletown, our column of some seven thousand dusty infantry turned south toward Gettysburg, still moving at an easy pace. I remember it was getting on toward noon and I was looking forward to our midday rest so I could devour the victuals I had stashed away in my knapsack when I first heard the "pop-pop-pop" of carbines down the road. Yankee cavalry vedettes had spotted our advance and were taking pot shots at our leading regiments, it turned out.

A bit later, as we topped a long hill, I heard what I would have taken to be thunder if it had not been such a clear day.

Colonel Ferro halted Nellie and waited for me. "That's artillery, sure enough, James," he said. "There is a battle going on to the south."

You could feel it in your bones. Something big was brewing. Without an order being passed, our men smartened up their ranks, got into step and speeded up their pace. The sound of the guns increased as we pressed on down that hill and then up a long grade leading across a wooded ridge. At the top of that ridge I could see General Rodes sitting on his horse. He was directing his column off the road to the right, deploying them along the crest of the wooded ridge, toward the sound of the guns.

When our regiment reached that spot on the crest, I could see the town of Gettysburg lying before us and could make out the crackle of sustained musket fire.

I stood beside Colonel Ferro as General Rodes spoke to him. "Iverson, O'Neal and Daniels will move their brigades along the crest of that long ridge there, taking care to keep concealed in the woods, until they reach that steep hill. The other two brigades should cross the crest and move along the western slope of the ridge, staying back as a reserve."

Colonel Ferro saluted and reined Nellie off the road to lead us across a field and thence along the opposite face of the ridge. It was hot. I was hungry but soon forgot my hunger as the noise of the battle grew.

That ridge along which we moved, I now know, was Oak Ridge, which led us to Oak Hill, overlooking the town of Gettysburg from the southwest. It also overlooked the right flank of the Federal I Corps, now hotly engaged with A. P. Hill's Confederate corps, which was approaching Gettysburg from the west.

As students of the Battle of Gettysburg know, the fighting got started by accident around daybreak when Yankee cavalrymen contested the advance of Heth's division of Hill's corps about two miles west of town. Napoleon wrote that when two armies are probing about, a battle can be brought on by a dogfight, and that is about what happened at Gettysburg as the cavalry scrap with Heth's skirmishers grew, with first Confederate and then Federal infantry coming into the action. The Yankees had been outnumbered during a morning of hot fighting, fighting that had seesawed back and forth until now the hard-pressed I Corps, about twelve thousand men, were holding a two-mile front along Seminary Ridge, which was really a low extension of the same Oak Ridge we were following. In fact, their right flank rested on the Gettysburg-Mummasburg Road, which ran along the south slope of Oak Hill.

It should have been easy for us to hit that flank and roll up the Federal line. It wasn't. Our regiment stayed back in reserve, but I had a ringside seat as I accompanied Colonel Ferro up to the crest of Oak Hill to reconnoiter. There was Rodes with three of his brigade commanders lining up over four thousand men for a flank attack. While he was doing this, several things were happening in the distance. What a sight! Hill's entire corps was drawn up in a two-mile line of battle, with his artillery giving the outnumbered Yanks merry hell from the front and taking a brisk fire in return. The Yanks knew trouble was brewing on their flank and were scurrying around to prepare for us, shifting men about madly and taking cover behind stone walls and trees.

Off to our left, just north of Gettysburg, there lay a fairly level stretch of open fields. A number of cavalrymen were fanned out across those fields to guard the approaches to Gettysburg from the north. And well they should have stood guard for far off we could see the long column of Early's infantry bearing down upon them along the Harrisburg Road.

Gettysburg appeared to be another one of those prosperous Pennsylvania towns that so excited our Southern envy. And its streets teemed with newly arrived Federal troops making their way through jam-ups of wagons and artillery limbers toward the north to relieve the cavalrymen. There were two buildings in the town with cupolas and from these vantage points the Yanks could see Early's men approaching, I am sure.

These newly arrived troops were men of the XI Corps, mostly German immigrants, the same luckless devils who got clobbered at Chancellorsville by Jackson.

While Rodes prepared his attack, his guns set up shop and began tormenting the Federal line. There we were on a high elevation looking right along the Federal line of battle. It seemed like shooting fish in a barrel. For the sake of the South, that Dickinson College professor should have talked to General Rodes instead of me back in Carlisle. For that gentleman warned me that the Union Army of the Potomac would be a different animal on Northern soil. A. P. Hill had already discovered that during the morning. Rodes was about to learn the same lesson.

William Ferro got off Nellie and nearly danced a jig as we looked out on this panorama of bursting shells and hustling units. "Oh, this is marvelous, James," he exclaimed. "I wouldn't miss this for the world. This is our great opportunity to beat the enemy in detail. We'll tell our grandchildren about this someday."

It should have been easy. O'Neal's and Iverson's brigades stepped out smartly and advanced down toward what they thought was the Yankee flank while Daniels' brigade moved to their left. I still am not clear on what happened, there was so much smoke and confusion, but it appeared that O'Neal faltered while Iverson marched right along with his own flank presented to a Yankee force concealed behind a stone wall. The slaughter was appalling. I watched in horror as Iverson's men fell in windrows amidst a blaze of musketry. Those who could retreated back up the hill, but the survivors of the two regiments closest to the wall threw up their hands and surrendered en masse. Just gave up on the spot. Never saw anything like it.

The remains of what had been a fine brigade of North Carolinians drifted back to General Rodes, who seemed in a fury at the miscarriage of his attack. He spotted Colonel Ferro and ordered him to lead the survivors back to join our brigade in reserve.

Rodes continued to probe around for the right spot to tear into the Federal flank. But those Yanks hung on like a case of the itch. We shelled them and sprayed them with musket fire. They had two advantages: they fought from cover and they were desperate. They wouldn't budge.

At last, Rodes recovered his composure and ordered his remaining two brigades into the action. Our regiment descended the hill and worked our way along the base of a ridge to get at the rear of the stubborn Yanks. I was kept busy relaying Colonel Ferro's orders to our company commanders as we rushed, fired, took fire in return and fired again.

While we were harassing the rear of the Federal I Corps, Early's division had deployed and come Rebel-yelling across a shallow creek about a mile north of us to smack into the flank of the newly arrived Federal XI Corps. By this time Rodes had spread his force out to effect a junction with Hill's corps, so Lee now had a continuous semicircle of five battle-hardened divisions battering away at the outnumbered Yanks. The cannon roared, the muskets crashed, men sweated and swore and died, and then the Dutchmen of the XI Corps caved in before Early's assault. They simply broke and ran back toward the town. The flank of the I Corps, at which we had been gnawing for two hours with a deadly crossfire, finally began to fall apart. We could see the bluebellies drawing back. Soon the entire corps began to abandon Seminary Ridge.

I could hear Early's men whooping and hollering as if they were on a coon hunt back in Virginia as they raced after the poor Dutchmen. They trapped hundreds of them in the streets of Gettysburg. The men of the I Corps were more dangerous adversaries, but we caught the spirit of Early's men as our regiment advanced along the Yankee rear, halting now and then to fire a volley when we met momentary resistance. We scooped up hundreds of worn-out Yankee prisoners as our advance carried us through the western edge of Gettysburg across the grounds of the Lutheran Seminary.

By dusk, what was left of two Federal corps had pulled back to the broad hill overlooking Gettysburg from the other side, leaving the battlefield, the town and several thousand prisoners in our hands.

Having been held in reserve so long, our regiment had taken few casualties, but we were exhausted from our march and our pursuit. And we were further burdened by our prisoners. I was glad when Colonel Ferro gave us permission to fall out and rest along the Fairfield Road on the edge of the town. I remembered the johnnycake and cured ham in my knapsack. Never did such poor food taste so good. As I washed it down with water, I looked up at the hill where the Federals were rallying on the other side of the town. I could see them moving artillery about and digging what seemed to be breastworks or lunettes. We had won a great victory, although it had not come easy. Tomorrow we would finish the job. That was my opinion and I heard it expressed by others. Little did we know.

To this day, I hear people criticize Ewell for not pressing on and taking that hill before the Yanks could fortify it and bring up reinforcements. That is hindsight. I didn't want any part of attacking that hill as tired as I and the men of my regiment were that night. Early's division had not marched as far as we nor been handled as roughly, but they had even more prisoners on their hands. They might have been able to take Cemetery Hill the evening of July 1, but then again they just might have met the fate of Iverson's brigade at Oak Hill. Too bad Johnson's division of Ewell's corps was not with us. It didn't get on the scene until late that night, too late. With them on hand, yes, Lee could have pressed on and seized Cemetery Hill in my opinion.

There wasn't a civilian to be seen in our part of Gettysburg that night. It was an all-Confederate town. After making sure our regiment was all in one place on the Seminary grounds, I found me a soft place under a tree and rolled up in my captured U.S. Army blanket and fell asleep thinking once more of Jane Ferro.

51

Those next two days at Gettysburg are confused and run together in my mind. We in the 10th North Carolina Volunteers felt destiny in the very air, I recall, a feeling even more intense than that I experienced at Sharpsburg. There could be no mistaking the brute fact that we confronted the entire Federal Army of the Potomac on their own soil, where they had to fight us down or withdraw into the fortifications of Washington City. One did not need a crystal ball to know that a great, pivotal battle was inevitable and that it would be fought out on the fields and hills just south of this town of Gettysburg.

They roused us early the next morning and turned us to, setting up corrals for the prisoners we had taken the previous day and establishing a strong picket line as near as we dared to Cemetery Hill. The Yanks on that damned hill had worked through the night to put up breastworks and dig gun emplacements. From their greatly strengthened position, they took pot shots at us with musket and cannon as the morning wore on, just enough to annoy us.

The town of Gettysburg remained shuttered and quiet. Occasionally you would see a woman skitter out into a back yard on some urgent errand; or an older man might scurry along the street. Generally, the traffic through the town was Confederate. Patrols searching for Federal soldiers hiding in cellars and foraging parties looking for food.

Johnson's division had arrived the night before and Old Ewell had ordered it to move through the town and beyond to face Culp's Hill, a wooded height east of Cemetery Hill. Early's division occupied the eastern end of town, facing the saddle between Culp's and Cemetery Hills. As for our division, we occupied the western part of the town and the line leading west to Seminary Ridge, which ridge ran south, roughly parallel to Cemetery Ridge. This Seminary Ridge was the Confederate main line. Hill's corps occupied the section just south of the Lutheran Seminary and eventually Longstreet's corps, the area farther south. That morning, however, two of Longstreet's divisions were encamped out toward Cashtown.

I get weary of reading about the Federals' "fishhook" position at Gettysburg but, damn it, I can't think of a better way to describe it. The eye of the fishhook was Little Round Top, a rocky height well to the south of Gettysburg. The line then followed Cemetery Ridge from a spot near Little Round Top two miles to Cemetery Hill and then bent east to Culp's Hill, the barb of the fishhook. In all, the line ran for nearly four miles, along mostly high ground.

George G. Meade had replaced Joe Hooker as commander of the Federal Army on June 28. Meade was a steady, cautious soldier. He clung to that fishhook position and wisely, too, for not only did it follow high ground, but also its shape enabled him to shift his strength easily from one point to another.

Lee, with a smaller army and without Stonewall Jackson anymore, had to cover a longer line. From my little reading of Napoleon's campaigns and such, I would say that was Lee's basic mistake at Gettysburg—trying to envelop an army of 90,000 with one of only 75,000.

Anyway, I wasn't thinking of Napoleon that second day of July 1863. Colonel Ferro sent me scurrying this way and that, carrying orders, making sure our mess wagons were set up and checking on the condition of our wounded at field hospitals.

Field hospitals! It made me sick to go near them. There at Gettysburg the surgeons had been busy through the night in barns and houses and the buildings of the seminary, sawing off limbs that had been mangled the day before and dressing other wounds.

Surgery in the war was a brutal business. Some of the sawbones became quite skillful with saw and scalpel. They developed amazing techniques for taking off an arm or leg and sewing up the flap quicker than you could turn around, don't mistake me. But how many thousands of men died because Lister was too late with his theory of germs? The existence of so many one-armed and one-legged veterans to this day is a tribute to the resilience of the human body. They survived in spite of, rather than because of, those callous men in blood-splattered smocks, those butchers.

We had relatively few casualties in our regiment the day before, no more than a score or two, but Colonel Ferro wanted a report on their names and conditions. He would have gone himself if he hadn't been so busy. He sent me to inquire.

I found the hospital set up on the grounds of the Lutheran

Seminary. Outside the building, two orderlies were loading arms and legs amputated during the night, loading them into a wagon like so much firewood. I turned my head to avoid the sight and went into the building.

The surgeons were done with their Confederate victims and, now that there was time, had begun dealing with the Yankee wounded left behind when their lines collapsed.

"Oh, Jesus Christ. Oh, Mother Mary. Have mercy. No! No!" an Irishman shot through both legs high up near his hip was screaming.

One of our sawbones was sharpening his scalpel on the sole of his boot as he waited for his two assistants to lift the Irishman onto a door set up on two saw horses.

"Shut up," he said to the Irishman. "We gave you a drink of brandy. Now stop your hollering."

"Chloroform. Can't you put me to sleep, for God's sake?"

"We ran out last night. We'd have to chase all over the countryside to borrow more. Now shut up. This won't take a minute if you'll quieten down."

One of the assistants wiped the poor man's face while the other tightened the straps. The surgeon pulled his straw hat down a bit to shield his eyes, got a better bite on his cigar stub and picked up his fresh-sharpened scalpel. He seemed irritated at my intrusion.

"Who are you and what do you want?"

"I am Sergeant, I mean Lieutenant, Mundy of the 10th North Carolina and my colonel has sent me to locate our wounded."

"Hell, man, I don't know one regiment from another. I don't ask questions of my patients. I worked from eight last night until four this morning. Had five hours' sleep and now we got to get through a pack of Yankee wounded before the fun starts again. Your men could be anywhere. Look around."

One of the assistants spoke up. "The 10th is in Rodes' division?"

"Yes."

"There are some of Rodes' men in a stable along the ridge the other side of the Chambersburg Road. Try there."

As I left, the Irishman began screaming again. I stopped outside the door in shocked fascination. His screams crescendoed and then stopped. Probably fainted from shock when the saw went through his thigh bone.

The surgeon's assistant was right. They had about twenty of our men in a stable with a hundred or more other men from Rodes' division. Most of our fellows were in a stupor, worn out from the ordeal of the surgeon's table and further stupefied from generous doses of morphine.

I took their names. Asked if they needed anything. And got out of there as fast as I could. It was a pleasure to walk back through the sunshine to where our regiment lay along the Fairfield Road.

When I got to the point where the Chambersburg Road crossed Seminary Ridge, I paused to look around me. Beyond the town, Cemetery Hill loomed, more forbidding than it had seemed the evening before for now it teemed with blue uniforms and bristled with cannon barrels peering from freshly dug emplacements. Here and there through the streets of the town, I could see groups of gray and butternut-clad men moving about. Reports of sharpshooters' muskets cracked intermittently.

Then I turned to look west toward the South Mountain Range. I was awed by the sight of thousands of fresh Confederate soldiers streaming toward me along the Chambersburg Pike to a point three-quarters of a mile away where the road crossed Herr's Ridge. At that point the column turned south through the fields. These were men of Longstreet's corps being moved over a roundabout route intended to keep them out of sight of the Yankees so they could be brought into position to attack the Federal left in the Little Round Top area.

Superb soldiers they were, never yet driven from a field of battle, and now moving like an implacable force to deliver sledge-hammer blows against our foes. I thrilled at the sight.

Closer at hand only a few hundred feet away I saw an erect,

bearded figure sitting on a large gray horse, watching the same scene. His face was turned away from me as he sat there with the slack reins in his gloved hands, watching those splendid soldiers moving to carry out his will.

I have often thought back to that scene and wondered what went on in General Lee's mind. The Yanks had been driven off this same ground the previous afternoon and now had taken another stand beyond the town. I wonder to this day if he had any inkling of the slaughter his orders would cause. I stared at him until he turned his face in my direction, and then, growing embarrassed, I crossed the road and returned to my regiment.

Colonel Ferro listened gravely to my report on the condition of his wounded. Then he thanked me, adding, "James, we must find you a horse after this battle is over. We can't have a colonel's aide running around on foot. Now please tell the captains to feed their men early. We're bound to see some more action before the day is over."

After delivering the message I sought out my old squad. Found them lazying about in the hot July sun, dozing, playing cards or chaffing each other, waiting for something to happen. Tom Shelton stood nearby, self-importantly scanning the hills with a pair of new field glasses.

"Well, if it ain't Loo-tenant Mundy himself," Harry McGee greeted me.

"So it is," I said as I seated myself in the grass.

"Are you sure it is proper for an officer to sit with common enlisted men?"

"Oh, lay off him," Noah Rhine said. "Jim is trying to be friendly. He ain't stuck-up."

"That's what you think. He has been Colonel Ferro's fair-haired boy all along. Rides his horse here and there. Writes to his sister. And now he is a genuine loo-tenant and runs errands for him." Shelton, hearing these gibes, lowered his field glasses and looked at us. I glared at Harry, but he didn't know when to stop.

"Jim deserves to be a lieutenant," Noah said. "He worked

hard as a sergeant and I for one am glad he got promoted."

"Aw, he ain't so much. His shit stinks just like yours and mine. Get him to tell about the nigger gal he screwed in Richmond."

My blood was beginning to boil. I had balled up my fists and was planning just where to hit him when a battery up on Cemetery Hill boomed out and four shells came sailing in our direction.

"Look out," someone shouted.

We flattened ourselves face down. The shells shrieked over our heads and exploded in the field beyond us.

Noah Rhine picked up his musket and fired at the puffs of white smoke on the hill. The rest of us followed suit. After a couple of rounds, we put down our muskets, our quarrel nipped in the bud.

From time to time during the afternoon, the Yankees favored us with a salvo of shells or peppered away at us with musketry. Once they pushed a skirmish line down the hill in our direction and then withdrew when we arose and poured a volley into them. We laughed and told tall stories and dodged artillery fire until nearly four o'clock in the afternoon. About that time there came a dreadful roar of artillery to the south, the guns booming and echoing for half an hour. Then came the Rebel yells and rattle upon rattle of muskets. Longstreet had launched his attack. The battle of Gettysburg had resumed in earnest.

Living as I have in Baltimore all these years, I have gone back to Gettysburg many times, and I have read much about the battle. So I know now that what we heard was Longstreet's assault against Sickles' corps in the peach orchard, one and a half miles south of our position there on the edge of the town. At the time, however, all we could tell was that a damned big fight was raging nearby.

Later in the afternoon we could see smoke puffing up from Little Round Top, followed by the sight of clumps of gray figures scrambling up the rocky face of the hill and then descending.

On and on the guns boomed and volleys of small arms

crashed. The noise crept closer to us and soon we could see clouds of smoke rising from Cemetery Ridge. Through breaks in the smoke, our men advanced and Yankee regiments ran out to confront them.

Colonel Ferro summoned me. "Pass the word to fall in and prepare to advance."

"Are we getting into the fight?"

"So I understand. Early is supposed to attack the northern face of that hill at dusk and we are to hit this side simultaneously."

I saluted and ran to tell the company captains.

It took a while to collect ourselves and get in formation. By now the sun was well behind the South Mountain Range. And Longstreet's attack had sputtered out. Early's division had a shorter distance to cover, so while we were still moving cautiously out we could hear the rattle of his muskets and see the angry flashes of the answering Federal cannon from the darkened crest of Cemetery Hill.

Our advance took us stumbling and cursing across an old farm road worn down by generations of wagon wheels and then over a field, where we halted, a long line of tense but eager soldiers. I tried to put the memory of Malvern Hill out of my mind.

One of our brigadier generals got out his field glasses and then called for a colonel. They pointed at the hill, shaking their heads. We waited, poised to charge.

We never made that charge. Our generals saw that Early's attack, launched before we were in position, had been repulsed and that the Federals were ready to receive us with their full attention. It would have been a useless slaughter for Rodes' division to have gone up against that well-fortified hill alone in the dark. But we did not return to our old position back along the Fairfield Road. Instead, Rodes posted part of his division, including our regiment, in that sunken farm road, just a few hundred yards from the Federal position on Cemetery Hill. The rest of his division was withdrawn to the rear as a reserve, but during the night General Ewell borrowed these men to help

Johnson make an attack the next morning against Culp's Hill.

So there we were, about 2,500 men under the noses of the enemy, and without any support from the rear in case of a Yankee sortie. At least we were protected by the lip of the roadbed.

As we settled ourselves for the night, some of the boys grumbled about the attack being called off. I didn't see anything to grumble about, however. I wish some general had shown the good sense to call off our attack on Malvern Hill the previous July. That Yankee artillery was hell on wheels, literally.

So we went to sleep that night, all huddled in the old roadbed. We would awake in the morning, but just a mile or so away, hundreds upon hundreds of Confederates and Yankees alike had begun their eternal sleep, the victims of Longstreet's late-afternoon assault on Sickles' corps in the peach orchard and the wheatfield. They were lucky compared to the other thousands who moaned and writhed in agony through the night, begging for water and crying out for their mothers. And the slaughter was not yet finished.

52

It was a short night's sleep for us, lying in that old sunken farm road, stuck between the two armies. Colonel Ferro awakened me around midnight to say he was heading back to the seminary for a conference. I went back to sleep, but before the sun appeared over Cemetery Hill, the muffled noise of a fresh battle broke out, coming this time from Culp's Hill to the east, on the Federal right flank where Johnson's division and part of ours had gotten a foothold the night before.

Our own troubles began after dawn. Our presence just a few hundred yards from their position was more than the Yanks on Cemetery Hill could tolerate. Their sharpshooters set out to torment us. They sent ball after ball whizzing down toward us, smacking into the earth along the edge of the roadside ditch or whistling over our heads. We huddled closer to the bank and endured their fire as long as we could. That was until they started potting shells down at us. Just a round now and then, doing no great damage but wearing to the nerves nonetheless, not to mention damaging to our pride.

Keeping my head well down, I duck-walked and crawled to a stone fence corner where Colonel Ferro had established a makeshift regimental headquarters.

"Boom!" a shell exploded several hundred feet above our heads, scattering fragments of casing about us.

"We can't let them get away with that, Colonel," I says.

"No, James, pass the word for the captains to assign their best marksmen to well-protected spots as sharpshooters and let's start returning their fire."

"Yes, sir." I started to go but, seeing the troubled look on his face, paused. "Is something wrong, sir?"

"Yes. I am concerned. This battle is far from over. And I am afraid it is not going well for our side."

"What do you mean? We put them to flight day before yesterday and took the town plus God knows how many prisoners. And from what I could see and hear yesterday, Longstreet handled them roughly down there around that high rocky hill. Today will tell the tale."

"It will, indeed, and I am uneasy about the tale it will tell. From the talk I picked up back at the seminary last night, Longstreet took some very heavy casualties. He drove a Yankee corps out of its position and back to that low ridge, but he paid a high price for a bit of ground. Damn it, these attacks aren't coordinated."

"We'll finish them off today."

"Let us hope so. Now pass the word about the sharpshooters."

I crawled around to all the captains. After a bit, our sharpshooters went to work. Each one had a spot where the ditch was deep or where a rock gave extra protection. They would slide the barrels of their loaded Enfields forward and leave them lying there while they peeked up from another spot to pick a target. Then they would sneak back to their weapons, take quick aim, fire and duck before their blue-clad rivals had time to respond. We gave our particular attention to their artillerymen, sending dozens of balls against each emplacement as its gun spoke.

The noise of the fighting from Culp's Hill ended about midmorning. Once a long skirmish line of Yanks ventured down Cemetery Hill thinking to bluff us out of our "thorn in the flesh" position, but when we poured a volley into them, they realized that we were somewhat more than a bold line of pickets. They turned tail and made their way back up the hill, our jeers following them.

After that it was a matter of lying in the July sun while our sharpshooters amused themselves. A few of our boys passed the time by sticking their hats on their ramrods and raising them above the shelter of the ditch until a Minié ball whistled past. I stopped that foolishness in my immediate area. Saw no point in asking for trouble.

It was out of the question to get mess wagons to our exposed position between Seminary Ridge and Cemetery Hill. So we swapped cold food out of our knapsacks and chaffed with each other or played cards.

The battlefield became quiet and I grew bored. Turned on my back to stare northwest to Oak Hill, where we had fought so hard the day before yesterday, then to the east at the spires and buildings of Gettysburg. It was hot in that road. I had slept little the night before. I wrote in my diary, bringing it up to date, and then, getting drowsier by the minute, dropped off to sleep.

A perfect storm of noise jarred me awake. It assaulted our ears, it shook the ground, it rocked our bodies. Never have I experienced anything like the next two hours as some 140 Confederate cannon emplaced along Seminary Ridge as far north as Oak Hill concentrated their fire on Cemetery Hill and the adjacent stretch of Cemetery Ridge. Soon the Federal guns nearest us began to reply, increasing the sound so we had to press our hands over our ears to save our sanity. There we lay, pinned in what would be called "no-man's land" in France today, with 220 rival cannon firing over our heads.

The blasts from their muzzles echoed back and forth between the two ridges; the air was filled with screaming and groaning from the thousands of shot and shell passing over our heads. And to this maddening racket was added the bursting of the Confederate shells around the top of the enemy-held heights.

Well, you might say, a little noise never hurt anyone, but we found ourselves in some danger from Confederate guns whose crews cut their fuses too short, or who did not load their weapons properly, making their shells explode over our heads or fall near our road.

It was impossible to talk. At least those damned sharpshooters had been silenced. Keeping my palms pressed against my ears, I got to my knees and looked up at Cemetery Hill. A bank of smoke from our shells and their cannon now obscured the crest, the white billows lighted by orange and red explosions. Other lads followed my suit, some even standing up, their mouths open, gawking at the inferno above them.

Back along Seminary Ridge, our guns flashed and boomed as if Lee had a year's supply of ammunition on hand and it was going out of style. God, what a sight!

Today they write about "shell-shocked" French and English soldiers in the trenches in France. I know what they mean. I don't see how a man's nerves can stand hour after hour of the physical noise alone, not to mention the fear.

We endured the ground-shaking noise for two hours. The smoke grew so thick we could not see the sun. Many of us finally got tired of holding our ears and lay down with our blankets wrapped around our heads. The sound let up a bit as the Yankee guns stopped firing. Then in a little while our cannon slacked off and at last stopped altogether.

Someone cried, "Good God Almighty, I wish you would look at that."

We poked our heads cautiously above the ditch. All along the face of Seminary Ridge stretched lines of our soldiers. For a full mile, rank upon rank were drawn up in full view of the enemy. And then they started to move forward, like a gray juggernaut across the open fields toward Cemetery Ridge, not hurrying, mind you, just walking with their muskets carried before them. What a sight!

"Sweet Jesus," Harry McGee said. "They're going right up against that hill."

"Hell," I said. "Nobody could be alive up there anyway after that bombardment."

What we were witnessing, of course, was Pickett's Charge, fifteen thousand of Lee's men moving forward to administer what he meant to be the *coup de grâce* against the Yankee army.

Seems to me that the quarter of an hour it took those fifteen thousand men to march from Seminary Ridge to the base of Cemetery Ridge represents the apogee of the tragic history of the South. The illusion of invincibility never shone brighter than in those brief minutes. How glorious the men of Pickett's and Pettigrew's divisions looked as they followed Lee's foolhardy orders to strike the Union center. And suddenly the illusion was shattered as the Yankee cannon came to life, throwing out round shot and shell tentatively. Our men halted long enough to dismantle a stout rail fence along the Emmitsburg Road which marked the base of the ridge. They reformed their ranks as they crossed the road. And then the slaughter began.

The Yankee gunners switched to canister, turning their cannon into giant shotguns on wheels which sprayed their deadly balls into Pickett's ranks. Our men fell like stalks of wheat before the scythe. The others broke into a run, screaming out the

Rebel yell. Again the guns spoke, followed by spurts of white smoke from a stone wall atop the ridge as Yankee infantry came out of hiding to join in the killing.

Pickett's men went down by the hundreds, but the survivors raced ahead. The cannon blasted and the muskets slashed, but still they pressed on, leaving the ground back to the Emmitsburg Road littered with their fallen comrades.

For a few minutes it seemed the charge had succeeded, for hundreds of our men went right up to the wall, some leaping over to club and stab the enemy.

The excitement was more than I could stand. "What are we waiting for?" I cried. "Let's get into it, boys."

With that, I take up a musket and start running toward the hill, pausing to shout again, "Follow me!"

Here and there men from Company H and others leaped up to join me. I could see Colonel Ferro frantically waving his one arm to signal me to come back. Still other men arose and advanced into the field behind me.

From the crest of the hill there came a hoarse Yankee "Hurrah" as their reserves rushed up to surround the points where Pickett's men had broken over the wall. A blue unit also ran out to fire into the flanks of the attackers.

I ran forward a ways and stopped as the survivors of Pickett's and Pettigrew's divisions began to turn around and sullenly walk back toward Seminary Ridge. They didn't run. They just walked away from their hopeless task. And the Yankees let them go in peace.

I looked behind me. Dozens of our men who had followed me out of the road now stood in their tracks, not quite knowing what to do. Officers were shouting at us to come back. Pickett's men were recrossing the Emmitsburg Road. I stood there feeling like the greatest fool on earth. And then it happened.

Something hit the barrel of my musket and almost simultaneously I felt a violent pain in my forehead. For a bare instant I was conscious of falling forward toward the warm, rich Pennsylvania earth. And then darkness.

BOOK TWO

1

When first I regained consciousness, it was pitch-dark. I was lying face down in a puddle of dried blood. The guns had stopped.

I tried to raise my head and immediately passed out from pain. I came to again, now lying on my back. The pain was still there, centered in the left side of my face and head. I could hear myself moaning involuntarily. I opened my eyes, or at least one of them. The stars made a spangled blue. I blinked and the dreadful hurting became even worse.

Hesitantly, fearfully, I moved my hand up to my face. My chin and left cheek were caked with dried blood and matted pieces of grass and dirt. My fingers fumbled higher till they encountered fresh blood and raw flesh. I fainted again.

Upon resuming consciousness I found my voice and called out for my companions, thinking they might still be back in the old farm road. No answer. I rolled over on my stomach again, and braced myself for the searing pain. I shrieked when it came.

It is beyond me to describe that ordeal accurately. I can only compare it with other experiences. Several years ago I passed two kidney stones the size of a grain of sand. The pain was excruciating. And when I was a boy at old Professor Mead's academy, I was struck in the cods by a hard-thrown horse-hair ball. That pain made me cry. But neither could compare with the torment I endured that night of July 3, 1863, as I lay in a field near Cemetery Hill.

Grinding my teeth in agony, I got to my knees and began to creep, moving as slowly as a turtle, with no sense of direction and no sense of time. In a bit I thought I heard voices and called out but got no answer. I crawled on until I could hear groaning and crying for water to my right. I crawled on in the dark, collapsed, came to and crawled again until I came to a rail fence. Exhausted and lacking the strength to get over the obstruction, I fell asleep.

"Hey, he ain't dead after all."

It was light. I looked up into the face of a Union soldier who was going through my pockets.

"Has he got anything?" Another soldier was leaning over the fence.

"Nothing except a pocket knife, a pencil and a diary. Oh, yes, and some of their damned useless money."

"Water," I could hear myself mumbling. "For God's sake, water."

"Hell, we can spare the poor devil a drink of water."

One of them lifted my shoulders while the other held a canteen to my lips. Never has anything tasted sweeter than those few swallows of lukewarm water.

"Now he can die easy," one of them said.

"I am not going to die," I said. "I refuse to die."

"Listen to him talk. He should see himself. Looks like half his head is torn away and he refuses to die."

"Aw, he ain't that bad off. The blood and stuff makes it look worse than it is. But his eye is sure a goner."

"Don't leave me out here, please."

"We don't want you. We got more Rebel soldiers on our hands now than we know what to do with."

"I'm not a soldier. I am an officer. A lieutenant."

"An officer? You don't look like an officer."

"I am aide to Colonel Ferro of the 10th North Carolina."

"Can you walk? Officer or no, we ain't going to lug you."

"Try. I'll try."

It took more determination than I knew I had to pull myself up and stand at last against the fence. The two pickets exchanged looks.

"What a bloody mess. Let's wash his face for him."

I felt a gush of water over my face, bringing on a fresh wave of pain, but I refused to cry out.

"There. See? What did I tell you? He got a busted eyeball and a split eyebrow. It isn't so bad. Okay, Mr. Rebel Lieutenant. You are our prisoner. Come along."

Once on my feet with some water in my gut, I recovered strength. Those two Yanks led and pushed me up the hill and turned me over to a provost captain who questioned me for a few minutes about my unit and the names of our officers. It never occurred to me not to answer. He acted as if he knew most of what I had to say anyway.

"Doctor. I need a doctor," I said as he put away his notebook.

"Yes, and so do several thousand members of this army. And they come first."

He walked away, leaving me to be led to a hillside thick with hundreds of Confederates captured during Longstreet's assault two days before and in Pickett's Charge the day before.

We crossed the area just behind the crest of Cemetery Ridge. This was where most of the shells fired during the great bombardment of the previous day had exploded. Dead horses lay all about, together with debris of exploded caissons and pieces of broken wagons and limbers. The ground glittered with thousands of shell fragments. It must have been a nightmare for the artillery reserves who occupied that ground. Evidently the infantry, lying behind the stone wall, had suffered few casualties.

Once in the prisoners' corral I lay down and put my hand over my good eye to keep out the sun. Someone came and sat beside me.

"You are in a bad way, son. What regiment are you in?"

"Tenth North Carolina. Rodes' division."

"Rodes? You weren't in our attack yesterday, then."

"No, they kept us back toward the town in an old roadbed. We saw the charge though. Took guts."

"Ha. Took a bonehead to order that attack. It was murder. They tore us to pieces. Of course it might have worked if your division had come up in time to support us."

I looked into the bearded face of an older man. About forty. Can't remember his name or much about him except that he was from Virginia and the father of six children. And that he was one of the kindest and most helpful chaps I ever met. He was a practicing Christian who never preached or tried to convert. He adopted several bad cases like me and spent his entire day going about and looking after us, like a father would look after his sons.

When the Yanks brought around our grub and water, he made sure I got my share. And he talked to me, getting my mind off my troubles. A thoroughly good, kind man.

An awful rainstorm fell the afternoon and evening of July 4. A gully-washer they would call it back in Oldham County. We were soaked through and through and there was nothing we could do except endure it. I would have given my good eye almost for a piece of canvas to shelter me from that driving rain.

That night I lay in the mud in my wet uniform with my head throbbing worse than a dozen abscessed teeth. I felt utterly miserable and hopeless. At last I broke down and sobbed like a little boy. It would be the last time I ever would cry for fifty years. Until my dear wife died a few years ago.

The sun came up hot and strong the next morning and began to dry out my clothes. I could see pretty well with my one good eye. My Good Samaritan friend sought me out.

"Mundy, we are beaten. General Lee is retreating. Heading back for Virginia, without us."

"Did we really lose the battle?"

"Afraid so."

"I suppose we must make the best of things now. Wish the Yanks would let a doctor look at my eye."

"I have been deviling the guards about the way you and some of the other boys need attention. But they say there are still long lines of Yankee wounded waiting. The doctors are working night and day. They say there are hundreds upon hundreds of Confederates lying about where they fell. Dying from lack of help. And they won't let me go out and carry water to them, the beasts."

"They are beasts."

"You cried last night. I heard you."

"Yes, I felt pretty down."

"I would have comforted you, but I figured it would embarrass you. Besides it probably did you good to cry. How are you this morning?"

"My spirits are stronger, but the pain just won't go away."

"Strong spirits, eh?" He laughed. "Odd you should mention them. Normally I don't hold with drinking, but yours is a special case. Look here."

He held up a bottle of rye whisky.

"Traded my watch to a guard for this. Am going to give it to you and some other lads who are in bad shape." With that he sloshed out a couple of ounces in a tin cup. The fiery stuff scalded my throat and stomach. In a few minutes a warmth crept through me. The pain retreated a bit.

"Aren't you going to drink with me?"

"No, I don't drink."

Well, that damned near made me cry again, that fellow trading off his watch to get whisky for me and others like me. There was a gentleman, although he was only a corporal as I remember it. That man kept me posted on the news. He drew me out, encouraging me to talk about my family and Jane Ferro. On the third day he scrounged up a piece of canvas and constructed a pup tent in which he put me and two other of his "patients," one a boy with a mangled arm and the other with a hole through his chest.

On the fifth day, my Good Samaritan came leading a guard in my direction. He pointed to me.

"This is the fellow."

"And he is an officer? He has no such insignia."

"He was promoted on the march. They made him aide to the colonel of the 10th North Carolina."

"You know our surgeons are worn out. They have worked

night and day on our own wounded. And now there are so many Rebs waiting."

"Sure, but they have to start on somebody. If you would just lead Lieutenant Mundy down to the hospital and let them see him, they can't turn him away."

"I don't know about that."

"Are we not fellow Masons?"

"We are brothers, yes. Come on, Lieutenant. I'll take you to the surgeon."

I never saw that old fellow from Virginia again. If there is a heaven, though, he is one man who surely belongs there. If St. Peter happens to be a Mason, I'm certain he is there right now. Those fellows stick together.

2

The hospital was set up in a large tent, the largest I had ever seen. Two weary-looking surgeons sat on camp stools drinking coffee while orderlies washed down a wooden operating table and bundled up bloody uniforms and rags for removal. The guard led me to the surgeons.

One of them, a large, genial-looking chap with mutton-chop whiskers, looked at me.

"Who is this?"

"A Rebel lieutenant, sir. We picked him up beside the Emmitsburg Road the day after the big attack. He is in a bad way, as you can see, and has had no medical attention at all."

"He does need some help." The big man looked at his companion, a sour-faced little man. "What do you think?"

"I am worn out. He's gone this long. He can wait until we have had a few hours' sleep."

"Please . . ." I began.

The big surgeon rose and looked closely at my face. "If he goes any longer, the wound may putrefy. That close to his brain it would kill him."

"Are you sure a Rebel like him has a brain?"

"Don't be unkind, Smith. We could fix him up in half an hour's time."

"We draw our pay to work for the Union Army. You can waste your time on a Rebel officer if you like, but I am turning in before I drop."

"Please . . ." I began again.

"Smith," the big man said, "I am a major and you are a captain, right?"

"Of course."

"So if I say we will patch up this poor fellow's eye before we turn in, then that's what we will do."

"In other words, that's an order."

"Exactly."

The little man gave me a disgusted look, but he wasted no more time. They laid me out on a wooden table. Two orderlies held my arms down while they washed out my eye socket and cleaned off my forehead and cheek. I twisted and strained but refused to cry out.

"Now for the chloroform."

In a moment a rag was over my nose. In another, the powerful fumes of chloroform filled my nostrils and burnt their way deep into my lungs.

"Count to ten, Reb, if you know how," the little surgeon said.

"One, two, threee . . . four . . . fiii . . ." That is all I remember. I awakened more than an hour later lying in a new canvas cot with a blanket over me. A cleaner, sharper pain was shooting through my face. I moaned. Someone was at my side instantly, wiping my forehead and saying, "There, there, don't move."

A woman's voice. Pleasant. Low. For a little while I was convinced Jane Ferro somehow had found her way to Gettysburg. Despite the pain, a euphoria settled upon me. Jane Ferro was with me, caring for me. Then I opened my good eye and looked into the broad face of a middle-aged woman with iron-gray hair.

"Who are you?"

"I am Miss Kelker of the U.S. Sanitary Commission. You are in good hands. The operation went well. Now you must promise to keep your hands off the bandage and lie very still. I'll be back to see you in a bit. When you get hungry, we'll bring you some broth."

The hospital was in a large new tent. It was run by Miss Kelker and several other maiden ladies from Philadelphia. Bless their kind, honest hearts. They treated me as well as if I had been one of their own. Maybe even better. They bathed me (from the waist up). They brought me soup and stewed chicken. I was the only Confederate in their charge and to tell the truth I became their pet. I saw they were intrigued by my North Carolina accent, so I set out to charm them. There were twenty-odd Yanks in the same tent and some of them didn't like all the attention the sweet ladies gave me. Most of them were in such a bad way they didn't notice.

The big surgeon came around the next day to lift up the bandage and inspect his work. "Good job, if I do say so myself. You just lie back and let nature take its course, son. We're working on Rebels entirely now. Maybe I should shift you over to a Confederate hospital but the ladies here seem to want to keep you. So we'll humor them."

I was impressed by the efficiency and the plenty around me. There was no shortage of food or medicines. The staff went about its work with a briskness one did not always see in the Confederate medical service. I wasn't supposed to leave the hospital area, but I did get up and move around the tent. Despite some show of hostility, I struck up conversations with some of the wounded Yanks. We even exchanged notes and opinions about our respective armies.

"Why do you Rebs make that curious yell when you attack?" a private from New York asked me. "Do they teach that to you?"

"No. It come naturally. Makes us feel like we are invincible."

"I'm here to tell you it is scary. A line of ragged bastards coming at you screaming like wild men. It does shake a fellow."

And there were the usual questions about slavery and secession. By the end of the week I was on a first-name basis with many of my tentmates. The nurses had fallen in love with me, calling me by my first name. My eye was healing nicely. Felt as secure and smug as a well-fed tomcat sitting beside a kitchen fire. But then I got too cocky.

I was lying back in my cot regaling Miss Kelker and another lady with my Oldham County stories when the little surgeon, Captain Smith, came into the tent.

"All right, Reb. Let's see your damned eye. Sit up, for God's sake, so I can get the bandage off."

He handled me so roughly I cried out.

"Oh, so our slave-driving friend isn't so fierce now?"

"I don't drive slaves."

"No? Thought you were an officer. A member of the slavocracy."

"My family doesn't own a single slave."

Miss Kelker spoke up. "Captain Smith, Lieutenant Mundy is the son of a Methodist minister. A fine young man. Don't you think you should be more gentle with him?"

"He's lucky to be in this hospital at all. He should be with his own kind."

I was beginning to boil. "What about my eye?"

"You mean where your eye used to be. We cleaned out the socket and sewed up the gash in your brow. Whatever hit you knocked a chip out of your skull just over the eye. You'll live. Of course you won't be much to look at, but an eye patch will keep you from turning stomachs."

Now I truly hated him. "Is that all?"

"That is all." He had turned to go when I said it.

"Then go to hell, you hateful son of a bitch."

He turned around, his face now white. "Why, you Rebel bastard. How dare you talk to me like that?"

"I'll talk to you as I please. You are worse than scum."

By now the little surgeon was hopping up and down with anger. Everyone in the tent was listening. I think he would have struck me if Miss Kelker had not been standing there. He sputtered awhile and then calmed down.

"So, you ungrateful Southern snake. You are well enough to insult a Federal officer. Then you must be well enough to leave this hospital. Yes, you are well enough to be discharged and take your rightful place, which is in a prison camp with other lousy Rebels. In fact, I will just attend to that right now."

With that, he strode out of the tent.

"Lieutenant Mundy, I wish you had not provoked Captain Smith like that," Miss Kelker said. "He is such a bad-tempered man. I'm afraid he will do as he threatens. And there is no one to stop him. The major has gone back to Philadelphia on leave."

The next morning two guards came and asked for me. They marched me through Gettysburg, across the town square and to the train station. A line of boxcars filled with "walking wounded" Confederates waited there. They squeezed me into one. Soon we chugged off toward Baltimore. Me and my big mouth.

3

It took us five hours to reach Baltimore via Hanover Junction. At the station they unloaded us and we marched, or I should say limped and hobbled, several blocks over cobblestone streets to an enclosed empty lot next to an old warehouse. The guards there were invalided soldiers from the Army of the Potomac, men wounded at Fredericksburg or Chancellorsville and not yet sound enough to rejoin their regiments. I was glad to be guarded by veterans. Except for some mild guying us about our loss at Gettysburg, they did not mistreat us as militia or recruits would have. They didn't have to prove their manhood. As Baltimore remained a pro-Southern city, I suppose they were well advised to watch their behavior, however.

That stinking, crowded prison lot was a far cry from the hospital tent at Gettysburg, with Miss Kelker and her sister angels bustling about to make me comfortable. I staked an early claim to a spot against the board fence and hunkered down to make myself as comfortable as possible in bad circumstances.

There was quite a mixture of Confederate types in that pen. Tough, lean Texans from Hood's command, easiergoing Louisianans with French names, plowboys from Georgia and prissy Virginians. The length and breadth of the South was there represented. For once my spirits ran too low to permit any easy socializing. I minded my own business and brooded about my family back home and Jane Ferro, wishing I had never heard of this damned war.

God, that crew stunk. We had big tubs set up around the lot to catch our bodily wastes. These had to be emptied several times a day. They fed us twice a day, mostly hardtack and thin soup. Miraculously, some of the boys had U.S. money and watches and such. Word of this got to the outside, and the next day after my arrival, peddlers showed up in the street outside our compound, offering their wares for sale or trade.

I watched the more fortunate of our prisoners press against cracks in the fence to barter with these enterprising street merchants. Out through the cracks passed money, watches, knives and stolen U.S. accouterments. In passed pies and sandwiches and even whisky.

Soon the supply of money and goods in our possession ran low and the trade stopped. I asked the fellow next to me—a Georgian with a wounded foot—to stretch out so nobody would steal my place and then walked to where the top half of a plank was missing. I looked out this space into the face of a short, broad man of about forty. He wore a round-brimmed black hat. Had a fringe of coarse orange hair and a full red beard.

"Hey, Johnny. You vant to buy somt'ing?" he asked in a German accent.

"I got nothing to buy anything with."

"No vatch? No pocket knife? No ring?"

"Not a frigging thing."

"That's too bad, Johnny. Got shot in the head, eh?"

"In the eye, anyway. At Gettysburg."

"That's too bad. Vere you from?"

"Near Meadsboro, North Carolina. In Oldham County."

"Ho, I know that place. I peddled goods through that part of North Carolina just before the war. I liked the people there."

"Sure enough? I wish I was back there right now."

"Poor fellow. Maybe you'll be back there soon. Maybe this foolish war vill end soon."

"It has ended for me."

Well, that German-born Jew stayed and chatted with me through the fence for half an hour. We both were lonely, as it turned out. I told him about my family. He asked my name and then said his was Emmanual Koning. Said he had left a wife and two children with her parents back in Cologne, Germany, four years before to seek his fortune in America. Said when he had made enough money he intended to send for his family to join him.

"Well, Mister Koning, you won't make any money talking to me."

"Call me Manny. And I don't mind. Vat do your friends call you?"

I grinned. "I won't repeat what some of them call me, but Jim will do."

He laughed. "Vell, Jim, tell you vat. I got two meat pies here that vill spoil soon. Since I can't sell them and you don't have any money, how about if I sell them to you on credit."

That just about bowled me over. He actually drew up a piece of paper for me to sign. I formally agreed to pay him two dollars when I was able. He had a twinkle in his eye as he examined my signature. Then he handed the pies through the fence. With that he saluted me and pushed his cart away.

I started to wolf those two pies down, but remembered the ailing Georgian who held my place beside the fence. Took those pies and gave him one. He could hardly believe his good fortune.

"Where did they come from?"

"Some Jew peddler sold them to me on credit."

Manny Koning came by every day to sell what he could. After trading stopped, he would look for me and we would chat. He was interested in the fact that I had received a good basic education at Professor Mead's academy.

"But you could not go to your state university?"

"My family didn't have the money. Anyway, the war would have made me drop out."

"But they made you a lieutenant anyvay?"

"Yes. Our colonel took a shine to me. I saved his life when he was a captain."

At the end of that conversation, he produced a cherry pie and solemnly accepted my I.O.U.

"Now, Jim, that makes six dollars you owe me. Ven the var is over, you got to come back to Baltimore and pay me."

I laughed. "Sure, sure, Manny."

He frowned. "I am serious. You must not joke about financial obligations. You must keep trust. And don't take money lightly. It is important. But somet'ing is more important."

"What is that?"

"Ve Jews call it chutzpah. It means vat you Tar Heels call 'Get up and go' plus guts. I think maybe you got chutzpah."

"I reckon that's a compliment, then."

"All right, Jim. Just don't forget Manny Koning. Or that you owe him six dollars."

He winked and set off down the street, pushing his cart before him.

4

Manny Koning came to see me one more time after that. I was standing with my good eye pressed to a crack in the fence when he appeared around the corner, without his pushcart and accompanied by a slender, dark young man.

They approached the broken plank. I went over to peer into the broad face of my friend.

"Ah, there you are, Jim. I have brought my Cousin Bernard vit' me. Bernard vent to medical school in Germany. He is not yet a doctor, but he has much skill. I vant he should look at your eye."

His cousin seemed shy. "If I may. Just put your face through here." I complied. Almost tenderly, he removed the now filthy bandage from my eye.

"Ah. It is healing well. A bad wound it was. Lean out more and let me cleanse it."

With that, he took some new cotton and a small bottle of wood alcohol from his coat and proceeded to wash my scar lightly. The alcohol stung. He apologized when I grimaced.

"I think you will be better now to leave off the bandage. Manny told me of your need. So I am bringing you this."

He held up a black satin eye patch.

"You just tie this around your head and it will cover the eye. Go ahead. It will fit loose so as not to chafe. See?"

The satin felt soothing.

"Thank you so much," I said. "How much do I owe you?"

"Not'ing," Manny said. "No paper to sign for this. It is a gift."

"I am mighty grateful for that favor."

"It is not'ing. Look, Jim." He bent close. "It is no good for you to be shut up like a chicken in a pen. How would you like to get out of this place?"

"You mean escape?"

"Yes."

"I'd give anything. But a one-eyed string bean like me, dressed in Confederate uniform—where would I go? They would catch me for sure."

"Bernard and I have just rented a little building not far from here. We gonna open a store there. Ve can hide you in the loft. There are men ve know who can sneak you past Washington back to Virginia."

"Sure enough? That would be wonderful, but they got guards with loaded muskets on the roof of the warehouse and at the corners of the fence. Even if I climbed over the roof, they would shoot me."

"You just vait. Listen. Tomorrow, I come and bring a little crowbar. I slip it to you ven the guards don't look. There vill be a moon tomorrow. You pick your time and pry off a board and I bet you can get avay. Just run to the alley behind our store. Ve vill leave the back door open. Here, I have drawn a map."

The upshot was that we agreed I would wait until five o'clock the next afternoon, when the guards would be passing out grub to the prisoners, and he would slip the crowbar through the fence. It would be up to me to get away during the following night.

Freedom! Its prospects inflamed my mind. What would have been another miserable night spent huddling against that fence was made bearable as my imagination told me how I would get through the fence, elude the guards and race to the alley that ran behind Manny Koning's store. After that, a bath, clean clothes, decent food and a bed. Then, after recovering my strength I could risk trying to return to Virginia.

The early sun flooded the prison yard. I crowded up to receive my miserable ration from a surly guard. The poor Georgian next to me noticed how chipper I looked.

"What you got to be so happy about in this lousy hell hole?"

"Everything. The world is a wonderful place."

"Wonderful, hell. You think it wonderful just because your Jew friend brings you a patch for your eye?"

"We should all learn to take happiness from little things."

"Tell me something I can be happy about."

"Maybe you won't have to look at my ugly face, for one thing."

"What?" He brightened up. "They gonna transfer you? Or . . ." He paused. "You figured some way to escape?"

I could have bitten my tongue off. "Don't be silly. I mean't you don't have to look at my filthy bandage anymore, now that I have an eye patch."

"Ha! Some big blessing that is. It'll take more than that to make me happy."

My dream of escaping that night lasted throughout the morning. It lasted until a Yankee colonel with a voice like a bull shouted for us to give him our attention.

"Now, listen. We are going to be moving you people to other locations this week. We will start with the officers. Those of you who are not enlisted men assemble over by the warehouse door. Bring your belongings over. Move along. Tomorrow we will deal with any sergeants among you."

There I was, a newly appointed lieutenant, but still dressed like a sergeant. I just stayed pat. To go off now with the officers would queer my chance to escape that night.

"Hey, Mundy," my Georgia friend said. "I thought you was a lieutenant. Ain't you going up? They'll probably give you special treatment."

"No. I'm not really a lieutenant. Just a sergeant who got promoted right before Gettysburg. I don't consider myself a real officer."

"Hell, what difference does that make? You are an officer. It is stupid not to take advantage of your chance."

Guards were moving through the crowded pen, hurrying along the captains and lieutenants among us. To my horror, the Georgian waved at these guards and drew the attention of one.

"This fellow here is an officer, but he is too modest to admit it."

"How come you are not in officer's uniform?" the guard asked.

"I'm a sergeant," I said. "I'm not really an officer."

"Yes, he is," the Georgian persisted. "He was promoted to second lieutenant just before the big fight at Gettysburg. They made him aide to the colonel of the 10th North Carolina. He told me all about it. He just didn't have a chance to get a uniform."

Another guard came over. To make a painful story short, they herded me across the prison pen to a group of Confederate officers, paying no attention to my protests.

The last thing I remember about that stinking corral was my Georgia friend's moonface beaming at me, full of self-congratulation over having done me a big favor. I could cheerfully have shot him.

5

I'll say this much for the Yankees: they put us on decent rail cars for the start of our trip to a permanent prison camp. The seats on our car actually had plush upholstery. Felt like heaven to sit on a soft seat.

Guards with muskets stood at either end of the car. They

couldn't or wouldn't say where we were headed.

On that car with me were a couple of colonels and majors. The rest were captains or lieutenants, like me.

No, not really like me for I was the youngest and, I suppose, the roughest cut. Most of those fellows were from families that owned slaves, either that or they had a better education than me. A few had light wounds, but I was the only one with an eye patch.

By the time we had got to Philadelphia we were well acquainted with one another and were getting it sorted out just what our places were on the social scale as determined by rank, seniority and status back home.

A white-haired colonel from South Carolina, one Simon Cruikshank, obviously outranked us all. He was older than the other colonel and he let it be known that he had thirty slaves back home. The other colonel, one Robert Williams, had been a teacher at a military academy. Tall, dark fellow who didn't talk much and seemed mildly scornful of the rest of us.

One of the majors in our midst had been an engineer; still another, a merchant who had lost his business because of the blockade.

I was at the bottom of this heap, so I kept quiet the first part of the journey. Besides, it took me all the way to Philadelphia to accept the fact that I was not going to escape to the store of my new friend, Manny Koning, after all. I was not going to be shepherded back to Virginia to rejoin my regiment. Instead, I was being hauled off somewhere to the North, where escape likely would be impossible.

At Philadelphia, they put us aboard the Pennsylvania Railroad but kept the same close-mouthed guards. We stayed in the rail yard overnight. The U.S. Sanitary Commission maintained a canteen there and some kind ladies brought us sandwiches and coffee.

The news that Rebel prisoners were in town had circulated and soon there gathered a crowd of small boys and not a few adults to gape at the horrid Rebel officers as we ate our grub.

The guards made us keep the windows closed in that sweltering car, but we could see the curiosity fairly shining from those faces as the people pointed at us like zoo animals. They seemed to pay particular attention to me, but I thought little of it at the time.

I marveled at what I could see of Philadelphia, which at that time was a city of some 200,000 population. It made quite a contrast with Richmond, what with its well-dressed people and a general atmosphere of wealth and booming business.

Our colonel from South Carolina, Colonel Cruikshank, took it upon himself to give us a formal address, reminding us that we were all Southerners, officers and gentlemen and how it behooved us to maintain discipline among ourselves.

"We have fallen upon misfortune, but let us not despair, gentlemen. If our Yankee captors mistreat any of you, they will have me to answer to. You bring any complaints to me and, as the senior officer among you, I will demand that the cause of the grievance be removed. I am confident that, despite our setback at Gettysburg, the Confederacy will prevail and that every one of us will be returned to our families."

Polite applause greeted the conclusion of this horseshit. We rearranged ourselves to sleep. I sat beside a filthy window, which was turned into a mirror by the dark outside and the glow of a hanging lantern nearby. Suddenly I realized why the small boys had stared so at me. The reflection of my face startled me for I resembled a pirate with my black patch, unshorn hair and haggard face. My seatmate, a captain in his thirties, was already asleep. I lifted off my patch and turned my face so the lamp glow illuminated the left side.

What a shock! Where my eye had been there now appeared an empty, sunken socket. A red scar disfigured my left cheek and puckered the brow above the eye socket. Where was the handsome face of Jim Mundy now? Unable to bear the sight of myself, I replaced the patch. I was glad when one of the guards came around and put out the lamp.

What a miserable, sleepless night I spent there on a Philadelphia railroad siding. A lonely night of shock and soul-searching. I felt I could never show my face again. What would Jane Ferro think of my disfigurement? Would she be disgusted? How my mother would grieve and my father pray, if they knew. Elvira Fincastle and Maria, the quadroon girl, would they think me so appealing now?

It was a relief when morning came. After the good Sanitary Commission ladies brought around hot grub and coffee, the train lurched and soon we found ourselves rattling out of the rail yard.

The guards still wouldn't say where we were headed, but even a dummy could see our direction was west as we passed through Paoli and Coatesville.

Soon we began to see the neat fields and vast, orderly barns of the Pennsylvania Dutch. This was Amish country, judging from the strange enclosed buggies jogging about the countryside.

One of our companions, a captain from Virginia, told us all about their quaint ways. His father had been an Amish lad who could not bear to live under their restrictive ways. He had run off to the valley of Virginia and settled there.

"Now ain't that the damnedest thing?" a major commented. "You hear about niggers running away north to get away from slavery. Sounds to me like your daddy went swimming against the tide when he headed south."

This touched off a general conversation about the Fugitive Slave Law and the perfidious Yankees who had failed to help enforce it. All the while this empty talk went on, our train rushed past rich farmlands, being tended by energetic free people, past little towns and busy small factories, through a land of plenty that did not know slavery.

For a while our train ran along the east bank of the Susquehanna, through Middletown and at last into Harrisburg itself.

They let us out at the train station, under guard, to stretch our legs and stomp our feet. The usual crowd of curious idlers gathered to stare at our bedraggled crew. I paid these gawkers no attention as I gazed beyond the nearby Susquehanna at the hills on the opposite shore. There, just across from the town, reared the height where the militia or whoever had built the fortifications meant to protect Harrisburg against our advance up the Cumberland Valley. Then, to the left, I could see another hill, the same one I had helped scout out with General Jenkins and his bunch.

"Well," I thought to myself, "you were so anxious to get to Harrisburg. Here you are."

We weren't there long, however, before they loaded us back on the train. We crossed the Susquehanna upstream several miles over the same stone bridge we had meant to destroy and thence into mountainous country. On and on we rolled until night overtook us.

We slowed down from time to time and pulled off onto sidings to let long trains have the right of way. Most of them were freight trains with cannon and wagons and such on their flatcars, but at least two trains carrying recruits for the Federal Army went by, headed for the training camp at Harrisburg, I suppose.

Our last stop was outside of Pittsburgh and they left us there for the night. I awakened the next morning when the train started hesitantly moving into the city. Soon all around us was fresh evidence of the industrial power of the North for the place abounded with the chimneys and buildings of foundries and factories. There was productive might in that one city such as the ordinary Southerner could not comprehend.

Even our vainglorious Colonel Cruikshank was awed into silence. I expect that if secession had been put to a secret ballot in our party just then, the results would have been negative.

They shifted us over, or I should say marched us over, to another line. There a new lot of guards took us over. They were dour fellows who seemed to look upon even Confederate officers as so much vermin.

Colonel Cruikshank was indignant when he saw they meant

to put us aboard a boxcar littered with filthy straw. "Why are you treating us like cattle?" he demanded of an impassive Union sergeant.

"Aren't you?"

"Cattle? No, we are not. We are officers in the Confederate Army. We are officers and gentlemen."

"Don't get yourself so worked up. This ain't a cattle car. In fact, it was just used to haul your very type."

"What do you mean?"

"It's a swine car and that's what we got now. A lot of gray swine."

The other guards laughed while our colonel spluttered.

"I am going to report you to your next in command. I will not bandy words with a mere sergeant. Who is your officer and where will I find him?"

"My company commander is Captain Josiah Charrington and you will find him at Johnson's Island."

"Just where is that?"

"You'll soon see for yourself. It's an island in Lake Erie. A prison camp just for Rebel officers. Now cut out the chatter and get in there with your brother pigs."

The sergeant looked at me. "Hey, you, one-eye! Take your hands out of your pockets and help Grandpa here into your swine car."

6

Johnson's Island. After more than fifty years, the name still calls up a feeling of revulsion. It lay in Lake Erie about two and a half miles from the town of Sandusky, Ohio, a one-mile-by-half-mile chunk of limestone covered by a thin layer of black earth and gravel from which sprouted a profusion of scrubby trees. That is what nature did to create Johnson's Island.

What man did to turn that low-lying, featureless dab of land into a hell hole was to enclose most of one end of the island with a 200-by-300-yard wooden wall standing fifteen feet high. This wall had a walkway around the outside so the guards could maintain a ceaseless patrol. Then at two corners of this palisade fronting on the lake they built guard towers and installed in them small cannon that could spray the camp with canister if need be. Another tower commanded the only gate into the enclosure.

Within the enclosure were erected thirteen two-story barracks or "blocks," crude structures which generally had one or two large common rooms on the first floor and several smaller rooms on a second floor reached by outside stairs.

One of these thirteen blocks served as a hospital. The other twelve sheltered over 2,500 Confederate officers; that many human beings were stuffed into a quarter-mile-square enclosure.

Each block was divided into two messes, and each of these groups was allowed to elect its own "chief" to see that we kept our quarters clean and ourselves fed.

I knew none of this, however, when our swine car rolled into Sandusky early one August morning. Our guards unceremoniously routed us from our beds of stinking straw. Some curious Sanduskians, mostly boys in their mid-teens, gathered to see us marched to a landing where a small steamer waited to transport us. I must say these Ohio citizens were not very hospitable. They did not make us feel welcome at all. Several young ruffians marched alongside us singing, "We'll hang Jeff Davis from a sour apple tree." And one of them pointed at me and shouted, "Hey, look at the one-eyed Reb. Ain't he a pretty sight?"

I longed to wade into those louts with both fists. Yet I must admit we were a ragtag group, dressed in stinking gray uniforms and carrying all kinds of parcels. The fact that some of us tried to assume an air of great dignity only made us look more ridiculous.

"Take no notice of them, gentlemen," our Colonel Cruikshank counseled us when he saw the guards would do nothing to stop the taunting. "They are only low Yankee scum. Take no notice of them."

Inside the gate at Johnson's Island a mild-mannered fellow named Pierson lined us up and explained he was the commandant and that we would be well treated as long as we behaved ourselves. Then he ordered us to turn over all our money to a Captain Charrington and his clerk.

This Captain Charrington was a tall Ohioan with a shock of black hair and a beak nose, and eyes as hard as two pieces of granite. His clerk was a pudgy little middle-aged fellow named Mason.

I was to get to know these two worthies better than I wished. In fact, I was to get to know Johnson's Island better during the next thirteen months of my young life, the most dismal period I can remember.

At that time, Johnson's Island was guarded by some four hundred men of a special battalion recruited in Ohio for the purpose of guarding prisoners. Imagine anyone volunteering for such duty. What a lot.

By the time our carload reached the island, the social structure of the prison had been pretty well established. They split our group up and assigned us evenly throughout the twenty-four messes. I found myself assigned to the first floor of Block Number 11. My mess chief was a feisty little major from Alabama, a chap named Watson. Major Watson showed me our wide bunks tiered three high along one wall, and he pointed to one on the very top.

"That's your bunk, Mundy. You are lucky. Chap who slept there went to the hospital last week or you'd have to sleep on the floor."

"Won't he be back?"

"Hardly. Poor fellow died yesterday. Hey, Funderburk. Come here!"

A square-built fellow with a blond beard separated himself from a card game and came over.

"This is Lieutenant Mundy, from the 10th North Carolina. Wounded and captured at Gettysburg. He's your new bunkmate. Mundy, this is Captain Funderburk, from Alabama like me."

Funderburk looked at me inquiringly. "You snore, Mundy?"

"I don't think so."

"Grind your teeth in your sleep, or thrash about?"

For the first time in days, I laughed. "No, and I don't wet the bed either."

He laughed, too, as he held out his hand. "Then I reckon you'll do."

God, I have no wish to chronicle everything that happened to me in that hellish place during the next thirteen months, not down to the last detail. Anyway, in general, life on Johnson's Island was not so bad during the fall of 1863. We still had hope of being exchanged. And while they took away our money, they did give us scrip in return, even crediting us for our Confederate currency at a rate of seven U.S. cents on the dollar. We were allowed to spend this scrip at the shop of a sutler who brought goods over from Sandusky.

This arrangement worked well at first. But we exhausted his supply of dried fruits, candies, canned meats and such delicacies in short order. He soon was reduced to tobacco, stationery and stamps.

Stamps? Oh, yes, we were allowed to write letters from the camp. They just had to be turned over to the little clerk, Mason, for screening. They wanted to make sure we weren't writing outside to invite help to escape. It was up to Mason to stop any such letters.

And mail did come in from the South, usually taking about two months to pass through Richmond and thence via the prisoner exchange bureaus of the two warring sections and finally through the U.S. Post Office. What's more, those of us from the border states or from occupied parts of the Confederacy could receive packages; those lucky individuals.

Now the food we got during my first few months was adequate, I must admit. The Yankees had built the camp the year before expressly for Confederate prisoners and they had provided good cooking facilities. Each building had its own stove. There was a central bakery that produced passable bread. Each mess got weekly rations of staples such as sugar, coffee, beans and rice. Four days out of the week we got fresh beef and on other days pickled pork plus occasional vegetables. Nothing fancy, of course.

It was up to the prisoners to cook their own food. It was up to us to clean our barracks and police the grounds. We likewise were supposed to air out our quarters and keep our persons clean. I am sorry to say that many of us lived like hogs. Ate like hogs, too.

No, the Yanks provided for us pretty well except in the matter of clothing. We simply were not prepared for the intense winters of that section, and our keepers were slow to find blankets or overcoats for us.

It got chilly in September. It got bitter-cold in October. Then it grew positively frigid in November. I can't find a word to describe the weather that gripped us in December.

We had three shallow wells as our chief water supply. The pumps froze, so we had to bring in ice from the lake and melt it. The ink froze on our pen points when we tried to write. We used to sleep with our canteens under our pillows. I awoke some mornings to find that the water left in my canteen had frozen.

The lake around us became covered with solid ice, so solid that it bore the weight of wagons bringing over supplies from Sandusky.

Sure, we had stoves in our blocks, but they did no good. The Yanks had hauled in green wood that produced more smoke than flame. The wind off Lake Erie knifed through the numerous cracks and drove us to our bunks to huddle there under our scanty blankets even during the day. Never have I experienced that kind of discomfort.

Before winter descended on us, however, some of us felt pretty feisty and there was much muttering of plans to organize an attack on our Ohio volunteers, overpower them and speedily convert our palisade into rafts to ferry us to the shore. Word of this got to Colonel Pierson and soon there appeared on the scene an armed steamer, the *Michigan,* the only armed U.S. vessel permitted on Lake Erie by treaty with Canada. That and an increase in the patrols around the enclosure put a temporary end to such schemes.

Prison life is a tough test of character. A considerable number of my fellow Southern officers and so-called gentlemen failed the test, for they lived like beasts. No, worse than beasts for they developed the foulest mouths that ever uttered an oath. I have used profanity all my life except in the presence of ministers of the gospel and my dear wife or other ladies, but I have always prided myself on some originality of expression. There was none of that among a certain class of our prisoners who communicated with each other by a perfect stream of obscenity from morning to night. It was enough to give profanity a bad name. No discriminating choice of words; no imaginative similes; no variety. Just a repetition of a half-dozen words.

These same fellows spent most of their time playing cards or dice and avoiding their turns at cooking or cleaning up.

Still another element spent long hours reading their Bibles, talking religion and listening to each other pray. They bored me as much as the first group disgusted me.

Still another group of wide-awake chaps realized how the human animal requires discipline and mental stimulation. They organized lectures, minstrels, poetry readings and debates. Their entertainments helped me keep my sanity.

I mentioned the little civilian clerk, Mason. What I am about to say of him is sordid, and I wouldn't mention it at all except that the incident was to have a profound effect on my life's course. It happened the first week I was at Johnson's Island.

This Mason would come around sometimes when our morning rolls were called, just standing about with his hands in his pockets, watching our faces as we answered to our names.

I noticed his watery little eye watching me at roll call one morning but thought nothing of it until the next day.

"Mundy," he said to me. "What is your education?"

"I went to an academy in North Carolina."

"You write a clear hand?"

"My penmanship is acceptable, I trust."

"I could use some help with my records. You would have a warm place to work when winter comes and you would take one meal a day, at noon, from the guards' mess. How about it?"

"When do I start?"

His little office was a corner room with its own small stove. I worked there for two days and each day the meal was hot and tasty. The work was not hard, consisting of copying off a list of the prisoners.

Mason was something else. He liked to talk, asking all kinds of personal questions. I told him all about my family and my life back home.

"You got any girl friends?"

"I have one. I intend to marry her when this war is over, if she'll have me."

"What is her name?"

"Jane."

"I guess you have had lots of other girls."

"Not really. How about yourself, Mason? You must be a married man."

"No. I support my mother and a sister over in Sandusky. That's women enough in one person's life." He smiled slyly and winked.

Well, I finished my work that day and returned to my block in time for evening mess. Felt like I had fallen in the proverbial pile of shit and had come up smelling like lavender water. That night my bunkmate, Captain Funderburk, listened to me brag about my soft job.

"Mundy, you watch that Mason fellow."

"What do you mean?"

"With all the educated men in this camp, why would he choose one of the youngest prisoners to work for him?"

"Hell, I don't know. Maybe because he figures an older officer would be hard to handle."

"Maybe. Just don't let him get too cozy."

I discovered what Funderburk meant the next day. Mason was busy outside while I did my copying in that snug, comfortable office. He brought me in a tray of good sardines with cheese and crackers at noon and hung about while I ate.

"Wasn't that delicious, James?"

This jarred me for until then he had called me "Mundy." I politely replied, "Yes, thank you, Mister Mason."

"Oh, you can call me Lester, if you like. I'd prefer that. After all, I expect we shall be working very closely for a long time. In fact, I've been wondering if you'd like to move your things over here and sleep in the room next door with me. Colonel Pierson might allow it."

I began to smell a rat. "Well, I don't know. . . ."

"I'll inquire. You know, James, they are such a rough lot, those prisoners, that a splendid young fellow like you ought to be protected from them."

"I can protect myself."

"Yes, but you should accept help when it is offered in friendship."

He came over and put his hand on my shoulder. "You are an unusual young man. It is a pity about your eye. You must have been even more handsome before you lost it."

And then he ran his pudgy little fingers through my hair.

That did it. I stood up, towering over him.

"What in the hell is your game, Mason? You are acting like a woman toward me."

He looked hurt. "I was trying to be kind to you, James."

"Just keep your frigging hands to yourself. What are you? Some kind of pervert?"

His face grew hard. "How dare you say such a thing to me? Is that the way to respond to an offer of friendship? You are most ungrateful. I have it in my power to make you regret you uttered such harsh words."

"So now you threaten me, you nasty little pederast."

He was angry now. "You will indeed regret calling me that, my friend. I should never have taken pity on you. You Rebels are all alike. You have spurned my offer of help and now you must suffer the consequences."

"What consequences? Giving up this pen-pushing job? I can bear that."

The soppy expression in his watery eyes had changed to one of cold hatred.

"You'll suffer far worse than that."

"How?"

"You will see. Get out of here and go back to your swinish Rebel friends."

That night as Captain Funderburk and I settled ourselves for sleep on our straw mattress, I told him about the incident.

"I was afraid it was something like that."

"Damn Mason and damn this island. I have got to get away from this place."

"You aren't alone in that sentiment. Now shut your mouth and tonight don't hog the covers."

7

Somehow I endured the rest of 1863 in that human pigpen called Johnson's Island. I endured it by taking part in the weekly entertainments got up in our mess. I endured it by writing long letters to Jane Ferro—directly to her, mind you, for now I didn't give a damn what her father thought anymore. And I devoted much time to keeping myself as clean as possible with cold water and very little soap. I still had my little pocket diary but for some reason could not bear to write in it anymore.

Some men were able to sit about with blank eyes hour after hour waiting for mealtime and bed, but not me. I determined that prison life would not get me down but at times my spirit burned mighty low.

Our mess chief, Major Watson, did the best he could to keep our quarters clean, our bellies filled and our hands occupied. But the poor fellow had no authority other than his own power of persuasion.

Our camp became a huge refuse heap as men threw garbage and trash out the windows. Our floors were covered with dark, sticky mud tracked in constantly. We emptied our bodily wastes into a number of sinks or long shallow trenches, but the limestone core of the island lay so close to the surface that the drainage was very poor. As a result, a stench hovered over the camp.

Cold. Boredom. Filth. Sloth. To this day I cannot abide these things. I learned to hate them at Johnson's Island the winter of 1863–64.

Despite our crowded conditions and lack of clothing, the

death rate at Johnson's Island could not compare with that at Andersonville in Georgia or Elmira in New York State. Still, during the intensely cold month of December 1863, eighteen prisoners died. And at one time in January they piled the corpses up between the buildings because they could not dig graves fast enough in the frozen ground.

When I started writing to Jane Ferro from Johnson's Island, it occurred to me that my old comrades in the 10th N.C. might be wondering what had happened to me after I fell there at Gettysburg. So I asked her to notify her brother William that I was alive and in prison. Started writing to her in August soon after my arrival and continued to do so right through the rest of the year . . . a long letter every week, which was all we were allowed. I reckoned that by the end of 1863 her replies might start flowing back to me. How I envied those of my fellow prisoners who did get letters.

Christmas—the bleakest I ever spent—came and went.

Then New Year's Eve. Somehow the boys in our mess got hold of a quantity of whisky and they put together a New Year's celebration. It was the coldest night yet, with a fierce, steady wind that drove our guards right off their walkway to huddle inside the guard towers. In our building, I and several chums got a couple of ounces of very bad liquor, bad but good enough to make us feel rosy and almost festive.

Captain Funderburk took his ration of whisky and offered it to me.

"What's the matter?" I asked. "You never struck me as a teetotaler."

"I'm not. My stomach feels uneasy tonight. So you drink my share."

I swallowed her down and pretty soon was leading a group in singing patriotic Southern songs and showing them how we danced the clog down in Oldham County. Felt like my old self there for a bit.

Then Captain Charrington and a couple of his bully boys came and ordered lights out.

Funderburk and I huddled back-to-back on our sour straw tick under two shared blankets. I went to sleep, my brain drunkenly reeling with thoughts of home.

I awoke at daylight to find Funderburk's side of our mattress empty. On his pillow there was a note addressed to me:

> Dear James: Me and three others are about to break out of this miserable hole. We have ropes and a grapple and extra clothes. We are going over the wall while it is too cold for the guards to patrol. I wanted to take you along but the others said your eye-patch would make you too easy to identify once we get to the shore. Wish me luck, James. You have been a good bunk mate. Come see me in Alabama after this damned war is over.

Shitfire! I kept my mouth shut, but at roll call the Yankees discovered Funderburk and the others were gone. By late afternoon a wagon delivered two of the four escapees back from Sandusky with frozen feet and hands. Getting over the fence had been a cinch, but the wind and cold were too much for their thin Southern blood. Funderburk and the other chap did get away, however.

The next morning Captain Charrington sent two guards for me. Made me stand at attention in front of his desk while the clerk, Mason, sat in a corner and watched the proceedings with a malicious look on his ratlike face.

"You mean that your bunkmate could gather all that gear for his escape and you wouldn't know anything about it?"

"I do mean that."

"The others said Funderburk concealed the rope under your mattress. What do you say about that? You slept on the same mattress."

"I never looked under his side."

His black eyes bored into me.

"How could he get up in the night and dress himself without your knowing anything about it?"

I couldn't explain about all the whisky I had drunk.

"I slept straight through the night."

"I don't believe you. The others said Funderburk wanted to take you along, but they vetoed the idea because of your one eye. I get the distinct impression you were an accomplice. So I am going to make an example of you to deter others from helping with escapes. You are going into solitary confinement until you confess everything you know about how they got their rope and grapple and extra clothing."

Of course there was nothing for me to tell. So off I went to an unheated cell measuring 6 by 6. Nothing in it but a straw mattress on the floor and a slop pot. I was able to take the two blankets Funderburk and I shared, however.

Those bastards kept me in that icebox for two weeks. Left me to shiver under my thin blankets, as sad and miserable a specimen as ever drew a frosty breath.

I kept my sanity through sheer determination. I recited every poem I ever learned. Did complicated sums in my head. Recalled the names of every person I knew back in Oldham County, color of hair and eye, shape of nose, every scrap of information I could bring to mind. Did the same thing with the men in my regiment. Found that I could remember whole sermons my daddy had preached.

And I thought of Jane Ferro. I had been alone with her only a few times. But I relived those experiences like some people play and replay those newfangled Edison Gram-o-phone records these days. Only, I would not allow myself to think about her until I had played other memory games, so as not to wear out the record, you might say.

I must admit that I let my mind dwell on Elvira Fincastle and that girl of pleasure, Maria, too.

They did feed me moderately well in my frigid little cell. The guards who brought the cold rations were under orders not to speak, which was all right with me.

I should say that punishment of this sort was not the usual thing at Johnson's Island. I laid the blame for my harsh treatment on the little civilian clerk, Mason, figuring it was his way of taking revenge for my rejection of his homosexual advances. He and Captain Charrington were thick as could be.

And so I went through two weeks of this ordeal until one bright, cold morning someone opened my cell door, and I looked up into the hearty face of a Union sergeant, a man I had not seen before.

"What they got you in here for?" he asked.

I explained about my bunkmate's escape.

"And that's all you did, or didn't do, honest to God?"

"Honest to God."

"Well, son, I am Sergeant Frederick Casper of the 23rd Pennsylvania Volunteers. We have relieved the guard contingent here. Their enlistments are up and they are being disbanded. I'll report your case to my captain."

"You mean those Ohio bastards are gone, for good?"

"Yep. And now you got real soldiers guarding you. We are veterans. We're in Sedgwick's corps."

"You at Gettysburg?"

"Indeed we were. And Chancellorsville and all the other big battles."

"I was at Gettysburg, too. That's where I lost this eye. And where I was captured."

In a bit the sergeant returned with a brisk captain who listened gravely to my story. At its conclusion he said, "Gather up your blankets, son, and come out of this miserable place."

So ended my solitary confinement. Although the Ohioans had gone home, the little clerk, Mason, was still about. His face bore a look of surprise and spite when he saw me free again.

Those chaps from Sedgwick's corps were a jolly lot. They chaffed with the prisoners and did small acts of kindness that made our lives a little less onerous. Between us and them there was a mutual respect of men who had been through the hell of battle together.

They remained with us until April, I believe, at which time they were called back to the Army of the Potomac to provide

U. S. Grant with cannon fodder for his drive on Richmond that was to begin in May. I was sorry to see that lot of stout lads go. We liked each other.

Their replacements were members of the Ohio State Militia, and in their own way they were worse than the original special guard detachment. Some of the militia were mere boys who had never shaved and others men too poorly to hold up in regular military service. And there was a fair proportion of fellows who looked healthy enough for any army; I took them to be slackers who joined the militia to avoid fighting.

Generally these militiamen seemed to feel they had to prove their manhood by bullying the prisoners or at least shouting at us and threatening to shoot if we came too close to the palisades. I think in truth they were afraid of us.

Anyway, their mean spirit was reciprocated. Talk of escape began spreading again. My new bunkmate, a wiry redhead from Virginia, one Nat Sladden, took up the subject one night in March as I was trying to get asleep.

"Now keep this to yourself, Mundy, but I know how we can get out of here," he whispered.

"Are you crazy? It's too late to walk over the ice. Besides, those damned militia are too quick on the trigger for you ever to reach the lake."

"A tunnel, Mundy. That's the answer. We can dig our way under the wall and swim over to the shore at night."

I was skeptical at first, but Sladden had it all figured out how we could pry up the planks in a corner room and dig down several feet, then run a tunnel forty or fifty feet under the wall. Then, using empty canteens or what have you to support us, we could swim ashore on the mainland.

"But that damned lake is so cold."

"It would be warm weather before we got the tunnel dug. Now how about it? You want in the deal?"

"Sure. Count me in."

It was a relief to have a project to keep myself from going mad.

8

Sladden and I went to great length to keep our project a secret but soon saw how impossible that was with over a hundred men in close confinement on one floor of a small building.

We started the tunnel in a small corner room closest to the palisade. By removing three short boards, one man could get down on his knees and dig away with a large spoon or cup or tin plate. The soil could have been worse to dig in. Our big problem was disposing of the dirt. With proper tools and plenty of eager volunteers as the word inevitably spread, we could have run that tunnel out in a week or so. But no, we had to work quietly, late at night, with makeshift tools and we had to dispose of the dirt in such a way that our captors would not notice.

Our way was to shove as much as we dared under our building, crawling to remote corners. We found that we could carry out a bag full just before lights-out and empty it in a sink as well.

The work went quickly on the shaft. Two or three men could work side by side while the rest of us played noisy games of cards in the little room, awaiting our turn to dig.

Within a week or so we had sunk our shaft; it was a hole like a deep grave. Then we called in a messmate who was an engineer and he figured out the direction in which we should tunnel. Now the pace became slower, for only one man could work at a time, in hourly shifts, on hands and knees patiently scraping away at the black soil and passing back plates of earth to the man at the entrance.

We moled away throughout April and into May. With the tunnel to occupy my thoughts I did not brood so much about not yet receiving replies to my letters from Jane Ferro, or anyone else for that matter. Nor did I dwell so much on the loss of my eye or the fact that the U.S. Government had halted all prisoner exchanges with the Confederacy as a way of applying pressure on the South's dwindling manpower reserves.

Northern newspapers kept us apprized of the horrible battles being fought between Lee and Grant in the Wilderness and at Spotsylvania and Cold Harbor, battles in which tens of thousands of Yankees fell. This was the period, too, in which Sherman maneuvered his way toward Atlanta with the wily Joe Johnston countering his every move.

While all this was going on in Virginia and northern Georgia, we pushed our tunnel along at the rate of half a foot or so a night.

I have never enjoyed being in close quarters and so it took all my courage to crawl into that tunnel for my turn at scraping out a few inches of earth. Of course the farther the tunnel extended, the harder it was to breathe. Found we had to slow down so we didn't exhaust the air down there.

By the end of May, our engineer adviser reckoned we were within ten or fifteen feet of the wall. By now the project was general knowledge in our mess, so the best we could do about secrecy was to threaten to cut the throat of anyone who spread the word outside our mess.

Fortunately, the militia guards were not very diligent about inspecting our quarters. The little clerk, Mason, only came to the door in the mornings to collect our letters for posting and take up the rolls.

About mid-May we started getting new prisoners, officers captured by Grant in the Wilderness. One of these was a fresh-faced lieutenant from South Carolina, a kind of mama's boy with flaxen hair and rosy cheeks. Before anyone could warn him, Mason had recruited him as his assistant. Several days after he had begun his clerical duties I drew him aside and tried to warn him. To my surprise he flared up, his baby face turning red as he said, "Don't say anything to me against Mister Mason. He is a kind person. He has told me about you and warned me not to associate with troublemakers of your sort." This in a mincing tone that turned my stomach.

I gave him a look of disgust and went about my business.

By early June we were drawing up lists of escape parties, giving first place to the six or eight of us who had done most of the work. It was obvious to Sladden and me that it would be impossible for our entire mess to get through the tunnel, down to the water and then two and a half miles to the mainland, not unless we had a boat waiting for us. Just to feed their hopes, however, Sladden worked up an idea for drawing lots for hourly escape parties. But we never got a chance to put the scheme into effect.

Two things happened, somewhat related, I suppose. Colonel Pierson, who had been commandant of the camp since it was founded, was relieved of duty because, I think, his favoritism to certain suppliers of fuel and meat in Sandusky came to the attention of Washington. His replacement was one Colonel Charles W. Hill, and from our point of view it was a disastrous change. Colonel Pierson may have been dishonest, but he was incompetent in a way we found to our benefit. Colonel Hill was made of sterner stuff. He came determined to make life more difficult for us.

One morning while we were lined up outside our block for roll call, Colonel Hill and a squad of musket-carrying militiamen marched past us and into our building. We stood in our ranks murmuring to ourselves until he emerged from the building and squalled for more militiamen to come with long iron rods.

They began thrusting these rods into the earth between our building and the palisade. It didn't take them long to locate our tunnel. By afternoon they had driven heavy posts down to block off the tunnel and had nailed the loose boards back in the floor of our little room.

That same day the little blond lieutenant from South Carolina moved out of our mess and into quarters with Mason. That night Sladden and I bought a flask of evil whisky from another prisoner and got quietly drunk.

9

God, that new commandant, Colonel Hill, was a bastard. The U.S. Government hanged his counterpart at Andersonville, poor old Wirz, but at least Wirz had the excuse of lack of supplies and transportation. Hill was just naturally mean.

The weather there on Johnson's Island warmed up somewhat in the spring, but then in June it turned chilly again. No difference to Colonel Hill. His calendar said June, so he ordered all stoves removed from the blocks, except for cooking ranges, leaving us to shiver.

Then he turned his special attention to those of us in Block 11 for digging that tunnel. He stopped our rations of sugar, coffee and candles. Later he extended this to the entire camp as more and more blocks incurred his displeasure. Also, he reduced our rations of beef to once a week.

Now the old colonel from South Carolina, Cruikshank, who was housed in another building, organized a petition from all the senior officers in the camp and presented it to Colonel Hill. The petition called for the restoration of our full rations.

Colonel Hill tore up the petition and threw the scraps in his face. The next day he reduced our bread ration.

The meanest thing he did that summer was the way in which he treated a Southern civilian, a chap from Tennessee, a fellow who made money importing medicine and other items through the lines into his home state and thence to the rest of the blockaded South.

The Yankees apprehended him on one of his buying trips in Cincinnati and they slapped him into our prison on Johnson's Island. I well remember him for he stuck out like a sore thumb with his full belly, red face and civilian outfit, just moping about the yard feeling and looking out of place among tough Confederate officers.

Somehow his wife and two children, a boy and a girl, made their way up from Nashville, hired a boat and crossed over to Johnson's Island, all without prior arrangements. They approached the gate, announced who they were and told how they had traveled all the way up from Nashville to see her husband.

The officer on duty carried the message to Colonel Hill, but he, that low-life son of a bitch, ordered that the woman be turned away.

By that time, word of the woman's appearance had spread to her husband's ear and he went to the gate, begging for a few minutes with his wife.

The officer went back to Colonel Hill, who flew into a rage.

So the poor woman had to go back to the boat. But the officer on duty was so touched by all this that, to his everlasting credit, he invited the husband to mount the guard tower so he could wave to his wife and little children as they drew away in the boat.

Word of Colonel Hill's callous behavior infuriated the prisoners more than his taking away our stoves or stopping our rations. That night there was much talk of murdering him, overpowering the militia and then tearing down the walls to be turned into rafts.

The very next day everyone in our block refused to answer to his name when roll was called. Our militia officer was furious. He threatened us with bread-and-water rations and all that, but in vain. Other messes, also lined up outside for roll call, began to shout, "Down with Hill! Down with Hill!"

This brought all the militiamen running up to the walkway around the top of our camp wall, with their muskets at the ready. The hubbub in our ranks increased, with more and more shouting and shaking of fists until some fellows closest to the gate began hurling stones and clods of earth at the militia.

Suddenly a volley of musketry sounded from one end of the wall. Two men fell, both badly wounded. We all took up rocks and sticks, and God knows what would have happened if the guards had not fired a blank cannon charge. We did not know it was blank, however, and we all fell flat on our faces as the noise echoed.

Then Colonel Hill, using a megaphone, shouted down to us, "You have ten seconds in which to stop this disorder. Our cannon are being loaded with double charges of canister. We will fire into you if you do not immediately empty your hands, reform in ranks and answer to your roll calls."

I looked up at those cannon muzzles glowering down at us and that solid line of trigger-happy militia.

Old Colonel Cruikshank yelled up to Hill, "If we obey, will you receive the colonels' committee again and hear our petition?"

There was a long pause, one of the longest I have ever experienced. There stood Hill staring down at us. There were nearly three thousand Confederate officers, angry desperate men. One wrong word now and the prison compound would have been turned into a slaughterhouse.

Hill shouted back, "Yes. I will receive you."

The crisis had passed. Hill did receive the colonels but did nothing about our rations after all that. Wouldn't surprise me if he was selling our beef ashore.

It was after this that we began killing and eating the wharf rats around our camp. Never thought I would be reduced to eating rats, but not only did I do so, I actually learned to enjoy the taste.

The rat population had grown by leaps and bounds during the

year I had been there. The rats had become fat and trusting, scurrying about under our barracks and coming right into our cooking area after lights-out. I got me a short, heavy stick and learned how to lay a rat out cold thirty feet away by hurling that stick a certain way. Sladden and I became adept at skinning those rodents. Found that if we hung them up to "cure" a day or two it improved the flavor. Don't knock rat stew until you haven't had any real meat for several weeks. It really isn't bad eating.

The mood in our prison became worse and worse as the summer wore on and the cause of the Confederacy grew more desperate. We had lost our great chance at Gettysburg. I did not realize this until long after the war, but Rodes' division had a ringside seat at a momentous historical drama that July 2 and 3 of 1863. Anyway, now it was out of the question for even a great general like Lee to crush a Union army and seize Washington. He didn't have the manpower. While his strength diminished, that of the North increased.

The last hope of the South that spring and summer of 1864 was to inflict such dreadful losses on the Yankees that they would grow sick of the war and in the November elections would reject Lincoln and make a peace candidate their President. Thus we received with joy the news that General George B. McClellan would oppose Lincoln in the election. Our hopes would have been further buoyed if we had known of plans certain Confederate operatives in Canada had for freeing us en masse there on Johnson's Island.

Few of us, if any, knew of this until September 21, but a band of escaped Rebel prisoners and C.S.A. secret agents planned to seize two steamers on Lake Erie and board the U.S.S. *Michigan*, then storm the camp, overpower the guards with our help, and haul us all over to Canada.

From reading the official accounts since the war, I know how unrealistic this plan really was. The Yankees got wind of the scheme somehow. They brought in extra artillery at Sandusky and alerted the *Michigan*'s captain.

September 21, 1864, was one of the blackest days in my life. That was the day we simultaneously learned that our friends in Canada had seized two steamers up at Beall Island, just a few miles away, and that they had abandoned them and fled when the *Michigan* appeared ready for them. This cast a gloom over our camp.

And September 21 was the day I tried to kill the little clerk, Mason.

10

The weather on that Godforsaken island, so unseasonably cold in June, now in September had become unseasonably hot. The air was muggy. Every prisoner seemed to have awakened in the same foul mood. The oaths were as heavy as the air as we stumbled about our morning toilets, ha, and ate our breakfast of stale bread, weak tea and a particularly vile lot of pickled pork.

At roll call, Colonel Hill chose to address us as we lined up, rank upon rank, in the compound in front of the main gate.

"It may not surprise some of you that your friends in Canada have been hatching a plot to release you from this place. Oh, yes, we know that communications have passed between some of you and those scoundrels across the lake. We have our means of discovering such things."

Scowls and looks of puzzlement passed between us as Colonel Hill let this news sink in. Then he raised the megaphone to his lips again.

"Those brigands have gone so far as to seize two vessels with a view to descending upon this place and carrying you off. Now don't, some of you, act as though you are surprised at this, for you have been a part of that very plot, I am convinced.

"But we have been kept apprized of the scheme. Why do you think those additional artillery pieces have been implanted over at Sandusky? Oh, we have been ready for your friends."

Someone shouted, "Oh, shut up, Hill, and get to the point."

He fairly spluttered at this insult. "The point is that the pirates who committed this vile act are either fled, drowned or in custody. Those who have been captured will be tried and most likely hanged. You can forget about being rescued!"

With that he turned away, leaving us to splutter in our turn.

It is quite possible that some few prisoners did know about the rescue attempt, but they sure kept it quiet from the rest of us. Anyway, the news that someone had tried to free us and had failed put us in a blacker mood than ever.

I went to my bunk, drew out my writing materials and poured out my distress in a letter to Jane Ferro. Time and again since my incarceration on Johnson's Island I had written such letters to Jane. I was troubled by my failure to receive any reply from her, or, for that matter, from my own parents, but assumed that the Confederate mail system between Oldham County and Richmond was at fault.

I took my completed letter, affixed the required U.S. stamps, and carried the letter to the clerk's office. The little clerk, Mason, was not there, which was all right with me. His sidekick, the blond lieutenant from South Carolina, was taking the mail that morning.

"How is our song bird this morning?" I asked as I handed him the letter.

"What do you mean, Mundy?"

"Why, last June you sang a tune to our Yankee captors and they discovered the tunnel from Block 11. Now, I suppose you sang again and they found out about the plan to take us off."

He turned scarlet. "Mundy, you don't know what you are talking about. I heard nothing about such a plot. How dare you imply that I informed on my countrymen?"

"Oh, shut up and mail the letter."

I notice that he put my letter to one side; he did not place it with the main pile, so I spoke up again.

"You heard me. Mail my letter. I know the boat is coming soon. I want my letter to go out with the rest of the mail."

"I cannot. Mister Mason is not here."

"What do you mean? What has he got to do with my mail?"

"Why, he must clear all mail. He must read it before it goes out. And he is in Sandusky today, visiting his mother. He particularly instructed me to hold any letters you might bring in."

I went away, confused and brooding. Lester Mason, the man who bore me such a grudge, had given special instructions for my mail to be held while he was away. Why me?

I brooded about this until that afternoon, when the boat that had carried the mail, minus my letter, returned to the wharf. Mason, looking tired and as wilted as the rest of us, came through the gate. I accosted him in the door of his office.

"Mason, why did you ask that my mail be held for your perusal?"

"I or someone in my charge must peruse all letters."

"Yes, but why did you give particular instructions regarding mine?"

He hesitated, avoiding my stare. "You are a particularly clever young chap who deserves particular watching."

I would not let him pass into his office.

"Mason, I have been writing letters home since August of last year, over thirteen months. The others who came with me after Gettysburg have been getting replies to their letters since January. I have not received a single letter."

"Don't complain to me. Perhaps your precious Jane does not reciprocate your sentiments."

"Damn you. That is not a satisfactory answer. You have no right to ignore my demand for an explanation."

He pushed past me, but I followed him into his office.

"Have you been stopping my letters?"

He refused to answer but he began to look worried.

"God damn you, answer me. Have you passed through a single letter I have written during the past thirteen months I have been in this miserable hell hole?"

I could read the answer in his watery eyes and his now trembling mouth.

"I don't have to answer you. Leave my office."

"I will not leave your office. You don't know what it is like to be cooped up here waiting, dreaming, in the hope that some word may come from back home. How could you do such a dreadful thing?"

"You chose to spurn my offer of help long ago, James." He said this in a quiet, hurt tone, adding softly, "You chose to suffer. I warned you at the time that you would suffer."

The rage came upon me like a summer storm. First I caught him by the lapels and shook him until his eyes rolled about.

"No, no," he gurgled, clawing at my hands.

I drew back my right fist and struck him across his nose. The blood gushed forth and he fell away, but I caught him and drew him upright. "I will kill you."

"No, don't. I didn't mean to . . . I didn't know how much it meant—"

This only made me more enraged. I shoved him into a corner and struck again and again, now with both hands, dealing smashing blows to his head and chest.

"Help!" he began to scream. "Help! He is trying to kill me."

I missed with a blow and he fell forward on his face, blood pouring now from his nose and around his eyes. I began to kick him, cursing insanely as I did.

"You rotten little bastard. You evil pervert. You had no right to stop my mail . . ."

The little blond lieutenant came running in the door and tried to pull me off, but I flung him outside. By the time he returned with two guards I had rolled Mason over on his back and was choking him. His face had turned blue. In another minute he would have been dead.

I recovered my senses somewhat after they had bound my

hands and slapped me into the same little guardhouse where I had stayed for two weeks the previous January. Only now, instead of a piercing cold I had to endure an equally unpleasant heat.

11

That terrible heat and mugginess continued right through the next day, made all the worse for me by the lack of ventilation in my tiny cell there in that little guardhouse. A guard brought me a cup of water and a chunk of stale bread in the morning and again that evening. Otherwise I was left alone, sweating like a pig and seething with rage toward Mason, Colonel Hill, the Union Army, Abe Lincoln and the U.S. Government, in that order. Never have I had such a sense of monstrous injustice.

By nightfall, exhausted, I fell asleep to the sound of a rising wind coming in from Canada across the lake. Some hours later, I awoke in the pitch dark to hear rain falling as though it were being poured from great buckets. I lay awake, wondering when I had heard it rain so hard.

Then came a sound like a great steam locomotive approaching, a roaring, whooshing noise as ominous as it was loud. My little guardhouse shuddered as the wind increased. Suddenly the storm burst upon the island amidst a swirling wind that filled the ears with its violent shrieking. First shingles and other debris began clattering against the guardhouse. I could hear muffled shouts of alarm from militiamen. My cell had a tiny window shuttered from the outside; that shutter disappeared as though some giant hand had wrenched it off and flung it away.

And then I felt the little building lift and myself go crashing into a wall. I lost consciousness briefly and then came to amid the sound of an oceanlike surf pounding nearby.

The building, its door now torn off, lay on its side on the beach. I put my head out but could not see for the blinding rain. The locomotive-like noise was gone and the wind began to fall away. I crawled out of the shed and into ankle-deep lake water. Fearing I might be drowned, I stumbled away from the noise of the surf. Through the slackening rain I could make out lanterns bobbing about in the dark. I veered away from them and made my way through some scrub bushes and low trees until I came to a clearing. I groped along until I struck against a wooden structure of some sort. Feeling along the planks, I discovered an opening large enough to crawl inside. A sickening sweetish odor filled the interior, but I was hardly in a position to be choosy. So I settled myself on the earthern floor and soon fell asleep.

I awoke at the first hint of dawn to find that I had taken refuge in the "dead house" on the edge of the burying ground for the prison. Four rough pine coffins lay along one wall. Through the door I could see rows of freshly turned mounds and could smell the odor of rotting flesh coming from the shallow graves. In months when the ground was frozen they had used the shed to store bodies. Now it held spades, mattocks and stinking blankets.

Through a crack in the opposite wall I got a good view of the prison. The storm had blown down a long section of the palisade together with the roofs of several of the barracks.

From postwar reading I know that a regular tornado had struck the island. At the time it seemed to me a miracle, but a mixed one. Although I was free from my cell, I became increasingly hungry and thirsty as the day wore on. But I did not dare leave my lair.

So I amused myself throughout the morning by watching militiamen and prisoners milling about the camp like ants whose nest had been kicked over. In the afternoon I saw a party of prisoners and armed militiamen marching out toward the cemetery, following a mule-drawn cart.

I barely had time to crawl in one of the coffins and slide the cover over me before the car drew up beside the shed.

"Shall we bring out the coffins?" one of the militiamen asked.

"Let's get the holes dug first. Over there. You there, Tennessee, get some tools out of the shed and let's get started."

I held my breath as someone entered the shed and rattled spades and mattocks about. Soon I heard the steady noise of tools striking rocks. As the prisoners dug away, two of the militiamen leaned against the shed, talking about the storm and the damage it had done to the camp.

"Did you see what happened to the guardhouse?"

"Yes, the wind carried the solitary-confinement shed right into the lake."

"Who was in it?"

"That crazy fellow from North Carolina. The one that tried to kill Mason day before yesterday."

"You reckon he drowned?"

"Sure looks that way."

"Come on, you lousy Rebels! We didn't bring you out here to lean on shovels. Get your backs into it!"

After half an hour, I heard a Southern voice call, "All right. Your damned holes are dug."

Someone came in the shed. I heard him grunt as he lifted one box and slid it out the door, and others complain as they carried it away. I could bear it no longer. I slid my coffin lid off a bit and whispered, "Hey, friend!" The stocky lieutenant whirled around, his face white as a burial shroud. "Christ Almighty!" he exclaimed as I sat up.

"Quiet. Don't give me away."

Lucky for me he was a cool customer. "What in the hell you doing in here?"

"Hiding. Don't give me away. I was in the guardhouse and the storm carried it off."

"I understand. Get back in there. I'll take another coffin."

I slid the lid back and heard him lift out another box as the guard railed at him for being so slow. After a bit the sound of earth being spaded into holes ceased and the car creaked past the shed.

"I'll put the tools back," I heard my lieutenant say.

He made a great deliberate clatter as he stacked the tools, saying to me in a whisper as he did, "I'm leaving my canteen and a chunk of bread just inside the door. Good luck."

As soon as they were out of earshot, I crawled out of my coffin and made the bread and water disappear in nothing flat. By nightfall I could see that the prisoners had been forced to erect a low fence across the gap in the palisade. By now the sky was clear and the temperature downright chilly. I waited until the sun was well down, then crawled out of my coffin and drew it outside the shed. Then I pulled up a short board serving as a grave marker, and put it in the coffin, which I began dragging across the cemetery, through the bushes and onto the shore.

Across the water, the lights of Sandusky gleamed. To my left, I could see the glow of lanterns in the camp compound. I stood there for several minutes, wondering how I might be treated if I turned myself in at the gate. Surely they would give me warm food. How pleasant it would be to sleep on my straw tick with a full stomach. How far away those lights seemed on the Ohio shore.

Yet how inviting they were. I took off my shoes and tied the laces together. I pushed my coffin out from shore until the water became knee-deep and then leaped into my craft and, using the grave marker, began paddling away from Johnson's Island and toward the beacons of freedom on the mainland.

12

That coffin made a very poor boat. It did not leak; its builders had joined the pine planks well enough. But the rectangular shape simply did not lend itself to easy handling. I tried to pace myself so as not to become exhausted. So I made little headway. The lights of Johnson's Island receded too slowly for my liking.

Remember, too, that I had eaten nothing but bread and water for two days and damned little of either. The result was that I soon used up my meager reserves of energy and had to lie down in my coffin to rest.

Not only was that rude box not made for navigation, it was not built to accommodate a body of more than six feet. So I had to double up my legs. Even so, uncomfortable as I was from the now chilly September night air and my cramped position, I felt a delicious sense of freedom, at first.

After a bit, I got to my knees and began paddling again. It began to bother me that I was slipping out from the direct line between Johnson's Island and Sandusky. My coffin was drifting and there wasn't much I could do about it.

"Oh, well," I says to myself. "It might be just as well if I don't come ashore at Sandusky. That place is crawling with Yankee soldiers. Another place on the Ohio shore might be even better."

So I paddled on until my arms felt ready to drop off, then lay down to gaze at the stars and rest. I lay there until I grew chilled again, then up it was to paddle some more. It went that way through the long night in my makeshift boat, me too weak to paddle effectively and too cold to sleep, and now too far away from Johnson's Island to turn myself in even if I wanted to.

I sang songs to myself. Tried to recite long poems but found I couldn't concentrate well enough to recall the lines. Later, when the wind freshened and the water became choppy, I prayed. Oh, yes, I made many a promise there in that coffin, on my knees bobbing along in the cold waters of Lake Erie. I repented of my sins, taking a certain amount of remembered pleasure in reciting them. I promised to reform my ways. I swore to become a better person. I even assured the Almighty that I bore no grudge against any man, all the while harboring a kernel of hatred for the little clerk, Mason, who had been destroying my letters all those months.

So the hours dragged by until I could see no lights anymore from either shore. I lost all sense of time and place, becoming a machine that knew nothing except to dip that grave marker–paddle over the side, pull against the water, and repeat the motion. I stopped even looking for the shore; it never occurred to me that I might be paddling in the wrong direction. I was, in fact, delirious.

A slaty-gray dawn came. As the light increased, I could discern no land. Hopelessness descended. My last shred of strength was gone. I could not paddle another stroke. So I lay down on my back and went to sleep. It was a numbed, fitful kind of sleep in which fantasy blended with reality. I dreamed that I was back in my rude upstairs room at home and that my little brother, Wesley, had pulled the covers off. Then I dreamed I was back in winter camp with the 10th N.C. at Fredericksburg and that our squad had let our fire go out. Then I was in the little laundry house in Richmond with Maria, the quadroon girl, and she was bathing me in cold water.

After a while I awakened and by sheer determination found the strength to raise my head out of the coffin. Still no land, but I thought I saw a sail. "Another damned dream," I thought, and lay back in a stupor.

Some time later, I thought I heard the slap of canvas and voices.

"It looks like a coffin."

"Anyway, it is a mighty big box. Shall we pick it up?"

"Looks like a good one. Let's get it."

I lacked the strength to raise my head. Then someone was attaching a boat hook over the side of my coffin.

"Son of a gun, Pa. It *is* a coffin and there is a dead man in it."

"Lemme see."

I opened my eyes. Two brown faces stared down at me, one of them framed by a gray beard and kinky white hair, the other that of a younger Negro.

"He ain't dead," the younger one said. "Hey, man, what you doing in that fool box?"

"Help me, please," I moaned.

While the old man held the gaff, the younger one caught me by the shoulders and drew me up and over the rail of their ketch. It wasn't easy, for I was dead weight. The old man helped by lifting my feet over.

As I lay there on the little deck they stared at me a long while, frowning.

"Pa, this here is one of them Rebel prisoners from Johnson's Island. Look at his belt buckle. Confederate."

The old man nodded. "You a Rebel, boy?"

"Used to be," I said.

"Used to be, hell," the young man said. "Once a Rebel always a Rebel. Let's go back to Sandusky and turn him in. There'll be a reward."

"Food," I mumbled. "Hungry. Nothing to eat for three days."

The old man sent his son to secure the tiller while he fumbled around in a box. He handed me an apple, which I ate, core, stem and all. Then he gave me a cup of wine.

"Still hungry?"

I nodded.

He gave me a thick pork sandwich and I devoured it in a flash, washing it down with a second cup of his wine.

A warmth crept through my body but, curiously, I began to

shiver so much he took off his own coat and put it around my shoulders.

All the while he was doing this, his son sat in the stern of the boat, eying me with pure hatred.

The old man was thick in the waist and heavy-shouldered. His eyes were a calm, clear brown.

"You from that prison camp, ain't you?"

"Yes."

"How you get away? They say in Sandusky can't nobody get off that island."

"Storm night before last. Big wind blew the guardhouse away and me in it. I hid in the cemetery until I could get away."

The two men exchanged glances.

"What was you in a guardhouse for?" The young man asked. I ignored him and his father got me off the hook by saying, "You let me ask the questions. I'm going to take this fellow in the cabin and let him lay down. You get the sail up again and I'll talk to you later."

He directed me down two steps into a small cabin and lit a lamp. The glow revealed two bunks heaped with blankets. Without asking his permission, I sagged into a bunk and lay down. The relative softness of the thin mattress, the warmth of the cabin and the magic of the two cups of wine gave me a feeling of delicious comfort.

"You stay there. I'll be back."

The old man closed the door. I could hear the footsteps of the two Negroes on the deck and their muffled voices as they went about lifting my coffin aboard and then raising the sail. In a bit the boat groaned under the burden of the wind, and began to move.

I was convinced that they were hauling me back to Sandusky or Johnson's Island to turn me in. But I was too weak. I was helpless to prevent it. Then the old man came below again and sat on the other bunk, his calm eyes studying my face.

"So you one of them Rebel soldiers? Where you from?"

"North Carolina."

"And you must be an officer or you wouldn't be in that camp."

"I just became a lieutenant right before Gettysburg. You know Gettysburg? There was a big battle there more than a year ago."

He snorted. "I know Gettysburg all right, white man. Twenty years ago when I escaped from slavery in Maryland, I made it across the Pennsylvania line and a family there hid me out for two days so the slave catchers wouldn't take me back. Oh, yes, I know Gettysburg."

"Well, I know Gettysburg because that is where I lost my eye and that is where I was taken prisoner," I replied.

It didn't occur to me until later that this was the first time in my life I had been in a serious conversation with a Negro, not counting my brief fling with Maria down in Richmond. And here I was not just talking to a black man but actually in his power.

I remember thinking to myself, "Hell, he's going to turn me in. There are two of them and I haven't the strength to tackle them, nor the skill to sail this damned boat." So I bided my time.

"You hold slaves down in North Carolina?"

It was my time to snort. "Hell, no. My family is poor as Job's turkey."

"Then what you doing in the Rebel army and an officer, too?"

"I was fighting for my country. Besides, everybody else was going off to war and I didn't want to get left out."

"Your country? Is that what you call the South? A country? And you are fighting to keep my people slaves just for the fun of it?"

There wasn't anything I could reply to that. He pressed his questions.

"If your family don't own slaves, how do you make your living down there?"

"My daddy is a Methodist preacher. And we ran a little farm."

"That's a joke. A preacher in slave territory. Preaching the gospel when human beings are kept in chains all around him."

The old man was beginning to get my goat and the wine made me feel reckless.

"I never saw any niggers in chains," I flared up at him.

He flared right back. "The chains are there whether you see them or not. You think losing an eye is something. Wait until you have had your freedom taken away from you."

"I have had my freedom taken away for the past thirteen months, old man. Forced to live like a chicken in a hen house. They even stopped my mail; everybody I know back home probably thinks I am dead because they pulled out my letters."

"Man, you just don't understand. You don't know what it is like to be considered a piece of property like a cow or horse. I'd rather lose both eyes and live in a real chicken house than to be a slave again."

My strength was beginning to build up again. If I could just keep the old man talking, maybe I could overpower him and then force his son to take me to Canada instead of turning me over to the Yankees in Ohio. I changed my tactics.

"I reckon us white folks don't understand what it is like to be black and a slave."

"You sure don't."

"Where were you a slave, anyway?"

"Eastern Maryland. The same family had owned my grandmother and my father. But they ran low on money and they sold me to a slave trader who was going to take me to the Deep South. I was thirty years old and I had a wife and a baby and they took me away from her. I couldn't believe that was happening to me. At Baltimore I knocked that slave trader on the head and set out north. The Underground Railroad picked me up at Gettysburg and passed me all the way through to Canada. I worked there as a free man for five years, saved every penny I earned, and hired an agent to go and try to buy my wife and baby back. He returned with just the boy. My wife had died."

"So you escaped from slavery. Would you like to go back to it?"

"You crazy, white man? Why you ask a crazy question like that?"

"I don't want to go back to Johnson's Island any more than you would want to go back to Maryland, old man. I want to escape to Canada just like you did."

My eyes began to wander around the cabin, looking for a weapon. Before I could spot anything, he was on his feet.

"I'm not going to waste any more time talking to a damned Rebel."

With that he left the cabin, closing the door and bolting it from the outside.

I lay back in my bunk, cursing myself for overplaying my hand. Up on the deck I could hear the father and son talking loudly. I couldn't make out their words, but they seemed to be arguing.

13

There was nothing for me to do except accept my fate. They would turn me over to the Yankees, probably at Sandusky. I would be hauled back to Johnson's Island to face punishment for assaulting the clerk. It was getting on to October. All prisoner exchanges between North and South had ceased. That meant yet another winter on icebound Johnson's Island with its filth and boredom. Why was I ever born?

Yet I have always been a believer in making the best of bad situations. Maybe at the last minute I could persuade my Negro captors not to tell the exact circumstances of my capture. If they could just say they picked me out of the water, leaving out what I had told them about hiding in the cemetery and all that, why, I could make it appear that the storm had flung me into the lake and that, miraculously, I had survived in the cold water for a day and a half.

Yes, that was it. Then the Yankees might decide I had suffered enough. Why didn't those blasted niggers come to the cabin door when I rattled it and shouted? Damn them anyway. I had nothing to do with slavery. It wasn't my fault the old man got sold away from his wife, or that she had died. Why did he have to take out his spite for the South against Jim Mundy? What I would have given never to have signed up for the Confederate Army.

Locked away under the deck, I could not tell how fast we were moving or in what direction. Indeed, I could not even judge the passage of time. No sensation of movement except a slight roll of the hull now and then and the creak of the mast.

Above me the sound of footsteps and shouts again. Then the rattle of a chain.

"All right, white man. Come out of there."

The cabin door opened and both Negroes stood outside, waiting. I stumbled to my feet, shielding my eyes against the sunlight.

"Let me say something to you," I began.

"Say it fast."

"Don't tell them I escaped, please. Let them think you just found me in the water. Otherwise they'll put me back in solitary on bread and water. I can't stand that anymore. Please."

I never thought that I, Jim Mundy, would humble myself to beg mercy from a nigger, but there I was, pleading with them.

"Shut up and get your white ass out here, Rebel," the young man said. "We can't waste any more time on you. Get out here or we'll haul you back to Ohio and turn you in."

It took a moment for that to sink in.

"Where are we?"

"Canada, you fool."

"What?" I rushed past them, onto the deck. An expanse of low, wooded land lay just a few hundred feet away.

"You're not going to turn me in to the Yankees?"

"Does it look like we are?"

"You are going to let me go free?"

"That's right, white man," the father said. "We are emancipating you. We are going to row you over to that shore and you will be on your own. Keep your mouth shut or we can get in trouble."

Well, at that I turned into a wild man, dancing a jig and clapping my hands. I even tried to hug the old man, who just stood there without changing his expression.

"Get in our little boat. I'll row you to the shore. There is a town half a mile that way."

He rowed me over to a pebbly beach. I tried to thank him again, but he interrupted me.

"Here, take this."

It was a five-dollar banknote.

"What's that for?"

"Your coffin. I can get ten dollars for it from an undertaker in Windsor where we live. I'm charging you five dollars for the boat ride. This is your change."

"Why are you doing this? I thought you hated me. Thought you were going to take me back to Ohio like your son wanted and get a reward."

"White man, if I had been headed toward Ohio instead of Canada, maybe I would have turned you in. Maybe. But it wouldn't have been because I hated you. Man, if I gave in to hatred, I would have died of it long ago."

"So you are helping me just because you happened to be coming this way. Is that the Lord's truth?"

For the first time he smiled. "No, that's not the truth. You say your daddy's a Methodist preacher who supports his family by farming. Well, I'm a Methodist lay preacher myself; only I support my son and me by fishing and hauling stuff across the lake.

One Methodist ought to help another, I reckon. At least we ought not to go out of our way to hurt each other. Now you get out of this boat and start moving."

I stepped into the water up to my ankles and sloshed ashore. The old man sat there, leaning on his oars, watching me.

"Thank you, uncle."

"You're welcome, son. You take care of yourself now, you hear?"

Before I could thank him again he started rowing back toward his ketch.

14

Hot diggety damn! I was free! It didn't hit me until I was halfway to the little straggle of houses and commercial buildings my Negro "emancipator" had called a town. I was actually a free man again. I was free of my Yankee captors. I was free of the Confederate Army. Free.

There on a rutted trace of a Canadian road, hundreds of miles from any battlefield, I stopped, raised my face to the late afternoon's pale sun and gave out with a Rebel yell.

There was just one place that called itself a hotel in the town. It really was a big boardinghouse presided over by a fat woman with tiny brown suspicious eyes. She seemed little inclined to accept me as a guest, and I couldn't much blame her for I was a sorry sight in my ragtag outfit.

She finally admitted that she did have a small room available for the night after I offered to pay her the advertised price of one dollar in advance.

"But supper and breakfast will cost you another dollar," she said after she already had taken possession of my five-dollar banknote.

I could tell she was dying to know just who I was and what business brought me to her place, but my eye patch and piratical mien must have given her pause.

The little room to which she directed me at the top of the stairs looked palatial to me, despite its narrow bed and mean furniture. I trembled with pleasure at the sight of that bed, which actually had a large pillow and clean sheets. Just to have a private room all to myself with space in which to turn around was worth my precious dollar.

As for the other dollar I had given her, I got full value for that at supper. I was one of half a dozen people gathered around her table that evening: two traveling salesmen, a pair of fishermen, and a couple from Montreal on their honeymoon. Madam Inn Keeper sat at the head of the table shouting to her bedraggled husband who shuttled the food out to us. At first she looked surprised as she saw the size of my helpings of her mutton and potatoes, not to mention the three slices of hot oven bread I took.

Later her face assumed an expression of alarm for I had cleaned my plate before most of the other guests had taken their second mouthfuls. I tried not to make a hog of myself, but it had been several days since I had eaten even a semi-full prison meal.

The other people seemed uncomfortable to be sitting at the same table with a wolfish-looking, one-eyed young villain, unshaven and unshorn, eating away with both hands. I was aware of the sidelong glances they were giving each other but couldn't help myself.

The husband of milady came out of the kitchen to watch. His wife looked glummer and glummer. Not only was she losing money with every mouthful I took; I was making her other guests uncomfortable.

They watched me in dead silence as I cleaned my plate for the second time.

"We seem to have no more food left," she said to the married couple.

"Pardon me," I said. "Thank you for an excellent meal."

"Don't mention it."

I could hear their conversation start up as I mounted the stairs. It was early and normally I might have taken a turn around that miserable little town, but my bed looked too inviting. I fell into it and stayed there for twelve straight hours of the sweetest sleep ever, just letting the strain and exhaustion of the past several days drift away.

At breakfast the next morning, I found that Madam Inn Keeper had outfoxed me. Our plates were already served, with eggs and wide strips of bacon, beans, biscuits and such. She had me stymied. The subject of second helpings never came up.

After breakfast I wandered out and found a barbershop, where the fellow shaved me, cut my hair and let me bathe in his back room, all for a half-dollar. Thence to a general store, where I haggled the clerk down to two dollars for a pair of trousers, shirt and some underwear and socks. That left me with exactly fifty cents. Suddenly I didn't feel so free anymore. Not enough left for another night's lodging.

"Where might a fellow find work around here?" I asked the storekeeper.

"What can you do?" he asked.

"Anything in reason. I've got to earn enough to get myself to Toronto."

"Toronto? Well, I'll tell you, Angus McQueen runs a big potato farm a couple of miles north. He raises potatoes and hauls them to Toronto every fall. He might use another hand."

So without returning to say goodbye at the hotel I hiked the two miles out to the McQueen place and presented myself to a hard-eyed old Scotsman. I explained my desire to find work and transportation to Toronto. He listened to me with a calculating look on his face.

"I can fill both bills. I'll be hauling two wagonloads of potatoes to Toronto in about a week. There is a lot of hard work to be done and I don't put up with slack workers. You used to hard work?"

"Born loving it," I lied.

"Can you drive a team?"

"Sure."

"In that case I'll guarantee you fifty cents a day, put you up and feed you, and give you a ride to Toronto. Is that a deal?"

"It's a deal."

A hell of a deal it turned out to be. That old Scotsman worked my ass off. Got me and his two near-grown sons up at 5 A.M. every day and drove us harder than any Southern slaveowner until dark, with just a half-hour for lunch. He didn't lose much money on the food. It was little better than the prison grub, washed down with blue John milk.

I wasn't used to all that bending and digging. The hard work I said I was accustomed to became an agony. The morning of the second day I might have accepted an offer to return to the indolence of Johnson's Island.

Old McQueen wasn't fooled by me for one minute. He knew I was an escaped Confederate and he let me know it. Started calling me "Reb."

Digging potatoes for six days on Angus McQueen's farm gave me a respect for physical labor that remains with me to this day. I respect it, but I don't want any part of it ever again.

On the seventh day, instead of resting, Angus had us load the potatoes onto two enormous wagons, drawn by two enormous horses each, and set out for Toronto. McQueen and I each drove a team and one son rode along with each of us. He never even bothered to say goodbye to his worn little wife.

It took us three days of traveling across the monotonous terrain of Canada West to reach Toronto. I entertained myself and one of the McQueen boys by telling him war stories. We slept in livery barns along the way, burrowing down in straw beds to keep warm.

As our horses plodded along, I sorted out my thoughts. I didn't have to return to the Confederacy. I could get a job in Toronto. Write to Jane Ferro and ask her to wait for me until the war was over. Or maybe I could work my passage to England; old Professor Mead had taught his students much about the mother country and I had often daydreamed about visiting it.

My mind was far from made up when we clip-clopped into Toronto, which struck me as a stark, cold kind of city. We delivered our potatoes to the market house, where McQueen and a fellow Scot haggled for half an hour about the price.

I waited until after he got his money.

"Well, Mr. McQueen," I says. "This is where we part company."

"It is that, young man. You'll be wanting your pay, I suppose."

"Yes, sir. Four dollars and fifty cents."

"How do you calculate that? You worked only six days. Do they use a different kind of arithmetic down in Dixie?"

"I worked nine days. Six days in the potato fields and three days driving a team."

"Well, now, that was transportation, not work. And don't forget I fed ye along the way. That was money out of pocket."

"Mr. McQueen, you are not being fair with me. You owe me four dollars and fifty cents. We use the same arithmetic in the Confederacy you do in Canada and I thought we followed the same rules of fair play. You are trying to cheat me."

"Oh, now, if ye're going to blackguard me, I'll just say good day to you. You can whistle for your money."

"I'll do worse than whistle if you don't pay up."

"See here now. Don't go making no threats. Ye don't frighten a Scot with threats. Besides, there is nothing ye can do anyway. Me two lads and I can't be frightened of a human scarecrow like you."

"I'll tell you exactly what I can do. I can go to the police authorities and turn myself in as an escaped Confederate prisoner. I can tell them I was hidden by one Angus McQueen, a potato farmer who is in town right now. Then you can have the pleasure of explaining how you harbored a fugitive."

"I would advise you not to do that. . . ."

"Good. I will tell them that I wanted to give myself up but that you urged me not to."

He faltered. "It's not worth fifty cents a day when you are getting a free ride to Toronto."

"I won't take a penny less. Pay up or be prepared to answer some embarrassing questions."

"This is extortion."

"It is simple justice."

How it pained him to count out another dollar and a half in silver. When I had pocketed the money and thanked him, with mock courtesy, his only rejoinder was "Ye were a damned poor worker, not worth even fifty cents a day."

"And you were a damned poor employer. Good day, Mr. McQueen."

The potato merchant had been listening to this exchange from just inside his office.

"Hey, Reb," he said. "Take this." He handed me a dollar.

"What is that for?"

"For the pleasure you just gave me. I have been doing business with Angus McQueen for ten years and that is the first time I ever heard anybody get the best of him. Also, it is so you won't think all Scots are as mean as he. Where did you escape from?"

"Johnson's Island, over near Sandusky, Ohio."

"I hear that is a tough place. Well, you will be among friends in Toronto."

"What do you mean?"

"Why, this town is crawling with Confederates. Agents of all sorts. The hotels are full of them. Downtown Toronto has become little Dixie."

"I could use some help, that's for sure."

"Easy as pie. You just go down to the Queen's Hotel. Ask for

Mr. Jacob Thompson. Understand he is a special agent sent here from Richmond by Jefferson Davis himself. Present yourself to him and your troubles should be over."

"How can I ever repay you?"

"You already paid me. Hey," he shouted to his partner in the next office. "I must tell you how I saw a fellow put one over on Angus McQueen."

15

Queen's Hotel was a splendid establishment. I found it with little difficulty. Getting to see Mr. Jacob Thompson was another matter. The desk clerk sent word up to his rooms and soon his secretary, a chap named Cleary, came down and drew me over to a corner of the lobby to explain, "Mr. Thompson has his hands full just now sorting out the business that took place on Lake Erie. He can't see anyone. Now where did you say you escaped from?"

"Johnson's Island."

"Really?" He looked as though he didn't believe me. "How did you manage that?"

I told him about the cyclone and floating off in a coffin.

"Incredible. I think Mr. Thompson should talk to you, but that can't be until tomorrow. Have you any funds?"

"Four dollars and fifty cents to my name."

"I see. There was a gentleman in Canada from Virginia recently, a Professor Holcombe who taught law at the University at Charlottesville. He assisted escapees like yourself to get back to Richmond, but he left Canada about a month ago. Mr. Thompson has his hands full with larger matters just now, but

I think he should see you tomorrow before he makes an out-of-town trip. Please come back about ten o'clock in the morning. Meanwhile, here is the name of a boardinghouse where they will put you up for a dollar a day, meals included. Tell the proprietor W. W. Cleary sent you."

Mr. Cleary didn't waste a lot of time with me. Clearly, I was on my own. After he hustled off, I looked around the lobby. The place teemed with men wearing broad-brimmed hats, sporting goatees or mustaches and speaking in Southern accents.

Poking my head in the bar, I overheard a fellow asking for a mint julep. I stepped up beside him and asked for one of the same. After two sips of a julep that outdid the one given me by the slave trader down in Fayetteville, I began to feel at ease. Didn't take me long to fall in conversation with my fellow imbiber or for him to extract from me the story of my escape.

"Son of a bitch," he commented when I had told my tale. "You got grit, son. There ought to be a place for you in Canada. What you planning to do?"

He was a lean fellow of about thirty with a lantern jaw and sad, hazel eyes. He listened closely as I explained I was to see Mr. Thompson on the morrow even though the Confederate commissioner was said to be very busy.

"I expect he is busy. He has got a mess on his hands with that *Philo Parsons* business."

"What do you mean?"

"Has to do with Johnson's Island, as a matter of fact. Come in the dining room and let me treat you to dinner. I'll tell you about it there."

He paid for my julep and led me off to a splendid meal of oyster casserole, genuine beefsteak and vegetables prepared with sauces I had never tasted, all washed down with wine as good as that I had drunk at the Ferros.

He made me run through my entire life history, questioning me closely about my experiences in the army and my imprisonment.

"Now what about this *Philo Parsons* business?" I asked.

As he explained it to me, Jacob Thompson had spent considerable in Confederate funds and his own time laying a complicated plot to seize the U.S.S. *Michigan,* free the prisoners on Johnson's Island, and then go about Lake Erie bombarding shore towns. A band of twenty men had seized the *Philo Parsons,* a boat plying between Detroit and Sandusky. They had shut the passengers and most of the crew in the hold and set out for Johnson's Island.

"But the way I understand it, they got there while it was still light. They turned back to an island to pick up fuel and kill time. While they were taking on wood, a smaller boat tried to tie up alongside and they had to seize it as well. To make a long story short, they put all the passengers ashore, scuttled the smaller boat, and set out to find the *Michigan* after dark. Got to within two miles of the ship about 9 P.M. and found her with her steam up, anchors aweigh and all hands at battle stations. So most of the fellows lost their nerve and refused to make the attack. Fellow named Beall was in charge. He was forced to take the *Parsons* back into the Detroit River and scuttle her."

"I'll be damn," I said. "Why, the *Michigan* is bristling with cannon; and the Yankees have guns on the island and over at Sandusky as well. How could they have thought twenty men could accomplish anything?"

"There is more to the story. You see, Thompson employed a spy to go over to Sandusky and pass himself off as a wealthy swell from Philadelphia. Made friends with officers and crew from the *Michigan.* Wined and dined them. Visited the ship itself. And on the evening in question he had arranged for the captain and certain of the officers to come to a big party in Sandusky. Planned to drug their wine so they would be passed out when this Beall and his crew came alongside the ship."

"What happened?"

"The Yankees got wind of the scheme. They arrested the spy, a fellow named Cole, a few hours before the party. Someone from Toronto must have tipped them off. This place is crawling with Union informants. Have to watch what you say. Now

Thompson is going to great lengths to prove that Cole was just an escaped Confederate like you so the Yankees don't hang him as a spy."

"I'll be damn. I would have been saved a lot of trouble if the scheme had worked."

"Well, it was pretty farfetched. You had no hint of it on Johnson's Island?"

"Not until the day or so after. The commandant taunted us with the news that some plot to set us free had been foiled."

"Well, some of the higher-up prisoners probably did know about it. Old Thompson spent a lot of precious gold on the plan and he is fit to be tied over its failure."

My new friend declined to tell me his name when I asked. "Don't mean to be rude, Mundy, but one can't be too careful. Tell you what, though. If Thompson can't help you tomorrow, look for me in the bar. By that time I may have something that could interest you. I am not free to discuss it just at the moment."

I bade my friend good night and made my way to the boardinghouse, where the proprietor showed me to a plain but comfortable room. With a stomach full of good food and wine, I had no trouble drifting off to a good night's sleep.

16

Ten o'clock the next morning found me rapping at the door of Jacob Thompson's suite on the second floor of the Queen's Hotel. The secretary admitted me to a small waiting room, inquired after my health and my opinion of my lodgings, and then ushered me into a large bedroom in which a peevish-looking, goateed gentleman in his mid-fifties sat at a small table littered with papers.

"Mr. Thompson. This is Lieutenant James Mundy."

Thompson looked up from the papers with an impatient cock to his head. "Who?"

"The man who escaped from Johnson's Island in a coffin. I told you about him last night."

"Yes, yes. Of course. Quite a tall story that. Johnson's Island. I wish I had never heard of that place."

"I feel the same way," I said.

"Quite. Now what can I do for you?"

"Why, sir, I am in Canada without any funds to speak of. I was captured at Gettysburg while serving with the 10th North Carolina as aide to its colonel. Technically I am still in the Confederate Army and subject to its authority. And I should think that the Confederate Government bears some responsibility for my welfare."

The secretary broke in. "I told Lieutenant Mundy that Professor Holcombe has left or he might have received assistance from him in rejoining his command."

"Professor Holcombe is gone, as you say. Why have you brought this chap to see me?"

"Why, sir, I thought we might have some special work for him as an agent or courier. He demonstrated considerable pluck in escaping from Johnson's Island. He might be of use to our mission."

Thompson regarded me coldly. "I don't think so. His eye. He would be far too identifiable with that eye patch. Those damnable Yankee detectives would spot him a mile away."

"But surely he has some possibilities for us."

"No, Cleary. He won't do. Now I have an oversupply of men with 'considerable pluck.' Too damned many with all kinds of fool schemes that cost money and time. You and I must finish packing or we will miss our train to Quebec. Thank you for coming around, Captain Sunday."

He turned his attention back to his papers. I wanted to strangle him.

Back in the small entry chamber, the secretary apologized. "Mr. Thompson really is being harassed about the *Philo Parsons* episode. You know he didn't want this job in the first place. He was Secretary of the Interior under Buchanan. He served as aide to General Beauregard at Shiloh. This assignment is hard on him because so much of it has to be conducted surreptitiously. Right now we are on our way to Quebec to try to see some high Canadian officials and we don't even have appointments. Everything has to be done informally. I regret he feels we have no place for you. I do wish you would take this."

He held out several banknotes.

"No thank you," I said. "I don't want private charity."

I wasn't feeling very kindly toward Mr. Jacob Thompson as I went downstairs. My low opinion of him was borne out years after the war when some high Confederates accused him of running off to France at the war's end with huge amounts of government funds entrusted to him personally by Jefferson Davis. So much for Jacob Thompson.

I needed a drink after that. My lantern-jawed friend of the evening before was in the bar, just as he had said he would be. He listened to my report with a smile on his long face.

"Oh, that Thompson is such a cold-blooded paper shuffler. As calculating as they come. Of course your one eye is a handicap, but that is a hell of a way to treat a loyal Confederate who has suffered as you have."

"Right now, I am not feeling so loyal."

"Oh? What do you mean?"

"Look, I fought at Malvern Hill and Sharpsburg and Fredericksburg and Gettysburg. I have been a good soldier. I love the South. I have been through hell and back again for my native country. Now I am in a foreign country and in need of help and my government's high commissioner here treats me in an off-hand, unsympathetic way. Like I was a common nigger."

"You do have a right to feel disloyal. You might feel even more disloyal if you knew some of the things men like Thompson are working on."

"What do you mean?"

He lowered his voice. "Don't get me wrong. I am a Kentuckian. But I think this war should be fought on the battlefield and not against innocent civilians. The gang that seized those two boats, they endangered the lives of several dozen passengers."

"I can't get excited about that," I said. "It was to release three thousand poor wretches like me."

"Oh, but there is more. There are plots to set fire to cities, to derail trains without a thought for the civilian casualties. And worse."

"Really?"

"Yes. There has been talk of introducing plagues like yellow fever or smallpox into crowded sections of Northern cities."

"That is going rather far."

"Indeed it is. Makes me ashamed to be a Southerner. Right now there is a rumor about a scheme for a band of Confederates to cross into New Hampshire or Vermont and rob banks, burn buildings and shoot down people on the streets. I ask you as a true Confederate soldier and officer. Do you condone such acts?"

"No, I don't."

"I didn't think you would. You know the war is going badly for the South. Sherman has taken Atlanta. Grant has a stranglehold on Lee in front of Richmond and Petersburg. Latest news is that Sheridan is laying waste to the Shenandoah. Naturally we hope that we can reverse the tide, but if we can't, just imagine the retribution that will fall upon the South if desperate ex-Confederates pillage Northern communities. It is an immoral, foolish piece of work."

"Well, I guess I don't want any part of that."

"What are you going to do?"

"I want to go home. I want to see my family. And then there

is this girl. She means more to me than anything."

"And Jacob Thompson didn't offer to help you."

"Indeed he did not."

"Well, you know it would cost you several hundred dollars to make your way to Halifax and book passage on a ship to Bermuda or Nassau. Then you would have to catch a blockade-runner into Wilmington. And you won't find life in the Confederate Army any bed of roses, for they are being hard pressed and on short rations from what I read."

"It wasn't any bed of roses in 1862 and 1863. But it is no bed of roses digging potatoes in Canada either. And if I don't go back, my girl will be lost to me. Her family would never let her marry a slacker, someone who sat out the war in Canada. How can a fellow get enough money to take a ship?"

"You mean quickly?"

"The quicker, the better."

"Let's go sit in a corner of the lobby. The bar is no place for this conversation."

My new friend sat me in a comfortable chair. Speaking in a low voice, he explained that he was backed by another "Southern force" and that he and influential friends were trying to keep tabs on men being financed by Thompson "to prevent excesses that would work to the detriment of the Southern people."

As he explained it, Confederate funds were going to finance a bank-robbing, town-burning expedition into New England.

"If I could find out their exact plans, I could take steps to head off the project. As I understand it, Thompson himself may not be in on the scheme. The money seems to be coming out of Montreal. Possibly from a fellow named Clement Clay, the junior Confederate commissioner in Canada. You see, he and Thompson can't stand each other, so they operate separately, each with his own funds in different cities. My friends would pay up to one thousand dollars if they could find out exactly what is planned in time to prevent their committing criminal acts that would bring down retribution upon our beloved South.

You could have that money if you are willing to take on the job."

"What exactly would I do?"

"One Bennett Young is thought to be the leader of the gang. I'd like you to locate him and offer to join him. Find out their plans and report back to me. Are you game?"

I reckon I was naïve. Even though I had been through the hell of Gettysburg and the purgatory of Johnson's Island, still I was an innocent farm boy in many ways. Looking back, I can see that this fellow's story about being financed by obscure "Southern forces" was full of holes. But he was so persuasive and I so homesick. And in that day a thousand dollars was a fortune.

Anyway, he finally told me his name was Parnell. This Parnell gave me $100 and the address of the St. Lawrence Hall Hotel in Montreal.

"You go and register there. Take immediate pains to meet Mister Clement Clay. Don't say who sent you. As I told you, Clay is the junior Confederate commissioner in Canada. He can't bear your friend Jacob Thompson. Leave me out of it, but otherwise just tell him the story of your escape from Johnson's Island. Be sure to emphasize the cold way in which Thompson treated you. Tell Mr. Clay you are willing to do anything to take revenge on the Yankee nation for the way you were treated in prison. That will give him an opening to tell you about his town-burning plot. Find out everything you can about the activities of this Bennett Young chap. He is up to something, but I need to know times and places."

"How will I let you know what I discover?"

"I will follow you to Montreal day after tomorrow. It is best that we don't travel together. I will register at the Empire Hotel. Just ask at the desk for Edward Parnell. I will have a thousand dollars ready if you can find out exactly what this Young chap is up to in time to stop him. Agreed?"

"Agreed."

That is how I came to sit up all night on a rattly train to Montreal. I had never been in a city where they didn't speak English. In Montreal, I finally found a porter who understood me well enough to direct me to the hotel.

I presented myself at the door of Mr. Clay's apartment. Not only was he in, but he saw me immediately. I found him a grave, sickly kind of fellow, with a high forehead sitting over concerned eyes. He questioned me closely about my experiences, going back to cross-examine me in a gentle way. I rather liked him.

"Incredible story," he said at last. "What an ordeal you have been through."

"I suppose you could call it that."

"How did you know to come to me?"

"Why, sir, Mr. Thompson was so unsympathetic that I figured I had better scratch him off my list and go see the next man in line. I am determined to strike a blow for the South."

"I am not surprised about Thompson. He can be awfully self-important. He has a fixation about Lake Erie. All kinds of harebrained ideas about controlling it and ravaging the coast."

"Isn't there some way to make the North taste this war as our people in the South have?"

"Yes, but it will not be through complicated plots that involve the capture of civilian ships and attacks on fully armed warships. Too many chances for slip-ups. No, there are simpler and more effective ways to punish the North."

"I'd sure like to know how. I would like to strike them a blow and make them suffer."

"Would you indeed? Would you be willing to cross into the United States and engage in activities that might be extremely dangerous?"

"Anything that my government or its agents consider right I would not balk at."

"Would you risk being hanged as a spy or bandit?"

"I have been through many a risk at Sharpsburg and Gettysburg. What is the difference?"

"I do admire such patriotism, Lieutenant Mundy. As a Confederate official in the public eye here in Montreal, I must be cautious in my activities. But I have contact with certain individuals who are far, far from cautious. One of them is a fine young man from Kentucky. About your age. Like you, he escaped from a prison camp and found his way over into this country. Very high type of individual. Intends to become a Presbyterian minister. Even attended university here until he and I made contact and worked out a course of action."

"Who is this gentleman and how may I meet him?" My heart was in my throat as I asked the question.

"You will find him at St. Johns, a small town south of here near the Vermont border. I will give you a letter to be delivered to him."

"Who is this gentleman?"

"His name is Bennett Young. Now don't let's waste time on questions. Do you have money?"

"Only a little. Earned it digging potatoes for that Scots farmer I told you about," I lied.

"Of course. I am going to give you a hundred dollars and provide you with a horse. The man who operates Poindexter Livery Stable on Afton Street is a strong Southern sympathizer. I'll give you a requisition and he will outfit you with a serviceable horse. You deliver this letter to Bennett Young at the address I have written down, in St. Johns, and then let nature take its course."

"May I wait until tomorrow night to depart?"

"You may not. You must go directly to the livery stable. Get your horse, leave this city and have this letter in Young's hand by tomorrow night. I don't want your face to become well known around here."

I started to protest, but he was adamant. "Get started now," he insisted.

To have argued any more would have blown up the entire scheme. I took his $100 and letter. I dropped by the hotel. They had a reservation for Parnell, but he had not arrived. So I left a sealed note saying I was on the trail of Bennett Young and that I would try to return with full information in a couple of days.

The man at the livery stable scarcely looked at me. He took

my requisition and brought out a large roan gelding already saddled up.

I signed a receipt, inquired about the road to St. Johns and headed my new steed south. Little did I know what I was getting into.

17

The roan gelding had some age on him, but he was a serviceable steed. With only three gaits, he was a far cry from Jane Ferro's little mare, Nellie. Still, riding him beat walking. His steady trot carried me safely over the magnificent Victoria Bridge to the south bank of the St. Lawrence. My mind hummed with a confusion of thoughts and fears. If I had had my druthers, I would have ridden that nag right across the U.S. border and gone clip-clopping down to Baltimore and then picked up the undercover route back to Richmond. But no, with my one eye and my North Carolina accent I could never make it.

I was troubled by the way the junior Confederate commissioner, Clement Clay, had rushed me out of Montreal, thereby preventing me from talking to Parnell before I set out on this mission. This way, I would have to meet Young, find out what he was up to quickly and then deliver the information back to Parnell in time to collect my thousand dollars. With that much money I could take a boat to Wilmington, via Bermuda. At Wilmington I could travel up to Oldham County and see my family and Jane Ferro. I could salt down a good portion of the money as a nest egg for Jane and me. Eventually I would rejoin my regiment wherever it might be. No matter how the war turned out, Jane would be waiting for me at the end. That was worth the risk I was taking.

My roan carried me south. I stopped at a country store and dined on cider, cheese and crackers. The countryside was different from my native North Carolina or any of the territory I had marched over in Virginia, Maryland or Pennsylvania. The houses seemed small and hunkered down against the cold. I had the feeling that thoughts of winter dominated the lives of the inhabitants even when it was summer. And there was more than a taste of winter in the air as I reached the town of St. Johns late that afternoon.

In a place of that size, it was no trouble to find the boardinghouse whose address Mr. Clay had given me. A nearby livery stable accepted responsibility for my horse. With more than a bit of apprehension, I knocked at the door of the boardinghouse and inquired of the landlady whether Bennett Young was in.

She regarded me with obvious suspicion.

"He might be. If he is, who should I say is calling?"

"The name is Mundy and I have something for him from a Mr. Clay."

I remained standing at the door until a well-formed, bright-looking chap of about my age strode across the living room to greet me.

"Mundy is it?" he asked as he held out his hand. "Come in. Are you a Confederate?"

I assured him on that point, adding that I was an escaped prisoner from Johnson's Island.

"Good. And you have something for me from Clay. It is about time. Here, come up to my room and let's talk."

Upstairs, in a large, pleasant room, he took the letter and ripped it open. To my amazement out fell a bank draft. I watched his alert face as he examined it.

"There. Fourteen hundred dollars. That is money enough. Now, let's see what Clay says in this note."

Upon finishing the letter, Young looked at me closely. "Clay thinks you would make a good partner in our enterprise. He says here that you are willing to take risks for the Confederate cause. Is that right?"

"Indeed it is."

"Then let me inquire about your background. You don't mind a few questions, do you?"

"Not at all."

His "few questions" turned out to be a tough line of inquiry that probed back into my childhood, my reasons for enlisting in the Confederate Army, my conduct in battle and on Johnson's Island. He put me through a regular cross-examination.

"Does anybody besides Clay know that you are here?"

"Not a soul," I replied, hoping he couldn't read the lie in my eyes.

"You are certain?"

"Absolutely."

"I have assembled a crew of bold, desperate fellows. All of them understand that anyone who betrays us will be executed. Do you understand that as well?"

I swallowed hard before answering, "Yes."

"Any one of us would shoot you between the eyes if you turned out to be anything but what you represent yourself to be."

"I understand."

"And if you were to be captured in the course of our mission, you likely would be hanged by the U.S. Government."

"Mr. Clay warned me of that."

"Very well. I'll introduce you to some of the other fellows tonight. We'll see what they say."

18

What a fix to be in. I needed that thousand dollars from Parnell. I lusted for the money. But I didn't need a bullet between the eyes from Young's gang. It was a mighty apprehensive Jim Mundy who came down to supper that evening.

The lady who ran the boardinghouse knew what to serve this crew. She set a table loaded with Southern food: good corn bread, fried chicken, rice with gravy, and brown-sugar-and-molasses pie. Normally I would have fallen upon such fare like a starving wolf, but I had no appetite.

Bennett Young introduced me to the other gang members present. As I recall it, there were half a dozen of them there that night, hard, determined fellows, every one of them. Each in turn stepped up and grasped my hand as Young introduced him. And each one looked as though he were capable of putting that bullet between my eyes were my true role to be revealed.

So while I sat at the table with a dry mouth and a nervous stomach, Bennett Young told his men about me. Their eyes hardly left my face as he described my being wounded and taken prisoner at Gettysburg and of my miraculous escape from Johnson's Island.

"I have extended an invitation to Mundy to join our little enterprise and he has accepted. Henceforth he is our brother and I think we are fortunate to have him."

Then there followed a long discussion of the latest war news. It was not encouraging. With Mobile sealed off by Farragut, Charleston and Wilmington were the only ports still in Southern hands, and both of them were closely blockaded.

"It is up to us to give the Southern people a victory way up North, in time to affect the presidential elections."

"We have been talking about this for a long time," a chap with cold blue eyes said. "Time is growing short."

"You are right," Young replied. "We must act. I have selected the place and now that Mundy has brought us the money from Clay we are ready."

By then we were through eating and our landlady had cleared the table. Young spread a map and we all stood up to look over his shoulder, I with my heart pounding away.

"Here," Young said, jabbing his finger at the maps. "Here in northern Vermont. The town of St. Albans. It has three banks and a clear road to and from the border. Town of about four thousand people. No soldiers around."

"When?" one of the men asked.

"This is October 7. I reckon it will take ten days to make arrangements, you know, equip ourselves and perfect our plans. Then we have to work our way across the border in small groups at separate spots pretending to be hunters, vacationists, horse traders or whatever. Finally we congregate in St. Albans and we pounce!"

St. Albans, Vermont, on or about October 20. I had the information I had come for, the information that would earn me a thousand dollars, passage back to the Confederacy and a nest egg for eventual marriage to Jane Ferro. But how could I get away from this crew? With my eye patch, I would be so easy to find. And these people had the run of Canada. If I sneaked away in the night, they would know the jig was up and they might hunt me down and kill me. Or even if they did not, they could so easily select another town to strike.

Later we sat in Young's big upstairs room, talking about life back in Kentucky and Virginia. Most of these fellows were out of cavalry units from those states. They were a high-spirited bunch who seemed to enjoy danger.

Bennett Young was a most unusual young man. I had expected to find in him a devil with horns, hoofs and a tail, but here he was, a personable, intelligent young chap full of imagination and charm, much like I would have been if I had been to the University and if my family had been part of the slave-owning aristocracy of Kentucky. It bothered me that I had agreed to betray such a splendid fellow for a thousand dollars. But then, when I looked at his friends . . . Anyway, it was a tribute to Young's skills of leadership that he was able to control some of the cutthroats in his gang.

That night I shared a room with two of these desperadoes. And I slept badly.

On my third day with these people, I had a brief opportunity to get away. As I was grooming my roan nag and waiting for the local blacksmith to put on fresh shoes, a farmer with a wagon-load of hay stopped to water his horses and buy himself a slug of whisky from the stableman.

"Where are you headed?" I inquired.

"Montreal."

"Don't suppose you could use a hand with your horses?"

"Nope, but I wouldn't mind some company. You want a ride to Montreal?"

Did I want a ride to Montreal! There formed in my mind quickly an idea of how I might burrow under the hay and let the farmer smuggle me back to Montreal. After all, Parnell had promised me the thousand dollars if I discovered what Young was up to and reported it back to him. No skin off my nose if they later struck another town than St. Albans. The trick was to get away from this gang safely and this farmer's load of hay was my chance.

The idea formed quickly and it evaporated just as quickly. One of my roommates came in the stable before I could accept the farmer's offer.

"Too bad I have other business in these parts," I said. "Hope you can find someone to give you a hand." Whew!

That night, around the boardinghouse table, I was glad I had not left the gang after all. We sat about reading the latest papers. They were full of reports of fresh victories of Sheridan over Early in the Shenandoah and of the Yankee project to burn out the valley south of Winchester so the Confederates could no longer enjoy its produce or its easy invasion route to the North. The level of indignation around that table was high as we talked of Sheridan's deliberate policy of burning—not just public buildings and bridges, but barns, feed mills and stored crops. He intended to make that lovely part of God's world into a desert.

"By God, we'll show them what it is like to suffer," one of the gang said.

"Let's see how the people in Vermont like a little fire. I wish we had a thousand men. We could lay waste to the entire state."

"We don't have a thousand men. We have only twenty," Young said. "We had better not get carried away. One town at a time, please. And let's keep our voices down. We are making ourselves too obvious around here. I got a fresh letter from Clay, just before leaving for Quebec. He warns me that fellow Parnell is back in Montreal and has been nosing around, asking about my whereabouts."

Parnell? I hoped the others could not detect my shock. I was glad one of them asked, "Who is Parnell?"

"He is a Yankee secret service operative. And, I am sorry to say, a fellow Kentuckian."

A chill crept over me. I dared not raise my eyes from the newspaper I held as they spoke of the very man who had employed me to undertake this mission. They went on discussing Parnell for some time, describing his appearance and so on, so that there was no doubt that he was the same man I had met in Toronto.

Here was a fine kettle of fish. What a fool I had been to swallow Parnell's story of representing Southern moderates who wanted to curb desperadoes. He was a Goddamn Federal spy. And he would pay me with Yankee blood money if I went through with the scheme.

What a shrewd bastard. He had known he could not persuade me to work against my own people as a spy. Instead, he had employed me as a "true Southern patriot," enlisted me under the guise of protecting the South.

Something else I had discovered made me feel even more confused. Young was not just taking the law into his own hands. He had been commissioned a first lieutenant by Richmond with specific instructions from the Confederate War Department to carry out a mission on a Northern town. Some of his men may have been bandits, but he was acting as a Confederate officer under orders from his government. And I was the damn fool who had been duped into working to betray him.

Confession may be good for the soul, but somehow, in these circumstances, I felt it would be decidedly bad for my personal well-being. I didn't dare tell Young that Parnell had hired me. And I couldn't just run away. Neither did I want to cross over into Vermont to burn and rob. All I wanted was to go home. How I longed to be on a ship bound for Bermuda.

19

My dilemma was still unresolved two days later when the time came for our crew to move out for the border. Young already had several men in Vermont. The rest of us he had outfitted in various garbs to cover our various roles. For my part he had bought me a heavy sheepskin coat and a cloth cap. The idea was for me to pretend to be a horse buyer. I was supposed to cross the border with two others to the east and swing around and come up into St. Albans from the south. Others would come in from the east and still others directly from the north, all pretending to be on hunting expeditions, fishing or just sightseers.

Young had things carefully planned, even down to the hotels and boardinghouses at which we would stay.

Young showed us how to use "Greek fire," a chemical that burst into flames when exposed to the air. And he issued us revolvers. The Colt navy pistol he gave me was the first weapon I had held since dropping my Enfield there at Gettysburg.

Young also had us speaking in the clipped way that Yankee voices sound to Southern ears. We had been practicing "talking Northern" for several days.

His plan called for us to strike the banks in St. Albans simultaneously after declaring the town under Confederate martial law. We would set fire to certain public buildings, seize extra horses and dash back into Canada, carrying all the gold and greenbacks we could stuff into our saddlebags.

The horns of my dilemma still impaled me even as we saddled up to start on our mission. It seemed that there was no way for me to get out of this business. Even if you granted that it was a legitimate military operation, I was far more interested in getting back to Oldham County, North Carolina, than in sacking the town of St. Albans, Vermont. And much as I had come to admire this Bennett Young, Jane Ferro and her love meant far, far more to me.

My situation looked hopeless as my steady old roan carried me along in company with two other raiders, heading east. We trotted at a good clip for several miles, until we came to a crossroads where one sign pointed left to Montreal, one right to Richford, Vermont, and another straight ahead toward Quebec.

"Mundy," one of my companions said, "you wait here for the next party and tell them to hold up for half an hour to give us time to get out of Richford. I am afraid that it will look like too many of us, all at once."

Suddenly, my situation did not look so hopeless as they rode off, leaving me on my own, free to do as I wished.

There I sat for several soul-searching moments at that Canadian crossroads. I could stay there until the next group came and then accompany them into Vermont on a mission of vengeance. Become a bank robber and a town burner, with the blessings of the Confederate Government, for what it was worth.

Or I could turn north and ride to Montreal. Look up Parnell. He could telegraph a warning that would save St. Albans. I could collect my one thousand dollars and take first-class passage to Bermuda.

Or if I had a bit more money, I could simply ride ahead to Halifax, Nova Scotia, and book passage there. Damn it, I did want that thousand dollars.

Bank robber or traitor, which would it be? I would have chosen the former if it would not have meant a delay in getting home and maybe a permanent delay at that.

My roan nag stamped his foot and tossed his head as if to tell me to get on with my decision. Then it hit me. The horse. I could sell him for enough to pad out my money and buy passage to Bermuda. He was the property of the livery stable in Montreal but, what the hell, let Clement Clay pay for him out of Confederate funds. That would be my compensation for spending several days working with Young and his crew.

Anyway, I'd rather be a horse thief than either a traitor or a bank robber. I had not asked to get in this mess. Get out of it and let events take their course.

With that I slapped old roan's flanks with the ends of the reins and off we headed, due east at a smart gallop.

I rode on for several miles, fearful that at any minute I might hear the hoofbeats of Young's men coming after me. Finally, to avoid exhausting my horse, I slowed to a walk.

Arriving in Cowansville that afternoon, I put my roan up at a livery stable, bought me a map of eastern Canada and Nova Scotia, and found a room at a cheap hotel.

That night, as I studied my map, I must admit that my conscience ate at me a bit. After all, I still had it in my power to head off the destruction of an innocent Northern town. A single telegraph message would do the trick. But then that could well mean the capture and possible hanging of Bennett Young and his crew.

I decided I would not interfere. The best course was to get myself out of Canada. From all reports it seemed that Halifax, Nova Scotia, was the most likely place to catch a boat. Halifax, more than five hundred miles away. I counted my horde of cash, looked at the map and made up my mind. Next morning I awoke early, ate a good breakfast, claimed my horse and headed northeast.

20

Looking back, I know I should have sold that roan in the town of Richford and taken the railroad to Nova Scotia. That way I could have covered the five hundred miles to Halifax in two or three days. But I was afraid of being seen along major thoroughfares and I wanted to husband my cash. How differently my life might have turned out if I had not spent the next two weeks riding my (or the Montreal livery stable's) horse along the back roads of Ontario, New Brunswick and, finally, Nova Scotia, sleeping in haylofts and eating rough fare at country stores.

My fears of being recognized increased as I read in newspapers along the way reports of the October 19 raid on St. Albans, Vermont, by a band of former Confederate soldiers. I read with horror how Young and his outfit robbed three banks of $220,-000, set fire to various buildings in the unoffending town, stole many horses and killed a citizen. Also, how a posse of angry Vermonters had pursued the raiders over the border into Canada and actually apprehended some of them before being forced to relinquish their quarry to Canadian authorities.

Young and fourteen of his crew were in jail, in Montreal. Seven others, I read with a chill, had slipped away. God help me if I encountered them on the road to Halifax.

It also gave me a chill to think what might have happened to me if I had gone along on the raid; I might be with Young in that Montreal jail, my chances of getting back to the South practically nil.

It was well into November when I finally reached the drab port city of Halifax on Nova Scotia's rocky east coast. I had never been in a seaport before. Everything about Halifax was strange. Wharves. Sail lofts. Ships' chandlers. Sailors with rough, red faces. Sea birds wheeling overhead. And the invigorating smell of salt water.

My first order of business was to dispose of my weary old roan. He had given me transportation across Canada, and I wanted to use him to swell my bank roll. He did not swell it very much. I found a horse trader who did not scruple to ask proof of ownership, but he sure as hell scrupled against paying a penny more than $75 for the nag. I took it and went back to scout the harbor.

Halifax harbor held a confusing variety of ships: large sailing vessels, smaller fishing boats, steamers with side paddles, and a few sleek, new craft with steam-driven propellers, mostly under British flags but some under U.S. and French.

I nosed around that harbor all afternoon, looking over the boats and asking questions of dock hands and sailors, hoping to find a blockade-runner scheduled for a direct trip to Wilmington. I found none. The best bet seemed to be a small combination sail-and-steam ship, the *Nairn,* flying the British flag. She was taking on a cargo of salt fish to be delivered in Brazil, but intended stopping over at Bermuda to drop off medical supplies to be run through the blockade to Wilmington or Charleston.

I made my way to her gangplank and asked to see the captain.

He was in his cabin, staring at some charts and drinking gin when I interrupted him. A great, bearded bear of a man he was, with bloodshot eyes and a red nose.

"Bermuda. Yeah. We are going there."

"I'd like to go along."

"We got no berth for any more hands. All the hands we need."

"I meant as a passenger."

"We don't generally carry passengers. You got any money?"

"A little."

"How much?"

My mind worked quickly. I wasn't about to tell him that I had well over $150 from the sale of the horse and left over from my advances from Parnell and Clay.

"Fifty dollars," I lied.

He snorted. "Not worth the trouble. I'd have to crowd you in with the second mate. I'd do better to pack in more stuff for sale through the blockade. More money to be made that way."

"How much do you want, then?"

"One hundred dollars U.S."

It was my turn to snort. "Be reasonable. You are making it impossible for me to go. I couldn't possibly pay more than sixty dollars U.S."

"You just finished saying you had only fifty dollars. If you look carefully in all your pockets, do you think you can scrape up seventy-five?"

"Maybe. Just barely. If I could, would you take me for seventy-five?"

He hesitated.

"Plus a bottle of rye whisky," I added.

That did it. He held out a huge paw and we shook on the deal.

"Be here tomorrow morning with your gear. And don't forget my bottle of rye as well as the money."

What a relief. I felt like skipping around that gray city in that far northern, inhospitable clime. Bought a bottle of rye for the captain and another for myself. Outfitted myself with a natty kind of yachtsman's cap and some canvas shoes. Even went so far as to buy some combs and silk handkerchiefs as presents for my mother and Jane Ferro. My worries were over, I told myself. I could relax and have myself a fine meal, then find a hotel and clean sheets.

And so, about six o'clock that evening, with my purchases piled beside me, I sat in a booth waiting for a waiter to deliver the lobster and beer I had ordered. Had never eaten a lobster and I was in the mood for a new food.

Yes, sir, I felt downright euphoric until I heard Southern voices asking the waiter for a table. The partitions between the booths were high and I sat with my back to the door, so I could not see the newcomers. I could tell from their voices that there was a pair of them and they took the booth right next to mine, near the door.

They began talking even before the waiter came for their order.

"What if we can't get a ship? They'll get us for sure if we hang around this town."

"I don't know about that. The Canadians might be just as happy if we got away. Save them another row with the Yankees about extradition."

"They seemed eager enough to slap poor Young and the others behind bars."

"Hell, they had to with that damned posse trying to haul them back across the border."

My ears perked up. God Almighty. It was two of my erstwhile friends from Bennett Young's gang. I recognized the voice of one of them as that of the chap with the cold blue eyes, the one I had felt the most likely to execute an informer.

The waiter took their order and they resumed talking.

"So you really think someone ratted on us?"

"Sure appears that way. The Canadian authorities seemed to be laying in wait to grab us when we crossed the border."

"Who do you suppose it was? Reckon the word could have leaked from Clay's office?"

"I doubt it. That one-eyed son of a bitch from North Carolina, that Mundy bastard, never showed up. He may have tipped them off."

"He did act peculiar. Like his heart wasn't in the game."

My waiter brought my beer, a bowl of melted butter and an enormous lobster. As he set all this in front of me, I motioned for him to bend low and I said in a Yankeefied whisper: "Where is your toilet?"

"Out back. Through that door."

"Just leave the lobster. I'll be right back."

I arose and, keeping out of the line of sight of the next booth, walked rapidly out into the back yard of the restaurant, leaving my packages but taking my cap. The yard was enclosed by a board fence, but I went over it like a cat. Took me only a few minutes to reach the dock where my ship was tied up.

The captain was on the deck, smoking his evening pipe and roaring at the seamen lowering cargo into the hold.

"What do you want?" he demanded of me. "We don't sail until tomorrow."

"I thought I might be able to spend the night aboard."

"This ain't no Goddamn hotel."

Fortunately, I had put the two bottles of rye whisky in my coat pocket or they would have been left back at the restaurant with my packages.

"I wanted to deliver this to you," I said, handing him a bottle.

"Ah, yes."

"Thought you might like to have it early."

"Thank you."

"And I thought I'd like to settle down in my quarters. Naturally I would pay a dollar, same as if I was staying ashore at a hotel."

"What the hell. I'll show you your bunk."

And that was how I escaped being shot by Young's friends in Halifax, Nova Scotia. Close call.

21

The *Nairn* was a dirty ship, about two hundred feet long, with a paddle wheel on either side amidships, and three splintery masts. Besides Captain Jenkins, her officers were a first mate named Hopkins, a sour, efficient man who seemed to despise the captain, and Pottlesby, the second mate, a timid young fellow who acted terrified of the skipper. The engineer was a matter-of-fact Scot, short and bald and rather strong in his opinions.

The crew numbered thirty, an assorted lot of Cockneys, Irishmen and mixed bloods, the scrapings of the great British Empire, stupid men who feared the captain, respected the first mate and scorned the poor second mate.

At a full tide in mid-November 1864, this unkempt vessel chugged her way from her moorings across the crowded Halifax Harbor into the Atlantic.

I was as excited as a terrier pup for I had never been to sea. I fairly trotted from the end of that dingy boat to the other and from side to side, watching the buildings of the Halifax waterfront recede, looking out at the line of swells marching in from the open sea, and feeling the lift and fall of the deck beneath my feet.

The cook was a foul little mulatto from the West Indies and his food was miserable. The captain tried to have me eat with the crew, but I explained to him that I was an officer in the Confederate Army, and he grudgingly gave me a place at the officers' table.

The conversation around that table was practically nil. We ate our food in an atmosphere of mutual hostility, which, oddly, did not get me down, I was so elated by the prospects of going home and relieved, too, at escaping from possible retribution by Young's bandits.

Things ran smoothly for two days, with the *Nairn* carrying a modest amount of sail to help the engines along. The seas were fairly calm and it appeared that we would make Bermuda in ten days.

The trouble came early one morning as the captain, second mate and I were having our breakfast of salt fish and bread. The seas had got rougher during the night. Neither the engineer nor the first mate was present; some difficulty with the engines and they were investigating.

Suddenly there was a muffled blast belowdecks and the sound of steam hissing, followed by shouts and running about. The captain went stomping out of the cabin, followed by the second mate. By the time I left the table, the ship had slowed down and the paddle wheels were no longer churning. Up from the engine room came four crewmen carrying the remains of what had been the first mate. He had been scalded to death, turned as red as the lobster I had never got to eat. A horrible sight.

The captain was in a rage, demanding of the engineer why he had allowed the boiler to split open; why he had not warned the first mate of the danger. But no matter whose fault it was, the first mate was dead. They sewed him up in an old piece of canvas with a weight in one end. The captain gathered us on the stern and read perfunctorily from a Church of England prayer book. Then two seamen slid the body over the rail and into the Atlantic.

The captain roared at the bo'sun to put on more sail and for everyone to get on with their duties. He retired to his cabin. Second Mate Pottlesby spent the afternoon making sure our sails were properly spread and that our course was set. When I went to summon the captain for supper, I found he had swilled most of the bottle of rye I had given him. He was in a maudlin stage of drunkenness. With a thick tongue he told me of his grief over the death of his dear friend, Alfred Hopkins, as fine a Christian gentleman as ever did sail under the British flag. He went on and on until I was ready to throw up at his hypocrisy, for I knew there had been no love between the captain and his mate. I had discovered, also, that the first mate, for all his tight, sour ways, was a first-rate sailor and a skilled driver of men. It now became obvious that the captain had envied the mate for his abilities but had never admitted to himself that he could not run the ship without him. Now, with Hopkins gone, he did not know how much sail to put on or how to direct the men other than by hectoring and threatening them.

I was amazed by the man's capacity for alcohol. He drank his way through his bottle of rye as he told me of how he had first met the saintly Alfred Hopkins five years before and what lovely, close friends they had been, although some undiscerning people might not have realized it.

He was interrupted in this discourse by the second mate, young Pottlesby, asking for instructions about a course change.

"Ye stupid little stripling. Have ye learned nothing? Set the course for 'Muda and don't dare come back 'rupting me wif stupid questions."

Pottlesby, his face scarlet, withdrew from the cabin.

The captain picked up his refrain. "Hopkins, bless his soul, never bothered me wif stupid questions. Told him what to do and he saw it was done. Oh, what will I do without him?"

At that he began to cry. It must have been many years since he had wept for he seemed to have a vast store of tears in that ugly, massive head. A regular Mississippi flowed down one cheek and an Amazon down the other, into his beard and dripping onto the table.

He did not sob; just produced a flood of tears. And then, the last of the bottle drained off, he put his head on the table and passed out. Pottlesby came in and together we put him in his bunk and covered him up.

Outside, on the deck, Pottlesby confided in me. "I do wish he wouldn't drink like that. The men are giving me trouble. Some of them feel we should head into Boston so we can repair the boiler there. They don't like to sail. But if we do that, our cargo of fish will spoil."

"Can't you handle them?"

"I could if the captain would stay sober. They are afraid of him, but they take advantage of me."

"Do you know how to sail? How to navigate?"

"Oh, yes. I have studied navigation since I was a boy."

"These fellows all experienced sailors?"

"Good enough. If they wanted, they could sail us around the world. But they have been spoiled by steam. Don't like the hard work of sailing."

"Maybe the captain will be sober in the morning."

But he was not. I awoke in my cramped bunk in the tiny cabin I shared with Pottlesby, feeling disaster in the air. My cabin mate was not there. I found him on the deck being bullied by a loud-mouthed bo'sun who refused to crowd on as much sail as Pottlesby thought necessary.

In the galley, the cook was smoking a pipe, sitting with his arms crossed. When I asked him for breakfast, he gave me a surly answer about not liking to feed passengers. I let that pass.

The captain could have come raging forth and straightened out the cook and bo'sun in about two minutes, for he was a formidable, if ignorant, man. When I looked in on him, however, a second empty bottle sat on the table. He had now polished off two bottles since the death of the mate.

I scrounged a cup of coffee, some bread and cheese from the cook and ate it alone. As I was finishing my food, in came Pottlesby, his face white with anxiety.

"What am I to do? The captain is passed out. The bo'sun says he had told the men to assemble at ten o'clock to decide whether to take the ship into Boston. He refused to follow my orders. Now the word is around about the captain being drunk and I can't control the men. Why did I ever go to sea?"

The poor fellow put his head in his hands like a bewildered schoolboy.

"They will meet at ten o'clock?"

"Yes."

"Perhaps something will develop."

He pulled himself together and went his timid way about the ship to check on the possibility that the engineer could repair the boiler. Without asking anyone's leave, I gathered up my gear from our cramped little cabin and carried it over to the larger cabin that had been occupied by the late first mate. One of his caps was on a hook and I found it a perfect fit. The others had been too preoccupied or superstitious to disturb his belongings, but I had no such scruples. Found pictures of a plump little wife and two robust boys plus a diary in which Hopkins had recorded details of the weather and the state of his religious life; also his great love for his wife.

His diary entries and an unfinished letter to his wife told me much about Alfred Hopkins. Beneath that cold, meticulous surface, he had been a sensitive, intelligent fellow. I was sorry he had died. I should have enjoyed knowing him.

At ten o'clock, the men gathered in front of the main mast while the bo'sun addressed them and poor Pottlesby stood by fidgeting and wondering what to say in response. The bo'sun told the crew that they could get into Boston Harbor in a couple of days under sail and there could have the boiler repaired quickly.

The engineer replied that if they would quit beefing and give him a hand, he thought he might patch the boiler so that it would carry a small head of steam. Pottlesby tried to explain that they would lose their cargo of fish if they went into Boston, but the bo'sun drowned him out.

All this was taking place about twenty feet from the door of the first mate's cabin, which sat on a raised deck looking down at the main mast. No one knew I was in it, listening. The bo'sun was saying, "We must vote. Only way to settle this. First mate is dead. Captain is drunk. And we got a green second mate that don't know his ass from a bunghole. Let's vote between going into Boston or sailing on to Bermuda."

That is when I stepped out of the cabin. I wore the first mate's cap and held in my right hand the Colt revolver given me by Bennett Young. They all looked up in amazement at my appearance. I raised the revolver and fired just over their heads, into the main mast, sending a shower of splinters over them. It was lovely to see them drop to the deck, thinking, I suppose, that I meant to murder them.

"On your feet, you scum," I shouted. "And pay attention."

They arose while I stood there, looking as tall and ferocious as I could manage.

"You aren't going to vote on anything. You have lost your first mate and your captain is incapacitated, true. But I have hired this ship to take me to Bermuda. Technically you are all in my employ. Second Mate Pottlesby is my representative and I will shoot anyone who fails to carry out his orders promptly."

A murmur arose from their midst and I raised my revolver again.

"You there," I said, brandishing my revolver at the bo'sun. "I am putting you in irons to be dealt with by the captain when he has recovered. I will shoot you if you resist. Here, you two. Bind that fellow's hands behind him and be quick about it."

In short order, I had the bo'sun shut up in a pantry, securely out of the way. I put my own bottle of rye in easy view on the table in the captain's cabin so he would see it when he came to. I followed Pottlesby around to make sure no one gave him any guff. I threatened to throw the cook overboard if his meals did not improve. And I assigned extra men to assist the engineer in trying to repair the boiler. By evening I had that ship reorganized and running smoothly again. The vessel's three masts were crowded with canvas and we were running before a good strong breeze, headed for Bermuda.

Over a hot supper, by far the best we had eaten since leaving

Halifax, Pottlesby thanked me for salvaging the situation.

"Don't thank me," I replied, patting my revolver. "Thank old Bessie here. She is the colt; I am merely the rider."

Pottlesby didn't get the joke.

22

The captain eventually sobered up, once he ran out of liquor. Fortunately his supply lasted until we had passed both Boston and New York. I didn't know what his feelings would have been about turning into one of these enemy ports for repairs and wanted to take no chances of ending in the hands of the U.S. authorities.

Seeing how well things were going, the captain followed my suit, using his natural authority to replace that of my Colt revolver, but still working through young Pottlesby.

That worthy began acting more and more like a man. Began to hold his shoulders back and look the men square in the eye when he told them what to do. He would never be the great bully the captain was, able to rule by fear, nor the ruthlessly efficient first mate, managing men through their respect for his knowledge, but still I could see that in time Pottlesby would become a competent, fair master of his own vessel.

The captain never referred to his breakdown. He let Pottlesby continue to fill the role of first mate, spending much of his own time helping the engineer patch the boiler. The captain did not question my occupancy of the first mate's cabin and I offered no explanation. I did take pains to point out what a good job Pottlesby was doing. Made it appear that he had taken more initiative than in fact he had.

During the remainder of the slow run under sail to Bermuda, I settled back and enjoyed the ride. I had never imagined it could be so restful and exhilarating to stride about the lifting and falling deck of a sailing vessel sliding through the water to the will of the sea wind. This was a far cry from my rude home in Oldham County, or from the camps of the Army of Northern Virginia, or from the fetid prison pen at Johnson's Island.

I lacked only one thing to be ecstatically happy and that was the presence of Jane Ferro. How I yearned to have her beside me, her arm in mine, the Atlantic breeze in our faces and the sun gleaming off her dark-red hair. I longed to sit on the capstan with her and tell her of what I had endured at Gettysburg, in prison and in Canada. She surely would not despise me for my blind eye. It was a happy daydream, perhaps even a silly one, but it did sustain me on the long sea road to Bermuda.

Curiously I experienced a kind of homesickness for the 10th North Carolina as well. That regiment had given me a sense of pride, of accomplishment. From a shabby performance under the inept leadership of Elmer Fincastle at New Bern, it had gone on to serve with valor at Malvern Hill, Sharpsburg, Fredericksburg and Gettysburg, not to mention doing yeomen duty in putting down insurrection in North Carolina and protecting the rail lifeline of the Confederacy between Wilmington and Richmond.

Where was the regiment now? I wondered. What had happened to Colonel William Ferro, Noah Rhine, Harry McGee, Captain Cadieu, yes, and the overbearing Tom Shelton? I longed to see them again and to swap tales of what had happened to them and to me since that afternoon of July 3, 1863, there at the base of Gettysburg's Cemetery Ridge when life had been rich and promising and when it still appeared that the South could vanquish its Northern enemies and enjoy a separate national existence of its own.

Back in Halifax, if I had known then what I know today, I might well have taken a ship to England and sought a new life there in the land of my Quaker ancestors. Alas, that is the daydream of an old man, yearning for what might have been.

About two days out of Bermuda, the Scots engineer announced that he had hammered and riveted a patch over the fatal split in the boiler and that, with the help of heavy wire baling, it should stand half a head of steam. He stoked up the furnace cautiously while we all held our breath at a safe distance from the boiler. To our vast relief, the paddles began turning slowly, digging into the water. The ship began moving forward with fresh energy.

Pottlesby and I beamed at each other. He came over and clapped me on the shoulder.

"How can I ever thank you, Lieutenant Mundy?"

"Easy. Get me into Bermuda."

The *Nairn* did just that on December 1, 1864. The low hills of the main island were in view by dawn. By noon we lay to off St. David's Island and signaled for a pilot. A lean, weather-beaten black man came out in a steam launch and skillfully guided us through the narrow channel into the St. George Harbor and to an anchorage in its calm waters, which were thronged with sleek gray side-wheelers lying long and low and larger, more cumbersome ships bearing names of English and French home ports.

The captain ordered a boat lowered over the side while I gathered up my few belongings. To my amazement, the engineer and the cook came up and shook my hand. Then one after another of the crew followed suit, all except the bo'sun who was still locked away in the pantry.

As the boat drew near the dock, the captain handed me an envelope. In it I found the seventy-five dollars I had paid him for my passage when I came aboard back in Halifax. I tried to thank him, but he looked embarrassed.

"Don't thank me. You earned it. All I want is for you to keep quiet about all this in port. No need for word to get around, is there? Man must guard his reputation, you know."

On the dock, I said goodbye to him and set off across the town square for the office I heard was maintained by the Confederate

Government to oversee blockade-running.

The two-story hotel on Duke of York Street was a busy place. I told my story to a portly, gray-haired clerk who acted rather blasé.

"You really want to get back into the country?" he asked.

"Sure. I want to see my family and I want to rejoin my regiment."

"That is rare patriotism, young man. If you have been out of the Confederacy since June of 1863, I'm afraid you'll find things have gone downhill somewhat."

"How do you mean?"

"Our money is almost worthless now. The country is badly torn up. Railroads in sorry shape. Supplies not getting to the army. Desertions from the ranks. Back country full of bushwhackers. The Confederacy is just barely hanging on. And have you heard the election news from the North?"

"No."

"Lincoln has been voted back in office for four years. That means the war will be pushed harder than ever. And the North has a growing advantage in manpower and material. What's more, they have found some generals to match Lee and Johnston. It will take a miracle to save our cause."

"Even so, I must go home. How can I?"

"Wilmington is your only hope. It is still open, barely. But the blockade fleet hangs about the entrances to the Cape Fear just out of range of the guns of Fort Fisher. Our blockade-runners can only get in at night. They used to be able to dodge about, running away if sighted to try again. Now the Yankees have fast craft of their own to chase after them. Our supply of good hard coal that leaves no smoke has run low. The smoke from soft coal gives our ships away. This time last year maybe one in five or ten of our vessels or the English were being captured. Now the odds are down to fifty-fifty. God knows how long it will be before the Yankees go ashore and take Fort Fisher itself. Then the jig will be up. For Wilmington and the Confederacy."

"But ships are still trying?"

"Sure. This business is so damned profitable there are still captains willing to try. A single run in with scarce goods and a run out with cotton or tobacco can make a fortune. Besides, most of these ships were built for this purpose; nothing else for them to do. Our difficulty is making the greedy bastards carry medicine and supplies the people need instead of fancy foods, wines and silks."

"How do I get on such a vessel?"

"I'll give you a note to the captain of the *Miriam.* He will make room for you. He is a good fellow, sympathetic to our cause."

"What will it cost me?"

"Maybe your life."

"Seriously."

"Seriously, nothing. That is what this note is about. You must promise to go straight there and talk to no one on the way. There are Yankee agents everywhere trying to get a line on what ships are leaving when. They signal Yankee ships lying about off Bermuda and they sometimes tail our ships across to the North Carolina coast."

"I'll keep my mouth shut."

"Good luck then. You'll need it."

How I would have liked to spend a few days in Bermuda. Its beauty took my breath away. Low, colorful houses and buildings with terra-cotta roofs designed to catch rainwater. Profusions of brilliant flowers. People of every complexion and race sauntering about the town. And all those ships.

Bermuda was a vast staging area where valuable goods were brought over openly from Europe to be transferred as quietly as possible to special ships for the dangerous run to Wilmington and Charleston.

I was tempted to delay my departure long enough to enjoy this semitropical paradise but the words of the C.S.A. agent haunted me. I had better get back to the Confederacy while there was still even a fifty-fifty chance of getting through the blockade. So I sought out the *Miriam* at dockside and presented my note to the captain.

Like the skipper of the *Nairn,* he was an Englishman, but the similarity ended there. This gentleman, and he was a gentleman, was tall, with clear gray eyes and a figure as taut as the contours of his sleek ship. He read my note without changing his expression and then spoke in a precise, well-educated way.

"Are you aware of the contents of this note?"

"More or less."

"It classifies you as valuable cargo to be transported as part of our required C.S.A. quota. Free of charge."

"So I understand."

"It also means that you must not go back ashore. You must go belowdeck and stay there until we clear this harbor. Can't risk your spreading the word of our departure."

"If you say so."

What a ship this was. Only two years old. Freshly painted a light gray. Two stacks that could be lowered into the hold in an emergency, to keep the silhouette low. Narrow beam that allowed very little cargo space and quite a bit of that taken up with luxury goods, bolts of fine cloth, ladies' combs, expensive tinned foods, coffee and sugar, also ingots of lead and boxes of cured bacon. One small section up forward contained sets of Sheffield surgical instruments, bottles of chloroform and reams of printed C.S.A. requisition forms.

I saw that she was already loaded, as the purser showed me to a narrow bunk in the crews' cramped quarters. I lay in that bunk for the rest of the afternoon while the polygot crew came and went, showing no surprise at the presence of a one-eyed Southerner with a Colt revolver in his belt. I suppose they had grown used to the sight of strange passengers.

Just as the sun was going down I felt the throb of the powerful engines and the ship sliding away from her moorings. I stayed below for more than an hour after that, until the captain sent word that I could come topside.

It was dark now and the pilot's launch was drawing away. The hills around St. George formed a dark outline spangled with lights from the homes. Ahead a mile or two, I saw the tall mast of a larger ship, also headed west toward the last glimmer of the sun.

The captain explained the situation to me.

"We are trying a new tactic on this trip. That merchantman is on her way to Havana. I have hired the captain to lead us across to within sight of the blockade fleet, then turn and speed south. I am hoping he will lure enough blockaders out of position to chase after her and leave a hole in their screen for us to slip through."

"Won't they seize her instead?"

"They probably will overtake her, but once they go aboard, see what she is carrying, and find all her papers have to do with the Cuba trade, they will have to apologize and let her go. Anyway, I have paid the captain a handsome fee to take the risk. I am taking rather a risk myself on this trip. We carried out a pilot on our last trip, but he took ill in Bermuda and I am having to risk this one with myself as pilot. Not to worry, though. I have been into Wilmington enough to know the ropes."

It took us five days to plod along at an easy pace, several miles behind that lumbering merchantman. And during that time I became well acquainted with our captain and the ways of the profitable blockade-running business.

23

That captain and I hit it off famously. His name was Mayfair and he came from the West Country of England, the youngest son of a vicar, who had gone off to sea rather than to the university as his father wished. He was the friendliest Englishman I have ever met. He gave me free run of the ship. Personally took me about the sparsely furnished deck and the engine room and explained all the ins and outs of blockade-running. Also, we had several interesting conversations about his business and about the war in general.

The *Miriam* had been built in Scotland in 1862 and had made her first run past the blockaders and up the Cape Fear River to Wilmington early in 1863. Since then she had made more than a dozen trips between that port and either Bermuda or Nassau. The owners already had recovered their investment several times over. Captain Mayfair got a large percentage of the profits for his risks. He was now a wealthy man and could retire to live on his interest, if he wished. I asked him why he kept at an increasingly dangerous game.

"I can't lose at this stage. Even if they catch me, and I suppose they must sooner or later, my financial future is secure. Besides that I feel some responsibility to your cause."

I expressed surprise that he should feel that way.

"It is true," he replied. "No matter what the right or wrong of slavery, I have come to admire the splendid spirit of you Southerners. It still amazes me that five million white inhabitants of the South have accomplished so much against such odds. You have created a government from nothing, have organized and equipped armies that have won impressive victories. You have improvised factories and have endured dreadful losses. You come from a gallant race, Mundy."

"The fellow at the blockade office thinks our cause is hopeless now. Do you agree?"

"Yes. It is very nearly hopeless."

"Not a chance of winning anymore?"

"Not in the sense of crushing Northern armies. You never did have the power to do that and to invade and occupy their territory as they have yours. But then, you did not need to do that to win your goal, which was independence."

"How do you mean?"

"All your cause required was to be allowed to separate in peace. But I fear that too many of you Southerners were itching for a fight. Had to prove your manhood on the battlefield. You lack patience. Then, too, some of your government's policies have been so wrong."

At my insistence he elaborated.

"Your leaders got it in their heads that your cotton was so important to the world that you could bring about foreign intervention by withholding it, by discouraging its production and by prohibiting its export. Stupid business. Just think of your financial position if during the first two years of the war, before the United States had built up its blockade fleet, you had continued to grow cotton and had shipped it out promptly to Confederate warehouses in England and France. It would be like having gold in foreign vaults. You could have used that white gold to back your currency. You could have financed a fleet. But no, you threw away your trump. And you didn't make your bid, which was foreign intervention. Our textile workers in the North Country, unlike some of our aristocrats, have been willing to suffer economically rather than support slavery."

"But damn it, there is more to this than slavery. I don't own any slaves. Damned few of the men in my regiment were from slaveowning families. We just don't want to live in a country where Africans can vote and hold office and marry our sisters. Slavery is a way to prevent that."

He smiled at that. "Mundy, inevitably slavery must end. The Negro is with you for all time. He is human just like you. Your government has been so shortsighted about the Negro, treating that patient, trusting people like farm animals instead of as human assets. Look, I have observed black people in Wilmington and Charleston and I see them differently from you. Your government should have employed them as soldiers in 1862 instead of passing your Conscription Act. With good white leadership, they would have fought as well as anyone else. But no, your government chose to let your white population bear all the sacrifices. Meanwhile, the Federals have turned your asset into a liability. They have signed up your slaves as soldiers and from all reports they don't do badly. Furthermore, Confederate use of Negro soldiers, assuming manumission as a reward for good service, would have strengthened your case in both Britain and France. It would have lent credence to the argument that your true goal was independence and not the protection of slavery."

I started to argue with him, but he cut me off.

"I tell you that throughout Europe the war is seen as a contest between slavery and freedom. I know how you Southerners prate of states' rights. If you had armed even a token number of slaves and given them their freedom, more Europeans would have believed you."

"I am sorry," I persisted. "Seems to me that would mean the end of slavery, to start putting guns in the hands of niggers."

"Slavery is being ended anyway. Everywhere the Federal armies go, the slaves desert their plantations and follow. Even now, if, by some miracle, the North gave you your independence, I don't see how you could restore slavery. How would you make those runaway slaves return to their masters? And what about the more than one hundred thousand ex-slaves in Federal uniform? It is unthinkable that they could be re-enslaved."

I soon got enough of this gloomy talk and excused myself to turn in for the night. The next evening I kept away from the subject of slavery by asking about blockade-running.

Captain Mayfair took me to his cabin, which was narrow and Spartan, like the ship itself. There he unrolled a map of the lower North Carolina coast. He showed me the inlets into the mouth of the Cape Fear and indicated the usual positions of the blockade fleet. He showed me, too, spots where sister blockade-runners had met their fates.

"Generally they run aground in the dark while trying to elude a pursuer. It is rare that a Federal ship actually destroys one of us with gunfire. We get in trouble trying to stay out of range."

I asked him about Fort Fisher, the huge Confederate system

of earthworks that defended the upper entrance of the Cape Fear.

"Thank God and the Confederate Government for Fort Fisher. That is a marvelous piece of work. We are all right once we slip in under the protection of those guns. All along here there are banks of sand thrown up with embrasures for eight- and ten-inch cannon. The sandy earth literally absorbs the shot and shell from any Federal ship foolish enough to run in close and exchange fire with Fort Fisher's guns. And the Confederates have added an English touch with a battery of breechloading Whitworth rifled field cannon. They throw a bolt up to five miles, accurate up to three miles. Small-caliber missiles that can do little damage, true, but they do keep the blockaders moving about and at a healthy distance."

Captain Mayfair was a good listener as well as talker. He seemed fascinated by my stories of our regiment's battles and of my prison experiences. Seemed impressed by my determination to return to fight for my homeland. I did not explain that my patriotism was tempered by an obsessive love for the daughter of an aristocrat far above my station. For me to have remained in Canada or gone to England would have been to write off any chance of taking Jane Ferro to wife.

We plodded along at little more than half-speed, just within sight of the masts of the slower merchantman that was serving as our guide and decoy. The sea remained calm for that time of year—December. I spent much of the time chatting with crew members off watch. They were apprehensive about running through the blockade, now that it was becoming so much better enforced. But they looked forward to visiting the fleshpots of Wilmington.

"Ah, those lovely coffee-colored girls," a young Londoner said. "I'd swim past the blockaders for a bit of that dark fluff." He rhapsodized about the delights of intercourse with high yellows until I grew weary of hearing him, forgetting about my own experience in Richmond with a girl of slight color herself.

On our last day out, the stokers in the engine room began

using anthracite coal so that we stopped trailing smoke. They lowered the stacks and erected a kind of small tent over the binnacle. The captain warned me that no light could be shone and that no one could speak above a whisper after sundown.

Meanwhile, the merchantman ahead of us slowed down and, if anything, seemed to produce more black smoke than ever before. We, too, began to slow down and run in circles. A sailor up on a yardarm with a telescope shouted down an account of what he could see.

"Four blockaders, just on the horizon a bit to the right."

"Can you see land yet?" the captain called up to him.

"Not yet."

In a bit, as the sun began to set, the lookout called again. "I can see the mound at Fort Fisher. And the blockaders are moving this way."

Our merchantman friend suddenly changed course, veering to the left so that he was headed south. He speeded up, sending forth a veritable bank of dark smoke.

"There. Two of them are headed after her," the lookout shouted.

"How about the others?"

"Still in position. And I can see more ships farther to the right and left."

"What about the fort?"

"They have lit the signal light on the mound!"

By now the sun was beginning to sink. The captain threw away his cigar.

"All engines full speed ahead," he commanded. In a moment the side paddles responded and the *Miriam* surged ahead like a horse with spurs thrust into its flanks.

24

The powerful engines of the *Miriam* thrust the ship through the dark water for the better part of an hour, until we could see clearly the light maintained by the Confederates. Then the captain ordered the engines slowed to quarter-speed. I stood in the dark as he quietly gave instructions to the helmsman and sent a sailor to the prow with a line and weight to take soundings.

"I had a choice of going north and running up New Inlet under the guns of Fort Fisher or turning south and coming in over the western bar. It's tricky business at night getting in the New Inlet. Narrow water there. But we are loaded so heavy I'd rather go that way than to risk getting stuck on the bar. Wait. What's that?"

He ordered the engines to stop. I could hear the whoosh of steam and the slap of another set of paddles in the near distance.

"A blockader on our starboard quarter. He is passing across the bow. They know something is up."

The shadow of a vast ship passed between us and the light from the lighthouse. I held my breath as that menacing bulk slid past us. "Any chance they will see us?" I whispered.

"Anything is possible. If he should turn or if another vessel should come behind us and see us against the light, we are in for it. We must wait a bit."

"How long?"

"We dare not delay too much or the tide will be running against us when we tackle the New Inlet. That would slow us down and also could increase the danger of running aground with all this freight."

He gave no orders now as we strained our ears for the sound of blockaders.

"There, she is turning to steam north again. Damn it, I hope he makes a tight turn or he may run right over us."

Another sailor padded up from the stern. "White rocket went up behind us, Captain. Couple of miles dead astern of us."

"My God. Listen," the captain said.

The first blockader's engines and paddles could be heard chugging and churning just to our left, sounding as if she were advancing right upon us. Louder and louder the noises came until the ship slid across our bow again, so close this time that we could hear the voices of crewmen shouting at each other. And just after she passed, a red rocket went up, up and then down into the sea.

The lookout from the stern returned. "I can hear the paddles of the ship astern now. Sounds as if she is coming fast."

"All right," the captain ordered. "All engines ahead half-speed. Right rudder." Then, to me, "Those damn rockets. That's the way they signal at night. And they change the meaning of the colors from time to time to confuse us."

The deck began to throb again and the paddles to slap the water far louder than I would have liked.

"I'm taking a chance, Mundy. I am going to follow the first ship and just pray that he doesn't discover we are trailing him. Or that he doesn't make another turn before we are ready."

For a nerve-racking hour, we followed that blockader's wake. Here and there about the western horizon signal rockets went up. During this time the captain was too busy to explain what they meant. He kept ducking under a canopy to consult his charts by a feeble lantern.

"Captain," a lookout whispered. "Look there, she is turning. See her wake?"

"Which way?"

"To the right."

"We'll have to take our chances. Left rudder! All engines ahead full."

He had hoped to steam ahead for another mile or so before turning squarely into the entrance to the New Inlet but now had to angle to the left and grope for the opening.

"They likely will hear us as we pass, or see us outlined against the light. But I have no choice. If I run back out to sea, their outer pickets will sight us in the morning. They have started using captured blockade-runners to run us down."

Sure enough in a moment a brilliant white light shown from our starboard side, illuminating our stern and stacks. Then a cannon flashed and a shell whined over our masts, exploding far ahead.

No more whispering of orders now as the captain shouted at the leadsman to keep up his soundings and down to the engineer to open his drafts and pour on the steam. The *Miriam* was racing through the water now as the light at Fort Fisher loomed larger and larger.

The blockade-runner fired several more times as she made her turn to pursue and once a shell burst close enough to rattle fragments down on our deck. Now I could see a second light winking faintly to the west of the first. The captain retired to his canopy and shouted for bearings to be taken on this new landmark.

The bow guns on the pursuing ship spoke again and again, their shells sounding like trains passing over our heads.

At last, the pursuing blockader gave up the chase and Captain Mayfair ordered his engines slowed to half-speed again. We were inside the narrow waters of the New Inlet now. I had started across the deck to congratulate the captain when the *Miriam* halted in her tracks, throwing me down and setting up a clatter of falling objects.

"We're aground!" the leadsman shouted.

"Christ in heaven," the captain said. "What rotten luck."

He tried everything to get us off. Reversed the engines. Turned the rudder this way and that. Tried to move ahead slowly and then thrust backward. But we were stuck fast and the tide now was running out.

The engineer sent up word that he was worried about ruining the engines. "All right," the captain replied. "Stop them. There is only one thing to do if we don't want to get caught here at daylight."

That one thing was to start dumping cargo overboard. First came crates of French brandy and boxes of food, barrels of sugar and sacks of coffee beans. Yes, and the medical supplies and various other items belonging to the Confederate Government. Finally "pigs" of lead meant for bullets. I worked right alongside the crew in a kind of bucket brigade that passed these valuable supplies, worth tens of thousands of dollars, up from the holds and over the side into the ocean.

All the while, the tide ran lower until the *Miriam* lay at a slight tilt. Leadsmen kept an anxious watch through the night while the tide ran out and then as the first suggestion of sunlight glimmered to the east began to run back in.

The captain and I stayed on deck, drinking coffee and talking.

"Well over fifty ships have been lost in the past year in this area and most of them were lost this way. Some are disabled by gunfire and some from equipment failure. But generally they run aground while trying to elude the Federal fleet. And it is happening more and more often. I should have tried the entrance south of Smith Island. New Inlet at night! What a fool."

We had kept our steam up throughout the night. As the light in the east grew stronger and the depth of the water increased gradually, we could see the masts of several blockaders several miles to the east.

"Matter of time until they spot us. When they do, they'll have another go at us with their guns."

He ordered the engines to start first half and then full speed astern, but the *Miriam* still would not budge.

I nearly jumped out of my skin when a lookout called, "Blockaders headed this way."

The captain swore. "Jettison the anchors. Signal gun, too.

Cast off the lifeboats. Bear a hand there."

Two blockaders were bearing down on us, almost within cannon range.

"All engines astern half-speed." The *Miriam* shuddered but remained stuck.

"All astern full." I thought the ship would shake to pieces as the paddles sent up a monstrous spray, but she still would not budge.

Then came the ugly shriek of a shell. It was a misfire that sent up a geyser two hundred yards astern. Then another that burst just ahead of us, a fragment of it sending the leadsman flopping to the deck with a lacerated scalp.

"Starboard engine half-speed ahead; port engine, full astern."

The ship shifted a bit.

"Port engine half-speed ahead now; starboard, full astern."

The *Miriam* shifted the other way.

There was a sudden deafening clang as a shell bored through the forward stack, followed by an explosion off our port side.

"All engines astern full speed."

The *Miriam* made one final shudder and broke free. A great cheer went up from the crew.

"All engines ahead full. Put on all possible steam."

Shells rained around us for a moment as the paddles sought their footing and then we began to race forward, our lightened craft aided now by the current from the swiftly incoming tide.

Guns now were flashing atop a great sandy mound to our right, the southernmost position of Fort Fisher, hurling shells out toward our two tormenters.

With one final salvo that fell short, the Yankee ships turned and steamed out of range, leaving us with a wounded sailor, a damaged stack and empty holds. The *Miriam,* after a close call, had got through the blockade. But the only item of any value it had to deliver to the failing cause of the Confederacy was a one-eyed twenty-one-year-old lieutenant. An item of doubtful value.

25

Three other blockade-runners were anchored in the lower reaches of the Cape Fear as we passed upriver after taking on a sour-looking old pilot. As explained to me, these ships were waiting for the opportunity to dart out and through the screen of blockaders. On our starboard side, we could see a group of Confederate soldiers waving to us. God, what sad-looking specimens they were from what I could see through Captain Mayfair's spyglass. Old men and young boys.

I tried to commiserate with the captain over the loss of his cargo, but he wanted no sympathy.

"I'll make money on the outward voyage. Cotton and tobacco are in great demand now. Not to worry. All in the game. Besides, it serves me right for trying to act as my own pilot."

It took us four hours to run the twenty miles up the Cape Fear to Wilmington. Five other long, low blockade-runners were tied up along the city's docks. And I saw a stubby, powerful-looking Confederate ironclad under construction.

A crowd of people of all descriptions waited on the dock as we tied up.

"What did you bring in?" one swarthy chap shouted.

"Nothing. Had to jettison everything," a sailor replied.

As this word passed through the crowd, a general murmur of disappointment arose.

Once our lines were fastened and a gangplank in place, Captain Mayfair, looking haggard and gray, said his farewell to me.

"What will you do now, Mundy?"

"Report to the ranking officer here and apply for a furlough home before rejoining my regiment."

"Here is my address in England. We have a home in the Cotswolds. Do let me hear from you, Mundy. And good luck, old fellow."

I had thought Richmond a rough, sinful city and Bermuda a polygot place, but Wilmington, North Carolina, in December 1864 outdid them both. The city reeked of greed and desperation. The sidewalks around the dock area teemed with sleazy characters. I was stopped a dozen times by men asking if I had brought anything in to sell. They couldn't believe that I didn't have a bagful of scarce items on which to turn a profit. And I was twice approached by pimps offering me my choice of complexions in women. What a debauched, miserable city Wilmington was; like a carcass surrounded by flies and carrion eaters.

Making inquiry, I learned that General Braxton Bragg had been sent down from Richmond by his good friend Jefferson Davis to oversee the defense of the Confederacy's last major port. It would be a simple matter, I assumed, to report to his headquarters, tell the story of my escape, get a month's furlough and make my way rejoicing to Oldham County, two hundred miles inland. Plenty of time, I thought, to rejoin my regiment.

Time, too, I thought to report to Bragg's headquarters. So I turned off into the least disreputable-looking saloon I saw, for a mint julep. What a coincidence that I should ask for that particular beverage for there at the bar stood the slave trader who had treated Noah Rhine and me to juleps back in Fayetteville.

"Why, Mr. Abernathy," I greeted him.

His shrewd blue eyes took me in without recognition.

"Yes?"

"I met you in Fayetteville a year and a half ago. You bought me and my friend a drink. Remember?"

"Of course." But obviously he did not remember me.

"It was right after a slave auction. My name is Jim Mundy, from Oldham County."

Now he remembered.

"Of course. But you look different."

"It's the eye patch. I lost my eye at Gettysburg."

"Lost an eye. How sad. This cruel war. I have suffered losses, too."

"What is the matter?"

"My nigger business has gone to the dogs. Had to give it up. The country is too disrupted to move about anymore. Impossible to travel to the Deep South. Atlanta has been destroyed by that devil Sherman. Now that wicked man is tearing up the interior of Georgia."

"What are you doing in Wilmington these days?"

"Oh, I am recouping my fortunes. I now run a line of wagons back into the interior from Wilmington. I buy cotton, bring it down here. Sell it to the blockade-runners and buy up stuff from Europe to take back for sale upstate. Everything is in short supply. A good time to be a merchant. The blockade is a blessing in disguise. Far more profitable what I am doing than the nigger business, actually. Niggers will get sick and die on you or run away. I lost ten in a single night down in South Carolina. Like to have ruined me financially. Wished I had switched over to merchandising two years ago. More dependable trade. What did you say your name was again?"

"James Mundy. Lieutenant of the 10th North Carolina. When we met before, I was a sergeant and our regiment was going to Robeson County to put down the Croatan Indians there."

"I do remember now. Alas, you should have shot every one of those redskinned scoundrels. They bushwhacked one of my trade wagons just last month. Lost an entire lot of silk cloth and ladies' hats intended for the trade up in Charlotte. What are you doing in Wilmington?"

I tried to tell him of my experiences in Canada and on the sea, but he listened with only half an ear until I mentioned the blockade.

"You are just in from Bermuda? What did you bring in to sell?"

"Nothing. And our blockade-runner brought in nothing. Had to throw the entire cargo overboard to get off a sand bar."

"Pity. What will you do now?"

"See my folks and then rejoin my regiment."

"Splendid, my boy. We need you. Things have gone against our beloved South this past year, but brave lads like you can reverse the situation. Yes, sir, General Lee has showed Grant that he can't take Richmond. Holding him off very well. Sherman will be dealt with in Georgia. I hear tell that Hood has marched his army off into Tennessee. Yes, sir, he is going to chase the Yankees right out of that state and maybe Kentucky as well. Fort Fisher is impregnable. We still have our communications with Europe. Brave lads like you make me proud to be a Southerner, you do."

"Well, sir, you do seem to be prospering."

"I have no complaints. Wilmington suits me, or it would if there weren't so many damned, grabby Jews flocking in here to profiteer. Oh, they are everywhere. Don't fall in with that lot, my boy. And let me caution you where you go at night. Desperate men here who would rob and kill you for a pittance. Murders here almost every night. Not safe for an honest citizen to walk the streets."

I finished my drink and shook hands with Mr. Abernathy, promising him to stay in touch. And I made my way to the headquarters of Braxton Bragg.

A young clerk with a clubfoot listened to my report. Seemed fascinated by my story.

"The 10th North Carolina, you say?"

"Correct. It was commanded by William Ferro when I was wounded and captured."

"Ah, yes. That unit is part of the forces defending Petersburg. You should report at Petersburg."

"What about my furlough?"

"Should be no difficulty. I'll just take the matter up with Colonel Fincastle and get his approval."

"Fincastle? Elmer Fincastle?"

"Yes. Do you know him?"

"He was the original colonel of the 10th North Carolina. What is he doing here?"

"Why, General Bragg brought him down from Richmond as a staff member. This should take only a few minutes."

It was more like a quarter-hour before he returned, his face red. "I'm sorry, Lieutenant Mundy, but Colonel Fincastle says you must return immediately to your regiment. They need every man at the front."

I was incredulous. "Why, damn it, I haven't seen my family for two and a half years. I have earned a month's furlough, surely."

"I told him your full story, but he was adamant."

"Here, I'll see him myself." I walked past that poor clerk and went directly into Fincastle's office. There he sat, not quite as fat and rosy as I remembered him but still a robust old fart. He wore an annoyed expression at my entrance.

"Look here, Colonel Fincastle. I am James Mundy and your clerk says you refuse to give me a furlough."

"Mundy, my dear fellow. Forgive me for not coming out to explain in person, but I am so burdened with paper work. Such a responsibility. Of course I remember you. But I thought you were a sergeant."

"I was, but Colonel Ferro promoted me just before Gettysburg. Never mind that. Why can't I have a month to see my family?"

"Oh dear me, I have no choice. My orders are to rush all men returning by way of the blockade directly back to their commands. No exceptions are permitted."

"I could have gone directly home and never reported here at all."

"You could have done that, but you would have had no papers and would have been liable to arrest as a deserter."

My voice trembled at this injustice. "I can't believe that you don't have the authority to make an exception. After all I have been through, surely . . ."

Before he could reply, the other door to his office opened. A stooped, bearded officer in the uniform of a Confederate major general spoke. "Elmer, I need to discuss these reports."

"Yes, General Bragg. I was just about through talking to this young man. Explaining to him why he can't have a furlough."

"What does he want with a furlough?"

Fincastle quickly told him my story.

"Makes no difference. We have a car with guards set aside for men to be returned to their commands. See that he is on it!"

With that, he left the office, closing the door behind him. I can see why so few people loved Braxton Bragg. That bastard.

To make a long story short, Elmer Fincastle had his clerk fill out orders, passes and so on for me to present at the station for transportation back to the army.

The clerk apologized. "Actually your colonel may grant you a furlough once you have reported. I am sorry about this."

"I am even sorrier," I replied. "But thanks for trying."

26

What a hell of a way to come back to the Confederate States of America. Welcomed back as a hero who had suffered agonies and endured hell for his country? No, ordered to return immediately to my regiment as if I were absent without leave. No consideration for what I had been through in the past year and a half.

I would have given Elmer Fincastle a generous piece of my

mind, would have reminded him of his own cowardly behavior at New Bern and his general ineptitude had it not been for my own sense of guilt about my brief fling with his ripe little wife back in Raleigh in the spring of '62. As for lacing into General Braxton Bragg, well, there was a limit to the gall even of James Mundy.

As I walked out into the crisp December morning, I considered the possibility of ignoring my orders and setting out for Oldham County, but there were some serious drawbacks. There were no rail connections from Wilmington to my neck of the North Carolina woods. And I had no leave papers. I could end up in disgrace if I were arrested as a deserter. And, truth to tell, I was as homesick for my regiment as I was for my family.

So, like a loyal officer of the Confederate Army, I presented myself at the Wilmington and Weldon station and was directed aboard a ramshackled passenger car filled with a mixed lot of Confederate soldiers. Many were drained and drawn fellows recovering from wounds or illness. A few were teen-aged boys going off to war for the first time. Others were robust chaps returning to the front after furlough. And one, his wrists bound and under guard, was being taken to Raleigh for trial as a deserter.

A bright-looking man in his early thirties made room on the bench beside him for me. He was a surgeon from South Carolina returning to hospital duty in Richmond after a furlough. A talkative, agreeable man, he filled me in on what had happened to the Army of Northern Virginia in the past year and gave me some idea of what to expect at Petersburg.

"It's not like the good old days when Stonewall Jackson and Jeb Stuart were alive and Lee could move about freely. Our army lives in ditches now where it is sure death to raise your head above the parapets. Yes, sir, our lines cover a distance of nearly fifty miles, starting above Richmond and stretching clear down below Petersburg. The Yankees have us pinned there. The armies sharpshoot back and forth at each other and throw mortar shells into each other's lines. There is plenty of food out here in the countryside, but our supply system has broken down so that little of it reaches the soldiers. You can see for yourself what sad shape our railroads have fallen into."

I could indeed see. Our locomotive was a rusty, patched-up affair, badly in need of an overhaul. It lurched along feebly, stopping frequently to take on green firewood or to repair broken tracks. And all through the once prosperous eastern North Carolina countryside, fields were overgrown with weeds and tree seedlings. In the towns, the people—white and black—were shabbily dressed, men in threadbare coats minus their buttons and women in patched dresses. The enthusiastic crowds that used to wave at soldiers and offer them cake or pie were no more.

My surgeon friend described the bloody fighting between Lee and Grant the previous spring and summer in the Wilderness, at Spotsylvania Courthouse, along the North Anna and finally at Cold Harbor, just north of Richmond.

"I tell you Grant lost more men in two months than Lee had in the Army of Northern Virginia, but he kept pressing his offensive. I can't remember a day in that period when the armies weren't in contact, when I was not working on the wounded. Grant could replace his losses and we could not. He gave up his overland drive against Richmond only to shift across the James and move up against Petersburg. Came within a gnat's eye of taking that city in July before Lee could counter him. In fact, your regiment may have had a hand in stopping the Yankees just outside Petersburg. The war would be over now if Petersburg had fallen. That would have cut Richmond off from the south."

"Would that have been so terrible? Lee then would have been free to maneuver."

"No, it would have been fatal. Richmond is vital to the Southern effort. Tredegar and other factories are making cannon, shells, carbines, torpedoes. . . . Richmond is like Washington and Pittsburgh rolled up into one. And the hospital where I work, Chimborazo, is probably the largest and finest military hospital the world has known. Not to mention the fact that Richmond is the capital of the Confederacy."

The surgeon went on and on, telling me the doleful story of unbelievably high prices in Richmond, of increasing desertions from the army, and the near starvation of the men.

"How come the army hasn't collapsed, then? How can it continue to hold the lines and keep Grant out of Petersburg and Richmond if things are in such a bad way?"

"One man is the answer. Robert E. Lee. The rank and file of the Confederate Army worship him. There is little scope now for his tactical genius, but his moral example is an inspiration to us all. Because of him and a kind of stubborn pride, a hard core of battle-tested veterans stays on, enduring poor food, mud, body lice and constant danger. In fact, it is because of Lee that I am returning. I left two small children back in South Carolina with a wife who begged me to stay home. But I have to see this thing through, I couldn't live with myself if I let Robert E. Lee down. Why are you going back?"

"It is simple. If I don't go back, I'll never win the hand of the girl I want to marry."

"Perhaps our situation isn't completely hopeless. The Yankees suffer in their trenches, too. Maybe Lincoln will come to his senses and give us some measure of independence. At any rate, we'll be able to tell our grandchildren some interesting stories of the war. God, when I think of some of the things I have seen done. The operations I have performed. One night at Spotsylvania I lost count of the number of legs and arms I amputated."

Along our hesitant, uncomfortable way, others in our unheated, broken-down car talked to me as well. From them I pieced out the story of the war since July 1863, a story of increasing numbers of Yankee soldiers and growing Northern resources pitted against dwindling Southern numbers, and, now, since the re-election of Abraham Lincoln, deteriorating Confederate morale. They presented a general attitude of grim resignation and hatred for Yankees, all except the deserter who sat there listening to all our talk with a mean look on his dark, bearded face.

"It is a rich man's war and a poor man's fight," he finally muttered.

"What's that?" I asked.

"I say let them that owns niggers fight for them. We poor whites should never have gone to war for rich planters."

Some of the other fellows grumbled at this sentiment but, once having started, the deserter would not be quiet.

"Who gives a damn about Robert E. Lee and Jefferson Davis? They ever follow a mule behind a plow? They ever see their children grow up with no public schools because the Goddamn slaveowners won't spend the tax money? Best thing could have happened to the South would have been to lose the war the first year. You all a bunch of fools to go back and keep fighting the rich man's war for him."

The mood in the car turned ugly. "Shut up, you damned slacker," one soldier said. "You are nothing but a sorry coward who don't love his country enough to fight for it."

"Shit," the deserter said. "I fought as hard as any of you for two years, until my eyes were opened. Worst thing could happen to the poor man and his family would be for the Confederacy to win. The slaveowners would become that much more powerful."

"What are you?" another soldier demanded. "Some kind of abolitionist or just a plain nigger lover?"

"Neither one. I hate niggers and I hate the men that own them. And I hate the Confederate States of America. And I hate Robert E. Lee. I wish he was dead."

This last remark brought half a dozen of my fellow passengers raging to their feet, surrounding the deserter. But his guard held them off by promising to gag his prisoner. From Goldsboro to Raleigh, the unlucky man sat with a dirty handkerchief in his mouth, its ends tied behind his head. They stilled his tongue, but his dark eyes continued to testify against the slaveholders and government of the South.

At Goldsboro, where they shifted our car over to the North Carolina Railroad, I saw something else that testified against the efficiency of the Confederate Government. Piles of potatoes and turnips, collected from area farmers as a "tax in kind," lay along the tracks, half-rotten already, awaiting transportation to the army by the inept Confederate Commissary. My surgeon friend shook his head at the sight.

"How we could use those vegetables at Chimborazo."

(The direct rail line to Petersburg had been cut the previous August. Normally we could have continued as far north as Stony Creek Depot, well into Virginia, and there taken a stage or wagon around the Yankee positions into Petersburg. But there were reports of cavalry raids in the area and so we were switched over to the North Carolina Railroad and thence on a roundabout route through Greensboro, Danville, and into Petersburg over the Southside Railroad.)

It took us three days to reach the battered, semibesieged city of Petersburg on the Appomattox River. I said goodbye to the surgeon, who was going on to Richmond, and sought out the provost guard. Petersburg had run down since I had last seen it. Now it was packed with sick, sad-looking soldiers, lean horses and hordes of unpainted army wagons. The once handsome city showed the wear and tear of a six-month siege.

A bald-headed major with thick spectacles looked over my papers, heard my story and told me how to reach the 10th North Carolina's sector of the entrenchments protecting Petersburg.

"Just go out the City Point Road about a mile and a half. The 10th is part of Ferro's brigade. It is holding the lines near the Appomattox River."

"Ferro's brigade? Who is the commander?"

"Brigadier General William Ferro, of course. He was promoted last summer after his regiment saved Petersburg."

"I'll be damned." I smiled. "Then who commands the 10th now?"

His reply wiped that smile right off my face.

"Shelton. Colonel Thomas Shelton commands what is left of the regiment. It lost over half its strength in one night in July. But it held Petersburg long enough for reinforcements to arrive."

This news made me so incredulous that I continued to stand in front of his table. Finally he looked up from his paper work.

"What's the matter?"

"Nothing. Just wondered how I might get out to my regiment."

"You might walk, if you haven't forgotten how. Or you can go over to the wagon depot and hook a ride out on a wagon. There is a steady traffic of supplies going out and wounded coming back every day. Just ask."

I did just that. A harassed supply lieutenant pointed to a wagon loaded with spades and sharpened stakes and drawn by two decrepit mules.

"That nigger is about to haul a load out to Ferro's brigade. He'll give you a ride."

Thus I soon found myself seated beside a talkative, middle-aged Negro wearing a faded Confederate overcoat.

"Yas, suh. I knows this road by heart. Could drive it in my sleep. Bet I have hauled a mountain of cannon shells and musket cartridges out here in the past two months alone. Yes and I brought back enough wounded soldiers to fill a hospital. Enough dead ones to fill a cemetery, too."

As his two bony mules drew us along, the sound of cannon fire came from our right. After a pause, a louder noise came from closer at hand as Confederate guns replied.

"There they go again. Don't know why they bother. Both sides is dug down in the ground so deep they can't hurt each other much."

I found the Negro amusing. Asked him about himself. Was he free?

"Oh, I belongs to a preacher in Petersburg. Me and my wife. Reverend got so poor he couldn't feed me anymore so he says one day, 'Cyrus, why don't you go get yourself a job?'

"I done just that. Presented myself to the Confederate Army and they signed me up as a teamster. Reverend lets me and my wife keep our room in the carriage house behind the parsonage. My wife does washing for army officers. I collects and delivers it. We getting rich. I'm free to come and go as I please and I keeps my wages, same as a free nigger. All I do for the Reverend is chop a little wood for him and the mistress. They boys in the army. And I brings in army bacon and flour for them, a little at a time. They good white folks. They old now and food costs so much they'd starve if it wasn't for me."

Throughout Petersburg and on the road out to the siege lines, I observed scores of Negroes driving teams for the Confederate Army or loading supplies. They seemed a high-spirited, independent lot who loudly abused their animals and showed no remorse when they splattered whites with mud. Remembering my conversation with Captain Mayfair on the blockade-runner, I wondered what these same teamsters would do if put in Confederate uniform and given muskets.

At the edge of a patch of woods, my driver let me out. "Ask the guard on the other side of the trees. You want to be careful, though. The Yankees could start shelling any minute. Or one of their sharpshooters might spot you out in the open."

Cyrus began singing at the top of his voice as he drew away.

"Oh, how I love Jesus. Oh, how I love Jee-sus," he sang in a clear baritone. Just then one of his mules shied and stumbled.

"You lop-eared son of a bitch. Watch where you going. Get your ass moving there."

He lashed the unfortunate beast across the rump and resumed his song. "Oh, how I love Jesus. Because he first loved me."

Laughing at the spectacle, I made my way through the grove whose trees bore the unmistakable signs of many shells having burst there. On the other side, I walked into the rear of a lunette protecting a battery of 30-pounder Parrotts, huge field cannon that could hurl a missile three miles. These long-barreled guns and their crews were shielded by an outer bank of earth and an inner one made up of stacks of sandbags.

"The 10th North Carolina?" an artillery sergeant said. "Yes, you will find them in the ditches ahead there about three hundred yards, just to the left. Regimental headquarters is under that pile of sandbags, see there?"

Through an embrasure, I could see a line of earthern banks stretching from the Appomattox River on my left far off out of sight to my right. And behind these entrenchments lay various dugouts or bombproofs and well-protected positions for mortars and light artillery. When I see pictures in the papers today from the Western Front in France, I am reminded of the works around Petersburg. Only in that day we did not have barbed wire or machine guns. And the soldiers did not wear helmets.

"Can I just walk down there?" I asked the sergeant.

"I'd suggest that you run. And keep low when you do. As tall as you are, some Yankee sharpshooter likely would see you."

"Are they as close as that?"

"Hell, yes. The Yanks are dug in about two hundred yards beyond your regiment. Your friends will tell you about them."

As we talked, the shelling in the distance increased. And, closer at hand, several musket shots rang out. I pulled my hat squarely over my forehead, ducked my head and started running.

"Spang!" a bullet zipped over my head. I fell to the ground as another shot passed overhead. I had forgotten what it felt like to be shot at. Several musket shots sounded from within our lines and someone shouted, "Come on in. We got them pinned down."

I arose and ran the remaining distance, unhindered, to where a man stood in a shallow communications trench outside the rear of the bombproof.

"In here."

He was a one-armed man wearing a major's insignia and he stood in the doorway of the sandbagged dugout. I leaped into the trench beside him and looked into the face of my old schoolmate, Noah Rhine, a Noah Rhine who had gone gray around his temples and whose face had turned leathery and whose eyes had become prematurely wise.

"Noah," I said.

He frowned. "Who are you? And what are you doing out here drawing fire on us?"

"Don't you know me, Noah?"

"Maybe if you told me your name, it would help."

"I am Jim Mundy. I was captured at Gettysburg, but I escaped."

I would not have thought it possible that a face as leathery and brown as Noah Rhine's could turn so white. His jaw dropped open and he literally staggered back against the door sill of the bombproof.

"It can't be. You are dead. I saw you fall. Your head was blown open."

"It was just my eye, Noah. I crawled off in the wrong direction in the night and the Yankees picked me up."

"I'll be Goddamn," Noah swore for the first time in my memory. "You aren't dead. Son of a bitch, Jim."

The Noah Rhine I remembered had not been a very demonstrative fellow, but this older version threw his one arm around me and hugged me till my shoulders ached.

27

Something like that same scene was repeated a dozen times during the next two hours. First, Noah Rhine sent a messenger for Harry McGee, asking him to report immediately to the bombproof.

"Harry is commander of Company H, or what is left of it. It

is down to platoon size. But Harry is doing a fine job."

Harry looked like a mud-splattered ghost when he saw me. Once it sank in that I was alive, he gave a Rebel yell and proceeded to pound me on the back.

Noah and Harry wanted an account of my adventures since Gettysburg. What a contrast we made compared to the three fresh-faced schoolboys who had got drunk together on that first train to Raleigh, three years earlier. Noah, a major with one empty sleeve; Harry, a mean, hard-looking captain; and I, a one-eyed scarecrow of a figure wearing a silly yachtsman's cap.

After hearing me out and accusing me repeatedly of lying or exaggerating, they told me of how, after returning to Virginia from our defeat at Gettysburg, the 10th North Carolina had been assigned to Longstreet's corps, had been put on a train and shuttled across the Carolinas and Georgia to arrive just in time to take part in the spectacular but empty Southern victory at Chickamauga, in September 1863; then of how they had marched across eastern Tennessee in a fruitless attempt to take Knoxville away from our old Yankee friend Ambrose Burnside. The regiment then had marched over the mountains back into North Carolina, where, in April of 1864 they had helped retake the coast town of Plymouth. They had missed out on the savage fighting between Lee and Grant in May but had been shifted into Virginia to "bottle up" General "Beast" Butler at Bermuda Hundred below Richmond. The following month, in June, they had been rushed down to Petersburg to save that key railroad town from an attack from the east.

"Ah, Jim," said Noah. "You never saw anything like the fighting. The Yankees outnumbered us two and three to one at times. We shot them down in droves, but they finally got possession of our works. Colonel Ferro led us in the counterattack. We went in and fought them hand to hand. Lost our colors there, but we captured two of theirs. Captain Cadieu was killed that night. So were Sam Elkins and Bob Miner. That's where I lost my hand."

"And that is where I split my musket stock on some Michigan

Yankee's thick skull," Harry interjected. "Noah is right. We never fought like that before. Lost about half our regiment, but we retook the position."

They went on to tell me of how Southern reinforcements had arrived just ahead of even more Yankees until finally about forty thousand Confederates were blocking the way of sixty thousand Federals and Lee came down in person to help them stabilize their lines with new entrenchments.

"That is the way it has been ever since last June," Noah said. "We are stuck here in these blasted ditches."

"Except for the mine. Tell him about the mine," Harry said.

They spoke, of course, of the mine set off under a Confederate strongpoint on July 30. The 10th then had occupied a stretch of the entrenchments next to the spot where a crew of Pennsylvania coal miners had dug a tunnel and exploded several tons of gunpowder.

"The explosion shook the ground like an earthquake. Sent cannon and men sailing up into the air and blasted a huge crater in our lines," Noah recounted. "Then the Yanks sent across four divisions, one of them black, intending to drive straight through to Petersburg. But we cornered them in the crater. It was beautiful. Like shooting fish in a barrel. They lost thousands before they withdrew."

"And since then?"

"Since then they shifted us over here and we have been living like moles in the ground ever since. It ain't the same war any more."

"How about Colonel Ferro? I hear he is a general now."

"Sure is. A brigadier. He is off in Richmond today to see about our getting new uniforms and better rations."

"But is Tom Shelton really our colonel? If I had known that, I would have stayed in Canada."

"He is our colonel all right. Not quite as big a bully as he used to be. He is home on furlough now."

After we three old school chums had done talking, Harry insisted on leading me, unannounced, through the communications trench and into the main defense work manned by our old company. A general hubbub arose as my old comrades recognized me.

Aside from Noah, Harry and me, only two men remained from our original squad of twelve. I looked in vain for the familiar faces of Bob Perry, Ed Engerer, and John Sutton. Only Frank Kugle and Jack Davis were left. But to my amazement, there, holding an Enfield musket and standing on the firing step of the trench, was none other than Hiram Winchester, the hard-bitten old miller from Oldham County, the same man who had been ridden on a rail back in May of '61 because he dared speak out against North Carolina's getting involved in the war.

"Cousin Hiram," I greeted him. "You are the last person I ever expected to see in the army. What are you doing here?"

"I'm standing guard duty, as any fool can see."

"But you were so against the war."

"I was against the war and I still am. But I never said I was against my own people. Bunch of damned fools got us into this mess. Figured it was my duty to help get us out."

"But you are too old."

"Nobody's business how old I am. Besides, a man is no older than he feels. They were going to conscript me into the home guards anyway and I told them hell no if I was going to be in uniform I would come up here and get into the real war. Wasn't going to run around chasing deserters and guarding prisoners at Salisbury."

"Don't you low-rate Uncle Hiram," Harry laughed. "He is the best shot in Company H. When he goes on sharpshooter duty, the Yanks all take cover."

"What did your wife say when you told her you were joining the army?" I asked.

"Said she always knew I was a damn fool so to go ahead. Now you quit pestering me. I can't shoot Yankees and talk to you at the same time."

What a stretch of filthy stinking ditch my old friends occupied. The floor of the trench was littered with peanut hulls and was slick with mud and tobacco juice. An open-air latrine pit, nearly overflowing, had been dug into one side. A firing step ran along the other wall. There were sandbagged portals for lookouts and sharpshooters along the parapet.

Harry McGee gave me a tour up and down the line. He told me what to do if a mortar shell fell into the trench. "If the fuse is long enough, toss it over the side, toward the enemy. If not, throw yourself down and cover your ears."

"They actually fall in the trench sometimes?"

"Last month they dropped one right in our shit hole and it exploded there. Worse thing ever happened to us. Took two days to clean up the mess."

Finally he showed me how to peer out toward the Yankee lines through a crack in a wall of sandbags. I looked out at a cleared space protected by a line of sharpened stakes set into braced rows and beyond to a long bank of earth behind which our blue-clad enemy huddled, or so he said.

"Are you sure anybody is over there?" I asked. "I see no sign of them."

"Give me your cap," Harry said.

Before I could stop him, he had taken the fine sailing hat I bought in Canada, put it on a stick, and raised its brim just above the lip of the trench.

"Crack!" A rifle spoke from the Yankee lines and the cap spun around with a hole in it.

"Bang!" Cousin Hiram Winchester's Enfield replied and the old man cackled, "By God, I think I got the son of a bitch. Saw his arm fly up like he was hit. Knew the bastard was over there. Holed up beside that tree stump."

He ducked his head as a fusillade of bullets smacked into his sandbags and sang over our heads.

"That calls for a fresh chaw of tobacco."

Harry handed him a twist. "Keep the whole thing, Uncle Hiram. I'll buy you a wagonload if you keep killing Yankees like that."

I went up and down that foul trench renewing friendships in

my old company and others of the 10th N.C. There were a few new faces among them, boys of sixteen or seventeen who had deviled their parents into letting them sign up. And a few older fellows like Cousin Hiram. Mainly, though, the troops manning those works were the battle-hardened remnant of those thousand-odd men who had left the field in panic at New Bern and who had gone up against the Federal cannon at Malvern Hill. I dare say that these same three-hundred men at New Bern would have made that battle turn out quite differently if they had been there. For despite their poor rations and bad living conditions, they were as mean and lethal a crew of soldiers as could be found. Efficient, single-minded killers of men they had become.

It did not take me long to make the acquaintance of a new set of characters. There had been an outbreak of body lice in camp at Fredericksburg, but we had kept them under control by boiling our clothes. Now the lice had the advantages. Every man and his garb in that trench was alive with the evil creatures.

"Don't do no good to scratch," Jack Davis advised me. "Just stirs them up. You can scrape them off, but they are just like the Yankees. Kill one and two take his place."

At supper that night, I, along with the others in Company H, partook of the normal rations, which were a cup of lumpy, half-cooked corn meal and a slab of fatback, carried down from a field kitchen behind the lines. As I ate, I thought ruefully of the tons of good bacon we had tossed overboard from the *Miriam* and of the piles of potatoes and turnips I had seen rotting beside the railroad in North Carolina.

I slept that night huddled in a louse-ridden blanket in the regimental bombproof. It was a fitful sleep, full of dreams of home and of my beautiful Jane Ferro.

As I was eating my breakfast (the same menu as for supper with the addition of a helping of molasses over the corn mush), William Ferro came into the bombproof. His hair hung to his shoulders and he wore a full blond beard. And he was dressed in a resplendent gray wool uniform, brand-new as it turned out. He was accompanied by Cassius, the black house servant who was married to Reba, the "mammy" of the Ferro family.

"James. I couldn't believe the good news. Had to come to see for myself. You are alive. My goodness, Reba was right."

"Reba?"

"Yes. She kept telling Jane you weren't dead. Said she dreamed you were alive but wounded. And that you would return. Isn't that right, Cassius?"

"Yes, suh. She sho did."

I remembered to salute, at last. "It is General Ferro, I hear. Congratulations, sir. How is Miss Jane?"

"Good, the last time I saw her. I was home briefly after we returned from Knoxville. Little Ernest has joined the North Carolina Junior Reserves and has been sent down to Wilmington. Father and mother are in good health. They insisted on sending Cassius back with me. Bring me up to date on yourself."

Noah Rhine, who was weary of my tale, left us alone. General Ferro sat down on a cracker box and listened closely to my story, interrupting occasionally to ask for more details. We talked for more than an hour.

"Incredible," he said at the end. "And Fincastle and Bragg refused to give you a furlough after all that?"

"They would not, sir."

"What a pair. They deserve each other. Well, I can fix things for you. Look, Tom Shelton is away on furlough but will be back in a few days. The regimental records are in bad shape. We never replaced you after Gettysburg. How about putting his returns in proper order and then you can have a month free to go home, see your family and Jane as well. Governor Vance has sent up a carload of new uniforms for North Carolina troups. You can go into Petersburg and get yourself a complete new outfit. Let's see, I made you a lieutenant just before Gettysburg, I believe."

"Yes, you did."

"All right, I'll use my influence to promote you to captain.

And upon your return from your furlough, I may find a place for you on my staff."

He went on to tell me of how upset Jane had been at reports of my death. "She had been steeling herself to speak to father about her feeling for you. How overjoyed she will be. I'll give you a letter to deliver to Father so you will have an excuse to visit Beaulieu. Things should be easier for you now. What a story! Come on, Cassius. We must continue our rounds."

So, for the next several days, I stayed with my old regiment there in the line outside Petersburg. At last, five days after Christmas, Tom Shelton showed up. His face was gaunt and he no longer held those powerful shoulders so squarely.

"So there you are, Mundy. Heard you were alive and back."

He didn't offer to shake hands. I saluted and tried to keep the sarcasm out of my voice as I replied, "Yes, sir, Colonel Shelton."

"General Ferro informs me that you want a furlough for thirty days. In view of the shortage of manpower here, your furlough can be only for two weeks, however."

I felt like smashing my fist into that arrogant face. "Two weeks? That is hardly enough time to get home."

"Sorry, but here are your leave orders. And a requisition for a uniform and back pay. And your commission as captain."

"Where is General Ferro?"

"He was called back to Richmond."

I knew I was defeated. Rather than to waste time arguing I took the papers and with a look of scorn on my face saluted Colonel Shelton and set out for the clothing warehouse in Petersburg. I thought nothing of it at the time, but when I reached the protection of the artillery lunette and looked back, he was still watching me.

In Petersburg, they outfitted me with a gorgeous officer's uniform made of the finest English wool, complete with a heavy gray overcoat and excellent boots. They even scrounged me up a good leather holster for the Colt revolver given me by Bennett Young in Canada.

And, at the paymaster's office, I exchanged my requisition for

$1,500 in Confederate bills representing one and a half years of back pay.

It was two hours until the next train on the Southside Railroad and during that time I had my photograph taken in a studio in Petersburg. I tried to buy some gifts for my family and for Jane, but the goods were so few and the prices so high I decided to save my money. They were asking $500 for a pair of boots. Imagine.

So it was that in the closing days of 1864, I boarded the train, my heart singing with hope and the pockets of my new captain's uniform bulging with Confederate money.

Hope. God knows how many sermons I have heard preached on the business about hope, faith and charity, always with the last-named virtue being extolled and faith running a poor second, with hope being left out of the contest altogether. But what miserable creatures we humans would be without hope. That neglected, unsung virtue had sustained me in hospital and prison. And my heart fairly burst with it as I rode in that rickety car across the red-clay terrain of south-central Virginia. At long last my hopes were near realization. Never mind the fact that the tides of war ran strongly against the South. Forget the near-worthless money, the shortages of necessities, the greed of profiteers, the dilapidation of equipment, or the grief of people who had lost sons and husbands, brothers and sweethearts. I, James Mundy, newly promoted to captain and all got up in a well-tailored new gray uniform, was returning to my home with honor. I was a hero. I was no longer a bumpkin of a preacher's son without status. I had been to Canada and Bermuda. I had been to sea, had even bossed a crew of cutthroat sailors and had held my own with sea captains. No one or no thing had been able to break my spirit. I had prevailed and now I was going home to claim my reward. Hot diggety damn!

28

That miserable train crept with many a halt across Virginia to the town of Danville. In Danville I changed over to the newly constructed Piedmont Line, built by the Confederates to close the forty-eight-mile rail gap to Greensboro, North Carolina. There I took the North Carolina R.R. cars for Charlotte. Required two days and nights to cover a roundabout distance from Richmond one of our modern Southern Railroad trains can travel these days in five hours.

In Charlotte the Confederate Government had established a naval yard. Put it there, far inland in the Piedmont, and brought in steam hammers and such equipment to produce armor plate for ironclad vessels and for the repair of steam engines. What I had known as an energetic little market town had become an industrial center, thronged with mechanics and with refugees from the coastal area.

It was late afternoon when I arrived. I had no desire to spend the night in a hotel. So I went around to the livery stable and found the owner, the fellow who so kindly had taken the trouble soon after the battle of New Bern to drive the wounded William Ferro and me out to Oldham County.

Took a while for him to remember me and even when he did he was not nearly so cordial or accommodating as he had been two and a half years before when the war had been young and wounded veterans were a rarity.

"Rent you a horse for a week? I have only got a pair of mules and one old saddle horse anymore. The damned Confederate Government has cleaned me out. I only keep this stable to board horses for other people. Have to keep the place locked and a shotgun near at hand or somebody would steal my customers' stock."

I explained my anxiety to get home.

"I have heard many such sad stories in recent months. You have proper leave papers, I suppose."

"Indeed I do," I said, holding them out with an offended air.

"Never mind. Did not mean to insult you, but some bastard in Confederate uniform hired my last good horse last month and I haven't seen him since. His name just showed up on a list of deserters sent out from Raleigh. I should have got a deposit in gold."

"You can hold my pistol and $500."

"Confederate?"

"The pistol is Union; the money Confederate."

He laughed. "Was afraid of that. Oh, what the hell. You have suffered more from this stupid war than I. It is not your fault Jefferson Davis is a damned fool. Just don't gallop my good old steed."

He led out a hip-sprung gray nag that looked ready for the bone yard.

"Haven't got a saddle for you. But we can strap on a blanket."

I turned over my revolver with the holster and gave him $500 in C.S.A. bills. He gave me a receipt.

As I mounted the horse, the livery stable fellow continued to talk. "He is what I call a Confederate gray. I have named him Joe Johnston, because he is so slow."

I gave him a polite laugh, dug my dangling heels into Joe Johnston's lean flanks and set off at a stumbling walk for Oldham County. I was glad no one I knew could see the ridiculous spectacle of a smartly dressed Confederate officer riding such a broken-down horse without a saddle.

Fortunately I knew the road well, for dark soon overtook me. On and on through the long, cold North Carolina night we plodded, me with dreams of what soon would be and Joe Johnston, I suppose, with dreams of his long-ago colthood.

North of Meadsboro a bit, I turned off for the Big Rock Camp Grounds area. And, just as the sun began to appear over the frosty landscape, I came in sight of our unpainted old house. Home! And then I was back in the bare yard where I had played as a tot.

I tied the gray to a chinaberry tree and tried the front door but it was locked. Had to knock three times before I heard the footsteps of my father in the hall.

"Who is there? What do you want?"

"Why don't you open the door and find out?"

The door opened tentatively and I stared into the face of my gentle old father. He stood there in his nightshirt, looking puzzled.

"Can I help you?" he asked.

"Father, it's me."

"Who?"

"Me, Jim. I'm home."

"Jim is dead. Killed at Gettysburg."

"No, he is not. He is standing here in front of you."

He opened the door wider and at last exclaimed, "Dear kind heavenly Father. It is Jim. Oh, my goodness. Mother, come here and see who it is."

With tears streaming down his sweet face that kind old man put his arms around me. Then Mother, her long gray hair hanging down to her waist, came into the hall, recognized me right off, gave a shriek and fell to hugging and kissing me.

It took me several minutes to convince them I was not a ghost. When it was settled that I was living flesh and blood, my father made us kneel in that cold hallway while he prayed out his thanks to his God of Mercy.

"Enough praying, Robert," my mother interrupted him. "James Mundy, what have you done to your eye?"

After that had been explained, they led me to the kitchen and had me sit in a chair while they walked around, viewing me from every angle.

It came my turn to ask a question. "Where is Wesley?"

"We tried to keep him back but they started taking sixteen-year-old boys in the Junior Reserve and he just would go. He went off last week to Wilmington."

They poked up the fire and, still bombarding me with questions, prepared me a breakfast of genuine ham, fresh eggs and grits.

"We can't get coffee and sugar anymore. Or salt. But we eat well enough," my mother said.

"The Lord provides for us," my father added.

So I was home, my heart full of happiness but my body worn-out with the fatigue of the train trip and my all-night ride on an impossibly slow horse without a saddle.

At last they let me go to bed. I slept until past noon. I awoke to find that my mother had made me a molasses cake and had brushed and pressed my uniform.

They were hurt that I wanted to set out for Beaulieu right away, but after I explained that I was under orders from General Ferro to deliver a letter to his father they stopped protesting. Fortunately Pa had an old saddle he used for riding his mule on preaching trips and he lent it to me.

I calculated that I would arrive at Beaulieu not so close to suppertime as to appear to be cadging a meal but still near enough so that an invitation could be accepted.

With my eye patch and hat firmly in place, I mounted Joe Johnston and pointed him south, toward the old Manawee Indian lands where the aristocracy of Oldham County lived.

There was a great surplus of womenfolk, many of them wearing shabby black dresses. I crossed the creek where the bully boy secessionists had dunked Cousin Hiram Winchester and past the courthouse square where I had first encountered Elmer J. Fincastle and where I had first laid eyes on Jane Ferro. There was the very spot where she later had stood when she discreetly kissed me goodbye.

Finally there came into view the long tree-lined lane leading to the great brick main house of Beaulieu. A cold wind swirled over the surrounding fields of corn stubble and around the house and its many outbuildings. I lashed my Confederate gray into something like a trot and rode him around to the stable at the rear.

"You are back. I told her you would come back."

Reba, the part-Indian woman and wife of Cassius, was coming out of the kitchen house.

"Hello, Reba. I am back. Did you think I was dead?"

"I knew nothing could kill anybody with as much gall as you is got. But Miss Jane didn't believe me. She tried to, but she couldn't."

"Where is she?"

"Inside. Tie up that sorry-looking horse. Now straighten your coat. Follow me."

She led me through the back hall and up the great stairway to the door of a small family sitting room. There, before a small fire, sat Jane Ferro, her head bent over her embroidery work. As she looked up, I had only an instant to study her face. The touch of little girl softness had disappeared. It was a sadder and more mature but even more touchingly beautiful countenance than I remembered. Her hair was as red as ever.

"Jane." My voice was hoarse.

"It can't be."

"Yes, it is," Reba, who stood behind me, said. "It is him. I tried to tell you."

"Oh, dear God." Her embroidery fell to the floor. She did not rise. I went over and stood beside her.

"It is me. I am back."

"It is not possible."

"I told you couldn't nobody kill that farm boy," Reba went on. "Told you he would come back."

"Oh, my soul, Jim. You really are alive."

Still she did not rise. Did not put her arms around me and kiss me as she had a thousand times in my imagination. She sat there, her lovely mouth half-open, her face stark-white and her eyes beginning to well with tears.

It remained for Reba to draw up a chair beside her. "Sit

down, boy. She has lost her manners, it looks like."

I sat facing her, growing confused by her failure to show any feeling other than surprise.

"I thought you were dead. William wrote that you had fallen at Gettysburg. He said you had been killed outright and left on the field."

"She wore black for a year after the letter came—" Reba began.

Jane cut her off. "Reba, that is enough. You may leave us."

"I thought of you a thousand times. I was in prison for more than a year. I wrote to you often but discovered they had not been sending my letters through."

I was in the midst of my story, babbling away nervously, when first her father and then her mother came in.

"So it wasn't Reba's imagination, Mundy. You are alive after all." Her father gave me a brief, formal handshake. The same self-assured, patrician air was there. How little he had changed as compared with his son, Noah Rhine or me, insulated as he was by wealth and geography here far from the war.

"I have a letter here from your son, from General Ferro."

"That was good of you to ride halfway across the county just to deliver a letter. Thank you."

Mrs. Ferro gave me a somewhat warmer but still formal greeting. They asked me a few questions about where I had been, all without mention of my very obvious eyepatch.

"As you can see, I lost an eye at Gettysburg."

"Too bad," said Mrs. Ferro.

"It has been a bad war," her husband said. "Harder than any of us expected, but Tom Shelton was telling us just last week that our lines are holding strong and that he thinks General Lee may have some surprises in store for Grant in the spring."

That name jarred me. "Tom Shelton?"

"Yes. Tom brought us fully up to date on conditions in the army. He doesn't think the Yankees have the stomach for more of the heavy losses we inflicted on them last spring and summer."

"Tom Shelton . . ." I stupidly repeated the name and then stood mutely while they waited for me to finish my sentence. At last Mrs. Ferro filled the awkward gap.

"Surely you know Tom. He is the colonel of your regiment now."

"Yes," her husband added. "And as Jane probably has told you already, she and he are to be married in the spring."

Mrs. Ferro stopped him. "I expect Jane would want to tell Mr. Mundy about that in her own way."

I shall remember to my dying day, with bitterness, the sound of Ernest Ferro's voice continuing, with what I later decided was a twist of cruelty, "Ah, since it has been announced in church, Jane's betrothal is hardly a secret."

Jane's face looked pained. "Father . . ." she started.

"Ernest," Mrs. Ferro said, "why don't we excuse ourselves for a little while and read William's letter? Mister Mundy, I am pleased that you are home safe and sound. I know your family must be overjoyed. Jane, we'll leave you to visit a bit, but don't forget that the Sheltons and the Liddles are invited for six o'clock."

At last we were alone.

"You are marrying Tom Shelton?"

"Yes. We announced our engagement last week."

"Jane. How could you? I thought we . . ."

She would not look at me. I continued.

"You have made a fool of me. All those letters you wrote. I used to recite them in prison to keep my sanity."

"Jim, don't."

"But you don't know how I suffered. How I hoped."

She raised her face. "And you don't know how I suffered or hoped, James. I felt like a widow when the news came last year. It is true what Reba said. I dressed in black and it made Father furious. I grieved for you for a year. And then I put away my mourning clothes. You men don't know what suffering is. And then I began to live again."

"But Tom Shelton. Why him?"

"Jim, I am twenty-one now. My mother was married at eighteen and her mother at sixteen. Did you think I would never—"

"Surely you can't love Tom Shelton."

"I am going to marry him. I must."

"Must? Just because it has been announced? Jane, I am an officer, a captain, now. I am as good as Tom Shelton. I am as good as your father. You can't treat me so coldly."

"I must."

"Is it my eye? You can't bear to think of being married to a one-eyed man? Or is it because of my family, because they are not rich? Is that it?"

"Please don't, James. I can't help what happened. And I did care for you deeply."

"But you care more for Tom Shelton. You really are going to marry that swaggering, overbearing bully. How can you?"

"I simply must. It is all settled."

I am ashamed of what I did next. There was that lovely face, more beautiful than I remembered, turned up to me, full of what I took to be either pity or disgust rather than love, and I slapped it so hard that she fell against her chair back.

My voice thick with rage, I swore at her. "You are a damned, spoiled, rich little bitch. To think I have spent three years of my life fighting so people like you can have niggers to fetch and carry for you."

She gasped. "How could you misunderstand so?"

"You and all of your family can go to hell."

I walked out of that house, past an anxious Reba, and mounted the old gray horse.

That livery stable owner did not know how his nag could gallop. I flogged that poor beast all the way to Meadsboro and beyond.

29

It was a good thing I had given my revolver to that livery stable chap as a deposit or I might well have shot myself in my rage and despair. I refused to weep. But I did not resist the cold rage I felt or the regrets. If only I had not been wounded and captured or if I had escaped in Baltimore or if that hateful little homosexual clerk at Johnson's Island had not stopped my letters home, or if by some miracle I had landed on the Ohio shore and had been able to travel overland to North Carolina or even if I had defied Elmer Fincastle and General Braxton Bragg and had made my way directly home from Wilmington.

No, damn it, the thing wasn't meant to be. If I had been from a better family or had not lost my eye, Jane Ferro would have called off her engagement to Tom Shelton without thinking twice. Damn her. She had treated me like I was a piece of dirt.

God forgive me for the way I in turn treated my parents. I withdrew from conversations with them, taking the edge off their joy at having me home. I could have stayed with them for a week, but after the second day of moping about, I told them I had just enough time to return to the army before my furlough expired. I could not tell them that I no longer had a home or a heart. The closest thing I now had to either lay with the Confederate Army. There at least with my new captaincy I would have status, and there I would have a job of killing Yankees. And I was in the mood to kill.

Sniffing back her tears, my mother packed me a great basket of roasted sweet potatoes, peanuts and apples. My father insisted on praying over me again. I kissed them goodbye and set out for Charlotte on my old rented gray nag.

The livery stable fellow gave me back my revolver and $400 of the Confederate money. Joe Johnston seemed relieved that he was free of the madman who had used him so roughly.

I took the cars to Greensboro, a distance of about a hundred miles. En route there, I found that one way to take my mind off the faithless Jane Ferro was to think hard about the first woman in my life, Elvira Fincastle. That helped my state of mind.

In Greensboro, I learned that there was a delay in the train to Danville but that another was about to leave for Raleigh. What the hell, I thought. I could make my way back to Petersburg by that route. And so, seven hours later, I found myself in the state's capital city. It was early evening and no trains to Richmond until the next morning. This put me in an even fouler state of mind. I walked out and bought a bottle of corn liquor, took a swig from it, and put it in my overcoat pocket. There was a depot in town where a Confederate officer could stay, but before applying there I decided to take a stroll around town. And so it was that I walked down the street past the little bungalow where Elvira Fincastle had taught me the delights of the flesh nearly three years before.

A light shone from the window. "Maybe whoever lives there now can tell me where she is; probably still in Richmond or else down in Wilmington with her fat husband."

I knocked and to my amazement the door was opened by Elvira herself, looking somewhat older and plumper than I remembered but still an attractive woman.

"Yes? What may I do for you?"

"Elvira, it's me, Jim Mundy. Remember me?"

I was prepared to run through my now practiced explanation of my return from the dead and all that, but then I remembered that she had had no news of me since April of 1862 when I had rolled naked out of her bedroom window and into a thorn bush.

"James Mundy. How could I ever forget you? Oh, my dear boy. Your eye. You look so much older. Do come in and let me look at you."

A baby boy of about two sat in front of the fire, playing with a kitten. He was a handsome little fellow with dark-blue eyes and black hair.

Elvira took my overcoat and made me sit down. Her eyes never left my face as she listened to my story.

"What an adventure. And your poor family thought you were dead all those months."

"Yes."

She became coy. "I seem to remember your saying you didn't have a girl friend. Did that situation change?"

"It did for a while, but she did not wait for me. She is going to marry someone else."

"You sound as though she hurt you."

Not trusting my voice, I nodded my head.

"Poor James. Serves you right though for never coming back to see me and after the way you led me astray, you naughty boy. You ought to be ashamed."

I had thought I would never again smile, but that woman's sly pertness, plus the warmth of the whisky I had drunk plus that of the fire all worked against my grim mood.

"James, how glad I am to see you. My husband is away helping General Bragg defend Wilmington. He sent little Elmer and me back here from Richmond in October. I really shouldn't be so bold, but I don't suppose there would be any harm in inviting a Confederate officer to stay for supper, would there?"

I winked at her. "I won't tell your husband if you don't."

"You are a devil."

Considering the shortages of the times, it was a good supper, tasty food prepared by a warm, feminine woman, and it did my spirits much good. I had had no appetite since visiting the Ferro house. I helped Elvira clean up the kitchen and together we tucked the little boy in his crib in the very room where Elmer Fincastle very nearly had caught me in bed with his wife.

Back in the snug living room, I produced the bottle of corn liquor from my overcoat pocket. Elvira made some hypocritical protests about drinking but then went and got two glasses while I put more wood on the fire.

We sat there in front of the fire like an old married couple, talking with mock politeness until after she had taken her second drink of my liquor and her tongue loosened.

"James Mundy. How many times have I lain awake at night thinking of you? You bad boy, not to come back to see me again after you promised. No, I take that back. You are not a boy anymore, but you are still bad, I'll bet." She giggled and winked.

"No, Elvira, I am not a boy anymore. The war has changed me."

"Me, too. It has changed us all. I was so innocent before the war, when Mr. Fincastle and I were married. I thought I was marrying a prominent politician. Thought he would go on from being a big preacher to something like governor or senator. But to tell the truth I know now that Elmer Fincastle has his deficiencies."

"He wasn't exactly the best colonel in the army," I began. I started to go on to tell her what an ass-kissing old windbag and incompetent he really was but checked myself.

"He wasn't cut out for the military life," she continued. "I thought he would make a good Confederate official, but it seems that after they get to know him people don't take him seriously. I know a wife should not run her husband down, but oh, why pretend? James, you gave me more happiness those few times you came to this house than I have ever known before or after."

She was on the verge of tears. "How I longed for you. Why didn't you come to see me again? Was it because of that girl who did not wait for you?"

"Yes, Elvira."

"And has she wounded you? Why didn't she wait for a splendid fellow like you, so tall and bright and good-looking?"

The liquor had loosened my tongue, too. Haltingly, I told her the story of how I had met Jane Ferro and of the growing intimacy of our letters. And then, barely able to keep back my own tears, I told her of our final meeting and of my learning of her engagement.

Elvira wept for me. She dried her tears to accept my offer of yet another drink. Then she came and sat on my lap, running her fingers through my hair and kissing me lightly on the cheeks, while murmuring little sounds of comfort.

She did not stop me when I began to unbutton her dress. At last, she stood up, stepped out of her bloomers and stood before me, plump and fair in her nakedness. I stood, too, and she helped me out of my uniform. Then she spread my heavy new overcoat in front of the fire and lay on it.

"Come to me, James," she said. "We need each other."

Later, after making sure the child was asleep, we got into the great brass bed and I made love to her again, this time like a savage, so that she cried out in fear once.

Then we slept and, just before dawn, we came together once more, gently.

"James," she whispered. "You really have become a man. So much better than I remembered or even imagined. I won't ask you where you learned."

We dressed quietly so as not to awaken the child. I stopped to admire the sleeping boy.

"Fine little chap," I said.

"Just like his daddy," Elvira replied.

She begged me to stay on with her. I lied by saying that if I didn't catch that train to Petersburg I would be declared a deserter. She cried and asked if I loved her. I lied again and said "Yes."

I thought it would be a long time before I could feel the kind of love I had experienced for Jane Ferro. I could go to a woman out of lust and loneliness but not out of love. Still, while I did not love Elvira Fincastle, I was grateful to that strangely sensual and yet innocent, generous married woman. She helped bring me back to life.

She wept again as I put on my overcoat.

"I can't bear to go on living if you don't come back, James.

Look, the Confederacy can't hold out much longer, can it? Come back and we can go out west. Take little Elmer and start a new life together."

"I'll think about it. I'd hate to break up a family; take a wife and child away from a man like that."

"You'd only be taking his wife, James."

"What do you mean?"

"You are stupid. When were you here before?"

"April of 1862."

"And what is this date?"

"Why, it is January 3, 1865. Happy New Year, Elvira."

"It is also little Elmer's second birthday."

"Yes?"

"How many months between April 1862 and January 3, 1863?"

"About nine months." It began to dawn on me.

"Look at my eyes. What color are they?"

"Why, a lovely shade of light brown."

"Yes, and you may have not noticed that Colonel Fincastle has dark-brown eyes. The color of horse turds. Whereas you and little Elmer both have blue eyes of very much the same shade."

"Elvira . . ."

"I can't be sure, of course, but you must admit that after sleeping with Elmer Fincastle for five years, it is strange I should bear a child only after jumping over the fence with you."

I didn't know what else to do, so I hugged her.

"Now do you promise to come back to me?"

"I promise."

And I half-believed that I would. That warm, trusting woman.

30

At Petersburg I went directly to brigade headquarters. Cassius told me to wait while General Ferro finished a conference with his five regimental commanders. I did not trust myself to look at Tom Shelton as the meeting broke up.

General Ferro, after expressing surprise at my early return, invited me to sit down and tell him about my visit home. I told him of my meeting with his parents and with Jane, everything except my slapping his sister.

"And Jane will not change her mind about marrying Shelton?"

"She said she would not. Hardly gave me a chance to plead my case."

He shook his head. "James, I am so sorry. I knew that Shelton and she had been corresponding, but thought nothing of it. They used to play together as children, you know. It was a shock to me when Shelton came back with the news they are formally engaged. I had hoped you would get there in time."

"I did not and now it is over between us."

"What can I do in such a situation?"

"Nothing. I only ask that you remove me from any contact with Tom Shelton. I couldn't bear to serve under him after this."

"This is no problem. Henceforth you will be on my brigade staff. Morale is not good. Perhaps you can help me restore it."

"My own morale is not so good," I replied. "But I'll try."

And that is how I spent the first three months of 1865 (and, as it turned out, the last three of the Civil War), serving as aide to Brigadier General William Ferro.

Our brigade returns for the first week of 1865 showed approximately fifteen hundred men present and more or less fit for duty. Only a fool could have argued that the South had a chance anymore. And the situation became worse with each passing week. The two sides sniped away at each other, exchanged shellfire between batteries, and lobbed mortar bombs back and forth. Hardly a day passed that one or more men were not borne from the ditches, dead or wounded from Minié balls or shell fragments. The unremitting danger and misery seemed to breed a die-hard kind of bravado amongst some men. They became careless despite warnings and threats from their officers. One wild fellow from the 10th N.C. actually climbed upon the parapet of his trench and stood there shaking his fist at the Yankees. Strangely, instead of shooting him, they gave him three cheers and yelled at him to come over and join them.

Worse than shot and shell was the cold, drenching rain that fell during January, rain so heavy that it washed away parapets, filled the ditches up to a man's knee, and caused bombproofs to cave in. Our poor men huddled in their fetid holes and ditches like miserable gray rats, cursing God and Abraham Lincoln alike.

All this was made worse by the bad news coming in from other fronts. First, that Hood's bold and foolhardy invasion of Tennessee with an inferior force had ended with a disaster in front of Nashville. Sherman had taken Savannah, Georgia, as a finale of his march to the sea, and when that news reached the Yankees facing Petersburg, they relayed it to us with a gigantic artillery salute that shook the sodden earth.

Later in the month they gave a similar salute to the news that Fort Fisher had fallen to a gigantic naval and amphibious assault. The Confederacy's last communication with the world was sealed off. All that was left of the C.S.A. was the state of South Carolina, which had started the war, North Carolina, which had come into the conflict belatedly, and a part of poor, long-suffering old Virginia. A broad section of the Deep South and Texas remained unoccupied, but their produce was of no help to us there in the trenches around Petersburg.

In a way the seat of Confederate resistance lay in the mind and spirit of Robert E. Lee. The some fifty thousand ill-nourished, desperate men of his Army of Northern Virginia were the flagging instruments of that one man's will. Only a fool could not see that the end was merely a matter of time.

31

Desertion had always been a problem in the Confederate Army. It was in the Union Army, too. We even lost some men in that way in Pennsylvania on the way to Gettysburg when the Confederacy seemed invincible. There was always the conscript who had never wanted to be in the army in the first place or the chap who didn't get along with his officers or was just plain cowardly. But there was never anything like the deserting that occurred in February and March of 1865.

It took two forms. Almost every night, in our brigade one or two fellows, hungry and low in spirit, would roll over the parapets, crawl between the abatis, and call out softly to the Yankee pickets to take them in. I might add that we got the odd Yank deserting to us in the same way, but I think they were mostly mental cases, for we had nothing to offer.

The other form of desertion was for three or four men, or, in one case, an entire platoon, after laying their plans carefully, to wait for a dark night and simply take off for the rear and home.

One of our five regiments had been recruited mainly from North Carolina's mountain counties and damn if half of them didn't go home in February alone.

The reasons would appear to be obvious: cold, hunger, constant danger and lack of any prospect of victory. The real reasons were the letters from home, relaying to the men the loss of faith of the people in the cause of the Confederacy. Those letters told of hunger, of children crying for their fathers, of roads made unsafe by bushwhackers, of overzealous state and Confederate tax men.

The problem was worst among North Carolinians because it was easy for a Tar Heel to get home. A Texan or a Mississippian had such a long way to go. Georgians had the same problem, but they got such pitiful letters telling of the way Sherman had devastated much of the state on his march to the sea that they ran the Tar Heels a close second in desertions.

Despite our poor conditions and the loss of morale, Lee's army was not to be trifled with. It remained well armed and the men retained their skills at killing. Bored and mean as they were, they were dangerous foes.

For my part, I was not eager for the war to end. What would I do with myself now that Jane Ferro would not be mine? It was soothing to my self-esteem to think that the voluptuous Elvira Fincastle was willing to leave her husband and take her child (and possibly mine) and go west with me. But how could a twenty-one-year-old man and a thirty-five-year-old woman make a life together? Besides, I had little money. Given a choice of going home to farm and staying on as a captain, I would remain the loyal Confederate.

So I threw my energies into helping William Ferro run that brigade efficiently. My returns were always on time and in proper order. I inspected the front lines, taking notice of details that needed correcting. I jollied up company commanders and joshed with privates. I worked out a screen of guards to stand picket duty *behind* our works to discourage desertions to the rear. And I developed a network of loyal soldiers who would talk up the cause in the trenches and report back to their colonels if they heard plans of desertion.

General Ferro and I made it a point never to flinch when a mortar shell fell nearby or a Minié ball sang over our heads. I always took at least one meal a day with the men, eating their same field rations. We did the best we could to get food, such as it was, up into the works while it was hot.

But it was just a matter of time.

Between me and William Ferro there existed a strain of embarrassment now that his sister had rejected me, but still we could talk frankly about the war itself.

In February, Lee was made commander of all the Confederate armies, which was rather pointless, General Ferro and I agreed, since the Southern forces were so widely scattered and in such poor communication with each other.

By that time Sherman had begun to move north, into South Carolina, from Savannah. Joe Johnston was brought out of retirement to oppose his advance with a force of odds and ends of units. There remained the faint hope that this wily, if overcautious, general might turn back Sherman or, failing that, Lee might detach part of his army to help smash the Yankee marauder and then bring Johnston's forces back to confront Grant.

"It would take a miracle," General Ferro said to me. "Look at the poor condition of our horses and mules. Can you see those half-starved creatures dragging cannon day after day? And our men. They have been cooped up so long they could not bear up on the hard marches that would be required."

"But it is still possible?"

"Perhaps. Just barely."

I have commented earlier about the Confederacy's failure to raise soldiers from among its black population. If this had been done in 1863 or even 1864, it could have made a tremendous difference, I feel certain. In March the Confederate Congress authorized the arming of 300,000 black men. A few companies were raised in and around Richmond, but to my knowledge they never got into any fighting.

And when this news of Confederate blacks reached the trenches before Petersburg, it was greeted with little enthusiasm. I heard enlisted men say openly such things as "I will go home and let Abraham Lincoln have the country before I will serve in line with a nigger."

Some junior officers, me included, saw a chance to command Negro companies or regiments of our own, however. In fact, William Ferro paid me the compliment of saying he would put my name forward as a major or colonel of black troops when the opportunity presented itself.

Of course, it never did.

Sherman walked right through South Carolina, burning Columbia on February 17. Four weeks later, he was in Fayetteville, N.C. On March 19, Johnston finally gave battle, stopping Sherman momentarily at Bentonville and Averysboro but abandoning both fields in the end to fall back on Raleigh, the state capital.

Time had indeed very nearly run out on the C.S.A. There was just time enough for a final desperate move and Lee made it early in the morning on March 25 along our front and to the right of our positions. With General John B. Gordon in tactical command, Lee assembled three divisions and made a surprise attack on the Federal lines around Fort Stedman. During the night, we sent out crews to quietly remove the obstructions in front of our lines. About 4 A.M. in the morning, a handful of carefully instructed men sneaked across the 150-yard "no-man's land" and shouted to the Yankee pickets that they wanted to desert. They were welcomed in and suddenly the trusting pickets became prisoners.

Larger parties, carrying axes, then emerged from our lines and proceeded to clear away the abatis in front of the Yankee works. At last, stilling their impulse to give the Rebel yell until the last minute, our boys advanced in clumped masses to pounce upon the amazed Yanks in and around Fort Stedman. Shots and sounds of struggles could be heard as our fellows spread out to the left and right, hauling in sleepy prisoners by the scores. By dawn we were in possession of a considerable part of the Federal forward works.

The plan called for us to press on into the depots and artillery positions to the rear of Fort Stedman, hoping to snap the besieging Federal Army in two. It was thought that the part between Stedman and the Appomattox River might retreat toward City Point and that part occupying the Weldon and Petersburg Railroad would be pulled back to try to plug the gap.

General Ferro and I stood on a parapet, straining our eyes in the early light to see what was happening. What we saw was the last offensive of Robert E. Lee fall apart. Our attack simply petered out. Our men found themselves burdened with prisoners; some stopped to loot the knapsacks of the Yanks. Units went astray in the faint light.

Meanwhile signal rockets began going up from the rear and nearby sectors of the Federal lines. And the Yankee guns, field pieces and mortars alike, came into play, tossing shell after shell into the works.

By 7 A.M. they had our attack well contained, with infantry reserves hustled up and pouring musket fire into the positions. The first of our men started stumbling back toward our lines, some wounded but many simply turning tail.

Now it was becoming safer to remain hemmed in there than to risk crossing the open space back to our lines. Hundreds of our men laid down their arms and surrendered.

Confederate losses ran high, close to four thousand men, men Lee could ill afford to lose. Our brigade was reduced to less than a thousand effectives. My old friend Noah Rhine did not return, good, steady old Noah. Lee had made his final gamble and we, his soldiers, had lost.

Only a fool could hope any longer.

32

We were allowed little time to lick our wounds. March 29 dawned chilly and cloudy. The day was made no more cheerful by the intelligence passed on to General Ferro that the Yankee cavalry nemesis, Phil Sheridan, his mission of crushing poor Jubal Early and laying waste to the Shenandoah Valley completed, had been put in charge of a huge mounted force and was feeling his way around our fortifications south of Petersburg. Grant had been extending his works along his left since the previous summer, thereby causing Lee to stretch his own lines thinner and thinner to avoid being outflanked.

As early as August, the Federals had closed off the Weldon and Petersburg Railroad around Reams's Station, forcing Confederate traffic from North Carolina to detour by wagons and thence into Petersburg on the Southside Railroad along the Appomattox River.

This latest movement by Sheridan, if unopposed, would sever the Southside Railroad and cut off Petersburg's last link to the eroding Confederate interior; also it would hem the Confederates in a semicircle against the Appomattox River.

"We're to move out of the ditches, James," General Ferro told me. "General Lee is sending Pickett's division down from Richmond and we are joining him tomorrow to keep Sheridan away from the railroad. Pass the word for the regimental commanders to meet here this afternoon to plan the march. Everything must be ready to move out early tomorrow."

There were a thousand details to be seen to in arranging for wagons and mules, teams for artillery, transfer of the sick. Our brigade had put down roots during the past nine months; it was not used to quick marches.

Added to Pickett's division and other units pulled from the Petersburg defenses, we made up a force of some ten thousand men. Lee was taking a gamble in withdrawing so many soldiers from his already thinly held defenses, but he could hardly ignore the threat to the Southside Railroad.

At any rate, it was good to get out of those stinking trenches. A semblance of our former high spirits returned as we swung into the line of march through Petersburg. Men chaffed with each other and skylarked like children let out of school. But I noticed that they shuffled rather than marched smartly as they had done in the past. And there was no band playing "Dixie" now.

William Ferro still had the little mare, Nellie, a different Nellie from the one I had ridden around Oldham County and up in Pennsylvania; her coat had grown rough and her flanks were not so sleek. As for me, I rode on the back of a mule-drawn wagon which contained brigade papers and a headquarters tent, me and old Cassius.

What a contrast Pickett's column made that cold and now rainy March 30, 1865, as compared to that scene in June 1863 when I had watched Ewell's mighty corps move like an invincible machine through Chester Gap on its way to Pennsylvania.

Our spirits weren't helped by that cold rain as we made our march out along the Southside Railroad into the countryside and as we set up our tents for the night.

About three miles south of the railroad lay a crossroads called Five Forks. Sheridan would have to pass Five Forks to get at the railroad. And that is where Pickett moved us on the last day of March, over the Ford Road to Five Forks.

Once there we found some old entrenchments and waited there while our cavalry fanned out to locate Sheridan.

They found the Federal cavalry well north of Dinwiddie Courthouse, two divisions of them.

I know from reading postwar accounts that Lee thought to

make a virtue of the necessity of defending the Southside Railroad, that he meant to smash up Sheridan and send him back behind Grant's lines with his tail between his legs, leaving the way clear for the quick removal of the Army of Northern Virginia to southern Virginia and a juncture with Joe Johnston.

This was easier said than done for not only were Sheridan's 9,000 cavalrymen armed with repeating rifles but, unknown to us, were backed up by two entire infantry corps, making in all 25,000 to 30,000 well-fed, well-equipped soldiers. And poor old George Pickett had only 10,000 ill-fed Confederates.

But for a while on Friday, March 31, it was almost like old times. Our gray lines pressed out in long ranks across the muddy fields and through rain-drenched thickets in search of the Federal cavalrymen. We found them on foot and, skillfully exploiting the gap between their divisions, poured volleys of musketry against first one flank and then another. Despite the advantage of their repeating rifles, they gave way. They would stop now and then to spatter us with balls from their quick-firing weapons, but things seemed to be going entirely our way as we neared Dinwiddie Courthouse and attempted a sweeping maneuver intended to bring us in on the flank and rear of a body of Yankee cavalrymen.

The situation changed in a twinkling for we found that we had turned our backs on a division of dismounted cavalry near Dinwiddie Courthouse. They began pouring a hot fire into our rear; we turned about-face and started giving it back to them. We pressed them back to the edge of the village, where they threw up log and rail breastworks and laid down such a heavy fire that we halted our advance in the growing dark and hunkered down for the night with only a hundred yards or so separating us from the enemy's line.

It had been a long and exciting day. We had shoved these dismounted cavalrymen back eight or nine miles. Harry McGee was exuberant when I crawled out to check on the lines after dark.

"By God, Jim, we did drive them, didn't we? Just like a herd of cattle. Who says the Army of Northern Virginia has forgot how to fight?"

"Keep quiet over there," Tom Shelton called out. "Keep your voices down."

"That bastard," Harry said under his breath. "He took your girl away, didn't he, Jim?"

"I don't want to talk about it. That is all over and done with."

While we slept on our arms near Dinwiddie Courthouse, a great mass of Yankee infantry was building up on our left flank. Sheridan had hoped to hold us in position while the infantry got around and behind us. Fortunately they moved so slowly in the mud that we had plenty of warning early the next morning and made a quick withdrawal back to Five Forks.

George Pickett was not one of the Confederacy's great generals, in my opinion, but he wasn't a bad division commander. The so-called Pickett's Charge at Gettysburg had not been his idea. It was Lee's. And it was not Pickett's idea to make a do-or-die stand at Five Forks. That, too, was Lee's.

So Pickett, carrying out his orders to hold Five Forks at all costs, set us to strengthening and extending the old entrenchments we had found there. He sited in his artillery and organized our lines. Meanwhile, he sent out a mixed lot of mounted and dismounted cavalry to form a thin three-mile screen on our left to cover the gap between us and the main Confederate works.

The scene reminded me of the one that had taken place three years before at New Bern, when the untested 10th North Carolina, under Elmer Fincastle, had lain behind inadequate breastworks in the rain waiting to be attacked by Burnside. Now, with barely more than two hundred men, under Tom Shelton, it lay in the rain waiting to receive an attack by Phil Sheridan.

The story is well known of how Pickett, thinking his lines secure enough to hold off any attack and that Sheridan would need another day to mount one anyway, was far to the rear eating shad with Fitzhugh Lee and Thomas Rosser, his two cavalry commanders, when all hell broke loose about 4 P.M. that April Fool's Day, 1865.

The Yankee cavalry advanced on foot and made the air alive with their repeating carbines, then retired before our slower but still deadly answering volleys.

General Ferro and I watched the action unfold from a position back among the artillery. Off to our left we suddenly saw a blue avalanche of Federal infantry, sweeping around our flank and brushing away our cavalrymen like so many flies.

Fortunately our trench line had been "refused," that is bent back at an angle to protect that flank. Our fire from this part of our line stopped the infantry advance momentarily.

All around us our cannon boomed and spent enemy bullets sang. Then the Federal cavalry on our front opened up again and Sheridan's horse artillery joined in the fun. The extreme left of Pickett's line, which our brigade occupied with another, became a decidedly uncomfortable spot.

A horde of infantry on our left; cavalrymen across our front. And Sheridan's horse artillery giving our cannon tit for tat. If we had been in our deep Petersburg trenches with abatis strewn in front of our positions and our artillery firing from well-protected lunettes, we could have held Sheridan. But we were mighty vulnerable in shallow entrenchments outnumbered three to one, and with our commander off at a shad bake.

"My God, James, look there," General Ferro exclaimed.

A tide of infantry now flowed around our flank and inundated the rear of the position. A fresh horde of cavalrymen burst through the brush and ran right over our left. Our line went to pieces. Men continued to fire and slash away. Some ran off to the rear and then stopped to fire back at the cavalry. The enemy got possession of three of our cannon on the extreme left and turned them on the center of our line. The men still left in the breastworks began to throw down their muskets and surrender, by the scores and hundreds.

The only thing William Ferro and I could do was collect our

survivors and lead them west, away from Petersburg and the intervening Federal infantry. We left behind at least half our brigade strength and all our baggage.

The next week was a nightmare. The very next morning after Five Forks we awoke to the sound of a stupendous bombardment in the distance, around Petersburg. Grant wasted no time after hearing of Sheridan's victory at Five Forks in ordering an all-out assault on Lee's lines, knowing that those lines were more lightly held than ever.

It was all we could do to keep our diminished brigade out of the Federal net, much less help hold Petersburg. Of course, after some initial repulses, Grant's attack succeeded. Leaving behind last-ditch defenders to man certain strongpoints, Lee withdrew his survivors with baggage and artillery across the Appomattox. And Richmond itself was evacuated after the Confederate officials and their records had been removed by trains to Danville.

A month or even a week earlier, Lee could have taken the Southside Railroad and the Danville and Richmond down to Danville and over to Raleigh to join up with Joe Johnston. But now Sheridan was astride the Southside Railroad. The best Lee could do was withdraw west. His futile attack at Fort Stedman and equally futile stand at Five Forks were even more costly than they first appeared.

The first day after Five Forks we marched due west. The few blue cavalrymen who came nosing around were easily discouraged when we formed up hollow squares.

General Ferro still had the mare Nellie. Tom Shelton had brought his horse out of the fight at Five Forks, but the other colonels were on foot now. As for me, I had managed to cut loose the two mules from our headquarters wagon. I rode one and Cassius the other after that.

On the third day, as we pressed northwest to join the rest of Lee's army, Sheridan's cavalry returned hot and heavy to our trail. They hung about on our flanks or followed at a safe distance. We laid little traps for them. Occasionally they would swoop in to snap up a straggler or a forage party.

Our ration wagons had been captured. Occasionally we would find a farmer willing to part with his precious store of corn meal. And once a stray pig had the misfortune to cross our line of march. Mostly we stumbled along, our eyes glazed with hunger like starved dangerous beasts.

Lee had ordered ration trains sent out ahead of the retreat into the Virginia countryside, but they went astray or were captured. Once we encountered a wagon with a broken wheel; its driver had fled with the team. To our delight, we found the wagon loaded with corn meal and fatback and our men fell on it like animals, eating it raw.

Late in the morning of the next day, on the sixth of April, William Ferro was riding Nellie at the head of our column with me riding my mule at the rear, when we came to a crossroads. A cavalryman nattily dressed in Confederate gray sat there on a strong, well-fed black horse.

I saw him pointing down the left fork of the road and saw the head of our column take that direction. General Ferro rode back to explain to me that a depot had been set up in the woods with hot food and coffee awaiting us. He asked me to remain with the rear regiment while he led the brigade to their repast.

As word of this good news passed down the ranks, the men gave feeble Rebel yells. For the first time in several days I observed smiling faces among them.

The road down which the cavalryman directed us was little more than a trail through second-growth pines and small fields of broomstraw.

After the general had cantered back to the head of the column, I sat beside the road on my ridiculous mule waiting for the 10th North Carolina to pass. Here were the remnant of the thousand-odd men who had been formed into a regiment at Raleigh three and a half years earlier, now ragtag, limping, bone-weary, hungry and desperate. General Ferro led the front regiment around a bend in the forest road. In the distance I could hear the rattle of musketry as another of Lee's columns fought off a cavalry sortie. Here in the woods, off the main road, all seemed at peace. Birds tried out their early spring tunes. The only jarring note for me was the sight of Tom Shelton riding an indifferent nag at the head of my old regiment. It occurred to me to warn him to post a rear guard, but I couldn't bring myself to speak to the man.

When my former Company H came along, Harry McGee was bandying words with brave Hiram Winchester, saying, "Uncle Hiram, I was afraid your legs would not stand a long march, but it seemed to me that you ran faster than anybody else back at Five Forks."

"When the spirit is willing enough, the flesh knows no age," the old man rejoined. A ripple of laughter ran through the ranks.

Harry's eye brightened when it fell on me and my mule.

"Dress up your ranks, boys," he called out. "There is our brigade adjutant and his royal steed. He's here to inspect our noble troops. Shoulders back. Get in step. One, two, three, four . . ."

Good old Company H or what was left of it. The boys spruced themselves up and marched past me in mock review.

"A cheer for Captain Mundy," Harry yelled.

"Hip hip hooray for Captain Mundy!"

"And three cheers for his mule."

They burst out laughing and cheering and I laughed with them as I swung my mule onto the road to follow them.

Looking back, I saw a second well-dressed cavalryman join the fellow who had pointed us to the warm food. As they sat there watching our progress, I wished I had joined the cavalry so I could ride a fine horse. Cavalrymen always got the best, I thought.

Our regiment had almost reached the bend in the forest road when I heard the rapid fire of what could only be repeating Federal carbines, followed by sporadic musket fire far ahead. Tom Shelton began yelling orders, and his lead companies broke into a trot toward the sounds. I heard the pounding of hoofs behind me and turned my mule off the road into a thicket.

Some two hundred blue-clad cavalry, carrying sabers, thundered down the road into the rear of the 10th N.C.

I rode the mule through the trees to the edge of a large clearing where the cavalry had caught up with the regiment and was scattering my old comrades like so many rabbits, giving them no chance to reload their muskets or get into any kind of formation. All the while there was more firing farther down the road.

I checked my impulse to charge into the fray with my old mule. The smoke cleared from the field so that I could make out Tom Shelton riding his horse into the woods and clumps of other men either standing with their muskets over their heads in surrender or scampering away into thickets where horses could not follow.

And then I saw old Hiram Winchester, his gaunt frame like a scarecrow's standing with his musket at the ready, bayonet fixed, and surrounded by a circle of Yankee cavalrymen, all laughing at his defiance.

They were still laughing when Hiram raised his musket and shot a cavalryman right out of his saddle. Another horseman, reacting more quickly than his comrades, rode at Hiram with saber upraised, but the old man thrust his bayonet into the fellow's stomach before he could strike.

Hiram wrenched the bayonet away as the cavalryman slid off his horse.

Now the other Yankees, no longer laughing, rushed upon old Hiram, striking at him with their blades while he dodged about, swinging his musket like a club, making their horses shy away and once knocking a cavalryman to the ground.

Enraged at his defiance, they crowded in too close to shoot him. At last a saber slashed across his forehead, opening a wound that gushed blood down over his beard until it gleamed scarlet. Still he fought back until another saber fell across the back of his neck and another thrust into his chest.

Hiram slumped beside the Yankee he had shot and the one he had bayoneted.

Sickened by this sight and ashamed that I had not gone to his aid, I turned my mule around and rode back through the woods, off the road, until I came near the crossroads. The two cavalrymen dressed in Confederate uniforms were still standing duty despite the fact that two hundred Yankee cavalrymen had just passed that point to strike the rear of our brigade.

I tied my mule to a sapling and crept closer, close enough to hear their conversation and their laughter.

"They fell for it hook, line and sinker. A whole brigade. Must have been five hundred of the bastards. You should have seen them smile when I told them hot food was waiting down the road."

"They got something hot, all right."

"Sure did. The ambush must have worked. Why don't you ride down and see? The firing seems to have stopped."

One of the bogus Confederates spurred his horse along at a smart trot. He had barely gone when I heard the sound of another horse nearby. Tom Shelton rode out of the bushes and right along the road to where the first fellow sat on his horse. Shelton's face was brick-red. He carried his sword across his saddle as he approached the Yankee in gray.

"What is your name, rank and unit?" he demanded in that big voice.

"Who wants to know?"

"Colonel Shelton of the 10th North Carolina and—" He never finished the sentence.

The "Confederate" brought his carbine up and shot Tom Shelton right out of his saddle. His horse reared and ran off into the woods, leaving Shelton stone dead on the ground. The disguised Yankee got off his horse, smiling, and began going through Shelton's pockets.

I drew out my Colt revolver and walked as quietly as I could toward him, my weapon cocked and leveled. He saw me out of the corner of his eye and reached for his own revolver. I fired, the bullet striking his left arm and nearly knocking him down. He kept tugging at his revolver and I fired again, shooting him square in the chest.

His horse was well trained. It did not run off. I caught the reins and held them while I went through the spy's pockets. Found them filled with greenbacks. And even more U.S. money in his saddlebags. From all that money and notes on his body, I concluded that he was a high-ranking Federal officer sent out in command of other spies to mislead and confuse our retreating army. He had earned his money that day, for his little trick caused the capture of almost all that was left of Ferro's brigade. Maybe he would have said it was worth losing his life for.

Anyway, I dragged his and Shelton's bodies over to a small gully and covered them as best I could with rocks and branches. That grisly work done, I set my old mule free to shift for himself and mounted the dead Union spy's fine black gelding. With my saddlebags full of sound U. S. currency, I galloped off northwest.

33

I caught up with a column of worn-out Confederate cavalry in the late afternoon, and they let me sleep in their camp and shared their meager rations with me.

It was an uneasy night's sleep with those saddlebags full of greenbacks for a pillow and my splendid gelding tied to my foot so that no one could steal him.

Even without my anxiety for my new-found wealth and horse, the recollections of the events of the previous day and all their implications kept my brain aflame.

Tom Shelton dead. I a rich man. My brigade destroyed. The horror of seeing poor old Hiram Winchester hacked to death. And all around me the once superb army of Robert E. Lee in disarray.

The captain of the cavalry with whom I camped gave me some of his hardtack and hot mush the next morning. There I sat eating that miserable stuff while, unbeknownst to my half-starved hosts, I possessed enough money to have bought us all caviar and beefsteak. How much money I did not know as I had not dared take the time or risk to count it.

In chatting about the condition of Lee's army that morning of April 7 with the cavalry captain, I learned that the disaster to Ferro's brigade was not the only one to befall our army the day before. In fact, it was a trifling one compared to what had happened at Sayler's Creek, where the Yankees had cut off Ewell's corps and captured six thousand men and nine generals, including Old Baldy himself.

"Nothing to do but surrender," my host said. "They would have been slaughtered if they had kept fighting."

I told him of the way in which we had been ambushed, skipping over the part about the spy and Tom Shelton for fear the chap might try to confiscate my horse if he knew it had been a Yankee's. He did invite me to join his outfit and fight as a cavalryman, but I declined.

"I must report to someone higher up just what happened yesterday."

So, taking my leave of him, I rode ahead until I overtook an infantry column. Far down that gray and butternut line of weary men, I saw a figure with one arm riding on a familiar-looking horse, accompanied by a black man on a mule. I put the spurs to my gelding until I caught up with the pair. They were surrounded by men from our lead regiments.

"General Ferro," I cried.

He turned his face toward me, looking at me with vacant eyes.

"Who is it?"

"Me. James Mundy."

"James. Yes. James, tell Colonel Shelton to rush the 10th regiment up and strike the enemy cavalry in the flank. We will hold them here. Hurry. It is an ambush."

I frowned.

Cassius caught my eye. "Mister William don't feel just right. He thinks we are back in the woods."

"Be quiet, Cassius. I am giving orders to Captain Mundy. And turn loose of my horse. You are taking liberties."

There were more than a hundred of our infantrymen marching along behind Nellie. One of them, a sergeant, motioned me to fall back, tapping his head with his forefinger as he did so.

"Do you hear me, James?" Ferro continued. "That cavalryman back there was a spy. He pointed us into a trap. But we can whip them if Shelton brings up his regiment immediately."

"Yes, sir," I replied. "I will convey the order."

The sergeant explained. "They let our front regiment pass and then they charged into the middle of the column. Shot us down in droves. The general can't get it in his head that he doesn't have a brigade anymore. He would have been captured if his old nigger had not led them through the woods. It is up to you now to command us."

I rode back and reported, "General Ferro. It is all right. Colonel Shelton is coming to reinforce us. He suggests that we continue on this road meanwhile."

"Good. Good. You have a new horse. What is his name?"

"Sheridan, sir."

"I is so glad you here now to help look after him," Cassius said.

Actually, William Ferro gave us little trouble. Mostly he rode along mumbling to himself, staring straight ahead, as I and the 130 men left from the old brigade pressed on to the west.

34

That afternoon we caught up with a wagon train of C.S.A. food and were able to give our tattered band half-rations. We marched on well into the night, slept briefly, and then trudged on through the next day.

Once we were ordered off to our south flank to help a hard-pressed cavalry unit hold off an aggressive thrust by Sheridan's relentless horsemen. Old Cassius stayed back on the road, holding Nellie's head, while we beat off the Yanks and returned to the line of march.

That night, Saturday, April 8, 1865, we fell in with the mass of Lee's army, some 25,000 men camped around a place called Appomattox Court House. All about us we could hear the sputter of musket fire. The Federal cavalry had got ahead of us and cut the railroad west to Lynchburg.

More ominous than the sounds of this firing was the way the night sky glowed to the south from the campfires of the Federals who had outraced us and now blocked the way by which we might have reached North Carolina and a junction with Johnston's forces there. Grant had us cornered.

Cassius and I made William Ferro comfortable, still humoring him with assurances that Shelton's regiment was on its way, that we had escaped from the ambush.

Then came Palm Sunday, April 9, 1865. The morning was the kind that only heaven and the upper South are privileged to experience and the South only in the spring. Balmy and bright.

To the west, we could hear Gordon's division skirmishing with Sheridan. We did not yet know it, but Gordon found that

Sheridan had been joined by fast-marching infantry and that it was impossible to clear the way to the west. Our first inkling came when white flags started moving back and forth throughout the morning.

Our camp lay near a collection of neat, widely spaced houses scattered about an unpretentious little courthouse. It was a town that had been spared by the war until then.

The rumors flew in our camp. Lee would personally lead a charge to break out of our trap. We would stand our ground and die. Even that Johnston had marched up from North Carolina and would soon join us.

Then Lee and some aides rode past our camp around noon, up to a two-story brick house with a high porch. It was the first time I had got a close look at him since Gettysburg.

There I had seen him in a dusty field uniform, sitting on Traveler beside the Chambersburg Road, watching Longstreet's corps marching to deliver that hammer blow against the Yankee left on the second day of Gettysburg. He had then held the fate of the country in his hands, poised as he was to strike with 75,000 fit, eager soldiers. Had he taken personal charge of Longstreet's column and led them across the fields and started that attack two hours earlier, what might have happened?

He had not and here we were, nearly two years later, surrounded and beaten.

"My God," I thought to myself as he passed. "How white his hair and beard have become."

His uniform was spotless, however. He sat on his horse erectly, a magnificent sword at his waist. An old and once powerful man going to do what he had to do with dignity.

That was around noon.

I have seen it happen in Baltimore that when someone is dying in a house, neighbors sometimes gather outside on the street to keep vigil, talking to each other in low voices. Something like that occurred at Appomattox Court House that Palm Sunday afternoon.

After a long wait and more white flags riding out toward the tightening Yankee lines, here came U. S. Grant and Sheridan and others. Grant, a rumpled, round-shouldered chap, and Sheridan, a peppery little bastard with a killer's shining eye. They dismounted and entered the McLean House, where Lee had been waiting.

At last, during midafternoon, Lee came out and stood in the yard, smacking his gloves against one hand before he re-mounted Traveler.

The word ran through our camps faster than it could have been telegraphed. What a scene. Men cursed and said they'd be Goddamn if they would surrender. Others wept, sobbing at the futility and the shame they felt. I saw men smashing up their muskets so the Yankees could not use them, as if they were even interested. Officers broke their swords.

And there rode Lee, not cursing, not breaking his sword. Hitherto, the men of the Army of Northern Virginia had felt a kind of awe for Lee. They would not have dreamed of addressing him directly or of touching him.

Now hundreds pressed around Traveler, touching the horse and rider alike, pleading with the noble old man to tell them it was not so, offering to fight on if he wished them to.

These were men who had not received any real pay in years, who had not been fed decent rations in months, the survivors of reckless, ill-conceived attacks Lee had ordered at Malvern Hill and Cemetery Ridge. And still they adored the man.

I, holding fast to the reins of my horse Sheridan, watched all this at a distance. My mind was already turning to the future. I had done all I could do for the Confederate cause. It was dead and there was no point in weeping around the grave.

At last they let the old man go about his business of arranging for the paper work of the surrender.

The Federals brought up captured cook wagons, and fed us with our own rations. Even before that their fellows swarmed in to give us food from their knapsacks and chat and banter with us, all in a good-natured way, exchanging stories of their life-and-death encounters on a score of battlefields, paying extravagant compliments for each other's valor.

It didn't take me very long to get the names of the survivors of our brigade and to help the Yankees pass out the paroles to the boys. One hundred and thirty men left, where once there had been several thousand. The rest lying in graves across bloody-old Virginia, in Maryland, Pennsylvania or Tennessee. Or rotting alive in Yankee prisons at Elmira, Lookout Point or Johnson's Island. Or in new prison corrals along the road back to Petersburg and Richmond. Or sitting back at home maimed and sick, waiting without hope for the war news. Or skulking about in thickets and backwoods hiding from C.S.A. authorities. Or, in the case of William Ferro, staring with glazed eyes, helpless. Could anything ever be the same again in the South? Did I even want it to be?

It would not be the same for me. No one knew about all that U.S. money in my saddlebags. I could have ridden away on Sheridan to a safe place to count and hide my loot but stayed on out of a sense of duty to William Ferro and to the men and, to be honest, out of a fear of being robbed out in the countryside alone.

Anyway, I kept our brigade together and marched them back to North Carolina as a body. I took great pains to see that our band had plenty of marching rations and then off we set. I on Sheridan, William Ferro on Nellie, and Cassius on his mule. It took us a week to reach Greensboro, traveling over country that had been freshly raided by Stoneman's cavalry.

At Greensboro, we encountered chaos. Jefferson Davis and his cabinet had passed through but had found so little welcome in that Quaker city they had taken the cars for Charlotte. Greensboro was filled with the backwash of Johnston's army and veterans of Lee's, like us. They were breaking into Confederate warehouses, getting drunk, bullying Negroes and there was nothing the state militia could do about it. Old Joe Johnston himself was over at Durham Station to the east, working out the terms for surrendering his army to Sherman. From what I saw of that rabble in Greensboro, he didn't have much to surrender.

It was at Greensboro that I dispersed our brigade. Before the men broke up to go to their homes in various parts of North Carolina I called on them to line up for a final inspection, with me and the still befuddled William Ferro riding along their ragged line there at the train station.

"Speech, speech," someone cried.

"Boys," I said. "General Ferro is still not well. I am sure that if he felt better . . ."

"You give us one, then."

Feeling somewhat foolish, I climbed upon an overturned hogshead and looked down into those thin, unshaven faces.

"Boys, they told us back in '61 that we could whip the Yankees before breakfast. That we could do it with cornstalks. They told us that one of us could whip three of them. It did not quite turn out that way. But by God, there is one thing: The Yankees know they have been in a fight.

A Rebel yell went up.

"The war is over, boys. It has been a hard fight. No one standing before me needs to be ashamed of what he did. You are brave, true men, every one of you. It is not your fault that the war did not turn out exactly as we wished. But by God you gave it all you had and then some."

Another Rebel yell.

"Now we must all go home and be good citizens. We have all been away from our families too long. You have got some plowing and fence-mending to do by day and, after being away from your wives and girl friends so long, some plowing and fence-mending to do by night as well, I expect."

Laughter and whistles.

"Don't ever forget our experiences together. That is one thing the Yankees can't take away from us, our memories of these past four years. God bless you all. And just one more thing. Try not to tell your children and grandchildren too many damned lies about what you did in the war."

Much laughter and side-slapping.

One by one, they came and shook my hand and then without speaking, tears coursing down their cheeks, passed by the uncomprehending William Ferro astride Nellie and touched his knee or gloved hand. And then they started for home.

"You gonna help me get him back to Beaulieu, ain't you, Mister James?" Cassius asked, perhaps reading my mind.

"Sure I am."

It took us two days to reach Oldham County. We made a strange trio plodding across the North Carolina Piedmont, a one-armed blond ghost in the uniform of a Confederate general, a one-eyed captain and an elderly Negro on a mule. We slept in a barn near Salisbury, bypassed Charlotte and reached Beaulieu late at night.

35

As we rode down the long lane toward the dark outline of the house, I said to Cassius, "I am going to get you to the yard and leave you. We brought him home."

"What you mean you gonna leave us, Mister James?"

"I don't want to intrude on the family. There is no point in my going in."

For the past nine days, Cassius and I had done very little talking and that little concerned only with the care and feeding of the confused William Ferro. Of course I had been busy with the management of the survivors of the brigade and he with caring for a helpless man. However, I had caught Cassius staring at me when he thought I wasn't noticing, sizing me up.

He had been courteous to me on the long ride from Appomattox, not groveling by any means but civil. He had seemed relieved that I did not abandon him and his master far from home.

His civility and circumspection dropped like a mask when we reached the circular drive in front of Beaulieu.

"How old are you, boy?" he asked.

Shocked by the abrupt change of his tone, I replied, "Twenty-two. Why?"

"You are a twenty-two-year-old fool."

I could scarcely believe it was he talking. "What do you mean, old man? Who the hell do you think you are calling a fool?"

"I'm calling you a fool and you are if you leave without speaking to the family. I been watching you ever since you came back to the army at Petersburg, trying to see what Miss Jane and my Reba saw in you. I seen you step in and put the brigade papers in good order. I heard Mister William praise your work to General Pickett. I seen the way you took charge of them soldiers after the ambush after Mister William lost his wits. I had about decided you is man enough for our Miss Jane. But if you go off now, then I say you a fool and you should not have her."

"You should not meddle in the business of white folks, old man. Your Miss Jane has rejected me."

"You *is* a fool. Look, I am getting old, but I know white folks better than they know themselves. Miss Jane was so crazy about you I couldn't believe it. She told Reba she would run away and marry you when the war was over, whether her father like it or not. When word came you was dead, that girl went to bed and cried for a week."

"Then why wouldn't she break her engagement to Tom Shelton when I came back?"

"I don't know. I wasn't here. Maybe it was because she had given her word. Anyway, what does that matter now? Tom Shelton is dead."

Confused and angry at his blunt talk, I spluttered. I had wanted to go home and count my money and spruce myself up. I was still ashamed of my behavior on my last visit.

"You are getting mighty uppity."

"No, I ain't. I just trying to help you. All you got to do is come in the house with me and let things take their course."

We never settled the argument for a light appeared on the porch of the house and I heard Reba's voice calling, "Who is out there this time of night? Is that you, Cassius?"

"Yeah, it's me, Reba. We home." He got off the mule and she ran to him. "Oh, you sweet man." She hugged and kissed him, then, "Now who is 'we'? Where is Mister William?"

Cassius dropped his voice so that I could not hear. Then Reba shrieked, "Oh, kind Jesus. James Mundy, don't you go out of this yard. Oh, Mister William, get off that horse and come to your Reba."

He was like a little boy as she embraced him and led him up the steps to the main hall, all the while ordering me to follow and for Cassius to put the horses and his mule away.

36

The house came to life as if by magic. House servants appeared in the entrance hall, where William Ferro stood with Reba holding his hand, then Mr. Ferro, Mrs. Ferro and, at last, Jane, wearing a long, full nightgown with her red hair hanging down to her waist, her face looking white and drawn.

Their cries of joy became subdued as Reba quietly signaled that William Ferro was not himself.

I felt devilishly out of place and wished I had not come in. I could see my presence made the Ferros ill at ease, especially Jane, who barely spoke to me.

Damn it, I did not belong there, not in those circumstances and not with an unshaven face and a filthy uniform. Damn that old Negro, anyway. I could have killed him.

Cassius entered the parlor, where William Ferro now sat, still mute. The old man handed me my saddlebags. "Here you is, Mister James. I don't think you meant to leave these out in the stable all night, suh."

The Ferros stopped clucking over William long enough to greet Cassius and long enough for the old man to say, "He has been this way about two weeks, ever since his brigade was tore up. Captain Mundy kept the men together after that and brought us all back to North Carolina. Don't know what we would have done without Mister James. God bless him."

That old black bastard. What was his game? I wondered as he explained how William had lost touch with the real world.

Jane listened to his recital of my bravery without looking at me. For my part, I was embarrassed by the old man's extravagant praise and suspicious of his motives.

"So we are in your debt again, Mundy," Mr. Ferro said with what I imagined to be a touch of irony.

"Yes," his wife chimed in. "This is twice you have saved William's life and brought him home to us. We are grateful."

Jane said nothing, staring at her brother, who sat dumbly in his chair.

"And William's brigade was badly cut up, you say?"

"Yes. Pretty badly. We were ambushed by Yankee cavalry east of Appomattox. We lost most of our men, I am afraid."

"Killed?"

"Killed, wounded, captured or simply missing. We had about five hundred men before the ambush. I surrendered only 130 at Appomattox."

"It was terrible," Cassius spoke up. "The Yankees took us by surprise. They had them repeating rifles and swords. Thousands of them. We never had a chance to fight back. Mister William blamed himself for letting it happen. That is how come his mind snapped, I think."

"Very well, Cassius. Let us not discuss this in front of William. What about Colonel Shelton. Did he come home?"

"No, sir," Cassius replied, although Ferro was looking at me.

"What happened to him?"

"You better let Mister James tell you." His dark-brown eyes met mine briefly. Damn that old nigger. I was not ready to go into that, not with Jane sitting there.

Now they were all looking at me. I cleared my throat.

"Colonel Shelton was killed outright. I saw him fall," I said.

Jane looked at me, her mouth open. And then she fainted, sinking to the floor before her father could catch her.

"Dear God," Mrs. Ferro cried. "My poor Jane. Poor, poor Tom Shelton."

The mention of Shelton's name touched a nerve in William Ferro, but her parents were too busy reviving Jane to hear him say, "Shelton. Tell Colonel Shelton to bring up the 10th. Quickly. Strike the enemy's flank. We are outnumbered. Captain Mundy. Go tell Shelton. What is keeping him?"

Cassius bent over him. "There now, Mister William. It is all right. Captain Mundy has sent word. Reba, you take care of Miss Jane and Mister James and I will put Mister William to bed."

After Cassius and I had led him upstairs and got him out of his uniform and in bed, I drew the old man into the hall. "You blasted old ape. They did not need to know about Shelton so soon. It could have waited until morning."

"No need to delay the truth that I could see, Mister James, begging your pardon, suh."

I started to flare up at his sarcasm, but he stopped me. "I do hope you find everything in good order in your saddlebags, young master."

There was no way for the Ferros to avoid giving me a bed for the night. I did not resist their invitation after they mentioned an outbreak of highway robberies in recent weeks.

Cassius lighted my way to the same attic room where I had spent the night three years before. I did not detain him, being suddenly anxious about my loot. After putting a chair against the door, I opened my saddlebags.

Dog-tired as I was, and with only a candle stub for a light, I counted and recounted the bundles of new U.S. greenbacks. They totaled over $3,000. Just as I had for the past two weeks, I slept that night with those saddlebags under my head and my revolver on the floor beside my low bed.

I awoke early, not sure at first where I was, and then lay quietly amid a crisscross of emotions. Jane must have loved Shelton, after all. Else why would she have fainted at the news of his death? I was rich, possessed over $3,000 in a ruined country where every dollar would be precious. What would I do with it?

Roosters crowed outside. I could hear the family stirring below me. Once I heard the voice of Mr. Ferro raised in what sounded like an angry tone. And then the stairs up from the second floor creaked under a heavy foot. I drew my revolver from its holster and cocked it. Was I becoming as mad as William Ferro?

Another creak and then someone was trying the door.

"Who is it?"

"Me. Reba. Open this door."

I arose to let her in, forgetting that I had the pistol in my hand and that I was wearing only my filthy underwear.

"Put that gun away. I want to talk to you." She motioned me to the chair and handed me a blanket. "Make yourself decent."

I obeyed and she gathered up my uniform and boots.

"Cassius has been talking about you. What are you going to do now that this fool war is over?"

"I don't know. Maybe go into business. I don't want to farm and I am not cut out to be a preacher."

"You gonna stay around here?"

"I don't know. There may not be enough opportunity to hold me."

"Cassius says you can do anything you set your mind to. And he says he thinks you got a lot of money on you."

"Cassius should mind his own business."

"Don't you low-rate my Cassius. This family is our business. I don't know where they would be without me and Cassius."

"Well, I am not your business. And this family is not my business."

"Humph. Maybe so. Anyway, Cassius will bring you some hot water and a razor. I will brush your clothes and clean these muddy boots so you will be presentable for breakfast. Try to have some manners at the table. Last time you was here you ate like a hog."

She left without giving me a chance to reply. Cassius soon reappeared with hot water, soap, towels and a razor. He even brought fresh underwear.

"Here you are, young master. Did you sleep well?"

I ignored his question. "How is General Ferro this morning?"

"He is still asleep. The doctor will come later. A little rest and he will be well again."

"How can you be sure?"

"He got this way once before the war. Had to send him home from Princeton with a breakdown. I helped cure him then and I reckon I can do it again. He is just high-strung. Only don't tell anybody I told you."

"You do a lot of talking out of school, old man. You told Reba about my money. You must have looked in my saddlebags last night."

"I didn't need to look. I knew you had something valuable in there, the way you watched over them."

Soon after I had shaved and had a good wash, he returned with my uniform and boots, freshly cleaned by Reba.

"Breakfast be in ten minutes."

Neither William nor Jane was at breakfast. Mrs. Ferro's eyes were red and her face was puffy. Mr. Ferro was reserved. They asked questions about the last days of the army and about the conditions I had observed in the rest of the state. It was from them that I learned that Lincoln had been assassinated on April 14.

"It is going to be hard for the South now. The Republicans have us at their mercy, I fear," Mr. Ferro said.

Lincoln dead. The man whose election had lit the powder keg of secession killed by a Confederate sympathizer.

"It will be hard. The man who killed him did not do the South a favor."

I told no jokes and attempted no small talk at that meal. The ghost of Tom Shelton seemed to hover over us, even though his name did not come up until I was taking my leave.

Mr. Ferro thanked me again in a perfunctory way and then stepped out on the rear veranda. "Incidentally, Mundy, the Sheltons might appreciate it if you would call on them and tell them what you know of poor Tom's death. It is possible they could recover the body and bring it home for burial."

"I could do that," I replied, thinking that by the same token, Mrs. Hiram Winchester might appreciate a call and the parents of Noah Rhine, too; yes, and the dozens of poor whites who felt just as deeply over their losses as pseudo aristocrats like the Sheltons.

I had not seen Beaulieu by daylight until then. I was shocked to see only charred foundations where great barns and shops had stood far to the rear of the house. And there were only a few children and old women around the row of slave cabins.

Cassius waited with my horse, Sheridan, in front of the stable, the only major outbuilding that had not been burned.

"What happened here?" I asked.

"They say Yankee cavalry came through. They took all the horses and set fire to the buildings."

"Where are the slaves?"

"They are not slaves anymore."

"Well, the darkies then. Where are they?"

"Reba says a bunch of them followed the cavalry. And some just went off on their own for Charlotte."

"What will you and Reba do?"

"Stay here and take care of this family. That is all we know to do. But don't you worry yourself about that, white boy. That is our business."

As I mounted Sheridan, I looked up at the great house and saw Jane Ferro peeking down at me. She drew back at my glance.

Strange people. To have lost their barns, their livestock and so many of their Negroes and yet be able to sit through breakfast with me without once mentioning the calamity. Well, I thought to myself, they have still got their land and their pride.

I slapped the reins against Sheridan's flanks and rode away from Beaulieu, never to return.

37

There were signs of depradations by the Yankee cavalry all along the road to Meadsboro. A burnt-out cotton gin here, a ruined barn or mill there. Very few people of either race were in the fields, but the town of Meadsboro was thronged with Negroes loitering about the courthouse or parading the streets as if on holiday. I suppose they were on holiday, from generations of slavery.

At home, both my parents were digging in the garden plot at the rear of the house. They threw down their hoes and came running when they recognized me. Yet another homecoming, as joyous as before, followed.

Wesley, who had been captured at Fort Fisher, had returned home just two days earlier. He was sleeping late but awakened at the sounds of my mother's rejoicing and came out to greet me. He had grown six inches since I last saw him and picked up weight as well. He was dying to tell me of his experiences around Wilmington and, amused by his exaggerations, I listened politely.

Father had been in town the day before and had heard the news of Lincoln's assassination. "He was a far better man than we realized. The South would have done well to have chosen someone like him."

I couldn't disagree with that.

After suffering through some more of Wesley's stories of his brief adventure in the Junior Reserves and giving me a dreary recital of the families that had lost sons and fathers in the past four years, my mother asked, "What will you do now, James? You know the county is full of nice girls and not nearly enough young men left to go around."

"Oh, Mama, I am in no hurry to get married."

"Have you thought of preaching?" my father asked.

"I am afraid I don't have the temperament for that."

"How about farming?" my mother inquired.

"That doesn't appeal to me either. Maybe I will go into business."

"Ah, but what would you do for money?" my father asked.

"Where there is a will there is a way," I replied.

Later in the afternoon, after Wesley had borrowed the ancient family mule to visit a girl and while my parents busied themselves with chores, I locked myself in my rude bedroom and counted my money again.

There I sat, my bed covered with good, sound bills, undoubtedly the richest man in Oldham County. It stood to reason that I could buy as much land as the Ferros themselves owned, or that I might scour the county for cotton left over from the 1864 crop and haul it down to the coast to make a killing. There were tremendous opportunities for a young man with that much cash in hand.

I should have been elated but was not. I felt empty. King Midas with his sterile wealth could not have experienced any more despair than I that afternoon. I almost would have preferred being back at Petersburg with my attention turned to army affairs or on the march to Gettysburg again with my heart filled with high hopes and expectations. It was a long, bleak, black afternoon.

At my homecoming supper, puzzled by my obvious gloom, my parents tried their best to cheer me up. Wesley ran out of tales about the heroic deeds of the Junior Reserves and pressed me with questions about Gettysburg, Robert E. Lee, Johnson's Island, Petersburg and the surrender.

Instead of cheering me up, my family's solicitude only depressed me further. How could I stay here in this bitter, defeated land for the rest of my life?

We were still sitting around the supper table in our kitchen when I heard the creak of long-ungreased wheels outside the house. My father answered a knock at the back door and I heard a woman's voice asking, "Is James Mundy at home?"

Reba stood on the dark porch, her brown face catching the reflection of our kitchen lamp.

"James Mundy, I want to talk to you in private."

I stepped outside and closed the door behind me. "What do you want?"

"You promise to hear me out now. Don't say nothing until I finish."

"I promise."

Reba told me that Jane Ferro still loved me. That she had loved me from the first time I visited Beaulieu three years before. That she had never stopped loving me. That she had quarreled with her father about our writing to each other but that she had told him she wanted no one else but me. That she had gone to bed, devastated by grief for a week, when the false report of my death at Gettysburg reached Beaulieu. And that, to her father's disgust, she had worn black for a year thereafter.

"Why then did she agree to marry Tom Shelton?" I said sullenly.

"Shut up, now. You promised to hear me out. What did you expect a pretty girl of her age to do? Never look at another man? Besides, Tom Shelton is dead and I say good riddance. He wasn't good enough for her."

"That makes a pretty story, but you saw how she fainted when she heard he was dead. And she never even spoke to me."

"You are a fool. You never gave her a chance. After the way you acted on New Year's, it wasn't her place to speak to you first."

"Oh, go on, Reba. I would be a fool if I believed that."

"White folks, they are all fools. You love Miss Jane, don't you?"

"I did once."

"I am not talking about 'did once.' I'm talking about right now."

"You don't expect me to go begging to those people."

"I am the one that is begging." Her tone softened. "I am begging you to take Miss Jane away and marry her right now."

"I am in no hurry to marry anybody. There is plenty of time."

"No, there ain't. If you want Miss Jane, you must take her now."

"What is your rush?"

She told me. Ferro would never permit me to come courting at Beaulieu, no matter what Jane's wishes. He would kill us both rather than suffer the disgrace of his daughter's marrying beneath her.

"But I have not asked her to marry me."

"She thinks you are just dying to marry her."

"Where did she get that notion?"

"I gave her that notion. I told her that you was crazy about her still and that you told me you want to leave this part of the country and take her with you as your wife."

"Why would you want to tell a big lie like that?"

"It was the only way I could get her to come with me tonight."

"Jane, with you?"

"She is out in the carriage around at the front, with Cassius.

She thinks you begged me to bring her. Don't you never tell her any different."

I ran out into the dark, around the house and stumbled into Cassius, who stood holding Nellie and his old C.S.A. mule which were hitched to the Ferro carriage.

38

Inside our kitchen with the three of them, I introduced Jane to my parents and Wesley. God, it makes my heart ache to this day to think how beautiful she looked.

That girl had never before entered the home of white people as humble as ours, but she could not have been more gracious. She and my mother got on famously. My family were charmed by her.

After some hemming and hawing, I said, "Pa, Miss Ferro and I wish to be married. Will you perform the ceremony?"

"When?"

"Right now."

That required some explanation, but Pa finally went and changed into his shiny black preaching coat and tie and had us stand before him in our kitchen. With my mother, Wesley, Reba and Cassius as witnesses, Jane Ferro and James Mundy were joined in holy matrimony.

My parents never understood why we wanted to leave immediately for Charlotte, or how I came to have the five hundred dollars in U.S. bills that I gave them.

Reba had packed a small trunk for Jane. Cassius and Reba rode in the carriage with Jane to Charlotte while I led the way on Sheridan.

It was a mild spring night. No more emptiness. No more despair for me. I rode with my revolver holster unbottoned and my saddlebags full of money in front of me.

Early the next morning, at Charlotte, I went into the train station for our tickets. Making sure no one saw me, I drew Cassius aside and gave him a packet of money.

"You must give this to William Ferro when he recovers. And you can present my horse to Mr. Ferro, with my compliments."

"That is generous of you, Mister James."

Reba and Jane were hugging each other and crying while Cassius and I unsaddled Sheridan and replaced the old mule with him in harness beside Nellie.

"You can lead the mule back. He might come in handy with the crops this spring."

"I expect he will."

"You and Reba are quite a pair, aren't you?"

"What do you mean?"

"I mean for a couple of darkies, you manage things right well."

"For a pair of Negroes, I guess we do all right."

"With that money on you and two good saddle horses, I am afraid you may get bushwacked on the way home."

"I ain't afraid. I got this."

He drew back a lap robe on the floor of the carriage to reveal a double-barreled shotgun.

"You know how to use that?"

"Indeed I do. I taught Mister William to hunt. And don't forget, I was in the army, too."

"So you were."

"Yes. I am not afraid to use this shotgun if I have to. I would have used it on you last night if it had been necessary. I will use it on you yet if you ever mistreat Miss Jane."

He grinned. I grinned back at him.

"You are something, Cassius."

"So are you, James."

We shook hands. Reba hugged me and made me promise to be good to "my baby girl."

Jane and I sat in the train looking out through a filthy window at the two black people in their ridiculous carriage with the mule tied at the back. They were still sitting there when the train lurched north.

At Greensboro, we spent the night in a hotel and hired a buggy and driver to carry us to Danville since the rail link between the cities was still unrepaired.

At Danville, we took the cars over the Richmond and Danville line. I pointed out scenes I could remember from our retreat to Appomattox.

We had agreed that we might settle in Richmond but found much of the city in ruins from fires set by mobs when the Confederates evacuated the city. All that I had fought for for three and a half years gone up in smoke.

The city was occupied by Federal troops, both white and black. To my humiliation, a cocky little blond Yankee lieutenant stopped me and demanded to see my parole papers.

He seemed disappointed that they were in good order.

"You still wear the Rebel uniform, I see."

"Your eyesight is good."

"It is, indeed. Good enough to see that you still wear Confederate buttons, also."

"What business is that of yours?"

"They are prohibited. You must remove them."

"Don't be silly."

"I will have you arrested if you refuse."

So I was forced to stand there with my bride beside me, my teeth clinched, while that little popinjay cut the buttons off my jacket.

"There. You may go now."

"Not so fast."

"What do you mean?"

"Give me the buttons or I will report you to your provost."

With a shrug, he handed them over and I passed them to Jane.

We found a hotel for the night and the next morning, thoroughly disillusioned with Richmond, booked passage on a small steamer up the Chesapeake Bay to Baltimore.

I still had not told Jane about my money. She did not ask how I was able to pay for hotels, carriage hire or train tickets.

In Baltimore, I found a good boardinghouse and, leaving Jane to rest from our hard trip, made my way to the location where Manny Koning, my Jewish benefactor back in August 1863, had told me he had a store.

39

Manny remembered me well. He had wondered what happened to me. I paid him six dollars to redeem the I.O.U.'s I had given him for the meat pies.

The upshot of our meeting was that he offered me a job helping manage his booming store. I told him I would never work for wages. Then he offered me wages and a quarter-interest in the store after the first year, if things went well.

I told him nothing less than a full partnership right from the start would interest me. He refused until I mentioned that I had ready cash. The very next day he put up a sign reading "KONING & MUNDY, GENERAL MERCHANDISE."

Like everyone else, he fell in love with Jane. He offered and we accepted the use of three rooms over the store for our living quarters.

Together we turned Koning & Mundy into a thriving business. Manny traveled about, buying up goods, and I spent most of my time bossing the clerks and haggling with the tougher customers or buttering up the bigger ones. We made a good team, the stocky Jewish immigrant and the tall one-eyed young Confederate veteran.

Jane lost a child, a miscarriage, early in our marriage and we did not have children for some years after that.

Just when Koning & Mundy had become a solid business with a new warehouse and several clerks, poor Manny fell ill with typhoid. Jane nursed him through his last days. Between attacks of delirium, he made me promise to look after his wife and daughters back in Germany; even though he could have afforded to bring them over, they had remained there because of her aged parents.

He died in the fall of 1871. The business had become so valuable that I could not raise the cash that would have been required to pay Manny's wife a fair price for his half-interest. I was getting tired of tending store, haggling over bolts of cloth or the price of work shoes; Jane was weary of living over a store.

So I sold out to another firm, lock, stock and goodwill, for a decent price: $50,000. After helping the new owners get started, early in 1872, Jane and I took half of the proceeds and booked passage to England, then over to Cologne, where we found Manny's frail, gray little wife living in a ghetto with her now senile parents.

She knew no English and I no German or Yiddish. Her daughter spoke French and so did Jane. Between them they communicated the happy news that Mrs. Koning would receive $25,000 from Manny's long sojourn in America.

After that Jane and I spent a wonderful two months in Europe. Back home in Baltimore, I bought up some printing equipment at a sheriff's sale and started in the printing business. Got through the Panic of '73 and built Mundy Printing Company, later Mundy & Son, into a prosperous printing house. One of the first companies to install the new linotypes, we were.

We bought our present two-story brick house with garden. I gave in to Jane's wishes and joined the Presbyterian Church; also became a Mason and signed up with the local Confederate Veterans organization.

Zeb Vance Mundy was born some seven months after we returned from Europe; draw your own conclusions. Estelle came along three years later.

I never went back to Oldham County except briefly to attend the funerals of my parents. Ernest Ferro died ten years after the war and Jane took the train down for the funeral and stayed for a month. She brought Reba back with her and she ran our household just as she had Beaulieu for so long. Cassius was dead by then. William Ferro had recovered his mental balance and married Tom Shelton's sister. Reba, who despised the Sheltons, couldn't get along with the new mistress of Beaulieu. She and I became good friends, always speaking our minds to each other as frankly as though we were not separated by age, sex and color. She did condescend to call me "Captain James," however.

Jane and I had a wonderful life together. She finally gave up her efforts to completely civilize me, settling for a halfway job with tender good humor. We became as close as two human beings can. When she died three years ago, I shut myself in my room, where Estelle and Zeb Vance could not see me, and cried for the first time in fifty years, since lying wounded in that prisoner-of-war corral at Gettysburg.

Since then, in the evenings, I allow myself one good strong toddy and a cigar. As I sit in my chair looking out on the side garden that Jane loved so well, my mind runs back to the first time I saw her, to those early days of the war, to the fiasco at New Bern, my brief affair with Elvira Fincastle, the scream of shells and buzz of Minié balls at Malvern Hill, Sharpsburg and Fredericksburg, the sight of the noble Robert E. Lee, and the fertile fields of Pennsylvania under our Confederate invasion. Yes, and the agony of lying thirsty and in pain at Gettysburg, the needless horror of Johnson's Island, the excitement of escaping through Canada, and running the blockade to Wilmington, right to the end at Appomattox.

As daylight fades and I doze, faces crowd across my brain, Noah Rhine and Harry McGee, Elmer Fincastle, Captain Cadieu, William Ferro, that quadroon girl in Richmond, the Pennsylvania artilleryman I captured at Malvern Hill, old Hiram Winchester, and Cassius and Reba. Yes, Tom Shelton, too. And my lovely, tender, loyal Jane.

All gone. All gone.

I set out to explain about the great American Civil War and my part in it. Guess I got carried away in places, but at least I have put it all down on paper.

It has helped an old man get through a lonely year.